W9-CQJ-653

A memory from long ago . . .

"I'm Sarah Beth Walker's daughter. Birth daughter, actually . . . She gave me up for adoption when I was two years old."

"Well," the voice hesitated and then rushed on, "I remember that time. It wasn't exactly like that. I mean she didn't really give you up—she fought hard to do anything but. She really wanted to keep—I guess I should say, there's probably more to the story than you were told."

"Oh . . ." Patsy didn't know what to say next. "Well, I know I wasn't adopted at birth like most babies. I was almost two years old. . . . My parents always told me my birth mother loved me, but couldn't take care of me." She paused. "But I have a hard time understanding why it took her two years to decide she didn't want to keep me."

Now the voice on the phone waited. "It wasn't that. Your mother—uh, birth mother—didn't want to let go of you."

Another long pause. "I—don't quite understand," said Patsy. . . .

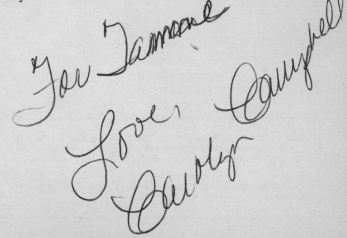

For Tamara
Love,
Carolyn Campbell

Most Berkley Books are available at special quantity discounts for bulk purchases for sales promotions, premiums, fund-raising, or educational use. Special books, or book excerpts, can also be created to fit specific needs.

For details, write: Special Markets, The Berkley Publishing Group, 375 Hudson Street, New York, New York 10014.

Together Again

True Stories of Birth Parents and Adopted Children Reunited

CAROLYN CAMPBELL

BERKLEY BOOKS, NEW YORK

If you purchased this book without a cover, you should be aware that
this book is stolen property. It was reported as "unsold and destroyed"
to the publisher and neither the author nor the publisher has received
any payment for this "stripped book."

TOGETHER AGAIN

A Berkley Book / published by arrangement with
International Locator

PRINTING HISTORY
Berkley edition / July 1999

All rights reserved.
Copyright © 1999 by International Locator.
Book design by Tiffany Kukec.
Cover photograph by Comstock, Inc.
This book may not be reproduced in whole or in part,
by mimeograph or any other means, without permission.
For information address: The Berkley Publishing Group, a division
of Penguin Putnam Inc., 375 Hudson Street, New York, New York 10014.

The Penguin Putnam Inc. World Wide Web site address is
http://www.penguinputnam.com

ISBN: 0-425-16454-3

BERKLEY®
Berkley Books are published by The Berkley Publishing Group,
a division of Penguin Putnam Inc., 375 Hudson Street,
New York, New York 10014.
BERKLEY and the "B" design
are trademarks belonging to Penguin Putnam Inc.

PRINTED IN THE UNITED STATES OF AMERICA

10 9 8 7 6 5 4 3 2 1

To my parents,
Cloyd and Mary Goates,
with love, respect, and gratitude

To Cameron,
May your story
and your life end
up as happy as
mine!

Love!
Carolyn

Looking for the Family She Lost

Chapter One

The phone never rang this early. As soon as she picked up the receiver, Patsy sensed tension on the other end of the line. A woman's voice said, "Mrs. Thompson, I'm calling from the hospital. It's about your father." Sounding stressed, the woman paused. Sighing heavily, she continued, "Frankly, Mrs. Thompson, I don't think this is the best thing for him. Your father's sister is going to transfer him to a nursing home. They're meeting this afternoon at one. You'd better do something right now if you want your daddy."

The words chilled Patsy. "What? Who is this?" she asked, a sinking sensation streaking through her mind and heart. Gripping the phone, she protested quickly, "I'm there all the time. I always talk to the nurses. No one told me about this."

"I don't know why that would be—" The woman hesitated. Patsy heard her shuffle papers. "I can only say that if you want to change any of the plans, you'd better be here at one o'clock today."

Patsy swallowed. "I'm on my way—please, don't let them do anything until I get there." After hanging up, she walked down the hall to her husband's home-based office. Barry was on the phone, and Patsy mouthed the word "emergency." Then she sat on the edge of a leather office chair and waited. As soon as Barry hung up, Patsy said, "I have to drive to North Carolina this morning."

"Again?" he asked. He looked at her quizzically, knowing she'd just returned the day before from spending the weekend at the hospital with her father, yet his smile was sympathetic and understanding of Patsy's caregiving tendencies.

Patsy said assuredly, "I need to save Daddy. Aunt Evelyn's putting him in a home. I'll feed the kids first, then I'll go."

Sitting behind his desk, her husband smiled up at her, then reached to squeeze her hand. "Don't wait until after breakfast. You'd better go now. I can feed the kids."

Patsy strode determinedly to the kitchen of the big antebellum-style house. She turned on the burner to heat water for grits, then set the big oak table for eight people. When the doorbell rang, she felt relief at the calm sound, knowing it signified the arrival of the Sorensens. These four extra kids were her best friend's children. Kathy Sorensen had died of a heart attack a year before. Worried about how their father would cope without his wife's help, Patsy had fed them breakfast since then and watched them after school, too.

"Hi, Mom," they said, settling around the table with Patsy's kids, Rodney, Chris, and Joy. All of them laughed and talked together. The sound of their happy, young voices made Patsy's heart rise. How could anything bad happen in a world where kids still had such energy and hope spilling over from inside them? For a moment she forgot the anxiousness in her heart.

"I told you I'd finish up here. You go on ahead, Patsy." Barry's hand rested on her shoulder.

She kissed him quickly, still trying to wrench herself from her morning routine. "Thanks for everything." She glanced up at Barry's face, then quickly looked down as her eyes suddenly filled. No time for tears. She had a long trip ahead of her.

Driving to the hospital, Patsy remembered the last serious discussion she had had with Daddy before the stroke. She could hear his words as if it were yesterday. She realized it was two Christmases ago, a year after her mother died. Daddy was never the same after losing Mama; it was as if part of him went to Heaven with her. Patsy mourned the aspects of her father that were gone and wanted to cling desperately to the fragile part she now hoped to save.

As she recalled that conversation now, she remembered sitting in the comfortable earth-toned living room at his house, an unnatural stillness in the room heightening her sense of his loneliness. She mentioned that she'd like him to come and live with her and Barry so he wouldn't be all by himself. Daddy had stared at her a moment as his round blue eyes filled with tears. A gentle grin faltered on his fair-skinned face. But then he abruptly changed the subject to another topic, one that was rarely spoken about during Patsy's growing-up years. Her adoption. The "big secret" in her life. Looking at her with an intense expression, his normally smiling face turned serious. There was an urgency in his voice that she never heard before. He said, "I'm not going to be here much longer, Patsy. It's time for you to start looking for your mother and brothers and sisters now." His voice lowered as his words rushed. "I couldn't talk about this in front of your mama. It really upset her. She wouldn't want me to tell you, but the fact is, she burned every paper that might help you look. Didn't mean anything by it. Just loved you and didn't want you to get hurt. But I think you should start looking now, Patsy. My time is getting short." His words brought a lump to her throat and an ache to her heart.

Because the stroke happened only two weeks after they talked, that last lengthy conversation was imprinted on Patsy's brain as if it were literally engraved there. Why didn't she ask him the questions that flew to her mind that day? Why didn't she guess that his time was almost up and they might never share a conversation again? You just never really knew when it would be too late, she thought. Too late could always come five minutes from now.

Reaching the hospital parking lot, Patsy felt a streak of fear the way she did the night they called to tell her about the stroke. She remembered the nurse's voice was emotionless and clinical. Massive, major stroke. Paralyzed on the right side. Couldn't talk or dress himself.

Patsy climbed out of the car, her dread mounting as she walked into the hospital. The cold air and medicinal smell of alcohol seemed to be in stark contrast with the warm spring day outside. Trying to calm her rushing emotions, Patsy walked to the elevator and rode up three floors to Daddy's room.

It was as if they were waiting for her. Aunt Evelyn, Uncle Tim, two nurses, and two women in "power suits"—maybe social workers, Patsy thought. Daddy was dressed in a white hospital gown and propped up so he could sit in a chair. He smiled innocently at her, the same smile that had made her feel safe all her life. Patsy felt her throat catch, and she was tempted to step over and hug him. But she knew this wasn't the time. The warm bond they had shared for forty years couldn't protect her—or him—from this.

"Aunt Ev, why would you do this? You know Daddy won't be happy in a home. What makes you think you can take him out of here without asking me?"

There was a long silence. Finally one of the power suits flipped through pages on her clipboard. She looked at Patsy and said coolly, "They have power of attorney, ma'am."

"What?" Now Patsy's eyes flew to Aunt Ev's face. "What is she talking about, Aunt Ev?" The slim, gray-haired woman stared back at her silently as her hands began to fidget with the strap of her black patent-leather purse.

When her aunt didn't respond, Patsy couldn't keep her feelings from spilling over into words. "This doesn't make any sense. I'm his only child. How could she possibly get power of attorney? Why didn't anyone ever call me?" Patsy directed this last question to the social worker, who, having made her pronouncement, now sat as still and impenetrable as a brick wall. Patsy continued gazing at the frozen faces. "I visit him all the time. I hate to say this, but I never see the rest of you here. This is ninety miles from my home and I come up here and sleep on the couch every other weekend. For six months! And now this. No one said anything to me!''

This time the silence felt leaden, weighted. A sick, sad feeling filled Patsy as she sensed everyone else in the room knew a terrible secret.

Suddenly Aunt Evelyn's voice groaned out like an iron pipe scraping against cement. "Dear, we thought that since you aren't his daughter—by blood and all—we didn't know if you would feel responsible to take care of him.''

The words hit as hard as stones. Patsy felt stunned as a sharp sadness rose in her throat. Her chin quivered, and moments later, tears pricked the corners of her eyes. No one had ever suggested that she wasn't Daddy's daughter. She knew she belonged to him in spirit, in love, in day-to-day caring—all the ways that count. Daddy and Mama themselves had always introduced her as "our daughter" and never, ever—not even once—as "our adopted daughter.'' Patsy was their only child, who came to them when they were in their forties. Patsy thought of years of home-cooked dinners, matching outfits, vacations, fun times. She knew she was a late-in-life present that they cherished. And even if Daddy wanted her to look for her birth family, Patsy knew it was only for the peace it would bring to her, not because he and Mama were anything but her real parents.

Patsy's tears dried as fires of anger rose within her.

"Aunt Ev, I can't believe you would do this to me. I can't believe you're trying to do this to Daddy. You know it's not what he wants. And I can't do anything else but try to stop you.''

Again, the power suit with the clipboard spoke. "I'm afraid the orders are already processed.''

Patsy's hand formed a fist and pounded against the night-stand. "Then stop them. I'm contesting them, whatever I need to do. I'll file a lawsuit.''

Now, finally, the other social worker spoke, directing her question to Patsy."You are—?''

"Patsy Thompson. His daughter. His only child. He is *my daddy*!'' Patsy said with an impassioned firmness.

The woman cleared her throat and consulted her clipboard. "Mrs. Thompson, feelings and relations aren't the most important consideration here. Your father's stroke took place a year ago. You don't recover from a stroke. You may or may not realize this, but brain tissue has been destroyed and it doesn't grow back. The truth is, he isn't going to get any better."

Patsy swallowed, then rushed to speak past the lump in her throat. "I'm not convinced of that. I think he won't get better if you put him in an institution, but—and my husband supports me on this—maybe I could help him if I took him home with me and his grandchildren."

Suddenly her father angled himself across his chair, leaned awkwardly forward, and squeezed Patsy in a lopsided, one-armed hug. A contented-sounding groan rose from his throat.

"See?" Now tears of delight coursed Patsy's cheeks. "He wants to go with me."

The social worker shifted in her chair. "It's not that simple, ma'am. The doctors examined him and wrote recommendations, and—"

"And I'll take him home with me before they're carried out." Patsy assured her, standing and looking for Daddy's suitcase. "Someone doesn't agree with those orders. Someone called me from here this morning and told me to come today if I wanted to help my daddy."

The woman cleared her throat again. "Whoever it was, that phone call was unauthorized and also inappropriate. As I said, it's not that simple. There would need to be tests to determine that he is of sound mind in seeking to reverse this decision. We would have to know that he understands what will take place and that this is what he wants and feels is best for his future." She stopped speaking and folded her arms across her chest.

"We'll do it. Whatever it takes. I'll bring him in for every test in the book." Patsy moved to help her father out of his chair.

"You can't take him with you without authority. The tests must be administered here at the facility. And frankly, Mrs. Thompson, I don't think he'll pass—"

"I think he will," said Patsy, furious at her throat for again suddenly closing with emotion. "He's my daddy. I know him. He's very determined and he's a positive person. He never stops trying. I just know he'll be all right."

The nurses and social workers gazed at one another and shook their heads. "You may be asking for disappointment, dear," said one of the social workers.

"Daddy's always been there for me. I know he won't disappoint me. And now, if you'll all leave the room, I'd like to visit with my father alone."

Chapter Two

Sitting alone in her living room the next week, Patsy reflected silently. What would happen to Daddy? How long would the testing take? She was filled with prickly emotions. For the first time ever, she felt like an outcast from the rest of her family. Daddy and Mama always told her that her relationship with them was no different from the relationships any of her cousins had with their parents. But today all forty years of her life seemed instantly called into question. It was as if she were a pariah—Aunt Ev and the others inferring that she didn't belong and wasn't Daddy's closest relative.

But if she wasn't an actual member of this family, which family was she a part of? Patsy's mind reached backward into her childhood where her recollections were fuzzy. She was adopted when she was two years old, but she knew that somewhere out there she had two half brothers, Brent and J. B., and a half sister, Mary Jane. Their faces were blank in her mind. As if she were looking through gauze, Patsy could vaguely envision a long-ago Mary Jane holding her, walking beside her, hand in hand. She knew Mama and Daddy had tried to adopt Mary Jane, too, but social workers decided they could only take Patsy. Tears rose in Patsy's eyes as memories of the long-ago separation flooded over her.

After her adoption, there had been intermittent visits from Mary Jane, J. B., and Brent. But when her family moved to Savannah, Georgia, while she was in third grade, the visits stopped. She couldn't remember the last time they were together. By then Mama and Daddy's love surrounded her like a warm blanket, eventually almost ebbing the inner ache at the loss of the birth family she now scarcely remembered.

Then a few years ago, while Mama was still alive, someone had called Daddy to tell him that Patsy's half brother had died back in Centerville, where she grew up. Daddy phoned her and practically whispered the news to her, as if he were afraid Mama might hear and be upset.

With a shiver, Patsy recalled the shock she experienced when she walked into the funeral parlor. The man who died wasn't Brent or J. B. When Patsy stepped close to the open casket, she recognized him instantly. His name was Allen Walker, and he owned a small grocery store where Patsy always took her children when she visited Centerville. They'd talked casually dozens of times. Why did she never sense the close family tie they shared? Why couldn't she guess that the auburn hair and round apple cheeks, like her own, were a family resemblance? Were there other half brothers and sisters she didn't know about?

Waves of emotion flooded her mind as she remembered that day. Standing over the casket, she'd felt ripples of shock and loss; she mourned not only the passing of this man whom she knew casually, but the fact that she had never known that he was her half brother.

Patsy had stared around her at the people in the funeral home, looking for other faces that appeared familiar from the days when she lived and visited in Centerville. She glimpsed a sixtyish, red-haired woman she thought she'd seen somewhere before.

"Ma'am?"

The woman smiled at her.

"I was so sorry to hear about Allen. Um, did he have other brothers and sisters—or half brothers and sisters . . . ?" Patsy let her question trail off vaguely.

The woman frowned slightly, stared into Patsy's face. Her reply was brusque. "Well, you know, since that horrible incident when they were children . . . There were ten of them in the family until that awful night—"

Ten of them? What night? Patsy wanted to ask. Instead, she squared her shoulders. "Do you know any way that I could contact Allen's family? I-I'm a relative of his, I think . . . sort of a long-lost relative."

To her amazement, the woman looked into her face again and asked, "Patsy? I thought that might be you."

Patsy was speechless.

"I'm Anne Walker. Your daddy used to bring you to talk to me at the county clerk's office when you were a little girl. His office was in the same building with us, you know. Girl, he was so proud to adopt you, he brought you into work and showed you around like you were a prize pig. My husband is your half brother, too. All ten of you were T. J. Walker's kids." The woman paused, looked into Patsy's face. "I think you're the only one from Sarah Beth."

"She was T. J.'s second wife?" Patsy asked.

"Third," Anne whispered as another mourner frowned at her. "Marvin's from the second."

Still swirling in a sea of emotion, Patsy managed to ask, "Could I meet your husband?"

"Oh, he just left." Anne Walker's voice was even. "Let me give you our phone number."

With shaking fingers, Patsy reached out for the small slip of paper. She looked at the name. Marvin Walker. Who was this man? Who was T. J. Walker? And where did she fit in this complicated puzzle? Patsy looked up and saw that the woman was waiting for her response. "Thank you," she said numbly, nodding and stepping away.

Moments later she sauntered over to the casket. Allen, she wanted to say, if I had known you were my half brother, I'd have set you a place at my Thanksgiving table. Had you out for summer barbecues. Let our kids play together while they grew up. Patsy couldn't think of a proper way to say goodbye.

Patsy walked out of the funeral home on emotional over-load. When she got home, she slid the phone number under a loose piece of Con-Tact paper on a kitchen shelf. As days passed, her mind continued to churn, and soon guilt accompanied her other emotions. What right did she have to pursue her curiosity when Mama and Daddy did all they could to be the best parents in the world? She remembered overhearing someone tell Daddy that if he did his job as a father right, she'd never even think about her biological roots lying somewhere else. Knowing how much Mama and Daddy loved her, and grateful for all they had done, she tried to forget about that phone number and put aside thoughts of searching for her birth family.

But now things were different. Daddy's stroke and the conversation they had weeks before it, brought to the surface the curiosity she buried years ago. And much as she hated to admit it, maybe the doctors were right. Maybe Daddy wouldn't get any better, and if he really wanted her to look for her relatives, maybe she'd best start now, so Daddy could see the results.

The next afternoon Patsy dug out the scrap of paper she'd hidden under the loose Con-Tact paper. Marvin Walker. Patsy gazed at the secret name written on the small white piece of notepaper. Just holding the paper with the name of the half brother she'd never known felt mysterious and scary. She stared at it for a long moment. "Daddy wants me to do this," she reminded herself as she studied the number, then picked up the phone.

"Hello?" a man's voice said.

"This is Patricia Thompson." Patsy suddenly felt flustered. How should she say something so personal to someone she'd never met? She'd never heard any etiquette for this type of occasion. Realizing that time was passing, she plunged forward. "I met your wife very briefly at your brother's funeral. I'm your . . . half sister. You might have heard of me as Patricia Diane Walker."

"Oh . . . yes. Patricia . . ." The tone of the voice revealed nothing. There was a silence as she tried to perceive his thoughts.

Patsy said, "I'm Sarah Beth Walker's daughter. Birth daughter, actually, the way they call it now. She gave me up for adoption when I was two years old."

"Well . . ." The voice hesitated, and then rushed on. "Sarah Beth was married to my father after he and my mother divorced. She was his third wife." A long sigh. "I remember that time. It wasn't exactly like that . . . I mean she didn't really give you up—she fought hard to do anything but. She really wanted to keep . . . I guess I should say, there's probably more to the story than you were told."

"Oh—" Patsy didn't know what to say next. "Well, I know I wasn't adopted at birth like most babies. I was almost two years old. I think I lived with my birth parents until then. My parents always told me my birth mother loved me but couldn't take care of me." She paused. "But I have a hard time understanding why it took her two years to decide she didn't want to keep me."

Now the voice on the phone waited. "It wasn't that. Your mother—uh, birth mother—didn't want to let go of you."

Another long pause. "I—don't quite understand," said Patsy.

"Why, she was afraid for her life. He threatened to kill her that night."

"Who—" Patsy interrupted, but it was as if her half brother didn't hear.

The voice continued. "He had a gun. She didn't have a choice. I was there."

Now Patsy waited, but the voice suddenly stopped. Her half brother sighed, then asked, "Is there any way we could meet? I feel awkward trying to explain this over the phone."

Meet in person? A shiver of apprehension touched Patsy's spine. The thought of entering what had always been forbidden territory somehow threatened to disrupt Patsy's relatively straightforward life. It was scary to think of her own version of her life story possibly being contradicted. But could she really go on without knowing who she was? What if one of her children needed an emergency medical transplant or other medical information? What if Aunt Ev and the others continued to leave her out in the cold? She reminded herself that Daddy wanted her to do this. And Marvin Walker sounded as if he knew something. She was groping for a response when she again remembered Daddy telling her that now was the time.

Patsy took a breath. "Yes, we could get together and talk. I'd really like to find out any information you might have. Would you like to come to my home? I live here in Quitman."

A pause. "Uh—why don't you come here sometime. I'm right here in Centerville where Sarah Beth was from. I might have some photos or documents I could show you."

"All right," Patsy said, then hesitated. "Could I come later this week?"

"That would be fine. But give me a call first."

Patsy felt another shiver of apprehension as she hung up the phone. What Pandora's box was she opening? Was she ready to face the demons she buried so long ago? No matter how wonderful her childhood had been, there was still the mysterious question of why she was given up for adoption. *Given up.* There was no way to escape the feeling of rejection in those words. Someone in the past hadn't wanted her and had turned her away. Though she hardly ever thought in those terms as a child, when she had, she couldn't help but feel a twinge of hurt and fear. As a little girl, there was always something scary about not knowing where she'd come from. Why didn't she live with the parents who gave birth to her as everybody else did? What was so different about her that she couldn't be raised in her own family? Was there something sinister or frightening hidden in her past? Most of the time Patsy shoved these unknowns to the back of her mind. And the fact was, her life growing up was a lot like most other girls her age— with an extra dose of love thrown in from her parents.

And now here she was digging up all those questions, and who knew what answers she'd find. Marvin said that

Sarah Beth had been afraid for her life. She had been threatened with a gun and forced to give her baby away. Patsy suspected the truth of her past was worse than she had ever imagined. Did she really want to know?

Chapter Three

Three days later Patsy fought to gear up her courage as she drove to the house where her half brother lived. When she phoned to tell him she was coming, he sounded reluctant, as if she brought back unwelcome memories. Patsy wondered how he could feel uncomfortable when she was the one who had been given away. As she thought about it now, the phone call seemed as if both of them were stumbling around in their shared painful pasts, wishing to move on, but knowing that history couldn't be completely forgotten.

Marvin Walker's home was well kept, the lawn mowed and the garden filled with a variety of spring flowers—daffodils, tulips, crocuses. The scene was friendly and inviting, yet as Patsy walked up to the steps, fear crept along beside her. Did she really want to know if someone hurt the woman who gave her life? And what did the man who lived in this pretty house think about a woman who ran away in the middle of the night and left her baby daughter without a mother? What was he likely to think of Patsy herself?

Patsy considered turning back, but then remembered that Daddy had asked her to search. She knocked and waited. A moment later Marvin opened the door, and Patsy saw that he wasn't much taller than her own five foot six inches.

She sensed recognition on his face as he looked at her.

"Come in. You must be Patricia. There's definitely a resemblance—the auburn hair. And you have the same shape face. I think I remember seeing you once before when you were little. You really do look a lot like her."

Patsy felt herself blush. What should she say to that? Her only pictures of her birth mother were the ones she created in her imagination. But now she wondered, if she ever happened to catch sight of Sarah Beth Walker, would she recognize her because they looked alike? Did Sarah Beth have the same high forehead Patsy always fought to cover with bangs? Did she have the same green eyes that people always said made them feel as if they knew Patsy from somewhere?

At her hesitation, Marvin gestured behind him. "Come out to the living room," he said. "Would you like something to drink? Isn't it warm for spring?"

"It is warm," Patsy agreed, settling on a velveteen sofa, "but no thanks, I don't need anything."

Marvin sat across from her. He seemed to stare at her in fascination, then he smiled gently. Was that pity in his face? Patsy wondered. When Marvin didn't speak right away, she forced herself to venture into conversation. "My father—my adoptive father—asked me to make this search. He knew some people who knew my birth mother. In fact, your wife told me he used to take me to say hello to her, at the courthouse where she worked. I was really little. I just remember a big building with an elevator and lots of hallways. Anyway, Daddy asked me to look for Sarah Beth during our last conversation two years ago, and now—" Patsy paused as she thought of Daddy. "Well, he had a stroke a few months back, and he's partially handicapped. Unable to speak. I'm just sorry I didn't look while he could still help me."

When Marvin only nodded, Patsy asked, "Is there any chance you've seen my mother recently? Within the past few years?"

Marvin's smile faded as he shook his head. "No, not

since that last night. It was . . . however long ago that you were two years old.''

Patsy waited. ''Thirty-eight years ago? Do you mean you last saw her the night she left our home?''

He paused and looked at the ceiling as if the answer were written there. ''No, it would be a day or two later than that.''

Surprised, Patsy asked, ''You saw her after she left our house?''

''Let me say, before I go any further . . .'' He stopped, stared at Patsy as if evaluating her. ''Her husband—our father—was what you'd call abusive,'' he said apologetically. ''I felt sorry for your mother from the first. I guess I kind of hung around, thinking she'd get beaten up the way my own mother did. I think she sensed I understood her. I have to tell you, your mother didn't want to leave you. Not at all. No. She left to save your life. I drove her in my truck. And she cried all the way. The last moment I saw her, she was still crying because she had to leave you and your brother.''

''My brother? Was it J. B. or Brent?''

''It was Paul.''

''Paul?'' Patsy tried to digest this news. Still another brother that she'd never heard of before. Shrugging aside her rising emotions, she shuddered briefly and said, ''You'll have to excuse my confusion. This is all new to me. Paul.''

Marvin said, ''He'd be close to your age. A year or two older.''

''Where did she leave him?''

Marvin lifted his hands with a shrug of resignation. ''I wish I knew more. I wanted to keep in touch. I thought she would.'' He sighed. ''And I didn't think she'd go away permanently and never come back. But she was so afraid. And it all happened so quickly. I didn't plan to take her with me until the last minute. She was going to go back to her parents' house.''

''That's where you were going?''

Marvin shook his head. ''I was heading to New Jersey

on business. She had a stepson—our oldest half brother—up there working. So she asked if she could ride up there with me. Really, it wasn't well thought out at all. She asked if she could go with me at the last moment, and I said yes. At the time I really didn't think much beyond that. I'm sorry. I should have. I know that now.'' He looked up at Patsy as if asking for forgiveness.

Patsy paused. ''Well, thank you for taking care of her that last night. I'm sure she appreciated it. It sounds like she was scared to death,'' Patsy said slowly. Then she asked, ''She never wrote after that?''

Marvin shook his head. ''But if you find her, could you do me the courtesy of asking her to call me?''

''Yes,'' Patsy said, a feeling of hopelessness spreading over her. ''I will.'' She stood, then stopped. ''So as far as you know, she stayed in New Jersey?''

''Uh, that's where I dropped her off. Trenton, New Jersey. I remember that. She was going to meet—'' He thought for a moment. ''Rex. That was his name. She was going to meet our half brother Rex.'' Marvin spoke as though this might be tremendously valuable information.

Patsy fought to keep her voice calm rather than urgent. ''His last name? Do you know Rex's last name?''

Marvin squinted in concentration. ''Most likely Walker, like ours.''

Patsy said, ''I never met Rex.''

Marvin sighed. ''I haven't, either. He was from our father's first marriage Anyway, your mama decided to go with me. I still remember I dropped her off right downtown. In Trenton, New Jersey.'' Marvin paused, then pointed his finger at Patsy. ''Oak Street. That was it. I dropped her off on West Oak Street.''

Patsy took a pad out of her purse and wrote. She looked up to ask, ''How can you remember that?''

''I recall that night like it was yesterday. Her crying the whole time. She never stopped. And the family's name. It's coming to me. The family where I dropped her off was Rogers.''

''Do you know who they were?''

Again, Marvin shook his head. "No. I just dropped her off. When she got out of the car, she said, 'Thanks, Marv.' I remember her saying thanks. And she was still crying. I recall that, too."

"Did she say who the Rogers were? Were they her parents?"

He shook his head again. "I'm sorry. I'm not sure. They could be, though."

Something urged Patsy on, though she could tell that the conversation had obviously worn Marvin down. "I really appreciate this, Marvin. I'm sorry to take so much time. But if I understand right, Sarah Beth left everyone behind that she knew in Centerville and moved to New Jersey."

"Yes."

"It was that simple?"

Now he shook his head vehemently. "Not simple at all. Probably the hardest thing she did in her whole life."

"Can you tell me exactly why it was so hard?"

Marvin looked at her, started to speak, and then stopped himself. "I don't want to upset you, dear. You came a long way and you're obviously a very sweet girl." He sat again for a moment, resting his chin in his hand. He sighed, then stood. "Guess that's all I have to say," he said abruptly. He walked to the front door, then opened it. "Just know that she loved you—enough to try to save your life by leaving you when she did. She cried the whole way there."

"You said something—when we talked before—about someone threatening to kill her."

"Yes, but after I thought about it, that's really all I know. They said he threatened her with a gun—but I couldn't swear to that. I wasn't there right then. There were lots of other people in the house that night. You should probably ask one of them that was there right at the time."

Patsy sighed as weariness spread over her. "But I'm here now. And you've been so helpful."

He paused. "I just don't want to misrepresent anything."

"Just tell me—who was it that threatened my mother?"

Marvin looked at her, surprised that she didn't know this. "I think it was our father. That's what they always said.

But I shouldn't say anything more. Don't take my word as gospel.''

"I—" Patsy started to ask, then realized she felt as if she'd been punched in the stomach. She felt tears start behind her eyes, and didn't want to cry where he could see her. "Thank you," she managed, then stepped out of the house. Looking back, she saw that Marvin watched as she climbed inside her car.

The next day, as she drove to the hospital to visit Daddy, Patsy continued to mull over Marvin's story in her mind. She couldn't help but think he was probably sincere. What advantage could there be for him in saying their father threatened to kill her mother and he rescued her? He really didn't want to talk to me, Patsy thought. He's hardly the type to crave attention or want to paint himself as a hero.

When Patsy arrived at Daddy's room, he was studying three photographs as a social worker held them up for him. Patsy recognized one picture as a portrait of her own family, the other as Aunt Evelyn, and another as his other sister, Ruth. The social worker explained, "Because of his limited speech capacity, we utilize other methods to determine his thoughts, opinions, and preferences.''

Patsy patted her father's shoulder. "I'm right here, Daddy.''

"Don't distract him, please," said the frowning social worker, who paused pointedly to look at her watch. "I asked him a question.''

Patsy thought of how her father had worked with technical data in his thirty years of employment at a government air force base. His mind had always worked so quickly, it seemed as if it was hardly work at all. She remembered him adding a column of numbers faster than she could sign her name. And how he had recognized everyone he ever met and smiled at them as if they were all old friends. But now Daddy frowned and squinted at the pictures, as if the effort to look at them was a frustrating struggle. Finally he lifted his good arm. Shaking slightly, he eased his hand forward to point to the photo of Patsy and Barry and the children.

Patsy turned and asked quickly, "What does that mean?"

Frowning, the social worker sighed again. She scrawled on her notepad. Then she looked down at the pile of charts on her clipboard rather than up at Patsy. When she spoke, each word seemed pried from her clenched lips. "We asked who he would want to live with after his therapy is over, and told him to point to a picture."

A rush of emotion that neared relief filled Patsy, and she reached to squeeze Daddy's arm. "See—see he *does* want to live with us. Oh, I'm so glad, Daddy. We want you to come stay with us, too. Your room is all ready." She turned to the social worker. "Now when can I get his things?"

The social worker exhaled with exasperation. "Mrs. Thompson. We told you before. This is only one of a battery of tests. We're nowhere near finished. I suggest you wait for the test results. Someone will notify you."

With his good hand Daddy awkwardly reached over and squeezed Patsy's fingers. He smiled conspiratorially at her, sensing she was being scolded.

Patsy couldn't resist smiling back at Daddy. But as the social worker continued writing in her notebook, Patsy said hurriedly, "I'm willing to take him with me today." She punctuated her comment with a thrust of her chin. "I don't need to wait for any more tests. I know what he wants."

"I'm sorry, Mrs. Thompson." Now the social worker turned her head to stare at Patsy in frustration. "*Legally,* I couldn't release him to you today if I wanted to." She leaned to close the test booklet with a snap. Then she dropped it in her briefcase and stood. "His testing will continue over the next few weeks." She looked at the clock, then left the room.

Patsy listened as the woman's footsteps faded away down the hall. When she felt sure the woman was gone, she turned to her father. "Daddy, my feelings would be hurt if you didn't pick me," she joked. Then she held his water glass for him. She eased the blanket over his legs up until it draped his chest. She sat back in the plastic visitor's chair and felt herself exhale slowly. It was always like this with Daddy, Patsy remembered, even when she was little. She remembered sitting in her miniature rocking chair while he wrote at his desk. Both then and now, she didn't have to say a lot, and just sitting with him felt comforting. But today she felt an unusual urgency because of her talk with Marvin. "Daddy, I went to see Marvin. My half brother. He told me my birth father made my birth mother leave. He said he threatened her with a gun. Did you ever hear anything like that, Daddy?"

Patsy waited, as if Daddy might suddenly speak to her. His bright eyes glanced back at her with the usual spark of affectionate recognition. All her life, he had listened to whatever she said as if it were the most interesting news on earth. But no matter how hard she hoped, since the stroke he didn't say a word. But Patsy still couldn't stop hoping. She sat still, her hands folded and her feet motionless on the blue hospital linoleum. A moment later she felt his hand touch hers, and she held his gnarled fingers and waited.

When she saw his eyes blink several times, Patsy knew her father was once again tired. "It's okay, Daddy," she said, gently setting his hand on top of the blanket. "I'll just keep looking. I'll let you know what I find out." She filled his water pitcher and shut off his overhead light.

Chapter Four

Patsy found the ad in the newspaper listed under Adoption.
Ever since her last conversation with Daddy, she occasionally read the Personals section of the classified ads, hoping
to miraculously see her own birthdate, with the notation
that a long-lost birth mother was looking for her. Instead,
she mostly read advertisements from hopeful adoptive parents, who all seemed to be rich, happily married, and cul-
turally well-rounded, able to offer a child anything from his
own horse to a Big Ten college education.

One day Patsy caught sight of an ad for an adoption
support group, for "all members of the adoption triad."
She saw the ad twice before allowing herself the possibly
idle hope that she might meet her own birth mother at the
meeting. When she phoned the number listed in the paper,
the support group leader told her that had actually happened
once. "Can you believe that the birth mother hid under the
table for about ten minutes when she realized it was really
her son in the room? Then she went hysterical, and couldn't
stop crying and hugging him. It was great . . . but a one-in-
a-zillion chance." Then the woman's voice turned serious.
"You're a thousand times more likely just to find information about how to search. And you'll meet people who
are searching like you are."

"Thank you," said Patsy. "I'll think about it."

On her first visit to the support group meeting two weeks later, Patsy was surprised that the room in the Quitman city hall was filled with people. If you were taking a first glance at this group, Patsy realized, there was no way you could tell who they were. They didn't resemble one another in any way. There were teenagers and senior citizens, men and women dressed in business suits, and others attired in Levi's and T-shirts. Their connection wasn't visible, but all had something in common—they were all looking for someone. Most were people like her who were adopted as children and separated from their birth relatives. Some were birth moms looking for the children they gave up who were now teenagers or adults themselves. As they introduced themselves, Patsy was surprised to see that the most hopeful looks were on the faces of adoptive parents who wanted to help the children they adopted and loved complete this very personal search. Some adoptive parents, she knew, were still threatened, and worried that their children would leave their adoptive families for their birth families. But these parents understood that searching wouldn't dilute their relationship and wanted to help their children. Like Daddy is with me, she thought. He knows I'm just looking for more about myself—not someone to replace him.

After the premeeting talk died down and they all introduced themselves, the leader, a petite woman in her forties with black hair and Charlene written on her name tag, opened the meeting for personal stories and inquiries. A slim young blond woman stood and walked to the front of the room. She shared some private words with Charlene before turning her hopeful gaze to the other members.

Charlene's shiny brown eyes and friendly smile seemed to put the entire room at ease. With the blond woman beside her, Charlene spoke. She said, "I'm asking for your help, guys. All we have is a lab test on this one. A hospital lab test from when she was a baby. If any of you know anyone who works in the hospital lab, let me know."

"What about nonidentifying information?" someone called out, referring to the recent policy of adoption agencies to release details that didn't give away the birth parents' identities.

"This was a private adoption. And the attorney who handled it is now dead. The lab test is all we've got. Anyone who knows someone who works in the hospital lab or the county records department, see me after the meeting." The blond woman smiled hesitantly and sat down. With a friendly wave, Charlene gestured that it was now the members' turn to talk.

A woman in her thirties with brown hair and brown eyes stood. "I called my birth father on the phone," she said. Everyone in the room gasped and sighed with empathy. Patsy's own stomach fluttered with anticipation.

The young woman's smile widened. "You won't believe this. I actually talked to his *wife*." More gasps and a giggle, with the young woman herself eventually joining in. "Now you'll really laugh," she said, and covered her own mouth to stifle her rising laughter. "So I call his wife. Here I am all scared to death, and guess what she says?" She leaned forward and glanced around the room, seeing if anyone would hazard a guess. "You'll never believe this. She says she's surprised I was the first. She was surprised that more of his kids haven't called." Now the room filled with laughter as the group identified with the irony of the situation. The woman went on, her voice turning suddenly sober. "And then it turned out he died two years ago." Sad sighs from the group, who knew that death was one possible result at the end of the birth-parent search. The woman continued, "His wife invited me over to their home. She showed me pictures of him, and I look just like him. She took me to see his grave. And now we still keep meeting for lunch. It's wonderful. Really. But I just regret that now I'll never meet him . . . and he was just like me."

"But it sounds like you established a connection," said Charlene.

"Yes," said the woman, smiling wistfully. "I'm not sorry I found him. And his wife and I are really getting to know each other."

Patsy felt an empathy with the blond woman, who obviously shared the confused emotions she herself felt—the feeling of knowing that there were people out there you were close to genetically, but complete strangers to emotionally. She couldn't let the woman feel as if she were alone in this odd plight.

Before the giggles died completely, Patsy forced herself to stand. She felt her knees shake, and folded her arms in front of her. "I'm looking for my birth mother," she said. "Just starting my search."

"Got a Social Security number?" someone blurted.

Patsy shook her head.

"What about a birth date?" the support group leader asked. "If you have a birth date, we can go to DMV. See where her last driver's license was issued."

"Don't have that, either," Patsy said. "I know her name—" and there was a hush among the group. The air was potent with waiting.

"Lots of us don't have that, do we?" said Charlene.

"And I know where some of her other kids are. My father made her leave when I was two, and now I just can't find her."

"Why do you want to find her?" someone asked. A strange question for this group, Patsy thought. The room began to buzz as the group members considered Patsy's situation.

Patsy paused and breathed. Though she felt her knees shaking, the words weren't as hard to find as she thought they'd be. "I want to tell her I love her. And that I'm okay. I want to let her know I don't hate her for anything. And she can come meet me and get to know my family if she wants—"

Charlene interrupted to ask, "How should we help this lady, guys?" The room continued buzzing.

A brown-haired woman in her forties raised her hand. At the leader's nod she said, "I think she should write to anyplace she can. Voter registration. School records. Stuff like that. The Social Security number might be on there."

Now the support group leader turned to face Patsy. "And you have a source most of us don't have. Those *relatives*.

Talk to them. All of them. One of them has to know something.''

Patsy nodded, writing like lightning in her notebook. Finally she looked up. "My daddy wants me to do this," she told the group. "It was the last thing he told me to do before he had his stroke. He said, 'Find your mother and brothers and sisters.' "

"Aaah," said the group collectively. Patsy sensed that her words recalled feelings they knew well. The blanket of understanding that just one relative's support could give. Patsy felt her heart beat as she looked around the room at their teary-eyed faces. "We all wish you luck," said the leader. Patsy suddenly realized that she was crying, too.

She was walking out the door when someone touched her arm and handed her a Post-it note with a phone number. "Call me," it was the woman who said Patsy should write for information. "I might have some ideas at home about where you could write. I've helped a few others."

"I will." Patsy nodded, the relief that she was not alone filling her like a warm and soothing bath. The feeling hovered as she walked out to the parking lot and found her car. Her thoughts were filled with hope as she drove on home.

Chapter Five

Another early-morning phone call. By the raspy inhalation of breath through the phone, Patsy recognized Aunt Evelyn was about to speak. "Your daddy has had a setback," she said. "They called me this morning."

Patsy's heart thudded. "What? Why didn't they call me?"

Patsy imagined Aunt Evelyn shrugging in both annoyance and victory. "Possibly they don't think you're being realistic about his condition."

"Oh, Aunt Evelyn. Come on. What happened?"

"I didn't go there yet to see. But they called me."

Patsy felt anxiety streak through her mind. "What did they *say*, Aunt Evelyn?"

"They said he had a setback. Probably another stroke."

Patsy closed her eyes in silent terror. "I'm heading out right now," she said.

It was the middle of the day, and Barry promised to be home when the kids arrived from school.

Patsy drove the ninety miles without turning on the radio, silently pleading with the universe that Daddy would be okay. The hospital rose like an oasis in the desert. Patsy parked and locked her car, then ran to the metal-framed front doors. She was out of breath by the time she reached the steps, nearly falling through the glass doors as she fumbled her way to the admissions desk.

She fought to catch her breath and speak at the same time. "My father—Jess McClendon. Is he in the emergency room or intensive care?"

The nurse looked on a computer screen. "Don't see him there. Oh, wait—he's in 334."

"That's his regular room," Patsy protested.

"That's where I show him," the nurse replied, equally determined.

Patsy rushed to the elevator, rode up three floors, and hurried to Daddy's room.

He was in bed with his eyes closed. His face looked flushed. Patsy felt his cheek. "You're warm, Daddy. I'll be right back."

She strode quickly to the nurse's station. "My father? Do you know anything about what's wrong with him?"

The nurse frowned. "His name and room number?"

"Jess McClendon. Room 334."

The nurse typed at her keyboard, then read the screen. She shook her head. "Nothing on my screen. But I'm headed that way. We'll check things out."

In Daddy's room, the nurse lifted his chart from the end of the bed. She flipped through the pages as Patsy held Daddy's hand. "He has a fever," said Patsy.

"That's what the chart shows here—the last nurse recorded an elevated temperature—but that's all I see."

"My aunt called me this morning to say he had a setback. She thought he had another stroke."

The nurse shook her head. "Nothing on his chart. And I really don't think so. He wouldn't be here now if he just had a stroke. He'd be in intensive care or possibly rehab." After placing the chart back at the end of Daddy's bed, the nurse left the room.

Puzzled, Patsy dialed Aunt Evelyn's number. At the woman's gravelly hello, she said, "I'm here at the hospital with Daddy, Aunt Ev. It looks like he's got a fever, but that's all. Who told you he had a setback?"

A pause, and then words coated with honey on gravel.

"When I called, the nurses told me he was ill."

"But who said he had another stroke?"

Aunt Evelyn sighed. "I can't remember, dear. But the point is, he got sick and you weren't there. He needs twenty-four-hour care."

"That's what I'll give him, Aunt Ev. He'll be in my home and I'll be there all the time."

"What about your children? You'll be gone with them. And won't they resent having him? He could take lots of your time."

"They look forward to having him, Aunt Ev. We have his room ready and everything."

"I still think he'll be better off in a home. . . ." the old woman's voice trailed off.

Patsy sighed. "Aunt Evelyn, if you call me like this again, I'll know to call the hospital first. And I know he'll be better off with me."

Aunt Evelyn said primly, "I don't think you know what you're getting into, Patricia."

Patsy set the phone down without saying goodbye. She walked out to the nurse's station. "Do you have my phone number listed as someone to call if my daddy gets sick?" she asked.

The nurse looked on his chart. "There's his sister's number, Evelyn Wilson, and then his brother, Aaron McClendon."

Patsy steeled herself. "I should be there—Patricia Thompson. I'm his daughter. His *only child.*"

She watched the nurse write her name and phone number above Aunt Evelyn's. Then she drove home and sat on the bed in the clean, empty room she had set aside for Daddy. There wasn't a speck of dust on the chest of drawers and the bed was made with sheets and a quilt she had sewn herself. There was a solid oak nightstand and a bureau with a mirror. The closet was empty and vacuumed.

Sitting on the bed, Patsy finally let herself release the tears she had been holding back. "Oh, Daddy, what if you did have another stroke? What if you die? Then I'd be all alone." Patsy cried for her father's ill health; she cried for her aunt's coldness; and she cried because she didn't want to lose the only parent she had left.

Patsy wiped her eyes with the back of her hand and took a deep breath. It had been a false alarm this time, but she knew the dreaded call could come at any moment. She wasn't ready to let Daddy go, but what could she do?

Patsy stood from the bed and looked at the clock. There was an hour before the kids would come home from school. She walked upstairs to the desk and drew out her notebook from the adoption support group meeting. Then she drove to the library and looked for the phone records for Trenton, New Jersey. She wrote down the numbers for the First Baptist Church, the fire and police department, voter registration, and something called Telephone Resident Service Center. Looking at her notes, she scanned the Yellow Pages and listed two New Jersey adoption support groups called Origins and Adoptive Parents for Open Records. Patsy felt dizzy and hopeful with the possibilities. Surely someone from one of these numbers would know something.

The next morning, Patsy started calling numbers on her list. First, the police department. "This is Patricia Thompson," she said, hoping to sound official. "Calling to see if you have a police record for Sarah Beth Walker."

"Have to call the court—" said the woman who answered, and then hung up.

Patsy glanced at the list of other numbers, then called the police department again.

"Could you please tell me which court I need to call to find a police record?" she asked again.

"Which county did the crime take place in?"

Patsy racked her brain, then she said she'd call back. She looked in the *World Book Encyclopedia* that she used to help her kids write school reports and discovered that Trenton, New Jersey, was in Union County. She called again. "Where would I call for crimes that took place in Union County?"

"Fourth District Court. 555-6784."

Patsy dialed. "Records," someone answered.

"I need to find some information about a court case involving Sarah Beth Walker."

"Do you have a case number?"

"No," said Patsy, a sinking feeling beginning to deflate her enthusiasm.

"Birth date?"

"No," she said again.

"Social Security number?"

"I'm sorry. I can't help you there."

The woman groaned, said she'd see what she could find, then set the phone down on the counter with a slam that hurt Patsy's ears. Finally she came back and asked Patsy to call back after lunch, when the office might be less busy and she'd have more time to look.

Feeling her frustration rise, Patsy vacuumed the main floor of the house, then got out an afghan she'd stopped working on a year ago, but now seemed a perfect project to keep her occupied. She stitched into the afternoon, her emotions gradually calming with the even rise and fall of the yarn.

At two o'clock she called the court again. When the woman asked her to call back in an hour, Patsy took the cordless phone and started dinner. She peeled potatoes and watched the clock inch to the time she needed to pick up the kids. She set the table. Finally she called a third time.

"Nothing," the woman said.

"Nothing?" Patsy asked.

"Nothing under that name in Union County."

Frustrated, Patsy hung up the phone and left to pick up the kids.

Chapter Six

The next morning Patsy drove to the Laurinburg court-house, where Marvin's wife, Anne, worked—where her own daddy used to work. Patsy recalled going there when she was a little girl, feeling so important walking through the big marble hallways, feeling so proud that her daddy worked in such an impressive place. Following a long maze of halls, she finally saw a sign that read COURT CLERK. "I'm here to see Anne Walker," she said expectantly, glancing back at the large room behind the clerk that was filled with filing cabinets and computer-topped desks.

"She's no longer with this department," said the woman, who sat frozen at her desk as if guarding a vast treasure behind her.

"Where might I find her?" Patsy asked hopefully.

"She's in the main building downtown," said the woman.

"Do you know her?" Patsy asked.

The woman nodded curtly.

"Anne and I are related through her husband, Marvin," said Patsy, hoping her calm-sounding voice belied her nervousness within. "I saw her at a funeral a couple of years ago. I'm looking for some of our other relatives. Did Anne ever mention her husband's stepmother, Sarah Beth, who left to live in New Jersey?"

The woman frowned at her, obviously annoyed at this nonbusinesslike question. "I couldn't release confidential information she mentioned about something like that."

A rush of hopefulness filled Patsy. "Then did she mention her? Are some of her records here by any chance?"

The clerk's frown was sour. "That information would be confidential as well. Her next of kin would need to make a written request that would need to be evaluated by a committee. What records are you seeking?"

"My father had a stroke and—" Patsy sensed this woman was about lose patience with her. She lowered her voice. "The truth is, I'm adopted and I'm trying to find my birth mother. Sarah Beth Walker is her name. My father told me to look before—"

There was a pause before the clerk's face turned scarlet. Patsy saw a vein pulse in the woman's neck before she said, "Now I know who you are. You're Jess McClendon's daughter, Patsy."

"Yes," Patsy answered, wondering why this information seemed to anger rather than encourage the woman. Staring at her flushed and frowning face, Patsy could practically see the woman's mind and the files behind her lock instantly. There was a feeling like a slap to Patsy's face when the clerk spoke. "I can't believe how ungrateful you are. I worked here when Jess brought you to see Anne. He used to flash you around like you were a ten-carat diamond. You were the light of Jess and Pearl's life. Their sun rose and set on you. Don't you understand? This other woman *gave you away*. She didn't care one bit about you. Why worry about whether you were born in a sewer if you grew up in a garden?" The woman stood and slammed a record book on her desk closed.

Patsy found herself trembling with anger. "My daddy asked me to make this search," she said, each word made of iron. "And I'm a forty-year-old-woman. I have three kids of my own, and I have the right to know who gave birth to me."

Tight-lipped, the woman stood, fists clenched at her sides.

Patsy continued, her frustration rising. "What could be so bad about my birth mother? Did she kill someone? Is she a criminal? Or is she just a living, breathing human being?"

The woman planted her hands on her hips. "She didn't care if you ended up a criminal . . . or even if you died. She left and never came back."

"She was forced to leave. Someone held a gun to her head."

"Think whatever you like," the woman said, rolling her eyes. "But I know Jess rescued you. After he brought you home, you were his first concern every day of his life. I still remember how his eyes lit up when he talked about you. And I wouldn't look for anything for you even if I could. I think it's time you learned to appreciate the parents who raised you."

"I do!" Patsy exclaimed, but now the woman turned and walked back into the file room without a word.

What made the woman so angry? If she really remembered Daddy, wouldn't she guess how he might accept his daughter's desire for more information?

Moments later the clerk returned with a tall, balding man dressed in a suit and tie. Looking over Patsy's head as he spoke, he said, "Above and beyond the emotional issues in this matter, ma'am, are the legal issues. The fact is, adoption records are sealed. You would need a court order to make such a request. Even then there would be no guarantees." He nodded briefly as their eyes met. Then he said dismissively, "Good day."

Feeling helpless and surprisingly angry, Patsy turned and left the courthouse building.

Sitting among her support group that night, Patsy recounted the scene with the court clerk. All of the group members smiled at her with a mixture of amusement, total understanding, and empathy.

The leader stood and faced the group. "What do we do, guys?"

A brunette woman in the front row raised her hand, then

said, "When we're asking for information, we say *anything* but adoption. We make stuff up."

The leader turned back to Patsy. "You'll have more luck if you say you're a reporter for a tabloid than if you admit you're adopted."

"I'm only looking for my own information. I don't want to disrupt anybody else's life," Patsy countered.

"They don't care. They never had the same need for information, so they don't understand," said the leader.

"If you say you're doing genealogy, they'll sing like birds," one woman said.

A man called out from the back of the room, "They deny us the most simple rights—our birth rights."

"Open records for everyone!" someone else shouted. The leader held up her hands as any decorum the meeting may have possessed dissolved in a sea of applause.

Later, sitting alone on her couch at home, Patsy realized that Lois Ferguson, the woman who gave her the Post-it note at the last group gathering, didn't attend this meeting. The next morning she dug in her purse, found the phone number, and made the call. After a few minutes of conversation, Patsy agreed to drive across town to Lois's house and bring all the information she had about Sarah Beth Walker with her.

Patsy was surprisingly nervous as she picked up her folders of notes and walked to Lois's door.

Standing in Lois's rose- and cream-colored living room, Patsy said, "The truth is, I'm discouraged. It seems like I have so much information that other adoptees don't—her name, my four half brothers' and half sisters' names and my birthplace. There I was, at the court clerk's window where my sister-in-law worked. Yet I'm still at square one. And look at how that clerk yelled at me . . . just for wanting my own information."

"I know. I've been through it. They take their information for granted all their lives, but they can't understand why we want ours. That's why you need to write letters."

"Letters? But that could take so long. Why can't they

just give me the information when I ask for it, when I'm there, in their offices?''

"There's something about a letter that is official—but nonthreatening. You've had time to think about this. But when you walk up and ask people in person, it's like you're throwing it in their face without giving them a chance to mull it over and decide whether it's the right thing.''

Patsy sighed. "I didn't think anyone else would care one way or the other. It doesn't hurt them.''

"They do care. It's a way of acting superior, or having power over us. They have something we want.''

"But letters take forever. It seems like I'm so close.''

Lois hesitated. "Do you know—even when you do find her—what your chances are of being accepted? You don't hear from people at the group whose birth parents turn them away and refuse to speak. Those people stop coming to the group. It's too painful. It's like being rejected at birth all over again.''

"But she kept me for two years. She didn't reject me then.''

"Lots more years have passed. Her life could be completely different. She might be married to a man she never told about you. She could have other kids, or an important job where she can't risk her reputation.''

"I wouldn't disrupt any of that.''

"Or she could be dead.''

Patsy swallowed. "I wouldn't hurt anyone's feelings then, would I?''

"A husband, maybe. Children who didn't know their mother could ever fall in love with someone else. It's a risk, no matter what. But letters are sort of a quiet way of sneaking in. And no matter what you get back, it's a clue.''

"What if they don't answer?

"Even that—it tells you to look in another direction. Try another name, another place. There's only one truly discouraging part.''

"What's that?''

"No matter how good you are at finding her, even if you're batting a thousand, the chances of her accepting you and forming a relationship are only fifty-fifty. Half don't want to see you, or they'll meet you once and that's it. But half do want a relationship. It's a gamble you take.''

"I know I could be disappointed,'' Patsy acknowledged. "But I don't think I can stop until I know.''

Now Lois smiled and leaned over and patted Patsy's shoulder. "Then you're one of us. We search until dooms-day. Can't go out of this world unless we know. Now I made a list for you, and some sample cover letters. Send out a bunch of these every week. Give yourself a day. Say Tuesday. Every Tuesday you send off five letters. And when you get back two no's, just think there are three out there that could say yes. Say whatever comes to your mind. Anything that sounds convincing. Just don't ever use the word *adoption*. Steer clear of it like it was incest or mur-der.''

"It was my father who asked me to do this, you know,'' Patsy said. "Right before his stroke.''

Lois leaned closer and smiled with something like rec-ognition. "I think he knows you better than you know yourself. He gave you permission to do what you really want to do inside.''

The next morning, after the kids were off at school, Patsy sat at the typewriter. Following the guidelines from Lois and the support group, she wrote, "Due to the Freedom of Information Act, I would like to obtain copies of both sides of my mother's voter registration.'' Then she rolled another piece of paper into the typewriter. She felt a twinge of guilt at what she was about to write. All her life Patsy was taught that dishonest people don't prosper, and what goes around comes around. Yet with Lois and the members of the sup-port group meeting, the most absolute rule was don't men-tion the word *adoption*. Recalling the instant rage on the clerk's face, Patsy typed, "This letter is in regards to ob-taining my medical records and those of my mother at the time of my birth. There is a genetic problem that needs to be addressed by my doctor for the sake of the future of my children.'' She paused, chewed on the end of her pen, then typed, "This letter releases you from any liability in submitting these records to me and my doctor."

After rolling the paper up, she typed her birth date, the hospital where she was born, and her address at the time of birth.

She wrote two other letters to school districts in Trenton, New Jersey, and another to a school district in Centerville inquiring about Sarah Beth Rogers, taking a chance that that was her mother's maiden name. Gazing at the letters, she understood Lois's feelings. There was a sense of purpose and accomplishment in just knowing that in this nonconfrontive way her voice might be heard.

In the group meetings she'd attended, Patsy listened sympathetically to adoptees who had no idea where they were born or what their birth parents' names were. They tried to help each other determine new ways of doing detective work to find the hidden names. But she was one of the lucky ones. She had information to pursue: the fact that she had lived with her mother for two years and the story of how one night her father held a gun to her mother's head. Patsy wondered about the sequence of events the night her mother left. Did the evening start out calm, with the family sitting in the living room, the way so many of her family's nights were spent? And how did anger escalate so that Sarah Beth left her home and never came back? Was it the first time her father threatened her mother's life, if that's what happened?

Could be that my mama really did leave to save my life, Patsy reasoned to herself. But why can't anyone tell me what happened to her after that? Was her life happy? And why didn't she ever come back to get me?

Focusing her mind back on the paper in front of her, she picked up her pen and wrote a P.S. at the bottom of each letter, saying that her records might be listed under Baby Girl Walker. She addressed the envelopes, gathered all the letters up, and left for the post office in Centerville.

Waiting in line to place them through the slot, she silently pleaded that someone who opened the envelope would write back with her mother's address, birth date, or Social Security number.

Driving home, she thought of the night her mother left. She mentally envisioned herself in Sarah Beth's place, with someone holding a gun to the side of her own head as she begged, "Don't make me leave my babies! Please, please, don't make me leave them here. I'll go—I'll go, but please let me take them with me." If she closed her eyes, Patsy imagined she could feel the cool metal of the gun against her skin. She shivered at thoughts of her mother's pure terror. Then she pictured her mother's dress soaring backward in the wind as she ran barefoot out of her own house into the dark, invisible part of the night. Thinking of her own three children and imagining herself in that situation, Patsy shook her head in horror before deciding what her own choice would be. She couldn't imagine leaving her children and not looking back. No matter what.

Chapter Seven

As the weeks passed, Patsy determined that she needed to speak to Marvin again, but would he talk to her? It wasn't until the next week that she managed to work up her courage and make the call.

She dialed Marvin's number and waited. His voice held the same reluctance it did at the end of their last conversation. "Oh, I thought we already went over all that," he said.

"Well . . . I thought of a few more questions," Patsy said. "I won't take too much of your time. I just want to make sure I understand the situation—"

"I don't understand it too well myself—no one did, you know. She just left that night. That was it. Now, you did say you talked to Paul, didn't you?"

"Paul. You mean—"

"Paul Walker, your brother."

"No—no, I haven't," Patsy said.

"He lives about ten minutes from me. On Hickory Valley Circle. I think he might have heard from Sarah Beth since she left."

"Really?" Patsy stopped herself from asking why he didn't tell her this before.

"I think I have his number."

Patsy waited. After getting her brother's phone number

and address, she thanked Marvin, then hung up the phone and dialed. When it was busy, she got in the car and drove.

The house, like Marvin's, was suburban and comfortable-looking. A blond woman was watering the flower garden with a hose.

Patsy sat in the car two houses down and watched. When the woman shut off the hose and walked toward the house, Patsy caught sight of a brown-haired man who stood behind the screen door and waited for her. After the woman entered the house, the man closed the hunter-green front door. Patsy climbed out of the car. I don't know these people, she thought, but everything I need to know could be in that house. With a quick glance at her reflection in the mirror, she strode to the front door and bravely rang the bell.

"Yes?" It was the woman, not opening the door all the way and peeking out with a slightly annoyed expression as if Patsy were interrupting her.

Patsy pasted on a smile she hoped looked sincere. "I know we haven't met before, but I'm Patricia Thompson. Your husband's sister. I just need to ask him a quick question."

The woman gestured that she come in. Patsy saw that the living room was ultra-tidy. Rose-colored carpet. Floral print chair and couch. Not a piece of mail or pile of newspapers anywhere. "Have a seat. I'll get him," the woman said. No smile or it's nice to meet you. Or I didn't know my husband had a sister I haven't met.

Patsy heard footsteps. The man's face looked stiff and resentful from the first moment. He kept his hands in his pockets and stood at the doorway.

"Hello, Paul. I'm Patricia Thompson—your sister."

"I know who you are," the man said flatly.

"You do?" Patsy was incredulous.

"I saw you at a funeral a few years ago."

"Oh, yes," said Patsy, not remembering ever seeing this man in her life. "I don't know if you knew that my dad had a stroke. Jess McClendon, the dad who adopted me. Right before he got sick, he asked me to look for my birth mother."

Now the man shook his head slowly and punctuated the gesture with a wave of his hand. "Don't want nothing to do with any of it," he said.

"What?" Patsy asked, puzzled.

"Don't want to talk about your mom. Don't want to think about her. Don't know anything."

"But she was your mom, too, right?"

"Yes."

"And you weren't put up for adoption, were you? "

Now the man hemmed and hawed. "No. But I ended up growing up without her, too. And I'm trying to forget that. So I don't want to talk about it anymore."

Abruptly Paul's wife pressed a large gold-framed picture into Patsy's hand. The black and white photo it held depicted a young, obviously pregnant woman with shoulder-length hair smiling down at a two-year-old boy that she held by the hand. "That's Paul," the woman said.

For a moment Patsy was distracted by trying to compare the two-year-old Paul with the sullen man standing with his arms folded across his chest. Then a chill grew inside her with the realization that the woman in the picture was her birth mother. The line of the face, the rounded chin, the eyes. She couldn't stop staring, but then she looked up suddenly. "She was pregnant with *me* in this picture," she said in amazement.

Paul reached out and roughly took the photo from her.

"Marvin told me you saw her since she left for New Jersey. Please," Patsy pleaded. "You had a chance to know our mom, but I didn't. You don't know what it's like to wonder all your life."

"Ha," Paul grunted, then looked up to confront her. "You had a good life. Why mess it up? What if you meet her and wish you hadn't?"

Patsy tried to control the fury that rose within her. "Sir, I don't believe you have the right to decide that for me. What could she do that I'd regret meeting her? Is she an ax murderess?"

When Paul shook his head, Patsy continued, "I know you have information that could help me. It won't hurt you to tell me. But I can pay a detective to get this information for me. You're not the only one who has it. But it won't cost either of us anything for you just to tell me. I promise I won't tell anyone I got it from you. I won't ever come back here again and bother you. What's the big deal?''

"I want no part of it." Again Paul punctuated his words with his hands. "And now it's time for you to leave." When his voice rose, he stepped toward her. His chin jutted out and his hands shook with anger. Patsy stood nervously, her hand on the back of the chair. "I'm sorry you're upset." She fought to make her voice as calm as possible. "But I don't think you have the right to make this decision for me. I have the right to know who my mother is and where she was from. If it were me, I'd help you," she said.

An angry sort of grin spread across Paul's face. This time he stepped menacingly toward her and pointed his finger like a knife. He sneered as he said, "Lady, you got no rights in my house. Leave now, or I'll call the police."

Patsy felt adrenaline cascade through her. Forcing herself to appear calm, she felt as if she were moving in slow motion as she picked up her purse and walked out Paul's front door. He slammed it behind her with a cracking sound.

Patsy lingered for a moment on the front porch, reeling as if she'd been physically hit. What was really going on here? she wondered. How could it possibly hurt this man to give her a few names and dates? Her mother's birth date and Social Security number were probably right inside a drawer in this house, Patsy realized. But now it was closed as tight as a tomb. Despite Paul's threat, she hovered on the front porch steps, reluctant to leave. What could she do now?

During the next four weeks, Patsy pondered why Paul held what seemed like a powerful animosity toward her and the mother they shared. He obviously made it to adulthood all right, didn't he? Was there really a secret she'd rather not know? As she watched endless T-ball games, volunteered at the school field day, and planted her spring garden, she debated how to search next.

The voter registration department wrote back, saying that the records they now kept only went back to 1967. The hospital's letter said that her mother's Social Security number and birth date were confidential information. Then she opened a letter from the school district in Centerville. The records office wrote that there was more than one Sarah Beth Rogers in their records, and they would need a Social Security number to distinguish between them. Patsy called Lois Ferguson in elation at receiving a first lead.

"Lois, there are two of them!" she said, not daring to express the excitement she felt rising inside her.

"Two of what?" Lois laughed good-naturedly.

"Two women with my birth mother's name at the school where she went." Patsy paused. A heavy sigh escaped her lips. "I just can't help but think that one of them might be the one."

"What does the school say? Did they tell you anything that makes you think it might be one or the other?" Patsy sensed Lois was trying to curb her own rising excitement.

"That's just it—they say they need a Social Security number so they can tell which one it is. . . ." Another sigh made Patsy's shoulders droop. Inhaling, she steeled herself. "So, help me think this through. I could guess what year Sarah Beth was born. . . ."

"And she went to kindergarten five years after that," Lois prompted.

"Maybe if I'm not too specific about the years—" Another sigh. "What child couldn't figure out what year her mother turned five?"

Lois interjected quickly, "Don't let them know you don't know that. And don't admit you don't have the Social Security number."

"But how can I figure out which one it might be?"

"Just don't let them stop you. If you admit you don't have the number, you're giving them an excuse to say no."

"But what else should I say? I know—anything but adoption. I'm just trying to think of—"

"Just give them everything else you've got. Write another letter. Put *your* Social Security number and birth date. Tell them you remember visits to Centerville, when your mom pointed out the school to you. Say fourth grade was her favorite. Or she told you about winning the spelling bee. Anything that makes you seem somehow entitled, but nothing they could check and prove you wrong."

"But information about *me* doesn't relate to *her*," Patsy protested with a frustrated laugh.

"You know that. I know that. But you'll make them wonder. Give them pause. And while they're pausing, you somehow rush in and get what you need." The two women laughed together.

"What do I have to lose?" Patsy conceded.

"If you want, call me and run your letter past me before you send it off."

Patsy thanked Lois again. After she hung up, she followed Lois's advice and calculated which years Sarah Beth probably attended elementary, junior high, and high school. She wrote to the school district again, not admitting she didn't have the Social Security number or birth date. As she dropped her second letter in the mail, Patsy hoped against hope that something in her words would draw the right response.

Chapter Eight

For several weeks, she tried to deny that she was feeling discouraged about Daddy. She dusted his room, put clean sheets on the bed, and tacked a grapevine wreath she'd made to the wall. She still visited every other weekend, sleeping on the couch in the hospital lounge. She phoned every Sunday to ask his condition. She tried not to admit her fears that Daddy might never come home to live with her. Why was the hospital keeping him so long when the tests were over weeks ago? Why wouldn't they release Daddy to her?

Patsy tried to shrug aside her weariness as she prepared for another weekend visit. Beside her on the car seat, Patsy piled books for Daddy to look at, along with his favorite homemade fudge. Maybe she should move to a closer town, Patsy thought, if she had to keep driving this far.

Reaching the hospital, she didn't even see the social worker who walked up behind her. Patsy only felt a hand on her shoulder before the woman said, "The doctor would like to see you."

Patsy gazed into the other woman's face. There was no smile, and the woman didn't wait for her response before striding faster and then turning a corner to the right. Patsy felt her inner alarm rise. What was happening to Daddy? A sick feeling spread inside her. Her own pace quickened as she hurried to catch an elevator door that was about to close.

She hurried into the doctor's office and saw that the nurse wasn't at her desk. After waiting just a moment Patsy glanced around, then sneaked past the nurse's desk, then back farther into the hall where the examining rooms were.

"Dr. Harrison—Dr. Harrison," she called out.

The doctor opened one of the examining rooms, peered out with a firm frown. His words were filled with lead. "Mrs. Thompson, go back to the waiting room until the nurse announces your father's appointment."

"He doesn't have an appointment. I'm here because the social worker said you need to see me."

The doctor hesitated, then shook his head irritatedly. "Go out there and sit down until I call you." Without waiting for her answer, he stepped back inside the examining room and shut the door.

Patsy sauntered back out to the waiting room. She picked up a magazine and placed it on her lap without opening it. What was happening to Daddy? She watched the clock, read Dr. Harrison's diplomas, and waited. In the waiting room, patients came and went as their names were called. Patsy continued to sit there, wanting to hear her name. Her fingers drummed on the chair and she tapped her feet. Once, she went out in the hall and called Barry, who told her to keep waiting.

Two hours later, she was startled to see Dr. Harrison walk into the waiting room wearing a jacket and carrying a briefcase.

"Dr. Harrison—" she called out in disbelief. "Aren't you going to talk to me?"

He again gave her an irritated look, then said, "Wait in my office—down the hall and to the left."

"How long is it going to be?" Fatigue sharpened Patsy's nerves.

"Momentarily," the doctor spat out, then turned away.

At least his office was a change of setting, Patsy thought. The tan leather chair was softer than those in the waiting room. She gazed around her at more diplomas, potted plants, rows of books, many with the word *geriatric* in the title. She stood and glanced at a photo of the doctor's wife and two sons.

With his jacket still on, Dr. Harrison strode in and sat behind his desk. His piercing blue eyes stared at Patsy. He cleared his throat, then said, "I need to tell you that the medical team has reached a decision. The nurse has the paperwork for you to sign."

He pushed back his chair as if ready to stand.

"*What* decision?" Patsy demanded.

"The nurse will inform you—it's detailed in the document."

"What decision?" Patsy felt her voice rise.

The doctor looked up at her and—was that the hint of a smile? Pressing his palms firmly on the desk, he looked straight at her. "After extensive testing, we're satisfied that your father is of sound mind, knows what he's doing, and knows exactly what he wants—which is to live with you."

Patsy never felt her feet leave the ground. She jumped into the air, flung out her arms, and said, "Thank you!" She might have hugged Dr. Harrison if he wasn't already on his feet and headed for the door.

Patsy ran up the stairs to Daddy's room. She didn't even want to wait for the elevator—she'd had enough waiting. Daddy was sitting up in bed, watching TV, and holding a plastic cup with water.

"Daddy!" Patsy grabbed her father's shoulders and laid her cheek gently against his. "Daddy, you get to go home with me! I'll be right back to get you ready, but I don't dare start getting your things until I sign all the papers." She kissed the top of his head. "Daddy, you wait here and I'll be right back."

Patsy made her way to the nurse's station and bit her tongue when she was told to wait. After about fifteen minutes, a pile of papers that looked thick as a phone book was placed in front of her. At first Patsy read each one through and looked at all Daddy's test scores. Some of them she didn't understand at all, and others looked like tests she'd seen her kids take at school. After about fifteen

forms she began to simply sign her name wherever indi-
cated. Finally she turned the last page.

"I'm going to go get him now," she told the nurse. It
was a relief, but felt strange to have no one say it was
impossible to take her own father home with her.

Patsy opened Daddy's door with a smile—but it looked
as if the room was empty. Patsy sat in his visitor's chair
and waited a few moments. Then she knocked on his bathroom door. No response. She visited the floor nurse, who
said, "I think someone already took him. He was gone a
few moments ago when I checked on him. I thought you
already left."

What? Patsy dashed back to Daddy's room. She opened
his closet. It was empty. She looked in the bathroom. His
shaving kit was gone. Patsy dashed down the halls, running
past nurses, gurneys, orderlies, and patients. After she raced
through every third floor hall, she proceeded to the second
floor, and the first. Her lungs ached and she was out of
breath from running, but she didn't dare stop. At the front
door of the hospital, a man in a wheelchair caught her eye.
She jolted to a stop, and a giggle burst inside her throat.

It was Daddy, facing the door that led to the street, looking outside and waiting for her to drive up in her car to
pick him up. Patsy started to laugh. Somehow Daddy had
gathered his belongings and wheeled himself all the way
down here. He had his hat on his head, his jacket slung
over the back of the wheelchair. Patsy walked up to her
father slowly. She saw he was leaning forward in the chair,
his one good hand tensed around the folded top of a lunch-
size paper bag as if he were about to take flight and didn't
want to drop it. With an outpouring of love, she studied
the visible anticipation in his posture. A tear traced her
cheek. Daddy was ready to go home.

"Daddy!" Patsy said, stepping up beside him. He looked
up at her and smiled knowingly with his lopsided half
smile. Patting his shoulder, Patsy again spotted the brown
grocery bag he now placed on his lap. Puzzled, she looked
inside and saw that Daddy had one-handedly arranged all
his belongings in this bag and another one on the floor.

There wasn't a wrinkle in any of the folded shirts, and the shaving kit was zipped closed. The tidy attention to detail reminded her of when she was a little girl, and he had tied her shoes in a neat bow or straightened her school papers in a line when he was through helping with her homework. Tears again pricked the edges of her eyes. She said, "Daddy, you stay right here. I'll be right back with the car. You're going home with me."

"Grandpa!" The kids all screamed with surprise when they came home to find him sitting on the front porch. That night the big antebellum house felt peacefully filled, as if everything was as it should be now that Daddy was asleep in the bedroom downstairs.

Chapter Nine

The next morning Patsy fed Daddy a bowl of grits and then wheeled him out on the porch, knowing how much he loved the fresh morning air. She sat with him as a peach-colored sunrise spread across the wooden porch slats. There was a peace about being with her father that reminded her of the old days visiting the farm in Centerville on the holidays.

As Patsy grew up, the few memories she had of her birth family seemed something like a recurring nightmare, and when she opened her eyes, she was born again within the warmth and love of Jess and Pearl McClendon. It felt like a rare and unique privilege to be Daddy and Mama's only child. Patsy always felt important in her parents' lives, whether she skinned her knee or her hair was coming unbraided and needed to be wound and fastened again with a rubber band.

As she grew to be an adult, she understood that she was indeed rare—the McClendon's only child, a welcome, beloved and long-anticipated gift. The McClendons were Methodists with a strong sense of the importance of family. On Thanksgivings and Christmases, the family returned to Centerville, where Pearl was from. Patsy remembered how holidays were spent at the old home place, a huge house in the country surrounded with woods and a creek. The men killed hogs and dried meat in the smokehouse for big family gatherings. Patsy and her five cousins ran in the woods, rode on the tractor, played in the creek, and chose a Christmas tree from their own land.

Patsy never felt different when she was with her cousins, even though she knew her biological roots lay elsewhere. She could still feel Daddy's hand on her shoulder, and remember how his voice sounded when he said, "This is my daughter, Patsy." Her parents always introduced her as "our daughter" and most of the time, she never even thought of herself as her parents' adopted child. When her mother filled out school medical forms, she simply checked "no" under the list of hereditary illnesses when the question at the top of the form asked, "Has child or a member of child's family ever had the following?" When someone asked where Patsy's talents for sewing and crafts came from, her mother always laughed and said, "Not from me," and the conversation usually took a different turn after that.

Even when she was little, Patsy had sensed that she was lucky to be with Jess and Pearl. She didn't want to rock the loving family boat by expressing her curiosity about her birth family. She knew intuitively even then that her feelings of wanting to know didn't stem from any lack at home. Yet, secure as she was, deep in the back of her mind the possibility lurked that if she looked for her birth family, maybe her adoptive family wouldn't like her as much anymore. *I want to be good so they'll always like me and keep me,* she had thought to herself. Her mind refused even to think the other, more terrifying possibility. *What if they find out I'm curious and decide to give me back, and then those other people don't want me, either?*

Days, months, and even maybe a year would pass without her adoption even crossing Patsy's mind. And now it seemed as if it was all she could think about. And the search certainly took up a lot of her time. Patsy hoped that once she found some answers, she'd be able to spend her time on what mattered to her most—Barry, her kids, and Daddy.

Patsy patted Daddy's gnarled and mottled hand as he sat

still and content on the porch beside her. She treasured these moments alone with him. There were so many things she wanted to say to him, to thank him for the good life he gave her. Looking at him, she forced herself to speak. "Daddy, now that I'm looking for my birth family, I realize you rescued me from a scary situation. I don't know where I'd be without you."

He half-smiled at her and she saw that the sun, rising in the morning sky, crossed diagonally and lit half his face. As she watched, he started to struggle, and for a moment she thought he might choke. His jaws worked, his Adam's apple bobbed, and he trembled. His hand gripped the wheelchair armrest so that his knuckles were white. Patsy took his other hand, felt his forehead. He didn't have a fever. While she gently patted and rubbed his back, a miracle happened. All his struggles with his throat and jaws emerged in a single word. "Bill." How long was it since Daddy could talk? The word sent chills down Patsy's arms. She jumped to her feet.

"Bill," she said, smiling and looking into his face. His expression was one of studied concentration. Patsy ventured, "Your brother Bill? I remember Uncle Bill, Daddy. Did you want to tell me something about him?" Daddy's face struggled again. His cheeks tremored, and she saw a vein pulse in his neck. "Bill," he said again, as if it were exhausting. He sighed with the effort.

"Yes," Patsy said to her father. "Bill."

She rolled him into the house and into the kitchen. She remembered how the hospital officials and Aunt Evelyn said he'd never talk again. And against all odds, he proved them wrong. Maybe she'd prove them wrong, too—maybe she would find her birth mother. Yes, there were many obstacles in her way, but Patsy was determined. After all, she was Daddy's daughter.

With renewed hope, Patsy sat at the typewriter and wrote a letter to the Bureau of Vital Statistics in South Carolina and the First Baptist Church in Laurinburg. She flipped through photocopies of phone book pages that she'd copied at the library from the directories for Trenton, New Jersey, and Centerville, North Carolina. The phone was in her hand when she remembered Marvin. Maybe if she talked to him and asked for more names, she could make five or six phone calls now, instead of fifty or one hundred later.

She was surprised to find that he seemed to put her off from the beginning of the conversation. "I gave you Paul's phone number. Have you talked to him?" For a moment, Patsy remembered the door being slammed in her face. Discouragement sat like a ton of bricks on her shoulder. "I just want to make sure I understand what you already told me."

"Well . . . this isn't really a good time for me. I have a lot of yard work this week—"

"I just need fifteen, twenty minutes tops," Patsy said.

"I don't know."

"I promise. Only fifteen minutes."

"I'm really not free this week, but . . . okay, how about three o'clock tomorrow?" Marvin's voice sounded frustrated and resigned.

"I'll be there," said Patsy, feeling torn because she wasn't sure who could be home with Daddy at that time. "I promise I'll be quick."

That night she went to the support group to ask how she could approach Marvin. "If I could afford it, it would almost be easier to pay someone," she said.

"It is," Charlene conceded, "but you have to be careful there, too. They know that adoption is close to your heart. So some of them charge a lot of money for nothing. Or for information you could get yourself with just a little research."

"I paid two hundred dollars just to get my mother's name. I called everyone I could find and I'm still no place," said one woman, who added, "I'm just about ready to pay someone else."

"Like the Seeker—" someone called out. A chorus of groans filled the room.

"The Seeker will do anything—legal or not," Charlene explained to Patsy. "He's heavily guarded with body-guards. He'll get what you want—but he'll break the law if he needs to and charge you five thousand dollars to do it.''

Patsy told the group about Paul's rejection, and her second chance at Marvin.

Beside her, Lois patted her shoulder. ''Get him to name names. There's no emotion in just a name. Get him to tell you every name he can.''

Charlene added, ''And when you call asking for the people, say that you have a friend in common. Just don't ever say that the friend is your birth mother until you actually talk directly to the person.''

After the meeting Patsy and Lois sat in the empty room and listed every place they could think of that she could write or call with the names she hoped Marvin would give her.

The next morning, Patsy fed the Sorensen children and her own. After the kids left for school, Barry rushed into the kitchen dressed in a suit and tie. ''Meeting downtown with a client.'' he said. ''See you tonight.'' Patsy felt panic stir inside her. She'd have to cancel Marvin without Barry being here to be with Daddy. As the hours passed, she thought about what to do as she changed the sheets on the boys' beds, made Crock-Pot chili for dinner, and folded Daddy's laundry. Forty-five minutes before she was supposed to meet Marvin, she helped Daddy put on a clean shirt. Then she helped him get into the wheelchair and rolled him out to the car.

Halfway there she remembered that Marvin's porch had three steps to the front door. How would she get Daddy's wheelchair up the stairs? She wound up walking to the front door, and when Marvin stuck his head out the door, she pointed to Daddy behind her on the sidewalk. To her surprise, Marvin came out of his house and wheeled Daddy around to the backyard.

''I think I told you my daddy's last request before the stroke was for me to find my mother and brothers and sisters,'' she reminded Marvin.

Marvin planted his hands on his hips and looked out at

the sprinklers watering his garden patch. "I just really feel like I told you everything. Can't think of anything else to say," he said.

"I just want to make sure that I understand," said Patsy. "I'm trying to square what you told me with what I remember," she said. "When I think back to that house, I remember a dark place. I know I was in that dark place more than once, and that it was a small, tight, dark place. And I remember that my brother was there—and he was holding me. And he was crying."

"That might have been Paul. Or it could have been Brent. You know there are six of us. Rex. Allen . . ." As Marvin racked his brain, Patsy scribbled frantically in her notebook. She stopped for a moment to pat Daddy's hand.

"J. B.—that's it," said Marvin. "And me. And four girls. Wanda, Dee, Mary Jane, and you."

"Were they all Walkers?" Patsy urged.

Marvin shrugged. "Mostly. Or Clark, I think."

"I don't remember all those kids," said Patsy. "I remember that dark place. And I remember arguments. People fighting. Sometimes only two people, and sometimes it seemed like the whole house was filled with people yelling at each other."

Marvin shook his head. "I know," he said. "Not too pleasant to look back on, is it?"

Wanting to change the subject, Patsy added quickly, "I remember the house, but back then, I didn't know where it was or anything. I mean, what town."

"Don't know," said Marvin. "Our parents were from Cheraw, South Carolina, or Laurinburg, North Carolina," said Marvin. "And they lived in Centerville. I think the church where your mother sang might have been in Cheraw."

"My mother *sang*?"

"Yes, with your sisters. At a church. Before all the trouble started."

"What church?"

"Well . . . it was Baptist." He wiped sweat from his forehead. "Whew, this heat. I can't be out here much longer. I'll be burned to a crisp and exhausted besides. Listen, I've got to get back to this yard work.''

Glancing to her side, Patsy saw that Daddy was tired, too. She mopped his brow with the handkerchief he kept in his pocket. ''You go ahead. I can talk while you work. And I need to take Daddy home soon, anyway.''

Marvin said suddenly, ''The Walker Singers. They were called the Walker Singers. Your mom and Wanda and Dee.''

Patsy wrote in her notebook. She remembered something else. ''That name you told me last time—Rogers. Do you remember anything more about that?''

''All I know was she was looking for Bertha Rogers on 129 Oak Street.'' This was more than he gave her before. As Patsy wrote feverishly, Marvin stood and walked to the shed in the back of his yard. ''You said fifteen minutes,'' he reminded her.

''129 . . . you didn't give me the number last time.''

Marvin shrugged and wheeled a lawn mower out of the shed.

Daddy's eyes were closed. He was asleep with beads of sweat on his forehead. Patsy felt both guilt and urgency assail her at the same time. Was there one last question she could ask that would reveal the one secret she needed to know?

''Schools—do you know where she went to school?''

Marvin turned the switch to start the lawn mower. After the engine caught, he started to move the mower across the lawn as he yelled back to her, ''Probably in Centerville or Laurinburg. Don't know which school exactly.''

The lawn mower motor rose to a roar. Marvin gestured at her apologetically. Glancing at her watch, Patsy saw they'd been there an hour. She'd stretched the fifteen minutes to its limit. She waved to him, smiled, and mouthed, ''Thank you.'' Then she touched Daddy's cheek and said, ''We're going home now.''

Chapter Ten

That night after dinner, when her family was watching a basketball game on TV, Patsy went back to work. She sat down with the phone book pages she'd copied from directories for Trenton, New Jersey, along with Laurinburg and Centerville. She began with an S. E. Walker in Laurinburg. Could that be Sarah Elizabeth—or Sarah Beth? Could it be that all her searching would be resolved with a single phone call? Patsy dialed.

The voice sounded hurried and abrupt. "Hello—"

"This is Patricia Thompson. I'm looking to speak with Sarah Beth Walker about a relative we have in common." Patsy breathed. She remembered the support group leader saying the phrase about a relative in common. Or mutual friends. Again, anything but the truth.

"Don't know her." Now the woman's voice slowed only slightly. "I'm Amy. My husband is Stephen Eugene. But there's a million Walkers."

Tell me about it, Patsy thought.

"Anyway, I'm sorry," said the woman.

"Do you know of anyone who might know her? Another relative?" Patsy asked, remembering how she was told to keep trying.

"I don't. I married Steve, but his family is from Pennsylvania."

Patsy tried S. Walker. The phone rang five times before there was a click. This time an answering machine with rap music. Patsy laughed. Somehow, she could not picture her birth mother listening to rap, but she left her number anyway.

She dialed the number for S. B. Walker. Could this be it?

"Hello." A man's voice. Businessy. Official.

"This is Patricia Thompson. I'm looking to reach Sarah Beth Walker."

"Wrong number," said the man.

"Do you know anyone who might know—" Patsy continued, but the man had already hung up.

Another answering machine at a number listed for S. B. Walker. This time the woman sounded as young as Patsy. Next, she called Sarah B. Walker. A young man answered. After Patsy asked for Sarah Beth, the young man said, "My aunt is Sally Beth Walker. Could it be her?"

Sally Beth Walker, Patsy thought. "Do you know when she was born?"

"I do. 1920. She always tells us about the Depression."

Too old, thought Patsy . Wrong name. She hung up, then wondered. Sarah Beth Walker. What if, after all she'd been through, Sarah Beth Walker changed her name? Or went by a new nickname? How would she ever find her then?

Patsy closed her eyes and rubbed her head. Would she ever find her birth mother? Where was she? Patsy tried to remember her mother's face, her voice. But no matter how she tried, Patsy's first memory of her birth family was of herself being shrouded in darkness. Like an out-of-focus movie, the blackness hung over her like a heavy haze. Where was she back then? Patsy wondered. She was in the dark place more than one time, she knew that. She also remembered arguments. She recalled her brother's arms around her, holding her. And she could hear him crying. But it was as if the camera was not only out of focus, but also not aimed directly at the scene in front of her. As much as she strained mentally, she couldn't see the complete picture, and what she could envision remained blurry. The only lasting image from those days was a scar on Patsy's chest the size of a quarter. She didn't know how it got there, or what form would make a shape like that.

The most distinct memory was later, when she was older, probably five. She remembered sitting on the edge of a bed where a man was lying. She spoke with him, she knew that. And she held a recollection that the man didn't look familiar to her, and she was scared of him because she didn't know him. There were people standing around, and somehow she knew the man in bed was her birth father. Possibly he was dying. She never saw him any other time, but she thought he was probably dead now. Though she couldn't bring the memories to focus, even now, when she was home alone, she always kept a light on. Darkness wasn't a terrifying fear, but a lingering unease that never quite went away.

That night at the support group Lois Ferguson couldn't hide the smiles that kept spreading across her round, happy face. Charlene said to the group, "You can probably tell Lois has some news for us tonight."

A chill shot through Patsy, who turned as Lois stood, hands shaking at her sides.

"I met my birth mother," she said, her voice breaking.

Oohs and ahhs filled the air in the municipal room building where the group met.

"Doesn't this give all of us a little more hope?" Charlene asked. "Now, Lois, tell us how this happened."

Lois was still shaking. Patsy reached out and took her hand. "We met at a Holiday Inn in Albany, New York," Lois began. "I took my mom with me so my two moms met on the same day." She wiped her eyes with her hand.

Someone asked if Lois looked like her birth mother. "The spitting image," said Lois. "Both of us have black hair, brown eyes, round face. She's a little bigger than I am. But I had a picture of her for a while before we met, so I knew what she looked like."

"What did you think about her?" asked Charlene.

Lois paused. "After hearing her story, I think the best

thing she could ever have done for me was to give me up—but now I know she loved me and never stopped thinking about me.''

"So would you meet her again if you had it to do over?" asked Charlene.

Now Lois stood still with determination. "It was the best thing I ever did," she said.

"What about your mom?"

"My two moms hugged each other when they met. And my mom said to me, 'I have to thank this woman. Without her I would never have you.' Then my birth mother thanked my mom for taking me and raising me as her own.''

"Well, it sounds fantastic, doesn't it?" Charlene asked the group. She turned to Lois. "Any surprises."

"Yes," said Lois. "My birth father, who has died, was a full-blooded Mohawk Indian, chief on the reservation for eight years."

"Ahh . . ." said the group again. Echoes of laughter.

Lois held up her hand. "And—" she said, "I am one of twenty-six children on his side."

Now the group broke into pandemonium, a sea of applause, laughter, and exclamations. Someone called out, "You can have reunions forever."

In the days following the meeting, Patsy recalled how Lois said she had a picture of her birth mother long before they met. Could a picture help her find Sarah Beth Walker? What if she had a picture to take with her as she searched?

Patsy took her phone book from the drawer and looked up Paul's number. When a woman answered the phone, Patsy realized she didn't even know Paul's wife's name. Inhaling quickly, she said, "This is Patsy Thompson." When the woman didn't respond, she continued, "I'm your husband's sister who came to your house that day. I know Paul isn't willing to help me find my birth mother. But if he feels that negatively about her, he could give me that picture you showed me. The one where she's holding his hand and she is pregnant with me."

Patsy took a breath. Silence on the other end of the line. Patsy sighed, then continued, "He doesn't even need to give me the real thing. I could go to a copy store and have a color copy made and it would be almost as good. I only need to borrow it for about an hour.'' When the woman still didn't reply, Patsy's throat tightened, and when she spoke again her voice broke. ''It might be the only thing I ever have of my mother's.''

At first there was a noise like TV static, and she wasn't sure if Paul's wife intended to cover the phone with her hand. Yet it was soon obvious they meant for her to hear exactly what they were saying.

''Paul, this is that Thompson woman,'' Paul's wife said. ''She's calling to ask if she can have that photo of your mother or borrow it to copy.''

Then the woman covered the receiver with her hand completely, and Patsy heard the two of them conversing in hushed tones. There was a shuffling, and suddenly she could hear their voices again.

Paul's tone was affected and filled with sarcasm as he pretended to be speaking to his wife. ''Hmm. I just don't know where that picture is. I don't know what in the world happened to that.''

Now his wife spoke into the phone. ''I'm sorry. We seem to have lost it,'' she said.

Patsy felt her blood boil and anger rise within. ''You tell your husband something for me,'' she said. ''Tell him that I don't need him. I'll find my birth mother on my own without him. And when I do, I'm going to call him and say 'I did it without you.' '' Patsy hung up the phone.

She wasn't aware that Barry entered the kitchen, but now he had his arm around her. ''Patsy, I need to tell you something. All those nights when you stay up until two in the morning and look through phone books and stuff, well, you think I'm asleep, but I'm really not.''

Patsy turned and grinned. Barry smiled back at her and kissed her on the cheek. ''I mean, back then when you were getting up with babies, maybe I slept through then, but not now. I hear you writing in your notebook.''

''I try to be quiet and not make too much noise with my pen.'' The two of them laughed together.

Barry stepped back, then sat on a kitchen chair and looked up at her. "The thing is, Patsy, I know you want this *real bad.*"

Patsy nodded sadly. "I do. I don't know why exactly, but I do."

"And I know it takes a lot of your time,"

Now her defenses rose. "I'm still getting everything else done. I take Daddy to therapy and all around town with me during the day. I still feed all of you, and this house hasn't exactly filled to the roof with dirt, either. . . ."

Barry took the hand she waved for emphasis and held it in his own. He squeezed her fingers gently until she finally met his eyes. Then he said, "That's not what I mean. I'm not saying that. Not at all." Now he waited, and his voice hushed and slowed. "It's you I'm worried about, Patsy. I don't want this to eat you alive."

Patsy's laugh felt like a tightly compressed valve releasing. "It won't," she said, shaking her head in her surprised consternation. She thought of Paul. "I might eat somebody else alive. But nobody's going to eat me."

Now Barry placed a finger to his lips. Then he turned his head both ways, peering around as if someone might be spying on them. Patsy frowned quizzically as he led her to a kitchen chair and sat down beside her.

Barry lowered his voice to a whisper. "Uh, the thing is, I asked a friend—and I'm not going to tell you who—to look in law-enforcement records."

"Barry!" said Patsy, mock-slapping his arm and knowing that in all the years he worked as a fireman and policeman, he always held to his ethics that law-enforcement records were confidential.

"Don't tell anybody." Barry again held a finger to his lips.

"So?"

"So, what?" Barry asked.

"So what did they find, you undercover cop!" Now Patsy playfully shook her husband's shoulder.

"Nothing."

"Nothing?" Patsy shrugged in disbelief. "All this like

there's a big secret and they found *nothing*.''

"Well, it's really strange that there was absolutely nothing. You can find *something* on almost everybody. But not Sarah Beth Walker. There's nothing in DMV. No driver's license. Or even a city ID card.''

A strange feeling filled Patsy. How could anyone exist today without a license or an ID card? How did Sarah Beth Walker survive alone in Trenton, New Jersey, without being able to drive? Patsy thought of the multitudes of times she was asked to show her driver's license to cash checks, use her charge card. Then her mind rushed to the scary possibilities. Was it possible Sarah Beth Walker was hiding on purpose for some life-threatening reason? Or that she died before she ever had a chance to get her driver's license? What if, after she said goodbye to Marvin, she rounded a corner and met sudden death? Patsy shuddered. Then she felt Barry squeeze her shoulder.

"But, Patsy—''

"Yeah,'' she turned to face him and fought to bring her mind back to the present.

"There was a name.''

"A name?'' Patsy was puzzled.

"A Sarah Beth Walker.''

"I knew it.'' She grabbed his hand and squeezed it good-naturedly. "You're holding out on me. I knew it. You found her and you're holding back.''

Barry grasped her arms. "We found a name. It's probably nothing.''

"You found Sarah Beth Walker?''

"Well—that name. Yes.''

"Well, what are you waiting for? Tell me. Where is she?''

"That's the thing, Patsy. We found the name at the state prison.''

Chapter Eleven

For weeks she felt bleak grief. Maybe it really could be worse to discover the truth than never to know. What if the Sarah Beth Walker in prison was her birth mother? Would she go visit her? Would she tell Barry, Rodney, Chris, Joy, and Daddy? Would she ever go back to the support group and admit what she found?

Yet, what if Sarah Beth needed her? Feeling as if she were in the middle of a movie script, Patsy wondered if her mother could possibly be in prison for a crime she didn't commit. Patsy wondered if she could possibly be the only person to save Sarah Beth. If she didn't look further, she'd never know. Maybe the reason for her search was bigger than she'd always thought.

Patsy couldn't decide whether it was the idea that the trail might lead to prison, or simply the fact that Barry's friend found nothing in law enforcement records, but something about bumping into this last dead end made her want to contact an attorney. The lawyer she called was a friend of Daddy's. She made an appointment for two weeks later.

Sitting in the attorney's office, Patsy thought that this waiting room was the most plush of any she'd seen. Thick forest-green carpet, walls with rubbed paneling, lush green plants. Much fancier than the hospital. She waited about half an hour before a secretary in an expensive-looking silk dress ushered her in the back office.

"Patsy," said David Benson, rising from his desk and holding out a hand for her to shake. He gestured for her to sit down. "Did you say Jess is staying with you now?"

"He is." Patsy sat. "We're thrilled to have him."

"Great guy." The words were sincere but rushed, as if they completed the required niceties and needed to get down to business quickly.

"I don't know if Daddy ever told you this, but he adopted me when I was two years old. I want you to know that he'll always be my daddy. He's my real dad. Both of us know that. But before his stroke, he asked me to look for my birth relatives."

The lawyer nodded. At least he didn't say she was ungrateful, Patsy thought.

"I tried some searching on my own, and think I need a little help."

"You know that adoption records are sealed."

"I know that. I want to seek a court order to get my birth certificate."

He nodded and leaned forward. "Could cost you a bit . . . maybe more than a bit."

"I've already spent a lot of time."

"Then you may have previously discovered everything I could find."

"I need to try this. I haven't found the basic stuff. Her birth date. Her Social Security number."

He jotted on a notepad as she spoke. "Let me have my paralegal check the database. I'll get back to you later this week"

Patsy stood. "You'll give me an estimate?"

The man reached out and gently cuffed her arm. "I'll check a few things out before we go that far. I owe old Jess a few favors."

"Thanks," said Patsy.

It was three days later when he called her back. She came home from Daddy's therapy to find the law firm name and number written in Chris's handwriting. She phoned immediately.

"Thank you for getting back to me so quickly," she said hopefully.

"I just don't want you to waste your money," Benson said.

"What?" asked Patsy.

"I'm sorry to have to tell you this, but I scanned the info on the database and there's nothing there. Just the amended birth certificate that says your parents are Jess and Pearl McClendon. I did notice—it looks as if your name wasn't legally changed until you were five years old. Do you know why that would be?"

Patsy envisioned a small version of herself in that long-ago hospital room. "Yes. When my birth father died."

"That might explain it. The adoption route was different from usual. No initial amended birth certificate when you were an infant. I wondered why that was. But I wanted to let you know not to waste your money. Someone could charge you big bucks to open the court files—and they're empty."

"But what about—" Patsy struggled to release the next words.

The lawyer cleared his throat, and she sensed the same rushed feeling as when they met in person. This guy wanted to finish business and hang up.

Forcing herself to go on, Patsy said, "My husb—uh, someone I talked to found my birth mother's name on a document at the state prison."

There was a silence. Patsy felt her heart thud.

"Patsy, I probably should have told you. I knew before you came in here that it was our firm that finalized your adoption. If you tell anyone I looked in the files and told you what it said, I'll deny it. But Jess was my friend. And sometimes lawyers and clerks get sloppy in adoptions. They leave the birth mother's last name on the papers, and call you Baby Girl Walker—or whatever the name is. Or sometimes there's a medical form left in there or info on the father or something like that. But not this time."

"Oh—" said Patsy. "Is there any way I could look at the file?"

"Absolutely not." The lawyer's voice turned crisp. "And about a prison document. What would make you think I have prison records here at my law office?"

"Thanks," she said. The word fought wearily from her throat. "How much do I owe you?"

"No charge—just don't let anyone else talk you into paying for your court file."

"I won't." There was a lump in her throat when she hung up the phone.

Patsy was discouraged, but wouldn't give up.

Two weeks later she was at the municipal building, looking for the room with a sign that read RECORDS.

"I need to find the records for a Sarah Beth Walker," she said assertively.

"Case number." The woman's pencil was poised on a scratch pad. She didn't look up at Patsy.

"I don't have one," Patsy said, trying to sound calm. She watched the woman's pencil move down to the next line.

"Birth date," said the woman, still not looking up.

"I'm sorry, I don't have that either."

"Social Security number."

"I'm sorry."

Finally the black-haired woman's brown eyes met Patsy's. "No way I can look it up without any of those." She appeared to peer closer. "What is this for, anyway?"

"I have her name," said Patsy.

The woman waved her hand. "Millions of Walkers," she said. Patsy realized that her knees were shaking. It was now or never. She looked back to a door that said Supervisor, where she glimpsed a man sitting behind the desk. "Could I talk to him?" she asked, pointing.

"Are you going to complain about me? Lady, I don't make the rules."

"No . . . no . . . it's just a long story, and it's . . . complicated. I just don't want to bother you anymore."

The woman eyed her warily. "Mr. Boggs," she said. "There's a woman out here who'd like to talk to you." The man stood, stepped out of his office, and came to look at Patsy. He wore a puzzled expression as if he were trying to determine how he knew her.

"Could I speak to you in your office?" Patsy asked.

"I can help you here."

"It's a personal matter."

He cocked his head. "Have we met before?"

"No, but you may know my dad, Jess McClendon."

Now he frowned, and it appeared to Patsy that he didn't want to acknowledge he may have forgotten her father. "Come on back," he said.

All the way back to the office, Patsy worried whether her only hope this time was to break the rules. Would that be the only way? And what could she lose?

She stepped through his doorway. "May I close the door?"

He nodded.

Patsy sat.

"How may I help you?" the man asked, clearly as curious as he was courteous.

"The truth is . . ." Now Patsy mentally envisioned the faces of her adoption support group, remembered their admonitions of what not to say.

"The truth is . . ." she began again, surprised to feel tears spring to her eyes. "I am adopted, and my dad, Jess, my real dad, the one who raised me, has had a stroke. He asked me to look for my birth mother and brothers and sisters." Now, this was the tricky part: how to say that a friend of Barry's made an illegal search?

"Someone told me—" she paused "—that my birth mother may have been in prison briefly."

The man was silent, gazing at Patsy with a penetrating stare. "Who gave you that information? Was it someone in this office?" There was an edge underneath the words that Patsy couldn't decipher. What was the right answer now?

"Possibly someone in my support group," she said,

thinking to herself that if her husband wasn't a form of support group, who was?

Now the man pulled out his own pad of paper. "Give me the information that you have." He wrote as Patsy dictated, then moved sideways to his computer on the other side of the desk.

Patsy tried not to stare even as she thought of standing so she could look over his shoulder. She looked away as she heard the click of his keyboard keys. When he stopped typing, she ventured a glance in his direction. He caught her gaze, then looked back at the screen. He then scrolled downward on the screen. Patsy felt that her palms were sweating.

Finally the man turned to her. "I believe I found the person your support group made reference to. And although this is public record, I'm not authorized to research it for you this way. If you tell anyone you got it from me, I'll deny it."

Her heart racing, Patsy said, "I won't tell."

The man squinted and looked close at his screen. He said softly, "There's just no way this woman could be your birth mother. She's not from this country and entered the United States illegally. Besides the time when the crime was committed, she has lived mostly out of the States. And in her case, Sarah Beth Walker is an alias—not her original name."

"An alias?" Patsy asked in disbelief.

"One of several," said the man, nodding.

"Thank you," said Patsy, suddenly filled with an odd mixture of relief and disappointment. Later, in the car, she tried to resolve her feelings. This Sarah Beth Walker wasn't her mom. For the first time, she was glad information was wrong.

When she arrived home, two letters sat on the coffee table in the living room. The first letter was from the Salvation Army, saying that they had no records for a Sarah Beth Walker, but she was welcome to resubmit her request at a later date. Primed for another rejection she opened the second letter, which was from the school district in Laurinburg. The letter was simple and contained only three sentences: *Records that may match those you are requesting have been located at Laurelwood Elementary School in Laurinburg. Please contact the school at your earliest convenience. We are sorry to take so long to respond to your request.* Patsy read the words again and again, her tears welling. "I've never been this close—this might be it," she murmured. "Maybe my birth mother is a real person after all."

She decided to drive to Laurinburg later in the week. Before then, she had Daddy's therapy appointment.

When the therapist asked how Daddy was, Patsy said, "He can say about fourteen words now. His brother's name was Bill. If he gets excited, he calls everyone Bill. But if we sit by him and prompt him with words—Patsy, Barry, Rodney, Chris, and Joy—he can say them after us. But it's hard work. We understand that 'Bill' is easier for him."

The therapist nodded.

"The thing that really surprised us is that he can sing. Words he can't ever say. Whole songs."

The therapist nodded again. "That's because that part of his memory is on the other side of his brain . . . the side not affected by the stroke."

Patsy continued, "We know he's as smart as he ever was. We take him everywhere. Six Flags. High school graduation. On trips. He loves to go. He was excited when we took him to Savannah, where he used to work. We have a garden plot for him, so he can grow a few plants. Flowers. Tomatoes."

"Obviously he's doing very well," the therapist said. After writing in her notebook, she put down her pen and touched Daddy's knee. "Keep up the good work, Mr. McClendon."

Patsy was wheeling Daddy's chair down the hall, when a nurse touched her shoulder. She motioned for Patsy to come closer. Then she spoke in a near-whisper. "The doctor didn't let on, but I think you should know. It's your love and his own determination."

"What?" Patsy asked.

"There's no explanation for why he can do what he's doing now, except his own determination." She looked closer at Patsy. "Your daddy must love you a lot. He's really trying hard for you. He's hanging on."

Patsy blushed. "He's been good to me my whole life," she said.

"It shows," said the nurse. "You're giving back what he gave you." Patsy's throat caught, and the nurse, seeing her patient's daughter was about to cry, patted her shoulder. Then she said, "More people should be like you." Then, whistling, she walked away, leaving Patsy to study a geriatrics poster until she felt her tears stop.

Chapter Twelve

The week passed quickly, and Patsy was anxious and nervous about her trip to Laurinburg and what could be her mother's school records.

Before she left, Patsy helped Daddy through the rituals she'd always view as miracles. It was 6:30 in the morning, and darkness was barely lifting off the sky. The heater started and hummed as Patsy walked down to Daddy's room. She knocked on his door and, without waiting for a response, stepped inside the bedroom to where she knew Daddy was lying awake, waiting for her. "Bill," Daddy said, smiling. He struggled in an effort to sit up in bed.

Admiring Daddy's determination to be as independent as he could, Patsy waited until he pulled himself into a sitting position. Then she eased her father's pants over his legs and helped him move toward the edge of the bed. She handed him his shoes, knowing it would take fifteen minutes for him to put them on and tie them by himself, an exercise of pure determination. His right side was still completely paralyzed. At first Patsy had thought that you could heal from a stroke; now she understood fully that once brain tissue died, it was dead forever. "Bill," Daddy said, again, thanking her for the shoes. Patsy knew if she sat on the bed next to him and said "Patsy" or "Barry," Daddy could repeat the words if he concentrated. But Bill felt comfortable on his tongue, and Patsy was used to it by now. Words were miracles, too; Daddy couldn't talk at all when he'd first moved here.

Patsy closed the door gently and left to finish breakfast. She never invaded the dignity of Daddy's fifteen minutes alone each morning. She only imagined what thoughts went through his mind as he put on his own shoes and shirt, and opened and closed drawers in the big oak chest.

As Daddy wheeled himself into the kitchen, Patsy recalled their long-ago conversation. The man who now smiled blandly at her had spoken with a determined urgency back then. Maybe he knew how hard my search would be, Patsy theorized.

"Daddy, I'm going to go look for my birth mother again today. I think I might have a lead this time," Patsy said, standing and watching him eat a bowl of cereal. "And if it's real, this is the first lead I've had."

Pausing over his cereal, Daddy gazed up at her and smiled again. "Bill," he said confidently, his face breaking into a dimpled grin. He and Patsy laughed together. When he wheeled himself over to make his two morning Pop-Tarts, Patsy patted his back, then stood to start making lunches. She'd made eight sandwiches when Daddy was ready for his banana. Then she wheeled him out to the front porch.

Patsy went to her closet. She donned the navy blue pantsuit she hardly ever wore except for when she took Daddy to the doctor or went to a PTA meeting or a fireman's company dinner with Barry. Her fingers fumbled as she fastened the gold buttons. She stood before the mirror and ran her hand down the front of the jacket. She ironed the suit last night, and laid out the earrings she rarely wore. Her nerves seemed to find release in blowing her hair dry. She needed a good hair day—it would be just one of many things that she hoped would work in her favor as she took this uncertain gamble. She put a notebook and three pens in her purse in case she discovered documents she couldn't keep or information she was unable to photocopy. She wished she knew what else she might need. A machine gun? A flashlight? A dictionary in another language? Patsy smiled to herself, thinking that her lighthearted thoughts kept her mind off the fear that lurked within.

Patsy heard Daddy wheel himself down the hall. She knew when she brought his laundry in an hour later to hang up his shirts, he'd be in the middle of making his bed. It sometimes took two hours for him to finish, but there was never a single wrinkle in a blanket or sheet. It was frightening, in a way, that this seemed so much like any other day. No one who saw her could ever guess that she might solve the mystery of her own life during this twenty-four hours.

She went downstairs and finished the sack lunches. She peeled carrots and dropped two chocolate chip cookies in each bag. She heard a blast of music from Chris's clock radio. She was filling a pitcher with orange juice when her three kids, one by one, came into the kitchen to give her a kiss and sit down to eat.

"Good luck today, Patsy." Barry came up behind her and kissed the back of her neck. She turned to him and felt a surge of affection. "Thanks for being my daddy-sitter," she said. "I don't know how long I'll be gone." They kissed again and Patsy gave him a lopsided smile as she left for what could be the final step of her search.

Driving to Laurinburg, Patsy's mind was a sea of nervous excitement. She fought to calm her fluttering heart as doubts rose like stop signs in her mind.

The night she ran away, it's possible my mama thought she would never see me again. Maybe her life changed after that, and she's someone else now. Maybe she won't want to see me.

How did it happen, Patsy wondered, that her mother cried so much on leaving her, and yet she ended up giving her away for adoption? She thought again of her only memories of the parents who gave birth to her—dark flashes like out-of-focus slides. Yet Patsy sensed that time in her mother's life was filled with extreme trauma and pain. If someone gives up a child, there is a powerful reason, she thought to herself. I'm not going to find my fairy godmother. I can't expect her even to know me. We probably wouldn't recognize each other if we saw each other face-to-face.

She drove into the asphalt parking lot of Laurelwood Elementary School in Laurinburg, North Carolina, where her birth mother possibly attended classes more than fifty years before. The redbrick building looked huge, solid, and impenetrable, like a fortress. Even the glass doors appeared heavy and forbidding. No children played on the painted hopscotch boards in front of her. Patsy felt small and alone in her car. She sat still and listened to the car's clock ticking. Now that she was here, Patsy felt as if she couldn't get out of the car. A surge of anxiousness filled her mind at the thought of the possible discovery she might make. Seconds later she mentally braced herself. She couldn't turn back now. But can I say what I need so they won't know I'm lying? What if I give myself away? Will they know what I'm thinking by looking at my face? She felt a drop of sweat inch down her side. I'm really almost there, she thought.

The wind whipped around her legs and hair blew in her face after she climbed out of the car. She stood with her fingers wrapped around the chain-link fence that barred the school from the street beyond. There was still no sign of life. It was as if all the teachers and children were locked in the building as securely as her mother's secret records. For a moment Patsy felt like a child again, when the older children and even the school itself seemed like huge, hulking giants. Patsy remembered feeling shy in school, and if a teacher ever called her name, butterflies of fear rose in her stomach. Now she was about to demand that the school surrender its secrets, in a time when confidentiality was shouted from every bureaucracy.

Turning away, she caught sight of a phone booth. Maybe it would be safer to call first. Standing in the booth, she fought to calm herself when a professional yet bored-sounding voice said, "Laurelwood School."

Patsy breathed heavily. "This is Patsy Thompson—I wrote you a letter about two weeks ago." She paused.

"You wrote back that you might have my mother's records." Wincing inwardly, she tried to make the lie she was about to tell sound plausible. "You know, my mother's house burned down and we're trying to have a family reunion." She paused again, gulped in air. The voice on the other end was silent, waiting. Patsy sighed and continued, "Mama lost everything in the fire, so we wanted to surprise her with something she had when she was little. Maybe—an old class picture of her—or her report card—something like that? Her name was Sarah Beth Rogers then—it's Walker now."

There was a long pause on the other end of the line and Patsy breathed in deeply again, then held her breath.

"What is your name?" the voice asked.

"Patsy Thompson," she said. "Patricia Diane Thompson."

Another pause. Patsy glanced at the leaves blowing on the trees above her. Spring and summer passed like lightning, and now the leaves were falling. She ran her foot along the pavement, a mixture of anxiety and dread churning inside her. She heard bits of muted conversation, as if a hand covered the phone on the other end. Then a different voice.

"Patricia Thompson. Oh. Yes. I remember receiving your letter. We don't get requests like this very often. I've never seen one asking for information more than ten years back. What is your mother's Social Security number?" asked the school office clerk.

Total panic. Patsy patted her jacket pockets as her mind rushed. What could she say? She pretended to fumble in her purse. "Not with me—" she said, as if she somehow forgot to bring the mysterious number she was hoping to discover.

A sigh on the other end of the line. "Just give me her birth date. So I can find the file in the right year."

Patsy nearly hung up, but couldn't let this question stop her now that there was something to be found. But what could she say? Of course, her mother's files would be with all the other children her age. And anyone would know her own mother's birth date. Her mind panicked. Her eyes squeezed shut in desperation as her hand gripped the phone.

"I need the date." Patsy thought she heard irritation in the clerk's voice.

"My mom went to more than one school." Patsy was amazed at her own words. Where did this idea come from? "I know she was probably a student there sometime from the late forties to the early fifties—maybe even a little earlier."

The clerk sighed. "I really don't have time for this. It's not in my job description to do background checks, and I need to count the lunch money."

Patsy breathed. "I'm here from out of town. My mom was really traumatized by the fire, and this was one of the few things we thought might help her."

Another irritated sigh. Patsy heard the phone receiver being set down on a counter.

She stood and breathed, studied the details of homes across the street, cars in the parking lot. She couldn't hear much through the phone. Clicks, rustles, the everyday noises of an office building.

"They're here—" The sound of a metal file drawer slamming.

"What?" Patsy asked incredulously.

"The records are here—"

"I'll be—" Patsy started to say she'd be at the office in five minutes, but the clerk hung up before she could answer.

Patsy slowly dropped the receiver to its cradle. She went back to the car and combed her hair while trying to form a calm expression in the mirror. She put on the lipstick she hardly ever wore at home. She sighed. There was no choice now but to go inside the school and face the woman she had angered enough to slam the file drawer.

The asphalt parking lot and playground seemed endless. At the doors of the school she stopped, panicked again. She was this close. She couldn't stop now. With renewed determination she opened the huge glass doors and stepped inside. Endless halls, signs with numbers, but without directions. A quiet buzz of classes in session. She walked, in search of an office, a main hall.

"Can I help you?" asked a tall, official-looking woman with precisely styled gray hair.

"I need to find the office," said Patsy.

The woman stared a fraction of a second longer. "Down this hall and to your left."

"Thank you." Patsy rushed away before the woman could ask her any questions. She reached the office. It seemed official and forbidding, filled with bustling clerks who didn't look up as Patsy pushed open the door. She waited at the counter, but no one seemed interested in helping her. She was looking for a bell to ring for service when a clerk finally looked up.

"Need to check one of your children out early?" the clerk asked.

"No—" said Patsy. "I'm here about records,"

The clerk pointed to another room. In this room there were two women who were as interested in reading papers on their desks as the clerks in the previous office.

Patsy knew that the longer she stood here, the more tense she would be. "Excuse me," she said finally. The voice that emerged from her throat sounded gruff, hoarse, unlike her own. "Could someone help me? I just have a quick question," she finished apologetically.

A woman in a black pantsuit stood from behind a desk, walked over, and loomed over the counter toward her. "Yes," she said, obviously resenting the interruption.

"My name is Patsy Thompson. I called about five minutes ago. About some records of my mother's." She willed her jaw to hold still and her knees to stop shaking.

The clerk stared at her a fraction of second long. "Your mother's name."

"Sarah Beth Rogers."

"Oh, yes." the clerk said, sauntering over to a file drawer. Seconds later she withdrew a manila folder. Patsy watched as the woman opened the folder and stared at the first document. Seconds seemed like hours. This is it, thought Patsy. She's reading that the information is confidential and can't be released to anyone.

Without looking up, the clerk said, "There is something strange about your mother's file."

Patsy watched as the woman flipped through the pile of documents. Her heart thudded and she held her breath. "Oh, really?" she managed to murmur casually, holding her body still as stone.

The records clerk stared at the first page a moment longer, then riffled through the brief file. "Unusual," she said.

Patsy could wait no longer. "What is it?" she asked.

The clerk shrugged. "There's supposed to be a whole stack of papers. It covers from kindergarten through sixth grade. But there's hardly anything in your mother's file. It's almost empty. I don't know where those other documents are. Just a minute, let me ask."

Patsy didn't dare breathe. She interrupted quickly. "That's okay. We'll make do with what you have. We'll make some arrangements with that. We really appreciate anything you can do."

The woman held a hand up as if fending Patsy off. "Just a moment," she said, and entered another door. Patsy could hear two women talking. Patsy closed her eyes briefly, then opened them, smoothed her hair. Licked her lips. She was aware that her hands were shaking as the clerk finally slid the slim manila folder across the desk.

"Thank you—thank you very much," she said, already stepping back and turning as she picked up the folder and walked away as fast as she could. The folder and papers felt light and flimsy in her hands, yet their possible relevance to her life seemed heavy and solid. She rushed outside the school building and finally exhaled, her sigh releasing years of pent-up waiting. Then she ran to the car and let herself drop in a heap on the front seat.

For several minutes she sat in the car and listened to herself breathe. Then she closed her eyes briefly, took another breath, and opened the file. There were just a few scattered papers, tattered and fading from years of lying in the closed file cabinet. They weren't in an ordered stack, but looked as if they were dropped in the folder one by one. The first folded rectangle was nearly as small as a playing card. Sarah Beth Rogers, it said on the cover. First grade. Age six. Tears sprang to Patsy's eyes as she realized this was her mother's first grade report card.

I shouldn't really be able to spy on someone else like this, she reasoned. But it was the only way I can get what I need. As she opened the card, black numbers seemed to rise up and shout at her. Birth date: April 3, 1933, the notation read simply. "Her birth date," Patsy said aloud, shaking all over by now.

For the first time she read her grandparents' names—her grandfather, Harvey Rogers, and her grandmother, Willie Rogers. "Willie," Patsy said, "short for Willadean or Willamina?" The next paper was a list of books her mother read in first grade. *Play Time* and *Play Fellas* and *The Music Hour*. Did her birth mother like to read like she did? "Sarah Beth—the first thing I ever touched that belonged to you," Patsy whispered to herself. "I know so much about you. Right now, I'm so close I feel like I'm holding you in my hand."

During the next days Patsy noticed that for the first time in her search, she was scared. How would she feel, she asked herself, if someone were secretly peering into her life? Was there any possibility that Sarah Beth Walker knew of her search, and was deliberately hiding?

Chapter Thirteen

For two weeks after Patsy visited the school, the folder sat idle on her bureau. It was like the discovery was so powerful that she needed more time to absorb its impact. Indian summer was once again bathing her house and yard with heat. She spent days in the garden with Daddy and started a volunteer job at the local hospital. She started crocheting an afghan for Daddy, and found herself thinking of Sarah Beth Walker while she worked.

Then the phone call came. It wasn't quite the middle of the night—only a little after 11:00 P.M. Patsy was hovering near sleep.

Her cousin Jane's voice took a while to wake her. She knew it was a woman calling, but didn't recognize the voice until she shifted in bed and half-sat.

"I'm sorry to call you in the middle of the night. I had to let you know that my mother died about two hours ago."

Jane's mother—Aunt Evelyn. In her mind, Patsy pictured the formidable woman she had found scary when she was little. Daddy's sister, who didn't think his daughter was really his daughter, or that she could take care of him. Or that he would live much longer.

"I'm sorry," said Patsy automatically, realizing that, deep down, she truly was.

The voice hesitated. "I know you had some conflicts

with her toward the end. I need to tell you that she really did love Jess. She worried about him.''

"He's fine . . . '' said Patsy. We won, she thought. Daddy and I.

"But isn't he quite disabled?''

"No,'' Patsy said simply. "He's fine.''

There was a silence when neither woman seemed to know where the conversation should proceed next. Finally Patsy said, "I didn't even know Aunt Evelyn was sick.''

"It was sudden. She just lay down and died. Probably a heart attack. I guess it was her time.''

Patsy couldn't think of a response, other than that she was surprised that Aunt Evelyn's time came before Daddy's. Aunt Evelyn, who could still walk, say any words she wanted on the phone, and dress herself in ten minutes instead of an hour. Aunt Evelyn was gone.

"It's hard to believe,'' Patsy said.

Jane said, "We all thought she was bigger than life. We didn't think she'd ever die. But her funeral is Saturday.''

"We'll be there,'' said Patsy. After hanging up the phone, she lay awake a long time. When she was little, she thought that people who died seemed ancient, bygone, almost from another era. Now they just seemed like people she'd always known. It was hard to imagine never hearing Aunt Evelyn's gravelly voice on the other end of the phone again. Daddy's sister. Patsy was trying to picture child versions of Daddy and Aunt Evelyn running and playing hide-and-seek when she finally fell back to sleep.

It was at least three years since she last saw Daddy in a suit. Somehow he looked younger, abler, more like the Daddy she remembered growing up, even though he sat still in his wheelchair. At the same time her two sons looked older dressed in the suits they rarely wore. Their walk was slower, more solemn. In the church Patsy recognized her cousins. The ones she hadn't seen in a long time appeared to have been lightly dusted with age. Some had gray hair at the temples, slightly wrinkled faces, tall children sitting beside them. Time was moving on.

Aunt Margaret came up and patted Daddy's shoulder.

"How are you, Jess?" she asked in a loud voice, as if Daddy were hard of hearing.

Patsy resisted an impulse to say Daddy was fine.

"Bill," Daddy said, smiling at Margaret.

Now Aunt Margaret spoke to Daddy, while looking at Patsy, as if Daddy's mind were vacant.

"No, Jess," she said. "Bill was my husband. He died."

Now Patsy's voice rushed. "He knows you're not Bill," she said quickly. "He just says that because it's easier to say. Margaret is a longer name."

Now Margaret looked down at Daddy. She took his hand. "I miss Bill, too," she said. "But they're all gone now. All except for you."

It was true, Patsy realized. Daddy had now lived longer than all his brothers and sisters. Would he somehow live however long it took for her to find Sarah Beth? Patsy turned to gaze at her father, who was now shaking hands with a man in a suit who also spoke too loudly. From the twinkle in his eye, she knew Daddy was enjoying himself.

She and Rodney were wheeling Daddy's chair out of the church following the service when it occurred to her, with an unease similar to a headache, that even though Daddy was still alive, he would be next. There probably wasn't time to put off her search if she wanted Daddy to shake hands with Sarah Beth Walker the way he was shaking hands with his own cousins now.

Yet during the next few days, she admitted to herself that part of the reason she was waiting to look further was all the people who said that searching for her birth family meant she was ungrateful to the parents who raised her. She had even seen a newspaper column the week before that said it was unhealthy for foster children and adoptees to spend too much time wondering "Who am I?" Her life really was good now, Patsy thought. What if she was some-how sorry when she actually found Sarah Beth Walker? She didn't want to cause Daddy any pain. Could she not tell him if she thought that what she discovered might hurt his feelings?

• • •

Two weeks later, Patsy drove into Laurinburg to pay a visit to the court clerk's office. She remembered that angry clerk who yelled at her the last time she was there. In her mind she could still hear the clerk telling her she should appreciate Daddy, and asking, "Why worry if you were born in a sewer if you grew up in a garden?" She did "grow up in a garden" she thought. There were charming old buildings, tree-lined streets, and an air of small-townness that still endured into the nineties. The courthouse bore rounded windows at the top, and the brick was a gray-green color that somehow appeared old-fashioned.

Patsy carried the folder with Sarah Beth Rogers's school papers into the building and found a door that read COURT CLERK.

She felt her heart thud once as she asked, "I'd like to buy a copy of a birth certificate."

To her surprise, the clerk said, "I don't think there's anyone back there in the public room, but you can go see if anyone's there to help you."

Patsy walked down the hall and opened a door with a sign that proclaimed PUBLIC ROOM. She entered a silent, high-ceilinged room filled with musty air, filing cabinets, and books. She called out softly, "Anybody here?"

When no one answered, she sat down on a chair behind a desk to wait. After a few moments she yawned and glanced at her wristwatch. Then she let her eyes follow the second hand twice around the clock. She was startled when the air conditioner sprang to life with a whistling rush. When it eased into a steady hum, Patsy idly let her eyes drift to a nearby filing cabinet. 1965, read one drawer, 1964, read the one beneath it. With a start, she realized that all the birth certificates for her brothers and sisters were probably in this room.

With a glance to either side of her, she stepped to the filing cabinet and found the year 1953. If Paul was two years older than she, his birth certificate would be in this drawer. She opened the drawer and winced as it groaned like a squeaking door. There were thousands of papers inside, and she knew that the clerk could return at any moment. She flipped through the W's, and was looking for Paul's name, when another name caught her eye.

It was natural that this name should grab her attention, she realized, seconds later. The name at the top of the document was her own. Yet the notation above it didn't say birth certificate—it said death certificate.

"What?" Patsy questioned. She lay the paper flat with both hands, then held it firm as she looked a second time to make sure the unbelievable words were real. Yes. There was no doubt. The black-and-white document looked official and exact, and it said that she died almost forty years before. Patsy gasped. "Dear God, I'm dead!" She sank back against a cushioned courthouse chair in the room where she was still alone. She felt suddenly weak. Her heart fluttered.

Closing her eyes quickly, she shook her head and then inhaled, squaring her shoulders. "Easy, Patsy," she said, trying to calm her racing heart. She stared again at the trembling paper in her hands. "It's my name," she thought to herself, touching the line of black letters that said "Patricia Diane Walker." The name below hers was her mother's name, Sarah Beth Walker. The Sarah Beth Walker birth date was the same as in the school papers. It had to be the same one.

Placing the death certificate paper delicately on the courthouse counter as if it were fragile, Patsy looked more closely at the document.

It was her name, but the wrong birthdate. Then it suddenly registered that the child on the certificate lived only eight hours. Understanding and relief flooded her thoughts in waves. She thought, Oh, then it isn't me.

Still, how could the certificate be so close, and not be her own? How could this certificate have both her name and her birth mother's? There had to be an explanation. It couldn't be a coincidence, could it? She examined the document a third time, and a chill brushed her spine at the irony of her new realization. "My mother had another child," she whispered. "The date is wrong because she was born two years before me. She lived eight hours and then died.''

Walking toward the photocopy machine, Patsy leaned her ear against the heavy wood door. When there was no sound, she turned back, and copied the two documents to take home to the piles and files of records she'd gathered in her years of searching.

She studied the birth certificate again and noticed something that gave her pause. Her birth mother's age was listed as twenty-two years old. Yet the space that asked, How many children have been born from this mother said "six." And the space beside it that specified how many children from this mother are now alive only said, "two."

Poor Sarah Beth, Patsy thought. You already lost four babies by the time you were twenty-two years old. Then you lost me, and then Paul, too. The certificate made the starkness of her mother's loss seem fresh and real in Patsy's mind. How did it feel to lose all those children? Could you go on with life as if they never existed? "Mama, if you're anything like me, you want me to find you. Something in me just won't let me quit looking," Patsy said aloud.

Suddenly the heavy wooden door flew open, causing Patsy to jump.

"May I help you!" The words weren't a question, they were an order.

"I was just looking for my birth certificate," Patsy stammered, and placed her hands behind her back. With one hand, she tucked the two documents into the waistband of her skirt.

"And did you find it?" asked the woman who'd turned on the light.

"I was still looking," Patsy said.

"Would you like me to find it for you?" the woman asked. "I'm sorry about the wait. But these are confidential materials. We can't let just anyone scour through them."

"I didn't find it," Patsy said again.

"What is your name and birth date?" the woman asked, pen poised.

"Patricia McClendon," said Patsy, before giving her the date.

She watched as the substantially built woman waddled over to the filing cabinets and opened the drawer that was marked 1955.

"Here it is," said the woman. She handed Patsy a certificate, a copy of the same one she had at home that said her name was Patricia Diane McClendon, and her parents were Jess and Pearl.

"Thank you," said Patsy.

"That'll be ten dollars," the woman held out her hand.

Patsy fumbled in her purse and handed the woman a bill. She could feel the papers tucked in her waistband as she walked out to her car, and hoped they were well out of sight.

It was dusk and Patsy was driving down Centerville's main street, when another thought struck.

Death certificate.

Death.

The cemetery.

After asking for directions from a gas station attendant, she drove to the Centerville cemetery. There was no one to ask directions or look up a name for her. A small shed was bolted with a padlock. She parked her car and began to walk. At first the cemetery looked small, but as Patsy actually stood at the entrance, it looked as if the green grass dotted with headstones stretched out forever.

There were lots of unfamiliar names on the first three rows. Dangerfield, Larkin, Potter. A row of Sorensens.

Patsy walked on. Henderson, Crause, Bentley.

The sun was dipping now, with shadows filling in the letters on the headstones. Bainbridge. Anthony. Tregeagle.

By now she had to bend close to read the names. Hewlett, Christensen. She walked farther. Campbell. Ernst.

Now there were some that she couldn't read. Patsy knelt and ran her fingers over the cool stones. Sparks. Lemmon.

Suddenly—Rogers. She traced the letters with trembling fingers. Ralph Rogers. Born 1885, died 1969. Wrong person. The next stone was his wife's. Amanda. Born 1889, died, 1965. Wrong again. The name on the next stone was Latimer.

By now Patsy could see stars in the navy blue sky above her, but she couldn't read the letters on the stones in front of her. And she was alone in a cemetery after dark. She shivered with an involuntary shudder.

With a sigh Patsy gazed in the direction of at least ten rows of headstones in front of her. She would have to come back. She turned, promised herself she would return. Possibly bring Barry with her.

Turning her back and trying not to think where she was, Patsy walked as quickly as she could, battling images of horror movies she'd seen as a child. Only all the new information she discovered today kept her fear at bay.

Chapter Fourteen

At the next meeting she told the support group about the cemetery, and finding the original birth certificate. Charlene, the leader, agreed to clandestinely check DMV for a current license. A man wearing a white shirt and tie raised his hand in the front row.

"Yes?" said Charlene.

"Databases," said the man.

"What?"

"She should try all the Web sites on the Internet. Lots of them are sites just for looking for other people. People-search, Bigfoot, all of those."

"And searchers have databases, too," said a man next to him. "They have lists of people who fall into different categories. Military service lists. Birth and death records. We pay them to look on the databases they own. But you can look on the Web yourself. And you can find searchers on their own Web sites."

That night Patsy brought up the Internet on Rodney's computer. She found Bastard Nation, a national network of adoptees. With the house silent around her, she read story after story of searchers like herself. Some happy, some sad. She signed the guest book, then connected with several links and wrote about her own search. I'm not alone, thought Patsy. I'm not the only person in the world who was adopted. Other people have these feelings.

Patsy drove to Centerville again. She felt a short rush of familiarity on driving down the main street—the sense that her secret might be hidden here and she would find it if she just searched hard enough. She visited the hardware store and spoke with a man so old and hard of hearing that she wondered if he would still remember Sarah Beth Rogers if he knew her years before. She visited the city offices with hopes of finding a deed to the mysterious house she still remembered in the back of her mind—the one with the dark place where she recalled hiding out. But there was nothing listed under Sarah's or her birth father's name.

"Possibly they just rented the house," said a sympathetic clerk. "Did you ask your parents if they owned it?"

"I'll try that." Patsy half-smiled, thinking it would probably be one of the last questions she would think to ask if she ever found Sarah Beth. She left the city offices and sat in her car, trying to think whether there was any other place in Centerville she could search. She drove through town, past the department stores and on to the residential section. She was deciding whether to stop for a hamburger when she saw the cemetery ahead in the distance.

The sun was bright now, just before noon. She could read the names on the headstones. Patsy drove through the open gate. She saw that the door to the cemetery offices was ajar.

A slim, blond woman sat behind a desk, talking on the phone. "Then he gave me another appointment for a Pap smear the next week," she said lazily, yawning, while staring at Patsy. She paused. "We'll go this weekend if it doesn't rain," she continued. Obviously, prompt customer service was far from this woman's concern, Patsy realized. She tried to quell her rising irritation as the long conversation continued. Eventually she sat in a folding chair and stared as the woman wrapped a piece of long blond hair around her finger. "Oh, I think so, too," the woman said. "Their prices are high. . . ."

With a sudden flash of inspiration Patsy drew a pad of paper from her purse. She wrote her grandparents' names on the paper, and then wrote above them: *Where are their graves?*

She handed the paper to the woman, who looked at her as if she'd been inexcusably rude. Without missing a beat in her conversation, the woman flipped away the lock of hair that was wrapped around her finger and turned to her computer.

Patsy stepped back and waited.

"Oh, I know," the woman said, "their sales are like nothing. They take two dollars off every thousand...." She gave off a feigned, nasty laugh. Patsy turned away and, moments later, felt a paper touch her hand.

She took the paper the woman handed her. The photocopy was blotched and faint, and it took Patsy a moment to understand that it was a map. Only the words *Main Street*, the road she just traveled before turning into the cemetery driveway, clued her in. She stared at the map, located the office where she now stood. What did this mean? She held the map up in the direction of the woman, frowning slightly.

"I'm sorry. I don't understand this," she said.

With a groan of disgust, the woman grabbed the map from Patsy's hand, slammed it down on the desk with an exaggerated gesture, and drew a circle with red pen. She thrust the map back at Patsy.

Patsy looked closer. She saw that the red pen circled a single yellow dot of ink from a felt tip pen. The dot was between a series of lines that appeared to be less than an eighth of an inch apart. Patsy frowned in confused frustration. She stared as the woman picked up the lock of hair to twist it around her finger again.

"What is this?" Patsy asked, breaking into the woman's conversation.

The woman frowned, covered the receiver with her hand. "That's where they are."

"These lines are graves?"

The woman clucked at Patsy's supposed ignorance. "*Rows* of graves."

"Then the ones I want"—Patsy angled the map and squinted—"are at the end of this row?"

"Someplace around there." The woman dismissed Patsy with a wave of her hand and turned away to concentrate on her lengthy conversation.

Despite her irritation, Patsy felt chills inside at the thought of what she might soon discover. Turning hurriedly, she rushed out of the office into the sunlight to where she could see the map better.

Minutes later a heavy wave of discouragement again settled over her. The map had obviously reduced a huge area to tiny lines that were practially indecipherable. Patsy gazed around her, realizing that one tiny row on the map stretched at least a block. She started walking in what seemed like the direction of the yellow dot on the map, then stopped again, admitting to herself that she still wasn't sure.

As disappointment slowed her pace, she moved forward, catching sight of a small white pickup truck in the distance. Patsy heard the engine running and stepped forward faster to catch up with the cemetery worker before he drove off. She was out of breath by the time she reached the driver's side of the truck.

The man stared at her, his face blank.

Patsy held up the map. "How do I get to this spot."

The man shook his head.

"This spot on the map—how do I get there?"

"No habla ingles."

Great, thought Patsy. She fought to remember her high school Spanish. Pointing to the spot, she said, *"¿Este? ¿Donde?"* The man took the map from her, studied it, and pointed to his left.

"Where is this row?" Patsy asked, but he shook his head, waved her off, and turned to drive away. Shaking her head, Patsy set off in the direction where he pointed. Why didn't the cemetery print a map with names, so you could check? Or number the rows? Patsy walked forward. There were large stones, a small one with a lamb for a baby. Tan stones. Gray. She took a step past the end of the row and felt despair begin to rise inside her once again. She turned, ready to head back to the car and home.

But something inside her made her stop and look down. At first she thought she was imagining what she saw in front of her. There they were. The headstones. The names seemed to shout at her. Harvey Rogers. Willie Rogers. Her grandparents. A feeling of butterflies rose in her chest.

She stood and stared at the names a long time, then sank to her knees. She ran her hands over the stones, felt the raised characters in the dates and names. She sat, waited. This is as close to each other as we will ever be, she thought, wiping strands of stray grass from her grandmother's grave. Many minutes later she wrote down the names and years in her notebook.

She stood and noticed that while some of the graves were topped by cans or bottles for flowers, these two graves were empty, as if no one had visited for a long time. "I'll try to come back," she said aloud, looking back over her shoulder as she finally walked away.

As soon as she walked in the door at home, the doctor's office called. "Mrs. Thompson, I'm sorry to have to tell you this. But there are fibroid tumors in your uterus. They are growing. You need to have a hysterectomy. We can schedule it as soon as possible—within the next two weeks."

"What?" said Patsy.

Suddenly the weight of the doctor's words hit hard. Fibroid tumors. A hysterectomy.

The doctor continued, "Female-related tumors, such as breast cancer, may or may not be hereditary. Did your mother ever have fibroid tumors?"

Patsy was instantly in no-man's-land. No, her mother didn't have tumors—but her genes didn't come from her mother. This was a sensation she'd experienced throughout her life. She'd feel very commonplace, as if she fit in with everyone else, and suddenly someone would say, "I look like my grandmother," or "I have the same allergies my dad has," and she would ask herself, "Who do I look like and what do I have that someone else has?" And she never knew the answer.

Now she said, "I don't know. I'm sorry. I'm adopted." Patsy swallowed. "I am searching for my birth parents partly to find my medical information. And for my daughter, so she will know hers."

The doctor was sympathetic. "I think that's worth doing. But this is urgent, too. So when can we schedule your surgery? I caution you not to wait."

Patsy fumbled. "I'll let you know. I have unfinished business to tend to first."

That night, at the support group, Patsy raised her hand. She stood and faced the group, catching Lois Ferguson's eye. She spoke to the crowd.

"I'm asking for help," she said. "I've written everywhere, called everyone, visited all the people I thought would know. I now know her birth date, and I saw her picture, but she's as far away from me now as she ever was. She's not listed with DMV, she's not in any microfilm or Internet phone directory. It's as if she dropped off the face of the earth. She could be dead, but I want to know that, too."

"It's a feeling we all know," said Charlene.

"And I feel like I have to hurry now. I have tumors in my uterus, and I need a hysterectomy. My daughter is getting older and someday she might want to marry and have children; we need to know our medical background. My father is hanging on to life, and he wants me to find out."

Lois Ferguson raised her hand. "You need a searcher," she said.

"But don't they cost a million dollars?" Patsy asked.

"You need to decide how much this is worth to you," Charlene said. "It's your father and your daughter's future."

"That's worth everything," said Patsy.

"Don't rush into anything. There are hundreds of people out there who will take your money. They know that adoption is close to your heart, and they know you want to find a solution."

"So how do I tell who's good and who's not?"

"The usual channels. See if the Better Business Bureau has any complaints. See if there are references they can give you. Call people whose searches they did before. Comparison shop. Or you could call or write to the famous ones, the ones who do shows on TV."

"It sounds risky," said Patsy. "And expensive."

"It is." Charlene nodded. "But you only need to use them once. And once you know, the longing you have now will go away. It could be replaced with other feelings that are just as painful. Sadness. Rejection. You could find someone who doesn't want to be found. But there's a peace that comes when you know the answer, whatever that answer is. In some ways, you'll feel like your friends who've always known where their roots are."

"I still think that's worth a lot," Patsy said again.

Around the room Patsy could see members of the group nodding and saying yes.

Someone threw a note in her direction. It landed in her lap. She waited a few moments. Then, when someone else was talking, she opened the unevenly folded slip of paper. *I'll take you to the Seeker* was written in uneven script.

Patsy looked back, into the sea of faces, but no one winked, smiled, or acknowledged that he wrote the note. She hung around after class, until only she and the support group leader were left. When she walked out into the parking lot, a folded paper was on her windshield. She opened it to find a phone number written in ink. Patsy gazed around the dark parking lot. The only sound was a flurry of leaves blowing at her feet.

The next day she wrote to the Salvation Army again and searched on the Internet. She thought about calling Charlene, the support group leader, but instead, she dialed the number on the scrap of paper.

An unfamiliar woman's voice answered.

Patsy said quickly, "This is Patsy Thompson. Someone wrote this number on a paper that was left on my windshield."

A pause, then the woman cleared her throat. She said, "If you are serious about searching for your birth mother, I can take you to the Seeker."

"I've been looking for years."

"But are you serious about this search? Are you willing to find the truth, whatever it is?"

"Yes," Patsy said simply. "How much does this cost?"

"Three thousand dollars a day. They pay him that much because he's worth it. He'll do anything, legal or not. He takes a lot of risks, but he always gets results."

An eerie feeling wafted through Patsy. She remembered Charlene's words. "Are there any references? How do I know that you're actually connected with him?"

"You have to trust me. He doesn't have to advertise for clients. People come to him—more than he can work for. I'm willing to do this for you because I heard your story in the group."

"And who are you?" Patsy asked. "What's your name?"

"Like I said—he'll do anything. But I have to protect his identity and my own."

"How do I know this is real?"

"If you want the answers badly enough, you'll take the chance."

"Can I call you back?"

"I'm not at this number all the time. In fact, today only."

"You won't be there tomorrow?"

"Never after today. You have one chance."

"Can I call you back this afternoon?"

"No calling back. I can't take the risk. We agree to meet now, and we hang up. That's it."

"My husband—"

"Alone—you meet me alone."

Patsy's instincts screamed that this wasn't safe, that she should say no. But part of her wanted to say yes. Then she thought of Barry, Daddy, Rodney, Chris, and Joy. She couldn't risk the family she loved to take a chance that might not even exist.

"I'm sorry. I can't," said Patsy.

The phone clicked instantly. It was too late. Did she lose her one chance?

That night she told Barry, who called his policeman friend. Setting the table in the kitchen, Patsy heard Barry's quiet voice as he talked in his office. Should she have said yes? What if this person was telling the truth?

She was making a salad when Barry finally emerged from his office. He took her in his arms, and seconds later she heard his voice in her hair as his lips neared her ear. "It was a con, Patsy. You did the right thing."

"You're sure?"

"The scheme's got all the elements. They promise you everything. You have to decide right now. You go alone to meet someone."

"I don't know. I could have been meeting my birth mother tomorrow."

"You could have been dead tonight. You go there alone and three men come and beat you up and take your purse."

"Someone from my support group would do that?"

Barry backed away, held his hands up. "The support group advertises in the newspaper, right? Anyone can come . . . anyone means *anyone*."

"But . . . the Seeker. I've heard of the Seeker."

"He's probably a con, too. Don't worry, Patsy. You're doing the right thing. If you're supposed to find this woman, you will."

Barry's words couldn't quell the eeriness that hovered over her as days passed. It struck her how close she had come. To death. Or to finding her birth mother. There was no turning back.

Chapter Fifteen

It was five days later when she saw the reunion talk show. A birth mother was told that she was brought to the show for a beauty makeover. The makeover began when a series of models walked past her dressed in the newest spring looks. One of the models was the daughter she'd never seen after giving her up for adoption as an infant. Patsy and millions of viewers watched as models in pastel skirts walked past the woman, who admired the clothes with a casual smile. Suddenly a young blond woman who looked like a younger version of the woman observing the show walked out. Patsy held her breath. The young woman stepped closer. The two women's eyes caught and held.

With a shriek, the woman jumped up, and the two embraced in a tight, unrelenting hug.

Tears flowed down Patsy's face. When the phone number of the search agency flashed on the screen, Patsy didn't hesitate.

International Locator.

She called the toll-free number and waited.

Moments later she was telling her story to a representative, the words spilling over with the emotion she held back all these years. As she talked, she kept reassuring herself that this person was three states away and couldn't possibly hurt her the way the unscrupulous con man might have.

Patsy said, "My reasons for searching for her are that I'd like to do this for my daddy and for my daughter; I'm concerned about her inheriting a tendency toward cancer."

Patsy stopped speaking to take a deep, calming breath. The woman on the other end of the line waited. No one said anything

Patsy asked, "How much would it cost to search?

The speaker explained that normally the charge would be fifteen hundred dollars.

Patsy was about to hang up. "I would have to talk this over with my husband to see if this would fit within our budget. I'll have to call you—"

"Wait!" said the voice. "I think my supervisors might be interested in your story. Could I have your name and phone number?"

Now Patsy was nervous. But reminding herself that she was nearly a thousand miles away, and that Barry gave out their phone numbers to customers all the time, she slowly recited the familiar digits.

"I'll call you back," said the representative.

An hour later the phone rang.

A friendly voice said, "Hello, Patsy? This is Arliene Dunn. I'm the vice president of International Locator."

"Hello," said Patsy, her heart racing. How would it feel, after all this time, to give her search away to someone else? To let them travel the paths she'd traveled, and look at the names and dates with fresh eyes and professional training? The thought made her giddy. She said, "Thanks for calling me back."

"I hear you've searched more than ten years," said Arliene.

"A long time," said Patsy, her heart still thudding.

"We'd like to help you, Patsy."

"That would be wonderful." Patsy swallowed. "But I have to say that I'm not sure I can get the fifteen hundred dollars together—that's a lot of money in my budget. But it would mean a lot to me—and to my daddy. He's had a stroke, and it was the last thing he asked me to do—to find my birth family. But I'll have to see what I can do. . . ."

She tried not to let disappointment or even realism creep into her tone.

"This won't cost you anything, Patsy. In fact, your expenses will be paid, because we're interested in your story. We think you could encourage other people who want to search. But there is one thing—"

"Yes?" In the phone receiver, Patsy heard her own anxious breath rush.

"We'd like you to help us."

"Really?" Patsy sighed. "What could I do? I'd be glad to give you all the stuff I found."

"We'd like you to appear on the *Sally Jesse Raphael* show. There are millions of viewers out there, and we'd like you to come on the show and appeal to them, ask them to help with the search. One of them might know something that would help us."

For a moment Patsy envisioned millions of people sitting in front of televisions across the United States. She thought of the slow pace of the letters and phone calls she made, and how she only reached one person at a time. The prospect of asking millions of people at once was dizzying— and scary. But she thought of Daddy, and knew there was no way she could pass up this chance. "I'll do it," she said.

"Wonderful," said Arliene. "I'll start putting the details together and call you back in a day or two."

It was only after she hung up that Patsy thought about how she would look on TV, what she would wear, whether they would ask her to go alone, or to take Barry, or the kids and Daddy. It was something like when she was a little kid and imagined being on a TV sitcom. It felt like a dream, yet she repeatedly found herself thinking about hugging her birth mother in front of an audience of millions. She was too excited to feel scared. For a long time she sat on the couch, replaying the conversation in her mind and wondering if the phone might ring again to tell her it was a joke.

She didn't know how long she waited before she stood and stretched. She glanced at the phone one more time, then walked down the hall to Daddy's room. She knocked, then entered his room a moment later.

"Daddy. You'll never guess who that was on the phone."

He patted her hand and matched her smile with his own.

"International Locator. You know, those people who do reunions on TV. They want me to go on the show and ask people to help them find Sarah Beth Walker."

"Bill!" said Daddy with enthusiasm.

Now Patsy sat, took her father's hand in hers. "Daddy, I wouldn't be doing this without you. If you hadn't asked me to find her a long time ago, this wouldn't be happening."

"Bill," he said again.

"Daddy, if they let me, I'd like to take you on the show, too."

Daddy's grin widened, and she thought of all the places he'd gone with her in her life. She tried to imagine how he and her mother felt when they first saw her as a two-year-old auburn-haired girl who needed a home. She thought of how Daddy and Mama reached out to her when she was too young to know how much she really needed them. She recalled how they were always there for her, no matter what happened in her life. Feeling her eyes mist, she leaned over and hugged Daddy. "I wouldn't have this without you," she said with conviction.

A few moments later she went upstairs and began making Barry's favorite spaghetti. When the noodles were nearly finished boiling, she walked into his office.

"Dinner will be ready in a minute, but I have to tell you something first."

He looked up at her with the same, warm open face as always, waiting to hear that Daddy's therapy appointment was changed, or that Patsy was going back to Centerville tomorrow to visit the cemetery again, or that she needed him to run a few errands.

"Intenational Locator called—that search agency—and they asked me to go on TV."

Barry stood and stared at her as a grin grew on his face.

"They want me to ask the viewers if anyone has any information about Sarah Beth."

"Patsy—" Barry said, with a mixture of excitement and disbelief. Now Barry stepped from behind his desk, rushed up to Patsy, and hugged her. "They want to know if anyone has any information? Did you tell them you have more than ten years' worth of information?"

"I told them I'd give them everything I found. And I said I'd go on TV."

Before he released her from his embrace, Barry said, "I knew it, Patsy. I always knew it."

"What?" asked Patsy, puzzled.

"You're going to be famous," Barry joked. "You know—Woman Helps Famous Search Agency Complete Impossible Search."

"Woman and her *husband*," Patsy corrected, with a faked stern expression on her face. "Woman and her husband and her father."

Barry said, "I knew you'd do it. I knew you wouldn't quit until you got it."

"I haven't found her yet," said Patsy, trying to be realistic in light of the rush of hope billowing inside her. "But this has to be a big step in getting there."

"My wife, the star," Barry continued.

"It's only one show—I'll be on ten minutes, if that."

Barry's tone turned serious. "But your life will never be the same after that."

Patsy didn't answer. She sensed he could be right.

"And I know they'll find her, Patsy. I've done enough investigations of my own. Professionals, like that—with all the money and technology behind them—it's only a matter of time."

Sensing that her eyes were brimming, Patsy turned and walked out to the kitchen. She waved aside the steam and saw that the spaghetti noodles were ready.

Then the phone didn't ring the next day. Patsy waited at home until noon, then left to run errands. There were no messages on the answering machine when she got back.

She took Daddy to his physical therapy, and when she got home, no one had called. That night she stayed awake late, reviewing her notes, wondering if there was a name or a date that would be more important than she realized. She waited and studied until after midnight, but the phone didn't ring.

The next morning she took Daddy out on the porch and began to read the paper with the cordless phone beside her. She lay the phone on the bathroom sink when she showered, so that she wouldn't miss the call. That afternoon she sewed, determined not to let the waiting paralyze her. Yet her anxiousness didn't ebb. Her nerves were on edge at the thought of being on the brink, of being almost there. It was like all the time and space between her and Sarah Beth was about to drop away. All Patsy's work was about to lead to the reunion she wanted. So what was taking all this time now?

Patsy's feelings alternated between impatience and gratitude. In a way it was a relief to know someone else was working on the search. Other brains besides her own were focused on the puzzle, and there was a feeling that the pressure was off her to find the answers. At the same time she wanted to lend a hand, give a progress report, do some of the legwork or make some of the phone calls. What was the delay?

When still another day passed, she told herself she could wait. Yet inside, the urgency never really left. She imagined professional searchers, with more knowledge and money than she possessed, trying to find Sarah Beth Walker. She pictured them following the same trails she had, but maybe knowing where to turn when the trail ended. She tried to set her anxiousness aside the way a mother tells a persistent toddler who is grabbing at her dress to wait a moment.

One more day passed.

Ironically it was Barry who answered the phone. He held the cordless phone to his head as heard the most momentous words of his life. His world suddenly stopped as Arliene Dunn, the vice president of International Locators, said, "Barry, I've got Patsy's mother on the phone." A sudden wave of emotion paralyzed him. The significance of the moment felt heavy—a pronouncement as profound as birth or death. He couldn't speak or breathe. Yet at the same time, he felt a weight lift from him. Moments later Arliene broke through the dead silence with a gentle chuckle, "Barry, are you all right?"

"Patsy," Barry was suddenly a sea of frenetic movement, waving his hand at his wife and darting around the bedroom. "The phone's for you Patsy." As his wife reached for the cordless in his hand, he held it up, out of her reach. Puzzled, Patsy stared down at the nightstand phone, then picked it up and held it to her ear. She frowned slightly, as if accusing him of rudeness for wanting to listen in on her phone call.

Barry's feet tapped nervously as Arliene said, "Patsy, how are you doing?" His breath rushed as the two women exchanged greetings and small talk. "On with it," he wanted to say. Just as Barry thought his heart would burst with emotion, Arliene said calmly, "Patsy, I've got someone on the phone who wants to talk with you—it's your birth mother."

Patsy instantly swung to face Barry. Her eyes widened and her hand that held the phone trembled. Barry watched the color evaporate from her face, yet seconds later she flushed with emotion. Her bottom lip quivered. A single anxious teardrop inched down her cheek, followed quickly by more tears. "Hello, Sarah Beth—Mrs. Walker—Mom," Patsy said, fumbling with possible terms to call this new presence in her life. "I've wanted to see you again since I was two years old. I know everything about you. I know what books you read in school, and that you had seven babies. . . ." Patsy's hand fluttered as she raised it to dab at her tear-drenched cheek. "I'm going to call you right back so this won't be on someone else's long-distance bill," Patsy was saying with a sort of thrilled desperation. "Now don't you go anywhere. I swear to goodness, I'm going to call you right back." Her hand still shaking, Patsy scrawled a number on a pad of paper. Then she put the phone down and jumped up, literally springing into the air.

She rushed to Barry and they hugged, half-jumping in a circle. Barry saw a flood of fresh tears on Patsy's face and felt his own eyes well up. Abruptly Patsy let go of him and sat at the phone again, smiling. "I've got to call my mama," she said.

Before she could lift up the phone, it rang.

"Hello?" Patsy said giddily.

"This is Arliene from International Locators," said a warm and friendly voice. "Your mother has a fear of flying, so we couldn't fly her to a show to meet you. . . ."

"Oh," said Patsy, "we'll go where we need to go." A rush of excitement suddenly filled her. "We'll drive wherever she is."

She and Barry leaped together for another hug, and she dropped the phone. Anxiously she rushed to pick it up. "I'm going to call her back and talk to her now. I'll tell her we'll come get her. Thanks so much, Arliene! How much do we owe you."

She heard the smile in Arliene's voice. "Nothing," she said.

"But I owe you so much. I've searched for so long and you—"

"This was going to be on a show—but when it couldn't be, we were just glad to help," said Arliene.

"I'll be grateful the rest of my life," said Patsy. "I would never have stopped looking, but I probably wouldn't have found her."

The next day Barry and Patsy set off for Georgia. Patsy packed her family pictures, the dress she wore when she was adopted, and a wreath she made to give her birth mother. All the way there, she had butterflies in her stomach. This was scarier than any search effort she'd made.

As they drove up, the house looked like any other. White brick with awnings. But when they rang the doorbell and an older man answered, Patsy could see that inside, this home looked just like hers. The living room was filled with crafts—needlepoint, wreaths, and embroidered pictures. The decorated walls caught her eyes, and it took her a moment to glimpse the woman sitting on the couch. When

Patsy caught sight of her birth mother, it was as if she were looking into the lens of a slow-motion movie camera. Her eyes captured the shape of Sarah Beth's face, the high cheekbones, the smile that looked like her own. Sarah Beth was smaller than Patsy, but had the same pillowy cheeks. Near her forehead, where Patsy had a few streaks of gray hair, Sarah Beth's hair was shining silver.

"It's you," Patsy sighed breathlessly.

"And you're my little girl," said her birth mother.

The two women laughed together—similar laughs that grew more high-pitched at the end. Patsy saw her mother wore a purple blouse the same color as one she had at home.

Then Patsy rushed to Sarah Beth and the two of them hugged. As Patsy's arms encircled her birth mother, an electricity filled her that created an instant bond. Neither of them wanted to let go.

"I've looked so long for you," Patsy said, leaning back to again gaze at her birth mother's face. There was Patsy's chin and forehead on a face she'd never seen before.

"I thought you were dead—I was afraid to look for you. I just prayed you were all right," said Sarah Beth. "I called an adoption agency, and they said if you were adopted, your parents probably gave you everything I couldn't give you at that time. That kept me going, and I gave you away to God—it was the only way I could go on."

"Are you all right?" Patsy asked suddenly. "I know you left at a very hard time. . . ."

Sarah Beth closed her eyes quickly, then opened them to gaze at Patsy again. "I survived . . . barely. Someone told me once that if you were adopted, I'd never see you again," said Sarah Beth. "I thought I'd have to do my best to go on without you."

"I couldn't let that happen," said Patsy.

The two women laughed again. In her mother's embrace Patsy glanced out the window of the white house. "What's that on your back porch?" she asked abruptly.

Her birth mother laughed. "Come see," she said calmly, taking Patsy's hand. On the back porch of the white house was a bird feeder, with three tiny birds placed in a flannel-wrapped bowl filled with straw. "Their mama died," Sarah Beth explained. "So I'm taking care of them. I feed them with a dropper."

How many animals have I taken care of? How many children? Patsy asked herself. She looked out across a garden that seemed miraculously similar to her own. "You have almost as many tomatoes as I do," she said suddenly.

"Plant 'em every year," said Sarah Beth.

"And look at your lettuce."

"Want some to take home?"

"I could have brought you some. But now, Mama, we're taking you back to meet your grandkids."

"I can't believe it. It's a dream I never thought could come true," said Sarah Beth, who excused herself, then emerged in a pink pantsuit that also looked like one Patsy would wear.

"I have lots of purple and pink in my closet," Patsy said.

"Come look at this," said Sarah Beth.

Patsy followed her birth mother down a hall to her bedroom. The clothes in the closet looked oddly familiar. There were more pantsuits and skirts and blouses than dresses. And floral patterns or solid colors rather than plaids or stripes. Lots of pink and purple, like Patsy often chose for herself. Patsy looked away at a quilt on the wall that eerily resembled the one on her own wall at home.

"I could live here . . . this house reminds me of mine."

"You can stay anytime," said Sarah Beth.

Patsy took her birth mother's arm. "Sometime. But not today. It's time we headed out to our place."

In the car they discovered that they both loved instrumental music, that they used similar expressions, and the same jokes made them die laughing.

As they turned on Patsy's street, she felt a new flutter of excitement in her stomach. As soon as they reached the big antebellum house, Patsy said, "Wait here, Mama. There's someone I want you to meet."

She went downstairs and found Daddy watching TV with

Joy and Chris. She helped him climb into his wheelchair and rolled him down the hall as she spoke. "There's someone I want you to meet, Daddy. Someone you've been waiting to see for a long, long time."

Daddy half turned and smiled over his left shoulder at her. When they turned the corner, Barry took Daddy's chair and slowly wheeled him to where Sarah Beth sat on the living room couch.

Barry said, "Sarah Beth, this is Jess, the man who raised Patsy. We call him Daddy. Daddy, this is Patsy's birth mom, Sarah Beth Walker." Daddy grinned broadly as Sarah Beth stood.

"Bill," Daddy said excitedly, in instant recognition. He pointed to Sarah Beth's chin. "Bill," he said again. Still grinning, he patted Sarah Beth's hand and kissed it.

Sarah Beth leaned toward Daddy and gently kissed his still-grinning cheek. "Thank you, Daddy, for taking care of my little girl all her life," she said. The two hugged each other.

"Bill Bill Bill," Daddy said assuredly. After they slowly released their embrace, Daddy reached up to a smiling Sarah Beth and held her face in his good left hand, turning it slowly from side to side. He gestured for Patsy to turn sideways, then started laughing. "Bill Bill Bill Bill Bill," he said assuredly, pointing to the two women's identical profiles. "Bill," he said again, as if casting a deciding vote.

Patsy alternately looked from Daddy's face to Sarah Beth's. Sunlight streamed down on them through the window. They looked as if they belonged together. Patsy knew, at that moment, that if Sarah Beth ever wanted to, she could come and live with them, in the big antebellum house. There would be room for her. When it was time, they would all be together.

In Search of a Life of Her Own

Chapter One

Allison McGarry shoved the suitcase out the window ahead of her, then clung to its handle until the last moment in an effort to let it drop silently. Easing her leg over the window ledge, she reasoned, I won't let them hit me again or give me one more bruise. They won't find me.

Three months pregnant and sixteen years old, Allison thought of her unborn baby that no one in her family knew about. She patted her stomach gently and whispered, "I'm doing this for you. I need to run away so I can start planning a life for us. I'll get us a place. We'll have a nice home someday. Don't worry. We'll make it."

She was still slim enough to wear pedal pushers and still sufficiently agile to angle herself sideways out the window and let her body drop quietly on the icy cool spring grass. She closed her eyes and listened as her breathing rushed in the black, humid Oakland, California, night. She sat still and nervously fingered the handle of the suitcase that lay beside her. Even after she'd crammed the suitcase with clothes, her closet was still full. The house she was leaving was filled with classy clothes, elegant furniture, and delicious food. Sighing, she understood for the hundredth time that no one who saw her house would ever guess that it also harbored hidden violence and betrayal.

Seconds crawled by, and she prayed that no one in the

house would suddenly wake. The house itself felt like a menacing hulk, as if the frightening memories it held might suddenly capture her, too, cutting off her escape. Come on . . . Allison thought. I made it out of here on time—now where are you?

Wait. Allison thought she heard a noise from inside the house. The click of a light switch? Someone sitting up in bed? She ran to the side of the house. Maybe if someone just looked out front, they wouldn't realize she was gone.

She hoped her mother, Victoria, would sleep, her long, blond hair splayed out in rays on her pillow, until morning, then wake up, get ready for work, and leave dressed as tastefully as the house was decorated, without checking Allison's bedroom.

Lost in thought, Allison shook with surprise when a pickup truck with its lights off drove smoothly up the street and stopped in front of where she sat. Without looking back, Allison stood, pressed the suitcase against her hip, dashed to the curb, opened the truck door, and threw the suitcase in before jumping in herself. She shuddered and gasped as she slammed the door behind her. Her thoughts whirled inside her head. Then relief washed over her in waves, bringing tears to her eyes as she sighed and exhaled.

Lynn, the young woman who sat in the driver's seat, glanced at Allison's intense expression. "Are you okay? Do you have what you need?" She peered closer and saw that Allison was crying. Then she asked, "Are you scared?"

Allison shook her head. "Too mad for that. I really am. Not kidding."

Lynn's stare lingered. "Are you sure? This is what you really want to do? We don't have to."

"Go—*go!*" Allison commanded, waving her arms forward as if urging a horse. "I can't stay here a night."

The gears in the truck abruptly ground against each other, sending her into panic. Suddenly a light went on in the house. "Get out of here!" Allison shouted anxiously. Lynn pressed her foot on the gas pedal. Allison leaned up and looked back as the house slid out of sight.

The light was still on. Was it her mother's bedroom or the bathroom? Now that she was on her way, she really didn't care.

Suddenly she remembered Antonio. "My boyfriend—he won't know where I am. Could you try to call him for me? I don't know when I'll get to a phone again."

"Write down his number. I'll try tomorrow after I drop you off," Lynn promised.

"He's in Arizona now. Call him in a few days. He should be back home then. I had to leave before I could tell him. I couldn't let them hit me again now that I'm pregnant."

"They wouldn't hit you if they knew, would they?"

"You don't know them. No one does. That's what so scary."

"We'll get you out of here," Lynn said. "And I'll try to find your boyfriend when he gets back from Arizona. I'll ask him to call or write or something."

Allison nodded. She sat back against the leather seat and waited. Tears and sweat swam on her face. "You know, I won't always be running away," she said. "Someday soon I'll have a house and I'll be married to Antonio, and our baby will be there."

When Lynn glanced sideways at her, but didn't speak, Allison let her thoughts drift to her one dream. She knew there was no way she'd ever let anyone tell her she couldn't have her single hope for the future. Again and again, she mentally pictured herself as Mrs. Somebody Respectable, with an immaculate house, and children she could hug and love. The house would be as beautiful as the one she grew up in, except it would be filled with love rather than hate. Her destination might be light-years from where she was now, but at least she was headed in the right direction. Folding her hands together atop the suitcase between her knees, she firmed her resolve. She thought, I want marriage, and I want a family, and no one is going to stop me.

She was startled when Lynn shook her shoulder and she realized she was still sitting on the leather seat with her suicase between her legs. Only now the sun was out, filling the old truck and its weathered interior with light. When did she fall asleep? She was stretching to try and chase the aches from her muscles as Lynn pointed to a wooden building with a sign that read COLUMBIA ORCHARDS. The sight of the fruit orchards lifted Allison's spirits. There would be work here, she thought. She could start saving money for the baby, and for the home she would have someday, and best of all, no one would hit her while she did it. Her life would be her own.

"There's the office. Just go tell them you're here. I've got to get going. I'm already late for my own work. I'll take the suitcase with me and pick you up at five-thirty."

For a moment, Allison just sat there. Lynn revved the engine. Allison shook herself, jumped out of the truck, and slammed the door behind her. Then, without looking back as the truck roared away, Allison walked up the two wooden stairs into the office. It was a cluttered room, with an overweight, balding man sitting behind a desk filled with piles of folders, envelopes, and invoices. He was talking on the phone and had a toothpick hanging out of the corner of his mouth. She was sure he glanced at her more than once out of the corner of his eye, but he didn't bother interrupting his conversation to talk to her.

Finally Allison sat on the lone, high-backed wooden chair in the corner of the room. Glancing around the walls at the business license, ledgers, and filing cabinets, she half-heartedly listened to the man's conversation with someone named Fred. She stood as he said, "Yep, gotta go."

"I'm Allison McGarry," she said, but the man's hand waved her away. He was already dialing another phone number, ready to plunge into a second lengthy conversation while he let her sit idle in his office. Thoughts of her baby plagued her mind. She needed to be earning money, not sitting here waiting. Allison stood and walked up next to his desk. Seeing her, he turned his head toward the other end of the desk, and she walked in that direction, so he couldn't avoid looking at her.

"Yeah, Dave. Yeah. Oh, 'bout five hundred or so—"

She leaned over the desk and stared into his face.

"Yeah, Dave. See ya Friday."

Finally the man hung up.

"Can I help ya, girlie?" He sounded annoyed.

"I'm here to work. I'm already signed up. I'm Allison McGarry."

"Don't need no junior high kids. Aren't ya sposed to be in school?"

"It's almost over. And I—I go at night," said Allison. "I'm here to work during the day. I'm already signed up."

"Ya don't *sign up*. You make an appointment, then you have an interview, and if I think you can do the job—" Allison felt the man's eyes on her small, slender frame, as he took in her flimsy V-neck sweater, pedal pushers, and short brown hair. His gaze seemed to dismiss her as insignificant and inadequate.

"I can do the job. I'm stronger than you think."

"You gotta be strong, all right, to pick those apples all day. Your shoulders hurt. Everything hurts. You ever picked an apple in your life?"

She hesitated. There was an apple tree in the backyard that brought forth maybe ten apples every summer. "Yes," she said, "and I need the work."

"Might be true, but question is, do I need you? Girlie, I got people employed been here year after year. *College kids*. Men needing a second job. Housewives."

"I'll work all day—and night," Allison felt her lip quiver and hated it for revealing her fear at this crucial moment.

"Don't need ya. I'm full. Ya can go now, let me get back to work." He turned to pick up the phone.

A sob rose from somewhere inside and her voice suddenly blurted, "I can't go. I don't have a ride until five-thirty." Now there was no mistaking it. The aches from riding in the truck, the exhaustion from being up all night, and the anxiety over running away all seemed to weigh on her at once. A tear inched out of her right eye, leading the way for others ready to burst forth.

"Ya gonna cry on me?" the man sounded exasperated. "I gotta get this work done. Can't have ya buggin' me all day. Well, if yer gonna be here all day, I might as well let ya pick a few." He got up, stamped out of the office.

When he returned, a tall man who looked about the age of her father strode in to the office behind him. A straw hung from his mouth, and he looked at her as critically as the first man had. He turned to the overweight man. "This is *her*? She's supposed to be a picker?"

"Yeah, I know." The two men laughed together. "Just let her try a few out there on the east end. She's stuck here till five-thirty. We could pay her just for the day."

"I don't know," the man said. The first man shrugged, then sat at his desk and shuffled through his invoices before picking up the phone again.

The other man sighed and walked out ahead of Allison. "Come with me, sis," he said.

They were right, Allison finally admitted at the end of the day. Everything hurt—her shoulders, her back, her calves, her hands. She had a headache and a blister on her foot, and even her eyes stung. When Lynn picked her up, she was too tired to talk, and she'd never been thirstier in her life. But in her hand she clutched three ten-dollar bills. She'd made thirty dollars. And the man in the office, whose named turned out to be Ray, said she could come back the next day if she wanted to. It turned out there weren't enough pickers out on the east end, after all.

Lynn's friends, some of whom were fruit pickers, too, lived in a wooden A-frame house. They said Allison could sleep on the Hide-A-Bed, and assigned her to take her shower at night. The hot water seemed to barely touch the aches that grew more penetrating the more tired she got. Her body felt heavy and filled with pain. Drying off after her shower, she put on her flannel nightgown and let herself drop on the Hide-A-Bed, which felt like a down pillow to her aching bones. Was it only one day since she left home? She fell asleep listening to Lynn talking to the guy named Harley and his wife, Celeste. Her last thoughts before she drifted to sleep were for her baby. What would thirty dollars buy? She knew she wouldn't be free to spend most of it the way she liked, but could she get a warm stretch suit for the baby? A used stroller? Even a very used crib?

Chapter Two

It was the fourth night. She'd just fallen asleep and was still dreaming about the orchard: green leaves in front of her dream-eyes; round, hard, smooth-skinned apples in her hands. The feeling of the ladder, the branches under her feet. Suddenly her shoulder being shaken.

"What?" Allison turned her head, shook away the dream images of bushel baskets and rows of trees. She blinked several times before she saw that a man who looked taller than an apple tree himself was now peering down at her. His voice was deep and held power, like a minister or politician.

"Allison McGarry?" he demanded.

Allison only sat up and drew the single blanket around her. She blinked and stared, fighting to feel more alert.

The voice sounded more insistent now. "Are you Miss McGarry?"

She nodded, then saw that the man was dressed in tan pants and a tan shirt. On his breast pocket was pinned a gold metal star. A sheriff. Standing here by her bed in Columbia. A shiver of fear heightened her consciousness. She sat all the way up and pulled the blanket around her.

"Yes," she said finally.

"There's an all-points bulletin out for you. I need you to come downtown to the sheriff's office with me."

"But—I have to work in the morning."

The man held his hand out for her, but she stood unassisted. "I'm Sheriff Anderson. You're coming with me," he said.

Allison glanced down at her gown. "Can I get dressed—please? It will only take a minute. I'll hurry." As she rushed to put on her pedal pushers and V-neck shirt, Allison sensed that everyone else in the house was awake and watching. What did she do to get the sheriff after her? Nothing but pick apples in the last four days. She had to get this problem with the sheriff taken care of so she could get back to work in the morning.

Ray would fire her in an instant if she were late. He'd say that one more high school kid had failed. It would give him pleasure, she knew, to tell her that she couldn't pick another apple and get paid for it.

Allison sat silent in the back of the police car, thinking again of her baby and the hundred and twenty dollars that she had quickly stuffed inside her bra.

In the sheriff's office Sheriff Anderson looked down at clipboard, then back up at Allison.

"You're Allison McGarry?" he asked again.

"Yes," she said. "I don't know why you want to talk to me. I haven't done anything but work for Columbia Orchards since I've been here. I just pick apples in the day and sleep at night."

He picked up the clipboard again. "I have a report here says you're a runaway. Someone named Victoria McGarry had the police down in Oakland put out an all-points bulletin on you."

Allison fought not to show that the name registered with her. She couldn't speak but folded her arms across her chest and sat straighter in the chair.

"That your mother, ma'am?" The sheriff bent closer to look into her eyes. "Victoria McGarry?"

Allison waited. When the man didn't stop staring, she finally nodded once. "Yes."

"We'll let her know that you're here, then, and she can come and pick you up. Can't be running away like that."

"Wait—" Far scarier than the sheriff, than the aches in her body, than the unknown that lay ahead, was the thought of seeing Victoria's face again. And the violent fury that would hover behind her frown. Allison cleared her throat. "There's something I need to tell you."

"Yes?" The sheriff's brown-eyed gaze was again leveled at her. He'd found out she was a runaway; now how could she possibly change his mind?

"I need to tell you that I'm an abused child. My parents beat me up."

Now Sheriff Anderson leaned back, put his hands on his hips, looked disgusted as if he heard this excuse every day. His jaws worked as if he were chewing gum.

"I'm not kidding," Allison rushed on. "I left because they hit me all the time. They beat me. Wait—" Shyly she lifted the back of her sweater, wondering if the bruise was there from the fight a week ago. Or if he could possibly see any of the scars from before that. When he made no comment, she let the sweater drop. "No one believes me because my parents don't seem like the type. We live in a nice house. They have money. They have jobs. My mom is a secretary for an important guy in business. She is the most beautiful woman I ever saw, and I love her. I do. But she hits me—and I can't take it anymore—" Allison's voice broke.

The sheriff stared at her, fingering a pencil on his desk. His face was as still as stone. Why didn't he believe her? "You're a minor. You're what? Fifteen?"

"Sixteen," Allison said. "Five months ago."

"Look," the sheriff started to say, "if you're a minor and your parents are still in charge of you—"

"I'm getting married. My mother doesn't know it, but I am."

"How could you get married without your parents' knowledge? Do you have your marriage license here with you to prove it to me?"

"No." Allison's face fell, but then she had a sudden thought. "But I have a job. With Columbia Orchards. I take care of myself."

The sheriff shook his head. "I'm sorry. I want you to know that I believe that someone has hit you. Those scars are real. And they're deep. You probably can't believe it, but I hear this story all the time. I don't want to let them know I found you. But it's the law. I don't have a choice."

Swallowing and gathering as much courage as she dared, Allison said, "I can't go home. I'm pregnant. I lived this long with them hurting me, but I can't take a chance with my baby."

The sheriff shook his head like he didn't want to hear another word. Then he stepped to the doorway of the office and quietly closed the door. Sitting down next to Allison, he spoke softly. "Look. No way I'm supposed to do this. But I believe you, kid. I'm going to give you *one day*. *One day* to convince me I shouldn't call that sheriff in Oakland right now."

Allison exhaled in a rush. "Okay—I'll just get a cab and rush right back to work and I can make it by noon and still work until five-thirty."

The sheriff shook his head. "Uh-uh." He stood and gestured with his hand for Allison to follow. They walked out of the interrogation room, down the hall, and through a heavy iron door that he opened with a full ring of keys.

Beyond it lay two rows of cells with barred doors.

"Oh, no," said Allison.

"You can stay here—in the jail. Or I can call Oakland."

The sheriff stood, waiting. Allison frantically racked her brain. What to say now? She thought of Columbia Orchards, where the apple-picking crews were moving on ahead of her, making money while she sat here in a room with the sheriff. She thought of Lynn, and the Hide-A-Bed where everyone would expect her to sleep at night. Lastly— and these thoughts burned in her mind—she thought of Victoria, and what would happen if she went back home.

Was that a hint of sympathy in the sheriff's brown eyes? For a moment she let herself wonder if he had a daughter, a mother, a life. Then she forced herself resignedly to meet his eyes. "I'll stay here," she said. "At least it's safer than my house."

Without looking at her face again, he walked ahead of her to the last cell on the left. A heavy, sullen-looking woman sat alone in the cell. He unlocked the door and gestured to Allison that she should go inside. "I'll be back to talk to you tomorrow," he said, locking the door and leaving. Holding back the tears that were threatening, Allison climbed to the top bunk, lay there, and tried to think how she could explain that she couldn't go home. Her hand fell to her stomach and she thought of her baby. She whispered, "This is so far from where I want us to be. I'll get us out of here. I will. Don't worry." Then she thought of Antonio, away somewhere in Arizona. She had to get out of here for him, too. Most girls who are put in jail would call their parents, she thought. But Victoria was the last person she wanted to see. Allison closed her eyes and turned over on the bunk as she thought of Victoria.

No matter how often Victoria hit or screamed at her, Allison never lost her fascination for the mystique that was her mother. She loved her deeply, despite the abuse. She recalled the night her father took her mother out for the evening, when she was dressed in a gorgeous dark purple wraparound dress and a picture hat. Her blond hair cascaded down her back, and elegant was the only word to describe her.

Every morning, after Victoria left for work, the scent of her Shalimar perfume hovered in the air. In the silence of the empty house Allison would open her mother's closet and peer at the jewel-tone colored clothes that accented Victoria's beauty and still carried a wisp of her scent. She stared at the delicate bottles on the perfume tray, lifted an atomizer, and sprayed her own wrist. When she was in elementary school, she put on her mother's ankle-strap shoes and played alone in the house. When she grew tall enough for her mother's classy knit suits, hats, and Pendleton reversible skirts to fit, she waited until Victoria left for work, then donned the clothes and wore them to school. She left her own clothes in the garage to change into before Victoria could discover her. Somehow, she hoped that wearing and touching the clothes could help her capture the elusive essence of Victoria's perennial beauty. The soft, clingy sweaters smelled so good, it was like carrying the mystery that was her mother with her. But the one or two times when Victoria caught her wearing the clothes, the mystique ended with swearing and slaps. Yet Allison never stopped wearing the clothes.

And now she feared nothing more than seeing her mother again.

A voice came from the bunk below.

"What ya in fer?"

Allison sat up. "Running away from home."

The woman smiled, and Allison glimpsed missing teeth. "Oh, yeah? You don't look big enough to run away."

"I'm big enough," she said.

The woman spoke again. "Guess your mommy and daddy will come get you any minute now, huh?"

"Nope. Never." Allison said, trying to sound tough. "What are you in for?"

"Drunk," said the woman, starting to laugh. "Ya ever been drunk?"

Allison sat back on the bunk. The truth was, she'd never been drunk. It was like she skipped that stage in her life. She thought of the dance where she met Antonio. It was at the YMCA, and the band played show tunes, not rock and roll. The dances she did with Antonio were the tango and the cha-cha, not the twist or the frug. Rather than handing her a beer in the backseat of a car, he took her out to dinner and treated her, for the first time, like an adult. He listened to what she had to say with total credibility. He opened doors for her, walked on the outside of the sidewalk so she could be safe nearer the buildings. Something inside her melted when she was with him. How could she explain the intoxicating headiness of respect, gentleness, and courtesy, feelings she never felt before from Victoria?

Even though she now sat in the dusty, grimy, starkness of the jail, if she closed her eyes, she could remember Antonio's hand on her shoulder. His kiss on her cheek. Meeting Antonio was the beginning of her dream, of wanting a house and a husband. She knew her dream wasn't like that of most girls she saw on TV or listened to in the school halls. She never longed to become a movie star or Miss America or to marry the president or at least the quarterback of the football team. But the fact that her wish was simple and plain only made her want it more, made it seem somehow more accessible and sacred, as if she could walk around the corner and somehow it would be there.

Thinking of Antonio and how she would soon be with him. Allison fell asleep in the jail cell. She was awakened by the screechy noise that was her breakfast tray being pushed under the slot. On a metal plate were scrambled eggs that were brown and sad-looking and a limp piece of toast. Climbing down off the bunk, Allison saw that her cell mate was already gone. She ate the breakfast, fighting mental images of the white china dishes and woven wicker place mat on her table at home. What could she say when the sheriff came to confront her again?

The day passed, uneventful until noon, when a lunch tray similar to the first, except it held potatoes and gravy, was pushed through the slot. Allison picked up her metal spoon and began to dip into the potatoes when she realized her hands were shaking. A sudden fear gripped her with an iron lock. What was it? Poised with a forkful of potatoes over her tray, she realized it was the smell. The scent that haunted her life was now here, in the jail. Shalimar. Allison took her tray and crawled under the bottom bunk. She covered her face with her hands. Moments later the heard the piercing click of Victoria's ankle-strap shoes. Then there was silence. She swallowed the last bite of potatoes and pressed herself against the cold and slimy wall of the jail cell. She held her breath.

The clicking again, getting louder. Allison couldn't press herself against the wall any harder. Then the tapping stopped. From her hideway beneath the bottom bunk, Allison peered between her fingers and saw her mother's white legs, perfectly shined shoes, and the hem of her maroon dress. She startled at keys clanking in the lock, followed by a long, pitiful squeak as the door swung open.

Her mother's voice, as sharp as steel. "Allison!"

Sixteen years of fear, pain, and anger compressed in Allison's mind and forced her body out from under the bunk. Now she shook with fury rather than fear. Unconscious of both her surroundings and the deputy who stood by her mother, she screamed, "What the hell are you doing here?"

Victoria didn't stop to breathe. She shot back. "What do you think I'm doing? I'm taking you back. Right now."

"I don't want to go!"

Victoria's face filled with fury, and Allison felt an odd satisfaction with the sudden understanding that her mother wouldn't dare hit her here with a jail attendant watching. "I signed the papers and they released you! They gave me your things!" Victoria stepped over and grabbed Allison's shoulder. Her long fingernails dug deeply into the girl's upper arm. As Victoria dragged her from the cell, Allison looked back at the barren room with an odd fondness, as if it were a school from which she was graduating. She wanted to go back and finish her sentence and then pick apples again. When Victoria started screaming as they got in the car, Allison knew the screams would last for two hours, all the way home to Oakland. She didn't dare think of her baby, or the physical punishment that lay only two hours ahead when Victoria got her home.

At first Allison tried to let Victoria's screams bounce off her, like misdirected bullets, as the car sped toward Oakland. But it seemed as if they nicked her insides, and jabbed at her anyway, despite her efforts to ignore them. "I wish you were never born. You're nothing but trouble, nothing but *trouble*!" Victoria shouted. "And when we get home, just you wait—"

Anger brewed inside Allison like water coming to a boil on the stove.

Without thinking of the consequences she spat out, "I'm pregnant."

Victoria inhaled sharply. Then her words held disdain. "Oh, you are not, you little tramp. You're just saying that to make me mad. Just trying to think of the worst thing you can say to upset me."

"I am. I *am pregnant*."

"I don't believe you. Just trying to drive me nuts like always. But if there's any chance you are, we'll drive right to the doctor and have him do something about it."

"No!" Finally Allison's voice raised to the same pitch as Victoria's. "I won't let you near me! It's my baby! Antonio and I are getting married. It's your grandchild."

Allison could practically see Victoria's temper rise to a fever pitch. If she weren't driving, she'd beat me right now, Allison thought. Instead, Victoria exploded, releasing another screaming accusation. "That wetback knocked you up! You'll never see him again. He's had his fun and now he's gone. And left you like this. Left you with *me.*"

Victoria turned and slapped Allison across the cheek. Yet Allison hardly felt the sting against her face. Victoria's last sentence bored into her brain, scaring her like nothing else since she'd left home. Was it possible Antonio would run away from her? She remembered his easy charm, the warm feeling of his arm around her neck, his passionate kisses. And now he was gone. Did he really go to Arizona the way he said? Was he actually coming back?

Was he gone forever?

Chapter Three

Walking into the big house she'd hoped to never see again, Allison longed for the Hide-A-Bed and her work in the orchard. A sick feeling rose inside her as she thought of the punishment Victoria would invoke. Mercifully, it didn't come. That night she slept fitfully, waking every hour or so and wondering if Victoria would walk into her bedroom and beat her.

The next morning she heard a knock, followed by her bedroom door opening with a rush of air while she was still half asleep.

"Someone is here to see you," said Victoria ominously.

Allison struggled to wake. She fought to focus her eyes in the suddenly bright room. She was startled to see that Dr. Newton, the doctor who took care of her while she had chicken pox and mumps, now stood at the foot of her bed. All the fear of him she had held in childhood rushed over her in waves. "I'm not sick," Allison protested, sitting straighter.

"He'll let me know what your condition is—"

As Allison froze in horror, Dr. Newton knelt, lifted her pajama top and placed a cool metal stethoscope against her stomach.

"Please don't—" she protested, as the doctor leaned forward, pressed the stethoscope deeper into her abdomen. Allison squirmed involuntarily as the metal edge poked harder, causing a cramp that made her writhe.

"Stop it! I'm not—"

"There's a heartbeat," the doctor said, turning to Victoria with a grave expression. A chill darted along Allison's arms. The sheer miracle of someone hearing her baby's heart brought a tear to her eye.

"You can arrange something, can't you, Dr. Newton . . . ? Get her in the hospital by the end of the week?" Victoria stepped closer, staring into the doctor's face.

"No!" Now Allison screamed. "I'll call the police! I'll run away again! I'll kill you!"

Dr. Newton set his jaw firmly, dropped the stethoscope in his bag, and closed it. "I recommend counseling for her, Mrs. McGarry. I can refer you to someone if you want. I don't feel I can schedule a procedure or refer you to an unwed mother's home until her emotional state is more stable."

"Never," Allison said, her chin jutting out in her mother's direction.

When Victoria only scowled back, the doctor lifted his bag and left the room. Allison stayed awake that night, and in the nights to follow, terrified that someone might come to take her away. Yet as days passed, she mostly sat in her room and waited for the phone to ring, for Antonio to call her to say he was back from Arizona. One afternoon she took the hundred and twenty dollars she'd stuffed inside a sock in her bottom drawer and went to a baby store. She spent it all—on stretch suits, receiving blankets, a used quilt. She found a used stroller for five dollars and a changing table for three. She hid them in the back of the garage, the musty wood odor reminding her of days when she'd hid out here to secretly change into Victoria's clothes. Looking down at her stomach with a mixture of wonder and sadness, she knew there was no way she could wear her mother's wool suits now. Her own pants pinched at her stomach. Her waist began to balloon out, in a loose and gentle way that fascinated her. She'd never thrown up, the way she'd always heard. But her shoes were tight, pinching at the toes and feeling snug and binding at the heels.

"Haven't heard from him, have you?" Victoria taunted her each night as they ate together at the dinner table. Allison suffered these words with a mixture of anger and compassion. Her own father had left and moved in with her mother's cousin when Allison was eight or nine. Desertion was something Victoria understood, and Allison sensed, in that unerring way that children sometimes have, that part of her mother's inflamed anger was actually pain turned inside out.

Victoria continued, "Haven't heard one word. And you won't, either. He won't come within miles of you. He's had the best of you, and now no one else will want it. You're stuck. Can't even go back to school."

Surprisingly, these words gave Allison hope. If her mother was right, and she couldn't go back to school, could she get a job? With forced optimism, she reminded herself that she didn't have to pay rent here, the way she would if she lived away from home. There was a closet to hang her clothes so they wouldn't wrinkle the way they did in the suitcase. Maybe . . .

But, as usual, Victoria dashed every ray of hope she might have with words that sent fear through her being. "I'll tell you right now, from the get-go, I'm not taking care of another brat. I had you and your sister and that was more than enough. I'm too tired and too old. You're not bringing a brat to my house, so you'll have to get rid of it or take it somewhere else."

The words seemed to shock Allison out of her reverie. The next day, after Victoria walked out of the house and locked the front door with her key, Allison walked out the back door. Riding the bus, she went to the high school, the YWCA shelter, and pregnant teen home. She scrupulously avoided Social Services and the one adoption agency she'd seen while driving downtown. When she got home, she felt as tired and discouraged as the moment she'd heard her mother's voice in the jail. How could she find her dream in a teen home or a shelter?

She was sitting down to eat that night when her mother

threw a flat manila envelope in her direction so that it landed on her dinner plate.

"Came for you today," Victoria blurted.

Hands suddenly shaking, Allison picked up the envelope. She saw it had been rubber-stamped many times with unfamiliar cities and postal codes, as if it went around the world and finally landed here, on her kitchen table. Her fingers still trembled as they slid under the flap and pulled open the envelope. An assortment of papers and folders slid out. One of them, she saw, was emblazoned with a bold red, white, and blue stripe. She flipped it open and saw that it held airline tickets. She fumbled with the folder and read the date.

"It's from Antonio," she explained, incredulous under the venom of Victoria's glare. "He's sending for me. I'm leaving for Mexico this Friday." Tears brushed her cheeks as satisfaction rose within her. It was as if the comforting blanket of Antonio's love once again rested against her spine and blocked off the stark pain brought by Victoria's anger.

"You're not going," Victoria spat.

Allison was stunned silent. How could this woman who, moments earlier said she would never allow her grandchild in her home, now forbid Allison to leave?

Victoria continued, "You're much too young to go to a foreign country like that all alone. Anything could happen to you."

"I'm going," Allison pounded her fist on the table.

To her surprise and ultimate horror, Victoria wrapped her own hand around the fist and said simply, "I'm going with you."

Again speechless, Allison fought mental images of Antonio's gentle charm, the one refuge in her desolate life, being annihilated by Victoria's vicious attack. She recalled the racial epithets her mother hurled against Antonio and the beatings and cruel remarks made toward her. She wanted to scream, to protest, as Victoria grabbed up the ticket folder and rushed to the phone to begin calling travel agencies to see if she could purchase another ticket. Allison left the table and ran to her room, leaving her dinner untouched on her plate. There was no way she could eat, or talk, or even think. She lay still on the bed as the sky outside darkened to black. Later, after midnight, she opened her suitcase, still crammed with dirty clothes from her work at Columbia Orchards. She threw out the sour-smelling, dingy T-shirts and pedal pushers and tentatively looked through her drawers for clothes to take to the town where Antonio lived. San Luis. That was the name of it. Allison realized she had no idea how far it was, what the climate was like, or how long it would take to get there. Remembering the few baby clothes she'd stuffed away in the garage, she realized she'd hadn't bought a single maternity outfit and had no idea if such things existed in Mexico. All of these thoughts, she knew, were trifles compared to the real issue. Was there any way that she could run away and somehow escape without Victoria?

As the week passed, Victoria seemed alternately furious with Allison for ruining her life and excited about what she viewed as an exotic vacation in a romantic locale. Throughout her mother's tirades of both anger and enthusiasm, Allison tried to keep reminding herself that she was going to be with Antonio, and that hopefully Victoria couldn't stay in San Luis with her forever.

Allison's first impression of her new homeland was that the weather in Mexico was warm. A gentle breeze wafted around her shoulders when she deboarded the plane in the middle of the night. A cautious surge of excitement rose within her, and she thought again of her dream. Now, at sixteen, she was taking on a new life as a wife and mother. She had visions of how she would love her children, beautiful babies with dark hair and dark eyes that she would cradle on her lap.

Antonio was waiting at the airport, and she flew into his arms, realizing how painful it had been to think she'd never be with him again. Even as she buried her face in Antonio's chest, she was aware of the Shalimar perfume behind her and the looming threat that was Victoria. Releasing herself from the hug, she said hopefully, "Antonio, this is my mother, Victoria McGarry."

Antonio's smile was open and accepting. When he lifted Victoria's hand to kiss it, Allison reveled in a rare smile from her mother. Then Antonio spoke in rapid Spanish and a woman dressed all in black with a black veil like a nun approached Allison. *"Mama, esta muchacha es Allison,"* he said, and the woman moved to take Allison in her arms. Her hug was encompassing and comforting, the way Victoria's had never been, even when she was little. The woman kissed Allison's cheek and said softly, *"Mi niña,"* which Allison knew meant, "My daughter."

After Antonio dropped Victoria off at her hotel, Allison felt another surge of excitement. The car felt airy and peaceful as Antonio drove off into the night. Suddenly shy, Allison wondered if she should try her few words of her night school Spanish on Antonio's mother. Moments later she decided to remain silent and stare out at the satiny blackness around her, trying to absorb the essence of this place that Antonio called home.

The next morning she realized that the hacienda where Antonio's mother lived was a large, windowless adobe house filled with air that felt as warm as the inside of a sauna. The walls were decorated with turquoise-blue ceramic tiles. There was a gaslight and a gas stove where Antonio's mother cooked tortillas on bricks. There was no indoor plumbing. Allison soon discovered that taking a shower required going outside and drawing the water up from a well into a cement cubicle before letting it it run in glorious rivulets over her body.

The warm breeze she'd felt when the plane landed turned into torrid heat in the daytime. All of her discoveries during the first day were tempered by the relief that the two mothers couldn't talk to each other because Antonio's mother spoke not a word of English. Maria, as Antonio told her to address her future mother-in-law, operated a dry-goods store out of the back of the house and, when she wasn't working, seemed to hug Allison regularly.

At least Victoria kept her silence during the daytime. It

was only at night that Victoria hissed at her in the silence of the room they shared now that Victoria conceded she was scared to stay alone in a hotel where she couldn't speak the language. As a flour mill in the town pounded like drumbeats and kept the two women awake, Victoria tossed negative thoughts across the room to Allison. "Marrying beneath you," she'd hiss in the dark. Moments later, "No bathroom for the rest of your life," she'd say. Or, "How are you going to stay here when you can't even talk to anyone?"

At the wedding Allison wore ankle-strap sandals and a wraparound skirt. She didn't understand a word of the ceremony, but knew all too well the surge of desire that rose inside her from the warmth of Antonio's kiss. Was that a tear on Victoria's face? If it were, Allison knew her mother would never acknowledge any emotion she may have felt, would instead become angry at her for mentioning it. "You're too smart to live down here your whole life." was Victoria's only comment as music filled the air and steaming tortillas were passed around on a tray to the two hundred guests who also consumed fresh fruit, hot rice, and empanadas filled with syrup-dipped cherries. Beneath her mother's words, though, Allison could see that her mother couldn't completely fault the Romero family. Allison held a quiet hope that their polished manners, hospitality, and instant acceptance of her daughter could somehow create a chink in Victoria's icy heart.

At the airport, when Antonio kissed her hand, Victoria displayed a chilly hint of a smile, but then turned away without a hug or goodbye to Allison, who felt bereft and empty, as if a package was suddenly yanked from her arms. "Goodbye, Mom!" she yelled, but it was too late; Victoria had already walked beyond the thick glass of the airport doors. As he squeezed her shoulders, Allison knew Antonio had no idea of the mixed emotions swirling inside her, of the love, hate, curiosity, and fascination that Victoria inspired.

Yet in the next months it was as if those broken feelings were smoothed like rocks in a river. Allison felt both frustrated and soothed by being the only person who spoke English within San Luis, the small town hundreds of miles away from Mexico City. Being a world away from the conflict that had held her captive all her life was like spending time in a balmy breeze. In the mornings she helped Maria in the dry-goods store, wrapping packages, measuring fabric, stocking shelves. Afternoons, the hacienda was hushed as she napped, read, rested, and grew as round as a plum. Allison thought she could live there forever. There was no phone. There were no letters from Victoria. Allison neither knew nor cared the date, the time, nor even the address of where she was now. It was as if she was wrapped in a warm, woolen blanket and didn't care if she ever emerged.

She was seven months pregnant when Antonio and Maria shocked her with a sudden request. One evening after dinner, while Maria was knitting in her favorite chair, Antonio draped his arm across Allison's shoulders. His mahogany-colored eyes probed hers. "You need to go back to the States soon. Mama and I bought your ticket for next week."

"What?" Allison exclaimed as fear and shock charged through her. What was wrong? How could he ask her to leave like this? Was Antonio becoming mysterious and darkly hateful, like Victoria? Did he now love and hate her, too? His pronouncement was interrupted by her own realization that she had visualized somehow staying here forever, with she and Maria alternately cradling her ebony-haired baby while the other one filled bins in the dry-goods store. She protested quickly. "Antonio, I can't go. The baby is almost here."

"Our child must not be born in Mexico. You must leave now."

Allison trembled in fear. "Antonio—don't do this to me. Don't send me away now."

He took her in his arms. "You'll be back soon, with the baby."

She hardly heard his words as Victoria's image swam in her head, saying, "I told you so, he really doesn't want this baby. Once he's had you in bed, that's it."

"I can't go," she repeated stubbornly.

"You have to—for our child. He must have United States citizenship."

For the first time Allison thought of the few things she missed about the United States. Being able to go into a store and speak to the clerk. Television shows. Her mother's cooking. The beach.

"Aren't there papers we can request? I am a citizen."

"No." Antonio shook his head sadly. "Not that the government in the United States will recognize. But, if the baby is born there, he will be a citizen of both countries. . . ."

Still, Allison shook her head. "Oh, Antonio—can you go with me?"

He took her in his arms. "You know I have no passport. And no way to get one. I could try to pass through the border—but if they caught me, they might discover that you are my wife. They could imprison us both. No. You must go alone. It is the only way."

At the airport she clung to Antonio as if he were her only safe harbor. Then Maria hugged her, patting her shoulder and then her cheek. *"Mi niña,"* she said simply.

Allison stared out the window as the plane rose, wishing to drink in the warm haven of Mexico, and somehow capture the peace of her smooth and even days with Antonio and his mother.

She dreaded the plane's landing, and even more, her mother's first sight of her rounded frame. She heard the familiar derisive tone before she even reached baggage claim. "Big as a house," Victoria's voice crept out of her mouth like a snake. "He lets you get as big as a house, and now he dumps you on your butt." Her tirade continued as they walked through the airport to the car. "Had himself a few more months of fun, but now you're too big, so he tosses you back to me."

Allison squared her shoulders, yet shook with fear. "Mama, it wasn't like that. He wants our baby to be a citizen of the United States. You should understand. You called him a wetback."

''Like he cares. He himself went in and out of this country like it had a revolving door.''

Victoria's wrath continued after Allison moved back into her own bedroom. She never referred to the baby as a child, only ''that halfbreed'' or on occasion, ''the bastard.'' Wanting nothing more than to distance herself as soon as possible, Allison didn't stop to remind her mother that her child would be legitimate—that Victoria herself had attended the wedding. From the moment she stepped back into her old room, Allison knew she had to find a way to move out, as surely as the night she crawled out of the window with the suitcase.

Chapter Four

Using the small amount of money Antonio sent with her, she began to stay in cheap hotels on odd nights. When she felt guilty about not saving the money for the baby and returned for a few nights at home, Victoria accused her of staying with men on the nights she was gone.

Allison didn't dare remind her mother that she was now eight months pregnant and hardly felt like a night on the town. She knew if she mentioned the baby, Victoria's verbal assault would take a new direction, and nothing she could say would quiet the attack or convince her mother to change her mind. Yet still, underneath a mountain of resentment, disbelief, and anger, Allison sensed she couldn't run away from Victoria completely. She remembered too well how quickly Victoria had found her in the jail. And somewhere, deep inside, her dream of having a happy marriage and family included her children having a loving grandmother. So she eventually moved permanently into a cheap hotel and visited Victoria on occasion, grateful only that her mother never questioned what her permanent address was now. Allison could only assume that the slight waning of her mother's criticism was due to Victoria's relief that, after all, the baby would likely not be coming to her house to live.

When she woke one night feeling as if her insides were

about to split open, Allison simply dialed the paramedics herself. She knew they wouldn't question what race her baby was or where his father happened to be.

She lay flat on the cool, smooth sheet of the hospital bed, trying not to move. Fluid from the spinal anesthetic fountained up to her brain, spilling over into headaches that seemed to reverberate throughout her being. The labor pains felt like a gigantic vise squeezing her body in an agonizing grip. It can't be much longer, she reasoned. He has to be almost here. She tried to comfort herself with inner glimpses of her dream. Somehow there would be a white-walled nursery for her baby with a warm quilt over the crib and a chest of drawers filled with matching sleepers, undershirts, and tiny socks. There would be a nursery lamp with a gentle light.

With another jagged, tearing pain, there was a sensation of weight leaving her body, as if the twenty pounds she'd been carrying rolled off like a pillow.

"Here he is!" the doctor exclaimed, and she saw him lift a bundle the size of a loaf of bread and wrap it in a white hospital blanket.

"Looks like a linebacker to me." The doctor's laugh was hearty. All her agony dissolved in the wonder of seeing her baby's face for the first time. She marveled over his warm olive skin, big brown eyes, and full head of wispy, soft brown hair. She gave him a name as Hispanic, exotic, and euphonious as his father's: Rafaél Simón Romero. Holding the warm weight of him in her arms, it was hard to imagine ever not knowing him. From that moment, Rafe represented an actual manifestation of the intangible hopes she'd held on to throughout her life thus far. His birth was evidence that her dream was beginning to come true. She had her son, now she just needed to keep persevering until her husband and home were also in place. It was a vision she promised herself she would never let waver, even for an instant.

She wasn't sure when she first realized that the money she'd brought back from Mexico was beginning to run out.

Looking through the drawer where she kept her folded bills, she suddenly understood that the pile was smaller, and Antonio hadn't sent any more. Her mind skirted around the despair she felt creeping in along with the realization there was no way to contact him. Understanding that there were no phones in San Luis, and that mail service was erratic, she didn't stop to agonize over how to get in touch. She was forced to admit, though, that soon she would need money. She had to get a job.

After going through the want ads and making a few calls, she phoned her sister, Susan.

As she waited for Susan to answer her phone, Allison felt her heart thud in her chest. There was no one else who knew Victoria's hidden violence the way her sister did. While Allison's more assertive personality made her Victoria's favorite target, it was impossible to live in their house and not endure their mother's venom. Susan had felt her share of slaps and snarls. Both sisters responded by surging into the world with a vengeance—Allison with her friends and future dream, and Susan with her pursuit of a college degree. As closely as they were bonded, being together refreshed their bitter memories, and they shied away from associating with each other. Calling Susan was a last resort. But what other person would understand and sympathize with her frantic desperation? Who else would know better why she couldn't ask for help from home?

"I need you to babysit. This morning. At eleven."

"What?" Rock music blared from the apartment where Susan lived with three other girls.

"I need you to take care of Rafe. I have a job interview."

"I have finals tomorrow. Everyone's studying here. I'd have to ask, and I don't think they'd say yes."

"Only an hour. I promise. Eleven to twelve."

"I'll do it at Mom's."

"What?" Allison felt hairs rise on the back of her neck. How many times had Victoria said, "No grandchild stays at my house"?

"She's at work. She'll never know. Meet ya there." The phone clicked in Allison's ear. For a full minute, she stared at Rafe lying on the couch wrapped in a receiving blanket. Then she picked him up, held his cheek to hers. She set him gently into his stroller, locked her apartment, and walked determinedly to Victoria's house.

When Susan opened the door, Allison felt forced to confront her with, "Mom said he could never stay here."

Susan had a pencil behind her ear, an open book in her hand, and stains from eating Victoria's cherry chocolates on her face. She said, "I tell ya, she'll never know. Look." Allison saw Susan had spread a huge quilt on the living room floor. "He'll just sleep there until you get back. No big deal," Susan said. "Now hurry. Get going."

Allison walked past Stadium Coffee Shop three times before she went inside. It was a no-nonsense small brick building where huge amounts of hamburgers, fries, and grilled cheese sandwiches were sold without the assistance of advertisers or interior designers. Allison herself had bought an occasional cheeseburger here and watched hundreds of other people carry white paper sacks and wax-coated cups down the block to the civic stadium where football games and concerts were held held year-round in Oakland's semimild weather.

Now a small sign in the window stated HELP WANTED.

Allison walked past the cafe one more time, and stopped before a vacant storefront. She looked in the plate-glass window that reflected like a mirror and combed her hair, then smiled to reveal her teeth. She suddenly missed Rafe, wondering what he was doing while he stayed with her sister. Was he hungry or crying for her? As a rising anxiety filled her, she understood there was no more time to waste.

She walked through the door of Stadium Coffee Shop and instantly smelled frying hamburgers and hot grease. She quickly poked her growling stomach, then wondered whether she should inquire about the job by standing at the cash register or near the order desk. Suddenly a voice that seemed to be at her elbow said, "Help you, ma'am?"

Surprised, she glanced down at a plump middle-aged woman with piercing brown eyes whose cascade of graying hair reminded of her of a rooster's comb. "Know what you want?" the woman said, in the same demanding tone.

The woman's gaze was intense. She seemed annoyed. Allison was tempted just to ask for an order of fries and leave.

"Yes," she said.

The woman's hand slammed onto her hip. "Well . . . yes what?"

"I know what I want," Allison felt her weight shift from one foot to the other. "I want the job."

"The job!" Now the woman flung both arms up in the air. Her crown of gray hair wiggled. She put both hands on her hips again and stared at Allison. "You want the job. I tell ya, this isn't the malt shop. You can't talk to boys and make root-beer floats. We need someone who can get the burgers out—look at this," she gestured angrily at the lines of people, the packed tables, the other people carrying out sacks spotted with grease from burgers and fries they contained. "I need someone who can help me get through the lunch and dinner hour. You work noon to six with one ten-minute break!" The woman looked as if she were accusing her of something.

Allison swallowed and said, "I can work days. I'm fast. I have a son who my sister will tend and I go to night school."

The woman raised her eyebrows, took a step backward, and surveyed her, studying her from head to foot. Allison looked off into the restaurant again, determined not to flinch. The woman was right: The restaurant was packed, probably always busy. It seemed to Allison as if this woman might be used to intimidating people, but now the two of them were engaged in a battle of wills. She refused to give in.

The woman spat. "You got a baby? I can't have someone always calling in sick or coming in late."

"I won't. My sister's there."

"Can you cook?" the woman demanded suddenly. "Get food hot and get it on a plate in under one minute?"

"I can," said Allison without a stammer, recalling how

she'd watched Victoria cook all kinds of foods: Chinese, German, Jewish, Hungarian. There was never a mix in their house—Victoria knew everything from scratch. She'd helped sometimes, too. Hamburgers would be nothing. "I can cook," she said again.

The woman nodded, eyeing her sideways. "We'll find out if you can."

What did that mean, Allison wondered, then noticed the woman's eyes traveling over her again. "You look like you're about an eight. I got an old uniform in the back that'll fit you 'til you buy one. Pay period starts Friday. You can work twelve to six. That's six at night. Have your late evenings free," the woman said, cuffing her on the arm. "Wear heavy shoes. Your legs will feel it worse if you don't."

Allison nodded, held out her hand. "I'm Allison Romero," she said.

"Bev," the woman said without taking her hand. Walking back to the steaming kitchen, she called out, "See ya Friday."

Chapter Five

Even though her legs ached from standing, and she grew tired of staring into hundreds of faces and counting change constantly, the work at Stadium Coffee Shop still wasn't as exhausting as picking apples. The days slid by as Allison sneaked Rafe into her mother's house after Victoria left, and Susan watched him. Allison always stopped a moment before she went out the door and gazed at Rafe's beauty as he sat in her sister's lap. She didn't dare linger long—the scent of Victoria's perfume and the memory of Bev's angry warnings haunted her mind. Some days it seemed less dangerous to take Rafe to work with her, to glance down at his contented, brown-eyed face as he lay on the floor on a blanket. She stood above him and peeled endless potatoes. The skins dropped in waves—limp, papery lengths falling into the sink. She rarely stopped to think that the job was boring and long, or lament that occasionally powdery starch flew up and stung her eyes. Her dream still lay at the end of the road, a beacon that blocked out all the struggle of getting there.

One night after work she was still dressed in her restaurant uniform and lying on the bed next to Rafe when the phone rang. It was late, after eleven-thirty. Panic prickled her thoughts. Could she have left a stray sock at Victoria's? A bowl of infant cereal in the refrigerator? Might Susan have betrayed her in a moment of frustration or fatigue? If she didn't answer the phone now, she knew, her mother might stay home late in the morning and call, increasing the chances of discovery.

She picked up the phone and, her heart thudded when she heard Antonio's warm, loving voice ask, "Allison?"

"Yes, yes, I'm here!" she said proudly, gazing down as tiny Rafe nursed at her breast. "You would be so proud of your son, Antonio. He is so beautiful, and already a man."

There was a pause. She was startled to hear Antonio's tone reflect not pride, but accusation. "What have you been doing while I try to come back to you? Where are you at night?"

A rush of anger filled her. Tears bit the corners of her eyes. She thought of the hours of standing on her feet, the nights when Rafe woke up crying and she couldn't get back to sleep, and the other nights, when she finished her homework, so late that there wasn't even time to go to bed. What was she doing? Allison's mind continued to flash images: the agonizing replay of the painful birth, the unending search for a place to live, and that perennial mountain of potatoes needing to be peeled. Her temper rose. "I have been caring for our son and working hard. I am making hamburgers and scraping the skins off potatoes in a restaurant."

There was a pause, in which she heard him inhale harshly all the way from San Luis. "Is that all?" said the melodic voice she now loved and hated passionately in the same instant.

"I am going to school, too. And I'm not even spending money for a baby-sitter. I sneak him into Mama's. I do more than enough. I do too much." She recalled the warm serenity of San Luis, the calm meals, the sound of the flour mill that eventually became as comforting as her own heartbeat. "That is more than you are doing," she said, her voice rising louder with each word until she slammed down the phone.

Instantly she regretted her anger and wanted to talk to Antonio again. She wanted to describe Rafe's wondrous brown eyes, his soft hair, the pure joy of holding his small, warm body in her arms. What was wrong with her husband? If he could only see her dedication, her exhaustion, the son she fought to save every day. Was it possible he missed her so much he was only trying to envision how she spent the days they were apart? Could it be a longing for her he disguised beneath his brutal questioning? For a moment she was angry with herself along with Antonio. Why couldn't she just tell him about his son?

Yet when Antonio called a few days later, an argument broke out again when he claimed that every time he tried to call her since the first time, there was no answer at her apartment. Allison fought her rising anger by trying to explain. "I told you. I work every day in the restaurant. It's by the stadium—there are always games and hundreds of people who want to eat. I have to feed them all. Sometimes Rafe is with me, lying on his blanket." Allison tried to speak quickly, to state her whole situation in a few words before Antonio could intercede with a harsh interruption. "When you don't take him with you, where do you go after work?" he accused.

"I go to my two night classes! And then I go home to him! With my feet aching and my back hurting and my hands raw!" She slammed the phone again, and once more wished she could pick it up and hear his voice. They just needed to be together, she told herself. Antonio needed to see his son, to hold him, and to watch Allison rush to work and care for her son at the same time. If he could see how she dragged herself through every day, he would know she had no time to misbehave.

Two months passed before Antonio returned to the States. The apartment they rented was larger, lighter, and airier than the musty room in the cheap hotel. As much as she felt a rush of valdiation that her dream was finally there, she sensed Antonio still did not trust her. While he shared her continuing fascination and love with the miracle that was their son, he continued to question how she spent her time.

One night, after a game, she and Bev both stayed at work an hour late to clean up. When she arrived at home at nearly midnight, Antonio rushed at her as she opened the door.

"Your work does not last until now! You have a lover! I know it! You were with him." To Allison's fury and astonishment, Antonio hit her, his fist a steel bolt slamming against her already aching arm. Instantly she felt all the fatigue and frustration of the past months rise within her. She slapped his face, the sound like wood cracking. "You son of a bitch. Get out of my face." She stepped closer to him, lifted her chin in defiance, and pointed her finger as if it were a knife. "Who do you think you are? You are the one who's illegal, coming into this country under a fake name. How dare you cross-examine me about my life! Get out! Get out!"

Surprised by her sudden rage, Antonio stepped backward.

"Out!" she shouted one last time before rushing to five-month-old Rafe's crib. The baby lay awake and gurgling, his eyes wide and looking almost black in the darkened bedroom. Allison didn't stop for pleasantries, or even to kiss him on the head as she usually would. With anger-shaking hands, she bundled him in his pram suit and knit cap, placed him gently, but quickly in the stroller. She wrapped him in blankets and surged out of the apartment into a waiting snowstorm. Her fury carried her down the street and across town. The snowflakes dropping on her head were hardly felt as her feet propelled forward. She paced clear across town from the northeast to the west side, stopping only when she arrived at a friend's apartment.

"Allison! What are you doing here in the middle of the night!" Even though she was obviously half-asleep, Terry's shock registered clearly.

"I'm leaving Antonio. He hit me."

As she and Terry chatted, she found the argument with Antonio loomed in her mind like a lingering headache. Half-heartedly listening to Terry's description of an evening of dancing and getting drunk, Allison held Rafe on her lap and thought of the home and marriage she still wanted so desperately. At first her mind pondered over the belongings in the apartment, wondering what Antonio would do with them if she never went back. Would he ache for Rafe the way she would if she were separated from him? When Terry finally sensed her distraction, Allison started to talk about the fight with Antonio. At first her words marched like storm troopers as her anger flared. But as she took the time to explain the argument, her furor died. Her dream of a family, after all, was still across town. Antonio hit her—and she'd never forgive him for that. But what was the source of his mistrust and anger? Was it possible Antonio still did not understand that she gave all her energy to help and preserve their small family? Did she need to explain this to him one more time?

She touched Terry's hand. "You're nice to listen to me. I'm sorry I talked so much. Could I use the phone to call a cab? I don't think I can walk anymore."

"You're going *back*?" Terry countered in disbelief.

"I have to. I just can't leave. Am I stupid or what?"

Terry shook her head. "You could stay here until morning."

"That's okay." Allison smiled, suddenly feeling weary and talked out, wishing she could mentally and instantly transport herself back to her own apartment living room. She called the cab, changed Rafe's diaper, and placed the knit hat back on his head. "I'm really sorry," she said to her friend. "I woke you up and took all your time. Thank you for listening to me."

"You're really going back. I can't believe it."

"Yeah," said Allison. But as she sat in the cab, her own doubts assailed her. Would Antonio think she now agreed with him, that her activities while he was gone were somehow suspect? What did he expect? Did he ever work both day and night himself? He never got up with Rafe in the night; he thought minding the baby was a woman's place.

As the cab dropped her off, she could see that the light was still on in the apartment, and somehow it seemed to reflect warmth, as if it were welcoming her home. The cab ride had lulled Rafe to sleep with his finger in his mouth and his knit cap drooped low on his head. Picking him up and putting him once again in the stroller with the blanket, Allison marveled that his skin was still warm. She dragged the stroller up the metal stairs, hardly feeling its weight through her hopefulness. With each step, she expected the door to be thrust open by smiling and apologetic Antonio. When she reached the closed door, she knocked and softly called Antonio's name. When there was no answer, she fumbled in her purse for the key.

"Antonio—" she said as she opened the door. Silence. She lifted Rafe from the stroller and set him on the floor wrapped in his blanket. "Antonio?" She called softly again; she didn't want to wake him if he were sleeping. But when he didn't respond, she stormed through the rooms, calling out his name in a voice that bespoke both anger and fear. "Antonio! Antonio!" Her voice rose with a scream that neared despair. She walked through the kitchen, the bathroom, Rafe's room, and finally the bedroom she and Antonio shared. The bed was made, the spread perfectly unwrinkled the way she'd left it that morning. When she stopped shouting, Allison's words echoed around her, both the recent screams and those from the fight hours earlier. The realization that Antonio was gone hit her as piercingly as Rafe's abrupt and somehow panicked cry.

Chapter Six

Each day the silence of the phone screamed at her. She flipped through the mail quickly, not even daring to hope. The advertisements and fliers seemed not innocuous, but cruel when she thought that none of the people who sent them to her cared whether she lived or died. And neither, it seemed, did Antonio. Now the days of going to school and working until there was time only to come home and change into her school clothes again seemed endless. There was no one to talk to. She was afraid Susan and Terry might abandon her if she burdened them with the full weight of her inner despair. She didn't dare tell Victoria of the despondency that crept over her weekly. The only relief was that she was so tired she was numb. Many nights she held Rafe on her lap or lay next to him on the bed until they both fell asleep. She awoke with unbrushed teeth, still lying beside him. But she also knew that nothing could compare with the warm feeling of his soft cheek against hers. She didn't want to increase her pain by trying to contact Antonio and feeling even more abandoned when there was no answer. Besides, there was no way to call or write—she didn't know where he was. She clung to Rafe as the one remnant of her dream. From her meager check, each week she bought something new for him. Beyond Bev's calloused frown, she sensed a small chink of sympathetic understanding: Her boss never complained about the nights Rafe spent on the coffee shop floor, even when he graduated from lying on a blanket to scooting around the smooth tile in his walker.

By now, when the phone rang, Allison didn't dare include hope in the emotions she felt. But her heart sank with despair when she recognized Victoria's smug, disparaging tone. "Left you again, didn't he?"

"No, Mom. He just hasn't come back here to stay yet."

"It's been—how many months? A year, hasn't it?"

"I don't know."

"Face the music. He's gone for good. And left you with a brat. You're stuck."

Sudden chills of panic prickled Allison's shoulder. "I am not stuck!" she cried defiantly, but she knew an edge of panic crept into her voice. Allison suddenly mustered her strength to say, "Goodbye, Mom." Then she hung up the phone and, for the first time since Antonio left, burst into tears.

Two days later Allison visited Margaret North, an attorney that someone told her about. The woman was famous, people said. Got fair settlements. Sympathetic to women.

"How may I help you?"

"My husband—" There was a sudden lump that threatened to close her throat completely. Two tears slid out of her eyes. How did she work all those months without a sign of emotion and now this?

The attorney waited, staring at her, Allison thought. She cleared her throat and tried again. "My husband—I think he has left me."

"He's moved out of the home?"

"No—" Allison shook her head as another tear threatened. "He's in Mexico. He's from there."

"Are you a U.S. citizen?" the lawyer asked.

Allison nodded, grateful for a simple question. "Yes. And he wanted our baby to be one, too. So he sent me back here . . . until Rafe was born."

"And he stayed there?" North's artfully arched brows frowned quizzically.

"Yes." Did she dare say this? "I met him when he was in this country illegally. He said he didn't dare risk that again."

"Did you believe him?"

With a sigh Allison nodded. "I had no reason not to. He flew me down there to marry him. If he wanted to abandon me, why marry me in the first place?"

North nodded mysteriously, as if she understood the situation in a way that Allison could not.

"So—you've been apart for how long at this time?"

Allison covered her eyes with her hands to block the flood of tears that now pushed out her eyelids like floods breaking through a dam. The weight of the exhaustion and worry of the past months now seemed to sit firmly on her small shoulders. "A year," she eased out, the words followed by a sob that cut sharply through her throat.

When she finally looked up, she found that she couldn't read the attorney's look.

"So what action did you wish me to take here?" the woman asked.

Again Allison sighed. "To file for divorce. After this long, I guess my mother's right. He's left me."

North looked down at the yellow pad where she was jotting notes. "If he comes back to this country, we can request child support, of course. But if not—"

Allison looked up in time to see the attorney shrug.

Months later she sat alone with North at her divorce hearing. The other side of the courtroom was eerily bare. North told her that letters she'd sent to San Luis, Mexico, were neither acknowledged nor returned. At least, she said, the divorce would be uncontested. It was as if Antonio had simply dropped off the face of the earth. In the months before the final decree was issued, Allison struggled to imagine Antonio's thoughts. Did he truly never want to see Rafe again? Were their fights really enough for him to want to sever the relationship completely?

One night after a late night at the coffee shop, Allison came home to find the divorce papers pushed through her mail slot at her apartment. It was a game night. She'd called Susan and begged her to take Rafe to her own apartment and stay with him until she got there. Then she stayed late to clean up and wash every tub, sink, and table surface. Susan muttered and frowned when Allison finally arrived home after two A.M. After her sister left, Allison's eyes felt grainy, and her legs, arms, and back ached. Her uniform hung limply and smelled of sweat, and her hair dangled like strings in her face. Yet she opened the papers, sat on the couch, and stared at the words as their impact pierced her soul. Her dream was gone. She was alone with an eighteen-month-old son, a job that wore her down to the nub daily and a mother who took perverse delight in her grim circumstances. Yet fighting the tears that began to slide down her cheeks, Allison stood angrily. She opened a drawer, dropped the papers inside, and slammed it shut so hard that Rafe stirred and groaned in his crib. She promised herself she would never look at those papers again.

Her busyness began to smooth the edges of her pain, at least so that there wasn't any risk of crying at work, or bursting into tears when she confided to Susan. With all her time taken up, there wasn't much space to pine or ponder as the days passed into spring. She worked, went to school, came home, and fell into a heap.

On her lunch hour three weeks before school ended, Allison celebrated in advance by deciding to eat out instead of sharing a salad and fries in the back room with Bev. Walking into a nearby seafood restaurant, she immediately noticed the cool calmness that seemed a stark contrast from the hectic steaminess of Stadium Coffee Shop. People here weren't rushed and pushing in line; they stood calmly and talked in soft, happy tones at tablecloth-covered tables.

While the difference felt as relaxing as dropping into a hammock, someone suddenly caught her attention. It surprised her that she would notice any man—it had been so long. But the tall blond man working behind the counter captivated her. He had one of those fresh, freckled American faces that are in every town in the United States. She found herself glancing at him again and again as she moved step by step through the line to the salad bar. What was so compelling about him? Did she know him from somewhere, but couldn't quite place him? Instinctively she sensed her awareness of him wasn't recognition from the past, but something else, something she'd wanted to avoid forever after her past pain. He was a good-looking man—that was all. Yet even after she understood that they'd never met, his calm stance was paradoxically powerful and intriguing, and held her gaze.

"How ya doin' today?" This man's easygoing, quiet, all-American air and manner bore a startling resemblance to the actor Dennis Quaid. From the first moment it was obvious that this serene appeal was worlds away from Antonio's fiery Latin charisma. As if reading her thoughts, he asked, "Aren't you Antonio's wife?"

"Yes . . ." Allison said, startled to understand that he seemed to know her though she was sure she didn't recognize him.

"Used to see you guys on Saturday nights." The man's grin was easy and constant.

She nodded in agreement, though she was still mystified. "From the YMCA dance," she said suddenly, and then somehow felt compelled to add, "He's my ex-husband now."

"Really? How did that happen?" His mock frown made her smile, and she actually felt a laugh inside, fighting to get out. Fatigue from half a day at Stadium Coffee Shop slowly evaporated like steam. Someone behind her nudged her shoulder, and Allison was abruptly aware of the huge line of people behind her as if they were a weight on her shoulders.

"Long story," she said quickly. "Long, bad story."

"Really? With Antonio? Hmmm. Seemed like a nice guy to me."

A man behind her said, "Lunch only lasts an hour, lady. Save the soap opera for afternoon tea."

Allison and the man laughed together. Flustered, she said

quickly, "Give me the fish and chips—and a side of fresh shrimp."

She sat alone at a booth, aware of her own inner tension rising at the same time she kept thinking she should feel calm in this cool, quiet place where she didn't have to worry about making conversation with anyone. Moments later the Dennis Quaid look-alike appeared with a tray in his hands.

"This space taken?" he gestured at the empty side of the booth.

Allison shook her head, then found her eyes involuntarily dipping down to the slice of lemon on her plate. She finally looked up when the man spoke. "Josh Morgan," he said amiably, extending a hand.

"Allison Romero." The name felt awkward on her tongue—she kept it only because she shared it with Rafe. Not wanting to explain her uneasiness, she reached out to take the man's hand, then sensed that he held her fingers a moment longer than necessary. Perhaps sensing her nervousness, he casually let go of her hand and sat across from her.

"So, like, you and Antonio are splitsville?" he asked jovially.

Allison nodded. "Looks that way." She pierced a piece of fish with her fork.

The man persisted. "For good?"

Now Allison shrugged. "I guess so. Papers arrived four months ago."

"He divorced you? Haven't seen either one of you at the dances."

Allison shook her head sheepishly. The dances. The days when she could dress up, head out, and dance to show tunes until after midnight seemed light-years away. She couldn't imagine how it must feel to dance all night without worrying about a baby or work and school the next day.

Interrupting her thoughts, the man asked, "Didn't we dance together once or twice?"

Again feeling flustered, Allison shook her head. She didn't want to say *I think I'd remember you.*

"Any chance you're going to go again in the near future? Say, Saturday night or so?"

"Oh, no," Allison said, again thinking how far away dancing seemed from her life now. But at the same time she couldn't deny the tingly feeling rising within, threatening to push aside the pain she'd worn like a shroud these last months.

"Come on," said the man, smiling at her. "Why not?"

"I couldn't," said Allison. "I have work and school." She didn't say, *and I have a son.*

The man smiled. "You have work and school on Saturday night? Tell me another one."

"Well—I do have work on Saturdays—sometimes." She looked at her watch. "Speaking of work, I have ten minutes to get back and not be late." She glanced down at her fish and chips and fresh shrimp, hardly touched. She'd be hungry tonight if she didn't eat now. It was a long time until eight P.M.

"Where do you work?"

"Oh, down the street," she gestured vaguely with her hand.

Now he grinned and her face reddened even more. "I bet you work at Stadium Coffee Shop."

It was as if he'd seen her without her clothes on. Her mind fleetingly imagined how she looked with her hair drooping, dressed in the sweat-and-catsup-stained uniform. "How did you know that?" she asked.

"You're not the only one who has to eat. I've seen you there."

"When?"

He shrugged. "Let me get you a doggie bag. You hardly ate a thing." He smiled at her knowingly, and moments later, when he handed her a paper carton, she found it hard to look up at him again.

"Thank you," she managed with a lopsided smile. "I have to say—this beats my usual Stadium lunch. I'll take it home and finish it after work tonight."

His shrug was good-natured. "You'll have to have lunch

with me again. Or we could make it dinner on Saturday night—before we go to the dance. . . ."

She felt tongue-tied again. Swallowing, she said quickly, "Sorry. I can't go Saturday. But thanks." Feeling his eyes still on her, she turned to leave the restaurant, not even looking back as he called out, "Call me here if you change your mind."

Surprisingly, the rest of her shift passed quickly. When she rushed home to Rafe, she was astonished to feel a flood of guilt drop over her like a wet towel because she'd intermittently let her mind slip away from him.

Through the next days she was surprised to find her mind warring between the unexpected lift the man's flirtation brought and her firm dedication to acquiring a home and family for Rafe. When her memories of that brief lunch kept interrupting her homework, her thoughts while peeling potatoes, and even her train of thought when she read to Rafe, she became determined to banish these interruptions from her mind.

One night, while Rafe lay asleep in his crib beside her, she lay on her side on the bed and wrote a long letter to Antonio. *I'm sorry I had to take this divorce action against you, but I have to think of our son and how I am going to take care of him by myself. . . . I still can't believe you haven't come back to be with us. . . . I still miss you, Antonio . . . and even though he doesn't know the words to say it, I know Rafe misses you, too. If you come back now, possibly we could still be a family.* She paused and thought of the warm sun, the plentiful food, the peace she found briefly in San Luis. She pressed the pen to paper. *Tell Maria hello for me. . . .* She sealed the envelope, thinking of how Victoria would ridicule her actions.

Chapter Seven

Still trying to forget the man's smile that brought her the same soothing feeling as a warm bath, Allison continued to work, then go to school, then study. She fell asleep at odd times, and woke on her couch, or on her own bed with Rafe beside her. The days passed in a blur. She was washing the kitchen floor at Stadium Coffee Shop one night when she heard a man shouting, out in the front where only two or three tables were occupied with customers.

"The service in this place is terrible! Can't I get a hamburger at this time of night!" she heard him say. Shaking her head and tuning out the man's voice, Allison mopped into one corner, then turned and moved toward the other. She jumped when someone firmly pressed a finger into her shoulder.

"Ya got a customer," Bev said, gesturing with her head.

"What? I'm mopping the floor. . . ." Allison protested.

"Out there." Bev jerked her chin. When Allison didn't put the mop in the bucket, Bev took it from her hands. "Waitin' for ya. Hear him yelling a few minutes ago?"

Allison frowned, confused. But she knew the only way to stay out of Bev's wrath was to move quickly. How could she possibly have a customer? She tucked her cleaning rag in her pocket and walked out to the front. No one was waiting. There were no customers standing by the order desk or the register. At first Allison only saw two couples eating leisurely at the restaurant tables. But then she saw a man sitting alone, at a table shadowed by the cash register island. He was leaning back so she couldn't see his face.

Allison felt a residue of excited tension bubbling up inside her as she stepped closer and saw the man in the booth was Josh from the seafood restaurant.

"Can't seem to get a burger in this place," he said, half-serious and half-smiling.

"We close in ten minutes. No one ever comes here at this time. People from the game went home an hour ago. Families with kids went home an hour before that. . . ." Allison was surprised how serious her own voice sounded, as if she were discussing peace talks or the national debt.

"Then how come you're still here?"

"Cleaning up . . ." Allison gestured with her hand at the booths, the floor, the counters.

"How about the dance tonight?" Josh lifted a bronzed arm and stared at his watch. "Exactly one hour and thirty-seven minutes left there."

Allison instantly visualized Susan asleep on the couch at her apartment and Rafe in his crib. No way could she stay out any later and force Susan to drive home after midnight. "Sorry. I can't." She stepped awkwardly back a step or two, mindful of the mop waiting in the back room with Bev.

"Why not?" He pounded his fist gently against the table and grinned at her. "Hey, I know . . . you want to change your clothes first. We'll stop by your place and be at the dance in twenty minutes."

Allison shook her head. "Still can't."

Now Josh paused and squinted at her. He angled his head. "Hey, are you thinkin' I can't take a hint? Is it that you wouldn't go out with *me*, no way, no how, no place, no time?"

Allison felt an unexpected blush rise to her cheeks. "Oh, no . . . it's that . . . ." She inhaled, then swallowed hard, guilt rushing heavy now at her own feelings of inexcusable shame. "See, it's that . . . I've got a son. He's almost two years old. My sister takes care of him. I need to leave now so I can go home and be with him.''

''A *kid*. You got a kid,'' he said.

She waited, but he stared straight ahead and didn't say anything else. When it felt as if her face was going to melt with heat, Allison turned and walked back into the kitchen and picked up her mop. When she and Bev finally went out later to lock up, they saw that he was gone. All the way home and in the next days, she told herself it was for the best—no more letting herself wonder what might somehow happen, no more being distracted by thoughts of his smile or the way he'd made her feel inside. It was only a lunch hour, she kept reminding herself. Only one hour amid weeks and weeks and weeks of pain and feeling alone. It showed how needy she was—her spirits would have risen at anyone who showed the kind of friendliness this man displayed.

As the next days passed, she was comforted by three things: Bev told her she'd passed probation at Stadium Coffee Shop and was now eligible for a raise; she'd convinced her boss she knew how to peel potatoes and make hamburgers. She now had only two months of school before she would receive her high school diploma just one year after the rest of her class. And she'd saved three hundred dollars toward the house she and Rafe would someday have. It wasn't everything, she knew, but at least she was moving in the right direction.

Her relationship with Victoria remained ambivalent, as she alternately avoided her mother and hoped, somehow, to see evidence of pride in how she was progressing.

''You have to admit he left you, just like I said,'' Victoria tossed at her one night on the phone after another long and tiring day. ''He used you.''

Allison wiped her sweaty forehead and said, ''Maybe, Mom, but I'm still not sure. Maybe something happened and he couldn't get back here to me.''

Victoria asked, ''Were you born yesterday?'' Allison didn't answer, admitting to herself that the idea of a terrible accident sounded hollow even to her own ears. But there was still an unfinished feeling. He'd never said good-bye, or that it was over. There was no reply to the divorce action. The attorney couldn't find him. She said aloud, "I'm not living at the same address. Maybe he couldn't find me." This argument seemed faint and pathetic. Victoria was living at the same address as before. Couldn't he just call there?

Victoria's laugh was harsh. "Grow up, girl. Don't be a stupid fool forever. It's time to move on."

Allison's throat tightened and she couldn't reply. " 'Bye," she choked out, too tired to fight her tears as she placed the phone back on its cradle.

The phone call came after she was lying in bed, trying not to think of the aches that were a residue from another night of standing on her feet until after midnight. Rafe was breathing blissfully in his crib beside her. It amazed her how her baby's simple breathing could be so comforting to her, its regular rhythm as lulling as a heartbeat. As long as his breathing flowed as smoothly as silk, the world must be all right, Allison thought. She herself was in that state of half-dreams that comes just before sleep. Then the phone rang. A phone call at this time of night spelled emergency to her. She didn't see any particular face in her mind, but began to sense the tinglings of blind panic. Not wanting to confront what lay on the other end of the line, she let the phone ring twice more before picking it up.

"Hello?" she said, softly and quickly, as if wanting to move swiftly past what lay ahead.

She was jolted awake when the words on the other end of the line seemed to make no sense. At first, it sounded as if she'd walked into the middle of someone else's conversation. A man's voice said, "About that business the other night . . . I'm sorry, it all just sort of took me by surprise, you know what I mean? And I didn't mean to just sit there like a dummy."

"What?" Allison asked, now sitting up in bed. "Do you have the right number?"

The man continued, lighthearted and friendly. "I mean,

I really screwed up there in the restaurant. I guess I just still wasn't sure if you were willing to go out with me and then after you said you had a kid, I didn't know if that meant you didn't want to go, or you needed a sitter if you did, or if you wanted me to pay for the sitter or make arrangements. I admit, I've never dated anyone who had a kid before.''

Oh. So this was the restaurant guy. Why was he calling her? How did he get her number? Lying on her back in the dark, Allison felt a smile creep over her face. His gentle voice after Victoria's harsh insults felt like a warm sweater wrapped around her. She wasn't sure if she wanted to switch on the light and clarify things or just drift back to sleep. Did she really want to invest the time and energy it would take to date someone? What about Rafe? Who would take care of him while she was out?

''That's all right . . . no big deal,'' she said simply, her mind arguing back that it wasn't all right, he'd caused her a bunch of pain, and wasn't she going to confront him with it?

''Well, the thing is, I'm still sort of mixed-up about all this. Were you telling me about your son as a way of saying you don't want to go out, or just as something to say, or what?''

Allison's mind warred with itself in the dark of her bedroom. How could she possibly go out with him? Her days with Susan as a baby-sitter were wearing thin. Victoria was not an option—she criticized Rafe for everything from his father's desertion to being a biracial child. Allison was determined not to let her child suffer the feelings of being an unwanted mistake the way she still did.

Yet she still remembered the warm-bath feeling of the one-hour flirtation, of spending time with someone who was no way involved with the painful, dead-end puzzle that seemed to be her future. She didn't want to admit to herself that this man was appealing to her, that part of the tantalizing sensation she couldn't stop feeling was the pricklings of rising attraction.

Not wanting to hang on and equally not wanting to let

go, she said simply. "Why don't you come to dinner at my house on Sunday at five o'clock?"

Now it was his turn to pause. "Dinner? Sunday?" There was a rustling sound. "Let me get your address." A wave of relief descended over her at having made a decision. She wouldn't take Rafe to the sitter, she resolved. And she wouldn't cook hamburgers. She'd make a dinner as grand as the ones Victoria used to make, and it would be clear that she was a hardworking responsible mom. Possibly she'd even tell him about the two dreams that took second place to her dream of being Mrs. Somebody Respectable— to someday become a poet and a gourmet cook. The evening might bore him to death, but at least he'd know her, and get a clue whether he wanted to keep hanging around Stadium Coffee Shop. Not very romantic, but them's the berries. Realizing that she might change her mind a thousand times before morning, Allison gave him her address, said she had to get back to sleep before work in the morning, and hung up.

All week, as she peeled, mopped, and shaped burgers, she thought about that weekend. And surprisingly, she thought of Antonio. Would he care at all to know that his son and former wife were about to entertain another man? Would the jealousy that caused his angry threats the last time they talked now rise over the idea of Allison and Josh sitting down to dinner in her apartment?

On Sunday afternoon every surface in her apartment was pristine, dustless, and sparkling. The table held cloth napkins in rings, place mats, and two forks for each of them. Rafe was dressed in his classiest one-piece outfit that somewhat resembled a tuxedo—royal blue pants with soft cloth suspenders, and even a fake bow tie at the neck. She was ready half an hour early, and spent the time straightening the three magazines on her coffee table, combing her hair and gently arranging the soft brown strands on Rafe's warm, round head. When the clock said five minutes after five, she was convinced he wasn't coming and decided to put everything away. Her thoughts raged angrily: I should have known better. How could I think I could count on him, someone I've eaten lunch with only once? I wasn't being realistic. I'm too dreamy—

The doorbell rang. Her heart thudded. She replaced the plates she was just about to put in the cabinet and glanced at herself in the mirror one more time. His smile was warm when she opened the door, as if they'd been apart a long time and he was glad to see her. She could tell his hair was freshly combed, and the light blue shirt he wore appeared to be recently ironed.

"Smells great in here," he said, grinning and walking in, handing her a single rose. Flustered, she scrambled for a vase.

Behind her, he was saying, "So this is the guy, huh?" in baby talk. When she turned around with the one vase she owned, from when Antonio sent roses back when they were going together, he'd already lifted Rafe out of his walker and was playing with the bow tie on his outfit. "What's this, huh? You're a good-lookin' guy, you know that? Have to beat the women off with a club in a couple of years. . . ."

She was speechless. This man was obviously used to children; actually, she realized suddenly, he was something like a big kid himself. He saw that she was staring and met her gaze with equal puzzlement. Finally she said, "You're used to kids."

"Oh, yeah—eight brothers and sisters. I'm the middle guy. Kind of the bridge between the older ones and the babies."

"But—the other night—when I said I had a son . . ."

"Oh." He covered his face in remembered embarrassment. "What it was, I just didn't see how you would have a kid, when I can't remember you being pregnant. I thought I saw you and Antonio at the dance about every week, well maybe every two weeks, and you . . ." When he gestured vaguely in the direction of her stomach, she laughed and blushed at the same time.

"We went to Mexico," she said.

"What?" He was obviously trying to understand how this could relate.

"We went there to get married. And then we lived there—but Antonio wanted our son to be a U.S. citizen, because he himself wasn't, so I came back here for Rafe to be born. . . ." Suddenly, her voice stopped and she understood that she would never, never have come back here and left the warmth of San Luis if she'd had any idea what lay ahead.

"So you and Antonio came back here to California," he prompted.

"No," she said. "Just me . . . Well, he was here for a short while. But then he left, and I didn't hear from him. So I finally filed for divorce, and I haven't heard from him since."

Embarrassed, she turned away and busied herself with dinner—burgundy beef tips, mashed potatoes, and green beans. She heard Josh still talking quietly to Rafe as she rushed to get the food on the table. She placed his plate in front of him, then sat down and looked at her own plate.

"Hey," he said, "I didn't mean to bring up anything to make you feel bad. Seems I'm really good at that."

"No it's me. I mean, the divorce is final. Papers signed. Been to court. I . . . don't know what comes over me." She shrugged helplessly and thought his smile looked equally off-balance. Now they both looked down, tongue-tied. For at least five agonizing minutes, the only sounds were of silverware clinking, and Rafe bouncing contentedly in his walker.

"Hey, bud . . ." She watched as Josh kept playing with her son. When he realized she was looking at him, he said, "This is really good stuff. Beats Stadium all to heck. Hey . . . why don't you come work in the seafood restaurant with me?"

Allison laughed, served the apple crisp, and lit the candles she'd placed on the table.

As they started dating, she tried not to be nagged inwardly by the fact that he wasn't particularly industrious and driven the way she was. Yet calm and easygoing had its own merits, and after a lifetime of Victoria's shrieks, temper fits, and malevolence, a man as comfortable as an old plaid jacket was hard to turn away. She tried to conquer her nagging doubts by reminding herself that his boss was going to get him started in logging. She imagined that this venture might be costly, or at least require some money, and if he didn't have faith in Josh's initiative, he wouldn't front him in the business. And there was something else that she'd never have guessed about him: Josh was interested in politics. Beneath his easygoing manner, she sensed that this was his own secret dream, that he himself wouldn't mind being a senator someday, could envision himself living in the governor's mansion if not the White House. The idea of being a politician appealed to him. This was a possibility, Allison thought. Didn't she hear once, a long time ago, that women still voted for presidents who were good-looking? Did you need to be a lawyer to get started politically? If so, Josh wasn't pursing a college degree. Maybe he didn't need to. She didn't know. Still . . . in her one dream, she and her husband were equally motivated, and there was no way she could pretend Josh was as conscientious as she was. But when he lifted Rafe on his shoulder and headed for the park, or took both of them to a drive-in movie, or helped her cook dinner, her doubts began to melt. It helped that she realized she'd fallen in love with him—not in the dramatic, exotic way she still, deep in her heart, loved Antonio, but in a comfortable way, the way you loved a boyfriend who got along with all of your family. His kisses felt natural and sweet, and when he held her in his arms, she felt as safe and comforted as if wrapped in a down quilt.

So when he asked her to marry him, she fought within herself for several days. She asked to meet his family and, surprisingly, gained more respect for him after realizing he came from a sea of dysfunction as powerful as her own. There was an alcoholic father, a string of marriages, suspected child abuse. How did this calm, all-American exterior evolve from such a tormented, nightmarish past? She looked at his familiar, freckled face with new wonder, thinking how far he'd come to be who he was now.

They married at his boss's home, the one who'd promised to get him started in a logging business. She wore an eggshell-colored linen suit with a hat, her hair flowing over her shoulders like Victoria's did at the same age. She left a halfhearted message with Susan to invite Victoria to the wedding. Then she didn't admit to herself that she breathed a sigh of relief when her mother didn't arrive. It crossed her mind briefly that no one gave her away at either wedding, an odd part of her dream that was mysteriously missing.

·

Chapter Eight

Josh's boss helped him find a home they could rent—and possibly buy later—in Novato. It was a two-story house, with an apartment they could rent out if they needed extra money. She joked that it was big enough for six children, then laughed at Josh's wide-eyed astonishment. Allison filled her home with elements from her lifelong dream. There were fluffy bedspreads, crisp sheets, matching kitchen towels. A peace settled over her as she surveyed the abundance of her surroundings and remembered the day she ran away with only her clothes. They would stay in this house, she reasoned, until Josh's logging business really turned a profit, and then they could look around for something even nicer. She pictured him waving at her as he drove the huge truck into the driveway. Like she did now, she would have dinner waiting for him every night as soon as he walked in the door. She envisioned him looking a bit disheveled from hauling logs all day, but never too tired to give her a hug and pat Rafe on the head. It was the scenario she'd imagined since the day before she climbed out the window with her clothes.

Why, then, was there this feeling like there was a rock in her shoe? A small rock that she couldn't find if she looked for it, but would eat away at her existence just the same. Why couldn't she relax in the peace she'd always longed for? Her dream had come to life as she always knew it would. Yet why was there this persistent nagging—this feeling that maybe she shouldn't be complacent just yet? How could something be wrong inside when everything felt so perfect around her?

She stopped thinking about the inner disquiet when she became ill. The symptoms were similar to those she had when she was pregnant with Rafe. She'd be bending over the sink peeling potatoes or watching TV at home with Rafe on her lap when a wave of nausea—like a subtle shift in atmosphere—wafted over her. There was no wondering if this could be the flu. She immediately called the doctor, who told her to wait three months before coming in. Deciding to trust her own instincts, she told Josh as soon as he arrived home that day.

"I have news," she said, hands on her hips.

His smile and eyes looked easy and ready, as if this were simple. A promotion at Stadium. Free tickets to a play. A friend in town for the weekend.

"Well, okay," he said, gesturing at her to come on and let the secret out.

Usually straightforward, Allison stepped up and put her arms around him. "I'm pregnant," she said into his chest.

"What?" He backed away instantly, now staring into her face with probing intensity. "You're what?"

"Pregnant," she said, simply, her eyes brimming over.

"You're sure?" his eyes widened in curiosity.

She nodded as he hugged her again, touched her tummy with gentle, wispy strokes.

"I can't believe it. That's great," he said, leaving the kitchen and walking into the living room.

Standing alone, Allison spoke, more to herself and Rafe than to Josh. "See, it'll work great. It'll be fine. I've thought about this. Rafe will have a brother or sister, and they'll just be three years apart. We can stay in this house and rent the upstairs until you get going with the logging." She paused and walked out to the living room to smile at Josh, holding up her arms in a gesture that seemed to indicate victory. "This was supposed to happen."

"Sure," said Josh. But what was it about his look that belied his words? Where was the smile that always buoyed her? Allison didn't stop to probe a sudden unease that rose within her. She went and sat beside him on the couch. "And I'll keeping working at least until the baby's born . . . probably afterward, too. I mean, I've done it this long, since Rafe was a baby . . ." The momentum suddenly dropped away from her words.

"Sure," he said again, this time patting her leg. "You'll do fine. You're great."

Right then Rafe fell on the kitchen floor and screamed. He lay there, his face seemingly glued to the linoleum. Allison ran to him, picked him up, held his face to hers, and thought she could feel his heart beating against her own. Yet her thoughts never quite left the living room, where Josh sat silently on the couch. She felt like there was something unfinished about their conversation. What was it that one of them wasn't saying?

She lay awake that night and thought of plans for the baby. He would share a room with Rafe, and someday, they would probably get bunk beds. They'd be close enough in age to play together, entertain each other. They'd always each have a friend. Or maybe she'd have a daughter. The thought brought chills. A daughter. Someone she would love and hold, and, if she dressed up in her clothes, not get furious the way Victoria had with her. A daughter. More of her dream was about to come true.

Then why couldn't she stop worrying?

As the months passed, Allison's worries continued. Josh started going to political meetings. Allison was glad he was finally pursuing his dream, but he was at the meetings until late many nights. Most times she was too tired to wait up for him, and went to bed alone. She reminded herself of how much time she took to work and go to school to pursue her dreams.

Still . . .

She thought of asking to go with him, but found she really didn't want to leave Rafe any more than necessary.

Was that it, or did she actually not want to find out what

he was really doing? She felt angry and frustrated with him during this time when she should have been mostly excited over having a new baby. She tried to calm herself by buying a few new layette outfits, more crib sheets, and one baby dress in case a miracle happened and she gave birth to a girl. But she felt as if she was pretending that everything was okay. Why didn't she dare confront him with her worries?

One night Josh left the couch where they were sitting, watching TV together. After twenty minutes passed, she stood, puzzled. What was he doing? She walked back into the bedroom and found him on the phone, talking in hushed tones. "Gotta go," he said as soon as he saw her.

"Who was that?" Her knees were shaking.

"Oh, just a guy," he said, then put his arm around her shoulder. As if he'd been gone only a moment, he asked about the TV movie. "Now was it the husband that killed her, or the man from the hardware store?"

Even though he sat on the couch with his arm around her for the rest of the movie and they made love later that night, Allison couldn't stop wondering. It happened a couple of other times. She was reading the paper one day, and looked up to find he'd left the room. She started dinner in the kitchen, and thought she heard his muted voice from the other room. On the phone again. Another day she came home from work and found him engaged in still another telephone conversation. He seemed startled to see her, as if he forgot she was about to come home. What was going on? People talked on the phone every day, she reasoned. But why did he talk so softly? Why did he feel as if he needed to hide it from her?

Then, just as she was beginning to tell herself the worries were all in her head, there was money missing. At first she thought she counted wrong. Then she counted again. It was fifty dollars one day, thirty-five another time. She had to confront him.

"Josh, why is there only a hundred dollars in the drawer? There was two hundred last night."

He looked straight at her. "For the campaign," he said. "I'm backing a candidate."

Her anger bubbled. Each word emerged sharp and distinct. "We told your boss we would put everything we get toward paying off the logging truck."

He shrugged, which made her more furious than ever. "He'll never know. I don't have a payment schedule with him."

"How is giving money to this candidate supposed to help our family?" She gestured to the bedroom where she could hear Rafe idly playing in his crib. In a few moments, she knew, he would cry for her to come pick him up.

Now Josh looked straight at her again. "I have to pay to get involved. I can't say exactly when this will put money in your pocket, but it's like paying dues to get a career . . . like you going to school."

"No . . ." she said, knowing instantly that it wasn't the same at all. "You're wrong."

Now he sneered. "Are you going to tell on me? Get me in trouble? Cut off your nose to spite your face?"

She had no answer. That night he slept on the couch for the first time. She lay awake until after two, thinking that if she went out in the front room to him, put her arms around him, he would come back and sleep next to her. And the money would still be gone.

The next week, when a twenty was missing from the drawer, and all the change was cleaned out of the jar next to the laundry basket, she didn't say anything.

Then one night he didn't come home all night. She lay on her bed beside Rafe's crib, waiting, looking at the clock. Where was Josh? Why didn't he come home? She tried to read a bit, but she couldn't concentrate and her eyes started to get heavy. When she woke the next morning, surprised that she could actually fall asleep amid her worry, she immediately rushed to the kitchen phone to call the police. She was startled and inhaled with shock when she saw Josh sitting on the couch as if he were a bean bag chair someone had dropped.

"Where were you last night?" she said, feeling all her worries condensing into a determined question. He didn't answer.

She stepped in front him, leaned over, and planned to lift his chin with her hand, but then actually settled for just looking into his eyes. "I asked where you were last night. You didn't get home until late and I wanted to talk to you."

Was that a shrug? He sort of shifted his shoulders, but he didn't answer. "Getting ready for the rally," he said finally.

Her words burst out like angry darts. "They didn't ask for more money?"

Again, no answer.

"Josh," she said, "I can't do this anymore. Our money belongs to us"—she gestured at Rafe, sitting on the floor with his toys. "What you earn is for our family. And we have to save it if we're ever going to get that logging truck—and we're going to have a baby. Do you know how much money a baby takes?"

Suddenly he sprang to life. "Okay, okay—you told me. Okay," he said again, frantically hurling himself to the closet and yanking out his jacket. "I heard you the first time."

The door slammed so hard she thought the walls would crash. Did she do the wrong thing? She looked at Rafe, who said, "Daddy." She thought of the baby they both anxiously wanted. Someone has to play the heavy, she thought. Someone has to look out for us.

Yet over the next weeks she told herself she'd miscounted when a ten was missing one night . . . a twenty and change was gone from his cuff-link box later that week.

Then there was a night when Josh said, casually, that he wouldn't be able to pick up Rafe after work. Susan would have to keep him a little later. He said it as calmly as if he might say his favorite sitcom would be on at seven that night. Allison felt like screaming at him. Instead, she shrugged and rationalized that he had to work late.

That night the game was rained out and Bev let Allison leave the coffee shop early. With Josh at work and Rafe with Susan, she thought she'd give herself a few hours of quiet time.

Although she didn't hear a sound initially, Allison felt a sinking sensation as soon as she stepped inside her front door at five P.M. What was different and out of order here? She stood still, then set her purse down on the floor. The living room looked as neat and organized as she had left it. Pillows straightened on the couch, magazines in a neat stack on a table. She could hear the dishwasher running. "I'm home, Josh." As she took her first step toward the kitchen, she heard a stifled, unfamiliar male laugh. Who was here?

In the kitchen three men sat at the table with Josh, holding drinks with ice.

"I'm home," she said again. "Where's Rafe? Why didn't you go get him if you were just going to hang around here?"

She was instantly aware of and didn't care about the picture she'd just painted of herself as a nagging shrew. What were these men doing in her home when she was out peeling potatoes to pay for it? She knew Josh had friends, but there was something different about these men. Something creepy that instantly crawled on her skin and made her want to throw them out right that minute. Looking around at the kitchen she'd decorated so carefully, her repulsion turned to anger.

"He's asleep—he's fine," said Josh, and spat out, "I called Susan. I *checked*."

"Well, what have you done all day?" She didn't care if he was embarrassed, humiliated. Her vibes were going off like an alarm clock. These guys were bad news, and now he wasn't just spending time with them, he brought them into her home, during the day, when he should be working on the logging truck while she was shaping hamburgers and scrubbing floors.

Two of the men started talking in hushed whispers, then stood, mumbling among themselves. "Hey, Josh . . ." they said.

"Wait a minute guys—" He held up his hand. "I'll be right there. . . ."

"We promised each other," Allison said, feeling as if she were hanging on to a cracking, breaking branch. "We said that we would work together to pay for the truck now, because I might not be able to after the baby is born . . . our baby."

"Your baby—" Josh said, yelling in her face in front of these men. "Your son . . . your responsbility." When she moved toward him with her hand raised, he grabbed her wrist. His voice was theatening. "Don't you tell me what I have to do ever again. These are my friends and I can have my friends in my house all day and all night if I want to."

"Ooh . . . can Joshy-boy come out and play?" said one of the men behind her, and Allison whirled in a rush. In that moment Josh ran ahead to catch up with the men in the living room. He'll tell them he's sorry he can't go with them today, that his wife is obviously too upset, Allison thought.

But she heard hushed voices, not a spoken explanation. Then the door banged shut. Though she waited, holding her breath, he didn't come back. She rushed to the driveway and saw that the logging truck was gone.

He came home in the middle of that night, smelling of beer and cigarettes. Allison was asleep when he entered the house, and woke only when he slid into their bed. She cringed with anger and pain and moved as close as she could to the edge of the bed. He didn't notice. They didn't speak for four days.

Should she throw him out? What did he do that night? Was all of this money going to another woman? She felt as if there was no one in the world that she could ask. Victoria would sneer in her face. Bev would want to know how this related to her work. Antonio was gone. Susan would wonder how, if she was so good at managing on her own, did she choose the wrong man twice. Was Josh the wrong man? Or was she wrong herself? She couldn't determine anything. So she waited.

As days and then weeks passed, she began to think that her enemy was really Larry.

Larry. That was his name. The man who, in the sea of sleazy men Josh befriended, seemed to be the main draw. And she couldn't imagine why. He had no wife, no family, no good looks, and seemingly, no job, although Josh said he was a consultant for the Democratic party.

A consultant. She admitted to herself, again, that she had no idea how politics worked. But as the weeks turned into months, she realized that she knew her feelings, and this guy made her feel sick inside. A deep, repellant kind of sickness. Yet she was also puzzled. Where was the clean-cut, all-American guy she'd met in the seafood restaurant all those months ago? How could Josh relate to Larry? Allison could fathom no similarity between them, no possible bond.

After she came home early twice, and Larry was there, she knew she could stand it no longer. She waited until they were in the middle of dinner, then said, as calmly as she could, "Josh, I don't ever want that piece of crap Larry in my house again. Do you understand me? No more Larry."

Josh gave her a long stare. She watched his anger rise, saw that a vein was pulsing in his neck. How did she ever think this man was calm? "Listen," he said venomously. "You mighta pushed that spic around, guy just barely off the boat, hardly spoka da English, but you're not telling me what to do."

"I have a right to keep slime away from my house. From my son. As hard as I work, I deserve—"

"Oh, give me a break. Like you're the only person in the world who ever had a kid and a job."

"It isn't just me. Your boss would fire you in a minute if he knew you were out every night with those losers."

"You don't know them. You don't know a one of them. I have to think about my future. You think a logging truck is going to make us rich? You want to lock me into that

truck and never let me out unless I get to baby-sit someone
else's kid.''

Those were Larry's words. She sensed it instantly, but
they stung just as sharply.

He stepped closer, stuck his face next to hers and poked
his fingers in her stomach. ''As far as that goes, how do I
know this kid is mine? Larry says it couldn't be. How do
I know you weren't with someone else all those times you
said I was? After all, I know I wasn't your first. . . .''

All of her hopes, dreams, and past hurts rose within, and
without stopping to think about it, she slapped him. The
noise the slap made was tremendously loud, and blood instantly gushed from his mouth.

''My teeth! My teeth, you bitch—''

She'd made his mouth bleed, but the realization didn't
dilute her anger. As she reached to slap him again, he
grabbed her wrist, yanked it so hard so that pain spread up
her arm like a burst of lightning. Her adrenaline was high
enough that she yanked it away, but the hurt didn't stop.
And she said something she'd never allowed herself to consciously think about, but somehow now knew all too well.

''That's Larry talking. He can't be any kid's father because he's a homosexual. The people he has sex with can't
ever have babies. Where's your brain?'' she said, tapping
the side of her head furiously with her finger.

Josh wouldn't answer, or look at her, but just stood by
the side of the couch and aimlessly flipped pages of a magazine. She felt her blood boil that he could be so placid.

She screamed, ''Don't you ever, ever, even think something like that about me again! I still can't believe you
would take that slime's word over mine!'' She picked up
a couch pillow and slammed it in his direction. Then she
fumbled frantically for her purse. ''I'm going out,'' she
said. ''And if I ever come home again and Larry is here,
I'm gone for good.''

She slammed the door, then stood silently before the
front window. Josh had already gone to the phone. Strain-
ing to understand his words, she could only tell that they
were calm, while she stood outside breathing hard and fast.

A few moments later she heard Rafe say, "Mommy," and she rushed to the door, then held her breath. She heard Josh hang up the phone and go to him. Good. She tiptoed down the walk, got into the car, and drove downtown. When she came back that night, the apartment was dark and silent; both Josh and Rafe were sound asleep.

After that, although they still slept in the same bed, it was as if they were two tenants renting out the same house. Allison tried to focus on Rafe and the baby that would arrive within three months. Growing more and more pregnant, she still mopped floors and flipped burgers, finding the work an emotional outlet for the turmoil she felt inside. Yet despite her preoccupation, she began to notice something odd: Their money was back. Not only was there no longer money missing, she would look in the drawer and find more there than before, when neither of them was anywhere close to payday. And she saw that Josh suddenly had new clothes—silk shirts, tailored pants, ties like swaths of fancy drapery fabric. Yet it wasn't until he brought home the new car that she guessed the source of their newfound riches.

"Got something to show you." Now he looked like the old Josh, with his smile filled with white teeth, freckles dancing on rosy cheeks.

They walked together to the front window and he pointed to the driveway. There, rather than the logging truck she'd dreamed of all these months, was parked a black, shiny sedan that filled her with instant dread. A sick feeling oozed like bile in her throat, and she turned to him and spat, "It's Larry's car."

"No," he said, his easy smile fading quickly. "It's our car."

"But he got it."

"Well, he helped me get it. We needed a car, with the baby coming."

"Not that car. What did you give to him so he would get that for you?"

He blushed, stepped back as if she'd struck him numb. "Nothing," his voice fumbled.

"Larry doesn't do favors for nothing," she said instinctively. "What does he have of yours . . . all the money we saved for the truck?"

Now his blush turned angry red. "You'd never get a car like that, never in a million years. All you know how to do is push me."

"Somebody has to," she said, "or you'd never get anywhere. Now tell me if you gave him our money."

He sputtered and pointed his finger at her. "You think I'll never get anywhere. You never appreciate how hard I work. It's no wonder Antonio sent you back here. You were too dumb to see he was getting rid of you. And if I were smart, I'd do the same thing."

She flew at him in anger, but he just pushed her away as if she were a rag doll. He walked out of the apartment without a word and came back sometime late in the night. He left before she woke up. She only knew he'd been there because the shirt he'd worn the day before was crammed in the laundry hamper. After that, both of them stayed in the apartment as little as possible. Although he still picked Rafe up from Susan's on the days Allison worked late, there was no discussion of the new car. The air in the apartment was heavy with tension, as if they did everything they could to be as far away from each other while living in the same place.

Chapter Nine

Looking back, she couldn't see that the day started any differently from any other. There was no shouting, no quiet disagreement, not even anything in the apartment mysteriously out of place. Allison went grocery shopping, mentally reviewing her work hours for the next week, Josh's schedule, and Rafe's current food likes and dislikes. That was it: She went shopping. She bought food. Not a loud word. Not even a calm disagreeing sentence.

But when she arrived home and asked, "Josh, could you help me in with the—" There was no answering hello, no shuffle of movement, no phone suddenly hung up.

He was gone. His absence screamed at her as soon as she walked in the door. Nothing about the apartment looked any different, except that its space all appeared larger and somehow more barren with him away. The books sat silently on the bookcase, the air conditioner hummed, the vacuum trails she'd left on the carpet still appeared undisturbed. Of course there were lots of times when he was gone—to work, to visit his grandmother, to be with the friends she so despised. But this time his being gone seemed stronger and more powerful than the others. This absence felt as if it somehow would not end. Allison felt strained and depleted, as if he had knocked the wind out of her without so much as a touch. The pain of Antonio's desertion rose again to her mouth, leaving the desperate taste she had forgotten while she was in love with Josh.

Feeling as vacant as the apartment now felt, Allison mechanically put away the groceries as she always did—canned goods together in neatly stacked rows, vegetables arranged in the crisper, meats in the meat keeper. She was putting a carton of ice cream in the freezer when suddenly it hit her.

Rafe—

Did Josh hurt her in the one way that would hurt more than no other, by taking Rafe?

She frantically flew to Rafe's room, and saw that he was sleeping in his crib, his eyes blissfully closed and hands folded together.

Josh left Rafe alone with no one to baby-sit him. She experienced instant visions of the house burning, burglars sneaking inside, Rafe falling and hurting himself with no one to pick him up and give him a hug.

He left Rafe alone. Somehow, she believed he meant to send her a message with this action. Was he saying that Rafe would miss his stepfather after he was gone? Or that she would miss Josh? That his presence, flawed and upsetting as it was, was far more valuable than his absence?

She couldn't guess. She ran to Rafe and hugged him, and he opened his eyes blearily and stared at her as if his sight were fuzzy. "Mama?" he asked. She stroked his warm cheek and his fine, soft hair. She leaned down to hug him as if he were as fragile as china. "Go back to sleep, darlin'. You're okay."

"Mama," he said, then reached out for her to hold him. As she lay beside him, too tense to allow her eyes to close, he breathed heavily, and his eyelids gradually drooped like sand slowly sifting through an hourglass. When he was back asleep, Allison left the bed and walked thoughtfully out to the kitchen. She remembered how Josh wrote names and phone numbers hastily on the phone book cover when she interrupted his clandestine calls—the names and numbers of the friends who tore her life apart by stealing her husband away. She'd felt annoyed at finding those numbers when she looked through the book to find her doctor's number, or to order a prescription from the pharmacy.

She found the list on the front and back covers of the phone book. Glancing at the scrawled numbers, she realized she felt such distaste for those men that she'd never bothered to learn their names. Which one should she call first? Which one did Josh consider his nearest and dearest? Which one could tell her where he was now? He knew better than to write Larry's name anywhere that she could find it. But there were others. Lee. Gary. Ted. Who should she call? And what would she say when someone answered?

She began with someone named Ben.

"Yeah?" the man's voice asked. The music in the background was loud, forcing her to raise her voice so high she worried that she'd wake Rafe.

"I'm looking for Josh Morgan," she said fluidly, making her request firm and straight, not to be possibly misunderstood.

"Josh—" The person paused. "Is this his *wife*?"

Now she felt like backing away, hanging up. But she had to find out. "Yes, this is Allison Morgan. I need to talk to him—it will just take a minute."

"Well, he ain't here."

"He's not there. Do you know where he might be? Where I could reach him?"

The person laughed softly. "Sure he's not home there with you and the kiddies?"

Now her anger rose. "Tell me where he is."

"Don't know. Don't care. Try Jack." The person hung up the phone with a snap that stung in her ear. Try Jack. She didn't know a Jack. She looked on the phone book cover again. Ted. Lee. Dave. She turned the book over, opened the back cover. There it was. Jack.

The phone rang and rang with no answer. During the next days, she called Jack's number again and again after she woke in the morning and after she came home from work at night. One night she dialed the number at almost midnight. She let the phone ring again and again, until she'd nearly fallen asleep with it in her hand. Then someone answered.

An angry hello.

"Josh? Josh Morgan," she said, abruptly drawn back to the task at hand.

"Wrong number." The voice still sounded angry, and now dismissive as well.

"Wait—" she called desperately. "Do you know a Josh Morgan."

"He doesn't live here."

She closed her eyes in desperation. "I know he doesn't live there. Do you have any idea where I could find him, or someone I could call who might know where he is . . . ?"

"No idea, lady. Think he moved out from Jean Manor. Don't know where he went now." The phone slammed into the receiver before she could ask who, where, or what Jean Manor was.

Tears sprang to her eyes at the same time that anger flared inside her like a lit match. Her fingers dialed frantically.

The phone seemed to ring forever. " 'Lo."

"You give me Jean's number. Right now."

"Jean who?"

"Jean Manor. I want her number right now. Or his. I don't know if she's a man or a woman."

The man laughed angrily. "Neither one. I'm hanging up on you, bitch."

Her mind fumbled quickly in desperation. "Wait—tell me where I can find her or I'll call the police. They're looking for Josh and I'll send them to you."

"You are so stupid. Do you think I believe you lady? I need to go back to sleep."

"Wait—just tell me or—"

"You'll do what? Come kill me with your bare hands? Listen, bitch. You got ears? Jean *Manor*. Not a person's name. A boardinghouse."

Allison's mind rushed. "Where? Where is it?"

"Oakland, bitch." The phone clicked.

As days and then weeks passed, Allison remembered Antonio, the months of waiting and wondering, the teetering between being still-married and now single. She couldn't fathom being back on that tightrope, always waiting, always hoping, trying to interpret every word and sunset as some sort of sign. She asked Bev for a week off and bought a bus ticket to Oakland.

The ride to Oakland on the Greyhound bus felt strangely peaceful, and Rafe leaned against her and gazed out the window as the scenery outdoors glided by. They shared snacks of potato chips, popcorn, and hamburgers. They basked in the brief, easy peace that food could bring. There was no feeling of anxiousness over when they would arrive at their destination. She simply relished the moments gently passing, like soft fingers on her skin.

She took Rafe to her sister Susan's home, then caught a cab to the name of the place the man on the phone had told her—Jean Manor. It was a huge, gray-bricked building. She went to the office and asked for the room number under the name of Josh Morgan.

"He's registered here. But we can't give out the room number information, ma'am. It's confidential."

"I—uh, have a package for him." She hesitated and a trickle of sweat inched down her body. "I can leave it here or take it up to his room."

"One moment," the concierge lifted the phone receiver. As sharply as she tried to angle her neck, Allison couldn't read which numbers the woman dialed.

Finally the concierge said, "A package delivery, sir. Do you wish it to be left at the desk or brought up to your room?"

Allison waited as the concierge listened to the voice on the other end of the line. Finally the woman shook her head in understanding, hung up the phone, and looked at Allison.

"Ma'am, he's asking you to bring it up and set it on the front porch of number 124. He says you can leave it there and he'll pick it up in a few moments."

"Thank you." Allison tried not to smile too broadly.

She walked up to Room 124, waited a moment, then

knocked briskly. There was no response. She knocked again. Allison put her ear to the door and heard nothing from inside the apartment. She leaned back and stared at the door, imagining herself breaking through it with her shoulder. Then she stepped closer and tried the knob. The door was unlocked.

After one more knock, she twisted the knob silently, then waited. No sounds from inside. Seconds later she entered the neat, if spare, living room and looked around. It seemed that no one was home, but didn't the concierge just speak to someone who was here? Allison stepped farther into the room, expecting Josh to pop out any minute. She imagined his easy grin, his nonchalant explanation, all the energy of her wrath draining into bewildered confusion at his familiar smile. She stopped in a doorway. The kitchen, too, was neat. There was the smell of cleanser along with spices. A dishwasher hummed steadily.

She opened her mouth to say his name, and it was like something suddenly held her back. Instead she stepped farther through the kitchen and down the hall to the only closed door in the house. She breathed. Was that a rustling behind this door? Was this the bedroom? Suddenly knocking seemed scarier than just walking in and facing whatever lay ahead.

The door opened with a squeak like an anguished whine. For a few seconds, her eyes couldn't adjust to the darkness, but then she recognized a bed with two motionless people lying under the sheets. Abruptly her heart pounded and her lip quivered as her brain finally registered that this was Josh and Larry, in bed, naked, together.

"What are you doing?" she screamed, a useless question, but the only one her mind could form.

The two men in the bed still lay unmoving, not even showing the slightest bit of embarrassment that their privacy was invaded.

"I knew it!" she shouted, although she'd really had no idea until this moment. "I knew he was slime, Josh. I knew he would ruin both our lives, and you let him do it."

Her throat filled with a racking sob so that she couldn't speak. She slammed the bedroom door, and slammed the front door, too. On her way out she thought she heard a man laughing.

Chapter Ten

She went to Margaret North, the same attorney who helped her get a divorce from Antonio.

"I am pregnant with my husband's child"—Allison gestured at her stomach—"but the man is homosexual. I've caught him in bed with another man." Drawing a breath, she said, "I feel like the bottom has fallen out of my life."

"You have a very good case," Margaret North reassured her, crossing her legs and swinging one atop the other. "As good as the first."

"The case might be good, but my life is falling apart," Allison protested.

The attorney couldn't argue.

One dark day after another passed with only empty pain. When she tried to conjure up her only dream of being a wife and mother, aches of despair rose within as she thought of the two husbands who left her. She felt like a failure.

She answered the phone one late night to discover it was Ken, Josh's boss.

"Josh there?"

"No," she said, not wanting to add anything else.

"Is this Allison?"

She sighed. "Yes."

"I hate to do this when you have a baby on the way,

but I don't have a choice. I can't keep Josh on the payroll any longer."

"But he needs his job. I have to take at least two weeks off after the baby is born."

"He hasn't reported in for a week and a half. I've been driving the route myself, but now I've got to assign it to somebody else."

"Do you mean he hasn't called or anything?"

"Not a word. I keep waiting to hear that there is some sort of emergency, but I can't wait any longer."

"Ken, I'd come drive that route myself if I could."

"Do you know what his problem is?"

She found no other direction but the truth. "He's left me, Ken." Saying the words aloud seemed to make them all the more true, and her tears flowed. "I don't know what I'm going to do. He's moved out."

"I'm so sorry." He paused. "But I really can't carry him on the payroll anymore. I'll send you his check for the last two weeks of this month, even though he didn't work any of those days. I wish I could do more."

"Thank you for trying to help him. I had no idea he would do this," she said simply. She hung up the phone and understood that her vision of Josh driving a logging truck into their driveway would never come true. And without his salary, there was no way to pay the rent on the house.

She was forced to move back in with Victoria, who immediately let her know how grudgingly she was welcomed. Victoria resented Rafe's clothes taking up part of her laundry room, his crying drove her nerves crazy, and she constantly reminded Allison that she'd spent too much time taking care of her own children to want to bother with another one now.

"Another man down the hatch," Victoria said. "Sure can't hang on to 'em long, can you?"

"It wasn't anything I did, Mom."

"Least I'm still here so you have a place to come and dump the kid."

Allison left the room in frustration and disgust. She took

Rafe to work at Stadium whenever she could, but he was now too big to lie contentedly on a blanket and watch her peel potatoes. One night she caught him inches from sticking a fork into an electrical outlet. Another night he burned his hand on hot french fries. She was waddling by now, and she couldn't rush fast enough to keep up with him. But if she left him with Victoria, she had to come home to an assortment of complaints about his very ordinary behavior.

Then, one night, she came home to find that Victoria's house was terrifyingly quiet.

"Is Rafe asleep?" she asked hopefully.

"I don't know," said Victoria, reading a newspaper through half-glasses.

"You don't know?" Shivers of fear darted through Allison's body.

"Nope. I called your father and we made a decision."

A sinking feeling filled Allison with dread. Since their long-ago divorce, her mother only talked to her father about life-and-death matters. What could this possibly mean?

"A decision?" she managed.

Victoria's eyes stayed on her newspaper. "Your father and I decided that none of us is capable of caring for him."

"What do you mean? I've worked so hard. I've been a good mother and Rafe loves me."

Victoria's stare was an angry dagger. "You have no money. His father's never sent a dime. You're pregnant again. You won't be able to work after this one is born. I can't keep him here—I can't stand his whining—and there's not enough room. What kind of life is that for a young child?"

"Where is my son?" Allison screamed.

"Your father came and took him to the Division of Family Services. They placed him in foster care after he showed them where Rafe's hand was burned. They assured us that he'll be well cared for."

Allison's scream turned to a screech. "You took my *son* away from me?"

Victoria didn't answer.

"How could you do that to me? You won't get away

with this. I'll get him back tomorrow, and we'll go where you can never see either one of us again."

Victoria didn't look up.

Allison immediately rushed to the phone. She called the police, saying that her son was kidnapped, but when she explained the situation, they told her that her only recourse would be to call the Division of Family Services the next day. She called the Excelsior, a boarding hotel near the stadium, and found there was one room left. Allison hurriedly threw everything she could into a suitcase and prepared, once again, to run away from her mother.

"I'm never coming back," she warned. "You'll never see me or Rafe again."

The room at the Excelsior was small and dingy. The gray stains in the sink looked as if they'd never come clean no matter how long she scrubbed them. The closet smelled of mildew and age. And there was no little boy to hold in her arms until they each gave way to slumber. Yet surprisingly, Allison fell into a deep, near-comatose sleep, not waking until after nine the next morning.

The Division of Family Services waiting room was filled with people who appeared as lonely, sad, and empty as she felt inside. Mothers with vacant, beaten looks, children who looked too tired even to think of play. Even the magazines held pages that were limp and wavy. Allison didn't even glance at her watch, but only sat, defeated, as minutes rolled past.

"Allison Romero Morgan," an official voice said.

Allison raised her hand, then followed a woman in a black, tailored business suit into a small office, where the woman sat behind a computer.

"How may I help you?" asked the woman, looking at Allison's obvious pregnancy with a sympathetic smile.

"My son. I need to see how I can get him back."

"Is this a custody matter?"

"No . . . my parents had him taken away. He's in a foster home someplace. I can't believe they would do this to me, or to him, but I've got to get him back. He is my whole life."

The woman looked at her skeptically. "Do you have his case number?"

Allison shook her head. "I didn't know there was any such thing as a case. I came home from work last night and he was gone, and my mother said—"

"I can try to find it from the name," said the woman. "What is your son's name"

"Rafaél Simón Romero."

The woman stared into the computer for what seemed like an eternity, then looked up abruptly. "I see here they made an accusation of neglect. But this is puzzling . . . It says that you are still a minor? And a single parent?" Again the woman's gaze drifted to Allison's very pregnant figure.

Allison considered. Amazingly, yes. Despite all she had been through in her short and eventful life, she was now only seventeen and she had already been married and divorced twice.

"Yes," she said. "I've been through one divorce and I'm going through my second. But I'll be eighteen in August."

The woman shook her head. "My dear. I'm sorry. But in that case, your parents are still in charge of you. There would need to be a hearing for you to be emancipated from them, and to be officially granted custody on your own."

"But I've worked so hard to take care of my son. And I have my high school diploma and a year of work experience. . . ."

"The law says that as a minor, your parents are in charge of you until you reach eighteen."

"But what about my son? I need to see him." Allison stood abruptly and shoved her significant girth against the woman's desk.

The woman moved her chair back, then leaned into the computer again. "There is one thing. You are entitled to visitation before the hearing. On weekends. The first time you could see him would be one week from Friday."

Allison was aghast. "Visitation? Can't I prove that I'm a good mother and then get him back?"

"If custody is awarded to you in the hearing, he will

come home to live with you. If I were you, I'd visit him all I could, and in the meantime, get the rest of your life straight so the judge will be inclined to award custody to you.''

''They took him. He's really gone and I can't get him back,'' said Allison in disbelief. As she watched, the woman wrote a name and address on a yellow pad. She said, ''At least you can call at this number and make an appointment to see him. Sometimes even knowing the location of the foster home is restricted information.''

''I have to make an appointment? To see the boy I've taken care of every day of his life?''

''Again, I'm sorry.'' The woman stood. ''But I have another appointment now.'' Allison saw she was looking past her to where another woman in a blue business suit was waiting with a woman and young child.

Allison waited until she was outside the building to read the name on the paper. Sarah Farber, 555-3028, 195 Oak Road. ''Oh, Rafe,'' she whimpered as she sat alone on a park bench outside the big, redbrick Family Services building. ''I know how it feels to be left. Please understand that I'd never in a milllion years let someone steal you away from me.''

On the appointed Friday she borrowed Bev's car and drove to the Farbers' home. She was anxious to see Rafe, but there was a part of her that feared what her son would do when he saw her. She was even more worried about how she would react. But it was the thought that she would soon hold Rafe in her arms again that enabled her to walk up to the redbrick house and ring the bell.

Sarah Farber looked like a million other housewives in the United States—shoulder-length brown hair, blue eyes, housedress, smeared lipstick. Who says this woman is more qualified than I am to take care of Rafe? Allison asked herself. But she forced a smile and extended her hand.

''I'm Allison Morgan. Here to see my son, Rafaél Romero. I have an appointment.''

The woman stared briefly at Allison, before saying,

"Come in. Excuse my house . . . tomorrow is my cleaning day."

Allison thought of her spotless room at the Excelsior. But she sensed a warmth about Sarah Farber, could see instantly that the house was comfortable, homey. This didn't seem like a woman who would scream at Rafe for spilling his milk.

"Do you have children of your own?" Allison asked as they walked down a hallway. She saw some clutter in the rooms, but the house was far from filthy.

"We do. A three-year-old and a baby. And two foster children—your son and Melanie, a little girl."

As they rounded a corner, Allison could see that all four children obviously played together in the family room off the kitchen. There were plastic toys and scattered doll dresses. A rocking horse. Suddenly all observations about her surroundings fled from her mind as she caught sight of Rafe. A shriek escaped from her throat and he saw her, and screamed, too. He ran to her and she caught him up in her arms. Her eyelids squeezed together in ecstacy and relief and she trembled at the electricity that flowed through her. She held and rocked him, kissing his cheek, his hair, his neck, rubbing the back of the unfamiliar white T-shirt he wore, realizing that his diaper was dry and had been recently changed. He didn't stir in her arms—both of them could have stayed there forever.

"Looks like you're pretty glad to see each other."

Allison abruptly realized that Sarah Farber was staring.

"Oh . . . you'll never know . . . more than I can say."

"I've never seen a mom be quite that emotional on a visit," said Sarah.

"Oh . . ." Allison still couldn't form a complete sentence. Moments later, when Rafe finally tired of being held in her arms and wiggled to get down, it was still hard to let him go. She watched as he went over to play with the other children, but kept glancing back to see if she was still there. After a few moments, he came and sat on her lap.

"Oh . . . is there any way I could just take him with me? Just for a little while?"

On her couch Sarah shifted uncomfortably. "We could both get arrested if I did that. I have to be in the same room, and I can't let you leave my house." A surge of anger erupted inside Allison, but she reminded herself that if she caused trouble, it could hurt Rafe. She forced herself to think from Sarah Farber's point of view. "Thank you for taking care of him. Has he been much trouble?"

"No." Sarah shook her head. "He's a darling little boy."

"What about sleeping?"

"First few nights he woke up . . . called for you. But now he's in the same room with Melanie, and he's doing okay."

Allison hesitated. "Can you call me? If he ever wakes up again? If you ever think he needs me?"

Sarah squirmed on the couch. "I don't know. I'd have to clear it with Family Services."

"You don't need to tell them . . . please."

"I'd have to . . . I don't know." Sarah looked at her watch. "We've got a doctor's appointment in half an hour. You better hug him once more, because we have to leave."

Allison couldn't stop herself. "You can go. I'll stay here with him. I always took good care of him. Please. I promise I'll still be here when you get back."

Sarah shook her head, blushing. "Sorry. It's not allowed. They're really strict about things like that.

"Come on Melanie, come on Rafe." Sarah stood, and Rafe rushed to Allison's side. She picked him up again, held him, was tempted to run out of this house and not look back. Rafe's face crumpled in terror and he began to cry. She pressed his head against her shoulder, her own tears joining his. When she felt Sarah try to pry him away from her, she was tempted to cling tighter.

Sarah said, "You better go . . . looks like he won't stop crying with you here."

The last thing Allison wanted was for this woman to become angry with Rafe.

"Rafie, Rafie," she said, talking to him as softly as she could. She sat him on a kitchen chair, pressed her cheek against his. "Rafie . . . Mommy has to go now. But I'll be back really soon.'' When she started to stand, he grabbed her again, but this time Sarah came and scooped him up.

"You really better go," she said, a new firmness in her voice that frightened Allison. "I'll have to call someone."

As she turned and walked away without looking back, Rafe's cries tore at her heart, and she gulped back her own sobs. She stood outside the house, hiding behind a tall bush, and waited. Five minutes passed. Ten. When she could no longer hear a noise from inside the house, she finally drove away.

As weeks passed, Allison fought to adapt to the protocol of visiting Rafe at the Farbers. She soon knew better than to ask to take him away for a visit or to make any comment about how hard this situation was for her. Allison discovered that mornings were better than afternoons to visit. Sarah Farber seemed like a slow starter. She was often in her robe if Allison arrived at ten, and welcomed a moment away from the children to finally dress and comb her hair. During this brief moment, Allison picked Rafe up, held him in her arms, and whispered to him how much she loved him. She always combed his hair and washed his face with a Wash'n Dri she brought in her purse. She also checked for bruises and scratches, and felt relieved when she never discovered any injuries. She stayed as long as Sarah Farber would let her, struggling to keep a placid, content look on her face. She expressed no opinions beyond comments about the weather. She didn't insist on play or any particular activity. Even if she only watched him eat a bowl of macaroni and cheese, the brief moment of being in Rafe's presence was momentarily soothing. She knew the empty ache she felt inside would never ebb completely until he lived with her again, but she was making every effort she could to bear up.

Then there was the day she felt like her world cracked in half. She was wiping the counter of her room at the Excelsior, then stopped to fold dishtowels as she waited for Sarah Farber to answer her phone.

"I'd like to come tomorrow at ten to see Rafe," she said,

fighting feelings of resentment at having to ask permission to spend a few moments with her own son.

There was a long pause. "Oh . . . Didn't anyone tell you?"

Fear gripped Allison's mind, and she held her breath. "Tell me what?" she asked, trying to sound calm and even.

"Rafe's been taken into permanent custody by the State. I don't have him here anymore."

"What? They said there would be a hearing. Did they have the hearing? What happened?" All the facade of trying to remain neutral and nonopinionated dissolved as she pleaded for her son.

"I don't know. You'll have to call Family Services," said Sarah, who immediately hung up

Allison rushed to the Family Services building and strode determinedly to the counter. When a woman asked if she could help her, Allison pounded her fist on the desk. "My son has been taken away from me illegally, and I'm going to call the police if someone doesn't get him back right now."

There was a flurry of activity during which the office staff whispered to each other and consulted papers, and then the social worker who talked to Allison before ushered her back into the same small office.

Allison didn't wait for preliminaries. "I called the foster home today and he's gone. You said there would be a hearing and I could be emancipated and file for custody."

"Let me get the file." The woman cleared her throat and went to a filing cabinet. She frowned as she looked into the manila folder. "It looks like the original hearing date was changed," she said.

"No one ever told me when it was going to be held the first time. Can we have another hearing?"

The social worker shook her head slightly. "I'm afraid the ruling's already been reached. You were denied emancipation. Your son has been surrendered for adoption placement."

"Adoption! But he's my child."

"Under the guidelines, you are not old enough to be

awarded custody for three years, until you are twenty-one.
The judge ruled that with the neglect complaint and your
not being able to take custody for that length of time, your
child would be best served if placed with adoptive parents.''

"I'll fight it. I'll show him that I'm a fit mother. Can I
talk to the judge?"

The social worker shook her head sadly. "The law is on
his side. You are not of legal age. There is nothing you can
do."

"There has to be something, a petition I can file. . . .
What about when I turn twenty-one?"

"I'm sorry. The decision is permanent. He is now living
with his adoptive parents. As I've said, there's nothing you
or I can do."

Overcome with emotion and unable to speak, Allison ran
out of the room and down the stairs until she pushed open
the heavy glass door that allowed her to leave the building.
Engulfed in sobs, she fought images of Rafe crying for her
every day. She pictured his despairing face, bewildered and
deeply hurt as he anguished over why his mother would
choose to abandon him.

Filled with a bitter sadness, she numbly continued to
work at Stadium as she grew more and more pregnant.
When her high school diploma arrived in the mail, it
brought no more joy than her divorce paper. She saw nothing ahead but bleak, empty days. Finally she told Bev that
she was resigning from Stadium Coffee Shop, and wouldn't
be back to work there after the baby was born.

Bev's careworn face reflected concern. "What will I do
without you? You make the best hamburgers. And no one
can peel potatoes for fries faster than you."

"I can't stay, Bev. I remember the nights that Rafe was
here with me. I keep thinking it's almost time to go home
to him. Then I realize he won't be there and and I start to
cry."

"But you'll still need to make a living. That new baby
will need to eat," Bev protested, but Allison saw that the
shiny brown eyes held sympathy. She walked over and

gave Bev a hug, the small woman's face reaching her breastbone. Allison touched Bev's hair, sticky with hair spray, and recalled how it reminded her of a rooster's comb the day they first met. The two women clung to each other, and Allison understood, not for the first time, that Bev's gravelly exterior hid a heart that cared too much.

"Now if you need to come back"—Bev waved a finger at Allison the way she had the first day—"give me one day's notice and I'll put your name on the schedule."

Allison swallowed. "Thanks, Bev," she said, smelling fries cooking as she walked out the door, unable to look back.

Chapter Eleven

As the day of her baby's birth grew closer, Allison's despair increased. She could hardly face waking each morning. It seemed like the only way to cope with her life was to escape from it. Yet at the same time, she felt a glimmer of hope at the thought of holding a newborn infant in her arms, of starting over once again. Then she told herself she had no business even thinking of a future with this child. All I have is love, and love won't feed a baby, she thought to herself. She made a firm decision: She couldn't do to this baby what she'd done to Rafe. There was no way she could get to know this child, and then have him snatched away, leaving both of them with painful, unending rejection.

She went into labor one morning when she was alone in her room at the Excelsior. Rather than call Victoria or Susan or even a taxi, she rode a bus to the University of California Medical School Hospital with her hands planted loosely on her turbulent belly. As each pain racked her insides, she was determined not to let the other bus passengers know that she felt anything other than the lilt of the bus. Her hold on this baby felt so fragile and tentative that she dared not disrupt it with even a sound.

In the warm stuffiness of the labor room, she waited, lying on her back and letting her thoughts drift. She felt both impossibly far and tremulously close to her dream with this second baby about to arrive. Allison mentally numbed herself to the desperateness of her circumstances in hopes that her first glimpse of this new baby would offer pure joy.

"There she is," the doctor called out, holding up a small bundle draped with a pink receiving blanket. A girl! Oh, could it really be true? Allison gasped at the first sight of her daughter's face. It was Josh's face. As she held the warm infant in her arms, she stroked the baby's hair, still wet from birth, which was the apricot color Josh told her his had been as a baby. The tiny eyes, when opened, reflected his steady blue gaze. She lay for hours with the baby, her arms not growing tired or stiff. Yet complacent as her body seemed, her mind soon roiled with anger and confusion. She made the decision to place this baby for adoption, yet how could she fathom never holding this child again? Never seeing her first smile, plaiting her first braids, hugging her wistful shoulders as she went off to college?

But I can't, Allison reminded herself. I have no right to keep this child when I can't even figure out life for myself. No matter how much love I have, I have nothing else to give. My family is gone. My husbands have left. And now I've lost my son. She pictured herself carrying the baby up the stairs to the room at the Excelsior. Trying to raise her there would be like cutting off her lifeline, she admitted. And who would watch her while I work? Susan was already hinting that she couldn't take care of the children. And Victoria said that Rafe and the new baby were born bastards because their fathers had left. Allison sighed with the understanding that there was nothing she could give this child.

Yet when a nurse with a sympathetic smile entered her room, Allison said, "Please leave her with me a little while longer—for the night if you can."

The nurse shook her head but left the room, and Allison placed her baby in the layette beside her hospital bed. When the social worker, dressed in a business suit and carrying a clipboard, bustled in Allison said, "I'm not sure yet. Can you please come back tomorrow?"

The social worker's smile didn't mask her uneasiness. She stepped closer and then sat on Allison's bed. "If that's what you want, dear. But I thought we'd pretty much talked about this."

Allison couldn't return the forced smile. "I'll let you know for sure tomorrow."

"Or you could call me later this afternoon. I'd be able to swing by then," said the woman, her earrings swaying as she talked. When Allison didn't answer, the woman patted her hand.

Allison sat straighter in the bed and tried to look rational, sane, and calm, as if this were a mere time delay. She said, "Okay. If you don't hear from me about coming back today, call me tomorrow."

"I will," the woman squeezed her hand and rose. "I know you'll make the right choice."

Allison nodded as her throat instantly filled with a lump, and a tears pinched out of her eyes. Yet later that afternoon, when the birth certificate recorder came in, Allison didn't interrupt her to say that there was a mistake, that this was an adoption and her name wouldn't be on the birth certificate.

"Baby's name?" asked the woman, her eyes on the form in front of her.

"Sara Anne Morgan," said Allison, picturing the girl the name might someday belong to. It was Sara because she liked it, and Anne was a remnant from her own Catholic heritage. Sam, she began to call the baby in her head, an acronym from her initials.

She recited the rest of the information in a daze: Mother's name, Allison Morgan; father's name, Josh Morgan; birthplace, Oakland, California.

After the birth certificate registrar left, Allison settled back into her pillows and wondered why she'd chosen the name Anne when growing up Catholic turned out to be so painful for her. It wasn't being Catholic itself that caused the pain. It was the fact that her father wasn't Catholic. She remembered throwing up and getting a headache every Sunday because she hated so much going to mass where she felt alienated and alone. She wasn't allowed in the homes of some of the Catholic children her own age, and wasn't accepted in the homes where she was allowed. Yet her father promised to raise her Catholic . . . a promise that evaporated like other commitments he made, including his vow of fidelity to Victoria.

She lay awake most of the night, and after the hospital was still, she walked down to the nursery. Her fingers touched the glass as she waved to tiny Sam. She watched as Sam's rosebud lips opened in a yawn. She thought of Rafe at this age. She looked again at her daughter. The baby had a few wisps of auburn hair and her skin was a golden peach. Allison shook her head, walked back in her room, and waited until morning.

The hospital ward was filled with tiny cries and the noises of carts being wheeled. Allison asked a nurse to bring Sam to her. She ate her own breakfast, and was holding Sam when the social worker arrived. She could see that the woman fought not to let her disappointment show on her face. She said, "I have the papers with me today."

Allison leaned over and kissed the top of Sam's head. She sniffed the baby lotion smell, and reached below the blanket to hold the tiny hand in hers. She said, oblivious of the social worker, "Sam, I'm sorry. I'm trying to think of you and your life growing up. This is the hardest thing I've ever done. But I know that the only way you'll have the life I want for you is if I give you up for adoption now."

She gingerly lay Sam back in her layette. She saw that the social worker's eyes held tears. The woman said, "I know how young you are. But it takes a pretty grown-up person to make a decision like this." She leaned over and gave Allison a hug. Then she handed her a clipboard.

Allison felt numb as she signed the papers. She read the first pararaph that said "termination of parental rights," then, finding the phrase painful, only looked further for the signature line. After her name was written, she said, "I hope she'll understand why I did this."

"She will." The social worker gingerly lifted Sam from

the layette, then leaned over to let Allison take a last look. "You've just given her a good life."

Allison felt empty and numb in the too quiet hospital room. She lay still for hours on the bed. It was evening before she got up and packed her things, feeling of loss, and yet relieved that she wasn't taking a new baby home to the musty barrenness of the Excelsior.

For the next weeks it was as if she were recuperating. She stayed in her room and went out only to buy groceries with the little bit of money she'd saved from working at Stadium. She bought a newspaper with part of her last five dollars and read the Help Wanted section. Below the long list of restaurants needing employees, her eye somehow caught on an ad that read Responsible Person at the top. Although *responsible* was far from the way she'd describe herself at the moment, she read the rest of the ad.

Responsible person to care for toddler boy, full-time, live-in, light housework, experience and refs required. At first, she wondered how she could even think of being around a child. Yet, as a few long, thoughtful days passed, applying for the job began to seem like the best thing to do. She wasn't anxious to rush back into the restaurant scene . . . long hours on her feet, memories of Stadium, peeling a million potatoes. And with the few post-pregnancy pounds she'd retained, her few dressy clothes didn't fit well. And she had twenty-two months of caring for a boy as *experience*. She didn't admit consciously that the job's big appeal was that it would take her away from the life where she'd experienced such painful loss. She wouldn't live at Victoria's or at the Excelsior. There wouldn't be reminders of the nights she came home late and greeted Rafe. She wouldn't pass the street where she and Josh met. And she wouldn't have to work in an office where coworkers expressed interest in her life and she had to constantly worry about saying the wrong thing. But what would she do about the request for references?

The woman who answered Allison's knock was pretty—blond hair piled up on her head, big earrings, long eyelashes. She smiled instantly. They talked about the weather, the traffic, restaurants, until Allison began to wonder if this woman were really in search of a baby-sitter. She was lulled into the ease of their conversation, until the woman asked the dreaded question, "May I see your references?"

Allison was surprised when the lie came to her. "I've been caring for my nephew . . . who has moved away."

The woman looked at her coolly, the smile frozen into an even line. "Do you have a letter from his mother that you could show me?"

Now Allison forced a smile that she hoped looked believable. "No . . . I didn't know I would seek this kind of work. I've been in the restaurant business. I only decided to change recently."

The woman left the room without speaking further. Allison glanced at the covers of magazines on her coffee table, but didn't dare pick one up.

She heard footsteps, then saw that the woman had returned with a toddler boy in her arms. His brown eyes were wide, and he bore the warm, sweet smell of recent sleep. Without a word, the woman came and placed the boy in Allison's arms, which naturally reached out and enveloped him. It was a familiar feeling that brought instant tears. At first the boy stiffened, but as Allison ran her hand soothingly along his back, he relaxed and leaned into her. She stroked his disheveled, yet soft and feathery hair, straightened the collar of his shirt, and rocked him in her arms.

"You are quite natural with this," said the boy's mother.

"He's a beautiful little boy," said Allison truthfully.

"You do know that I am looking for someone to live here with us—in the other half of this duplex."

Allison nodded and rocked. The woman stood and gestured for her to follow. They walked out her front door and around the side of the house to the other half of the duplex. The room was clean, spare, and looked like a palace compared to the Excelsior. The woman, who by now had introduced herself as Petra Sbatos, showed Allison the closet space, the bathroom, the laundry room. It seemed to be heaven. They walked back to Petra's living room.

"Now," said Petra. "Tell me what you would do with my son all day while I am working."

Allison haltingly responded with a typical account of a day she would spend with Rafe, trying not to let the memory spark her tears. What would this woman think if her account of a child's typical day made her start to cry? She mentioned coloring, reading, going for walks, the lunch she would likely prepare. She was becoming lost in her recollections when Petra interrupted her with a payment offer that was twice what she was making at Stadium. Allison's face registered how startled she was.

"It's not enough money?" said Petra with a confused look.

"No . . . well, yes," said Allison, a giggle rising at Petra's bewildered frown. She forced herself to be serious. "That would be acceptable," she said, trying not to sound overly enthusiastic.

"I saw my son is comfortable with you," Petra concluded. "That is worth money to me."

Allison could not think of a reply. When Petra stood, crossed the room, and shook her hand in agreement, a soothing feeling filled her.

Allison loved caring for Petra's son, Michael, although in many ways, being around and tending to him reminded her of the two children she lost. As she stirred Michael's spaghetti, yanked T-shirts over his reluctant head, and pushed him in the backyard swing, her memories flowed relentlessly. Yet caring for the young boy was also a way to cope. As she cuddled him, she wished upon the universe that someone somewhere else was doing the same for Rafe and baby Sam. She was somehow closer to her children by being close to Michael. Too, it helped to see no familiar sights. No Excelsior. No Stadium Coffee Shop. No seafood restaurant where she and Josh had met. She wrapped this new life around her like a cape into which she crawled to heal.

One day, Allison and Michael sat in the yard playing ball, she heard a hearty male laugh from the yard next door. At first glance, he reminded her of Antonio with his black curly hair and brown eyes. Yet he was older—his hair bore gray streaks, and his laugh brought crinkles to the corners of his eyes. "Your son—he will be playing in the stadium soon?" asked the man. He spoke with a rich foreign accent that again made her think of her first husband.

She cleared her throat and said, "He might play in the stadium—but he isn't my son. I take care of him while his mother works."

"Sorry. My mistake," the man said, his smile still as big and friendly. To her surprise, he came near the fence and began to sing a song to Michael in a foreign language that instantly captivated the young boy. Michael rushed to the fence, his fingers wrapping around the chain link as his mouth opened in an O. Allison fought against her own enthrallment with the rich voice and odd-sounding words.

The man's accent was Hungarian, he told her after they shared several conversations on days when she took Michael out in the yard to swing or play with his ball. The man's name was Nicholas Kovacs, and he'd come to the United States as an army machinist fifteen years before.

At first, Allison despised hearing the lilting melody of her dream in the back of her mind when she was with Nick. Yet, like the two men she was married to in the past, he was dashing, good-looking, and represented the possbility of a stable home that she had sought since the day she crawled out the window. And this man actually owned his own home—he wasn't a foreigner who had no place like Antonio or a man who couldn't get a start and was on the wrong track like Josh. Allison's mind warred. She reminded herself that she was still recuperating from the devastation of losing both Josh and her children. She was in no shape to start a new relationship.

At first she didn't acknowledge to herself the disappointment that fizzled inside her when it rained and she and Michael couldn't play outside. Another day, when she felt her heart lift in anticipation of seeing Nick, Michael just didn't want to play outdoors. He wanted to finish putting together a puzzle and watch *Casper* cartoons. Allison dusted his mother's duplex, washed the dishes, then waited.

She combed her own brown hair and reapplied her lipstick, feeling foolish. Moments later she smiled at herself in the mirror, wondering what Nick would think when he saw her.

Then when she and Michael finally went outside, Nick was in his yard with a woman.

Allison instantly felt like a young teenage baby-sitter. Color flooded her cheeks and continued to warm her face when she thought of her earlier giddiness. This woman was near Nick's age, which Allison estimated at ten or fifteen years older than her own twenty-two. Like Petra, the woman wore her hair upswept, and her sundress held a bold, jungle print accented by her gold beads. Allison couldn't say she was beautiful, but there was a classiness about her, and familiarity between the two of them as if they'd known each other a a long time. The two spoke easily, and as she pushed Michael in his swing, she couldn't help but listen.

"Remember—that night at the restaurant," the woman was saying, "when you—"

The two of them burst into gales of laughter.

"No," Nick said, "I thought the best one was that time at the concert."

As they laughed together again, Nick caught Allison's eye. She felt a stab of humiliation as he stepped up and stood by the fence. "Allison—come over here. I want you to meet someone."

Chills prickled her arms. She wanted to pretend she didn't hear, and just abruptly walk back in the house and close the door. Instead, she grasped the swing straps until it gradually stopped moving. She took Michael's hand and, without looking up, led the small boy to the fence.

She finally glanced up to see that Nick was grinning, white teeth flashing. "Allison Morgan, I would like you to meet my old friend, Sophia Lupinsky."

Sophia held out her hand, surveying Allison coolly. "You are Nick's friend?" she asked, as if such a possibility were ridiculous.

"Sophia, this is my neighbor Allison," Nick said as the two women shook hands.

Allison rushed the introduction and excused herself as she led Michael back into the house. She continued to hear an occasional raucous laugh from outdoors. Each one felt like a knife-slice to her insides. After a while she went in her room and counted the money she'd saved while working at Petra's. She tried to focus on her plan to someday buy her own home where she could bring Rafe if she ever found him again. She'd already written a letter to the Division of Family Services, saying that if his new home with his adoptive parents did not work out, she was now twenty-two, and would love to take him back at any time. She thought rarely of Sam, because to remember the tiny warm bundle in her arms was to ask for waves of lingering pain.

Chapter Twelve

Allison decided to avoid Nick, but it was impossible. Michael wanted to play outside at least once a day, and she could never guess when Nick might be there, ready with a floppy wave and hearty laugh. Even if Michael became captivated with a cartoon in the afternoon, eventually the sunshine outside caught his eye.

One day she turned quickly to chase a ball that Michael threw high, over her head. She stumbled, then looked over to find Nick staring at her. Somehow, it was obvious he'd been watching for a long time.

"Good catch!" He laughed, amused that she'd nearly fallen on her face.

She found herself filled with sudden fury. "Would you like to come over here and try it?" Allison glared angrily, but Nick easily hopped the fence. The three of them played catch until dark.

Later that week Nick called and asked her to go out to dinner.

Despite her misgivings, they started dating. She discovered that he was compulsively neat, his clothes were arranged by color and type—all shirts hanging the same way in his closet, and his rolled underclothes and socks neatly standing in rows. He was old-fashioned in thinking the man should have power; this both reminded her of Antonio and was a refreshing change from Josh. Nick was a take-charge man. She became addicted to both his personality and his accent, and relaxed in the lull of his firm command.

They dated for two years. He never told her he loved her, so his proposal came out of the blue.

"Marry you?" she said, surprised.

He laughed at first, then looked hurt. "Say yes," he said simply.

Her mind whirled through the possibility of once again living her dream. He already had a house. A good job. He wanted the kind of wife she always thought she wanted to be. Domestic. A good cook. A mother. She would be Mrs. Somebody Respectable. Mrs. Kovacs.

"You would not have to move far," he said, laughing again, gesturing toward Petra's house next door.

She made a skeptical face, indicating that she wasn't quite convinced.

"You would have your own home," he reminded her.

"Your home—your home," she joked, poking him in the chest until he started to laugh.

"I would take care of you—pay your bills, keep a roof over your head."

"I can do that myself," she said simply. "I've done it since I was sixteen."

Now his smile turned wicked. "We could have a baby. Or lots of babies. You can't do that alone."

I did, the painful thought surfaced in her head. I had Sam alone. I raised Rafe alone. I was never more alone than when I had my babies.

He must have seen the sadness in her face. "Or we don't have to have a baby right away. You are still young. Very very young.

"Twenty-four next month," she reminded him.

"So you still have lots of time. But I'm asking now. What do you say?"

"Yes," she said simply.

"Yes?" he repeated, obviously prepared for an argument.

"Didn't you want me to say yes?" she asked.

He took a moment to laugh heartily before he kissed her.

The marriage began more conventionally than either of her others. She and Nick were married in a Unitarian church with his family and her sister present. But then, the marriage that seemed so much more on the right track began to derail. Nick obviously wanted to be boss. He told her what to cook and how to cook. For someone who grew up in a house with nary a mix and had worked at a restaurant for two years, these instructions were not only boring, but infuriating.

"No—" Nick held a breaded pork chop up to her face so close that she could see the rippled veins in the meat. "This is all wrong."

"What's wrong with it?" Allison asked with a mixture of exhaustion and anger. She brushed a wisp of hair out of her face. "I followed your recipe exactly."

Fuelling her anger, he picked up the chop and sniffed. "No no no," he said, and she felt her fury rise. "The breading does not taste right. You have not added enough salt, and there is too much sage."

Allison closed her eyes in exasperated fury. Her anger surged when she heard him lift the chops out of the pan with a spatula. She gasped as she saw him place them on a piece of old newspaper.

"No!" she shouted. "That is our dinner! Nick, I'm exhausted."

He frowned angrily. "We can't eat these! The flavor isn't right."

"I can't cook again, Nick. I'm too tired."

"You will cook again. I'm hungry and you are my wife."

She sighed and looked out the window at Petra's yard. If she were still living there, she could make a ham and cheese sandwich, read a book to Michael, and then be free to relax until she fell asleep. It was now nearly seven P.M., and she had to start over. Wearily she opened the freezer, longing for TV dinners.

An omelet. Possibly she could somehow find the strength to make an omelet, a dish she'd prepared with ease since she was ten years old. She'd begun stirring the eggs in the pan when Nick surged up like a wave behind her.

"Was that pan prepared properly?" he asked.

"I greased it with margarine," Allison spat.

"No—no—no!" Nick shouted. "Nonstick spray and then butter." With a roar of anger, he picked up the half-full carton of eggs. Glaring at her with fury, he slammed the egg carton against the counter. The lid flapped open; eggs flew up and hit the ceiling, then settled in cold, crawly dribbles on Allison's head and neck. She looked up to see a clear membrane of egg drip down Nick's forehead.

"I'm not making anything else," she said. "If you know how to cook so wonderfully, go ahead. I don't care if I'm your wife. I'm not your slave."

He glared at her in anger and disbelief.

Then he thrust his finger at her accusingly. "Is this how you treated your other two husbands? Is this how you chased them away?"

Allison shook with anger. She ran to their bedroom and locked the door. It was only a brief respite, she knew. He would say that she was his wife, and should be by his side, every night, every minute. To say she felt smothered would be a hopeless understatement. And, like in her other two marriages, both a sad and happy event had occurred. In the midst of understanding that her marriage was seriously troubled, she gained another, more simple understanding. She was now pregnant for the third time in her life.

After the first shock the pregnancy served as a lifeline that she clung to. In keeping with her own and Nick's expectations, she cleaned the house fastidiously and prepared the nursery elegantly. She bought all the things she'd dreamed of the two times when she was pregnant before. A nursery lamp with Mother Goose characters, a miniature chest of drawers, a well-appointed changing table. She filled the baby furniture with all the layette items she'd read about in women's magazines for the last ten years.

This baby was coming to a secure home, where it

couldn't be more wanted and loved, at least by its mother, Allison reasoned. And true to his word, Nick did take care of her in the old-fashioned sense. Bills were paid and home repairs were completed. He answered the phone and asked who was calling before he handed it to her. When they walked on the street together, he always walked on the side nearest the street, to protect her in case a car splashed water from the gutter.

He was there when she went into labor, mopping her forehead with a cool cloth, and lifting her wrist as if he were about to take her pulse. He led her to the car, and elegantly ladled her into it, as if they were a prince and princess heading out to a ball.

The pains like an ice pick poking were familiar, and brought sad thoughts of Rafe and Sam, who would now be nine and six years old. As needles of pain continued to bore into her body, Allison thought of her two children, wishing they were here with her now, so she could gather them in her arms to welcome this new baby. Instead, there was only Nick, sitting with dignity in a straight-backed chair at the end of the bed. Occasionally he leaned over and took her hand, or mopped her brow. He was her first husband to be there when she gave birth, and these small gestures were appreciated for their rarity if not their warmth. For hours they sat in the labor room, until he left to have dinner.

He was sitting at the end of the bed again, a drumstick in his hand, when a pain tore through her that felt as if her body were shredding in two.

"The doctor, Nick. Now." He bounded up off the chair, dropped the chicken leg into the plastic-lined wastebasket, and dashed out into the hall. It was certainly more comfortable to give birth with a partner, Allison realized. She was still reflecting on the comfort of having her husband with her when a nurse and two attendants dashed into the labor room. The nurse fumbled with Allison's hospital gown, then felt for her cervix with a hand coated with a surgical glove.

"The little head—it's right down there. Take her to delivery."

The little head. At those words Allison pictured her baby for the first time, a little doll with round cheeks. She looked up to see Nick loping along beside the gurney. There was an urgent, worried look on his face that she found oddly touching.

When the doctor asked her to push, she grabbed the rails at the side of the bed and pushed until she was shaking with a violent shudder.

"Again," the doctor said simply.

She thrust downward once more, her fingers trembling as they gripped the rail.

The doctor felt her stomach and glanced under the sheet. "One more time," he said firmly.

Allison pushed and felt her baby slide out like toothpaste out of a tube.

Nick lifted his fist and cheered, "Yes!" and looked down to grin at her. Allison saw he had tears on his cheeks.

The doctor held the baby up. Beautiful, mahogany-dark hair. Alabaster skin. Big round black eyes, open and peering out.

"A beautiful girl," Nick proclaimed

A girl, Allison breathed in ecstasy. Rafe and Sam, you have a sister. I have a daughter, who is finally mine to keep. Her tears were warm as they flowed down her cheeks to the flimsy cotton of her hospital gown. She took the small warm bundle in her trembling arms, and held the infant close to her, as if she could never let go.

Her own baby. Her daughter. She gave the baby all the girls names she could think of at that moment, names she stored up in her mind as the years passed. Brittany Margaret Christine Kovacs. A name for a princess.

Each joy of motherhood was precious to her. She basked in sitting on the couch as Brittany nursed calmly at her breast. There was no time clock to punch, no baby-sitter to find, or worry over, or pay sweat-earned dollars to. She could relax and give Brittany her bath, gently caressing the tiny round belly and plump arms with a water-warmed washcloth. She could nap on the bed beside her tiny daughter's crib. And there were days when she didn't dress all day, until she realized there was only an hour left until Nick arrived. That was her only tension. The house had to be perfect, and dinner must be ready the instant his key turned in the lock. It was work, yes, but not as hard as Stadium, and she could shape her days to fit her own terms.

Then she found the letter. It was tucked neatly in Nick's sport coat pocket, when she was searching the pockets to send the coat to the cleaners. Before she even read the address, she smelled rich, heavy perfume. The stationery was delicate and thin, like onion-skin. The return name and address said it all—Sophia. Without a thought for whether this was legal or proper, Allison instantly slid the letter from the envelope. As she read the words, a feeling settled over her similar to when she overheard conversations in Nick's backyard. Innocent words with a mysterious overtone of intimacy. Now that she was Nick's wife, the feeling was infuriating. Yet she knew if she confronted him, he would be angry with her for reading his mail.

As days passed, she couldn't stop thinking about the letter. Was it the first Sophia had written to him in the three years they had now been married? What was her husband, with his strict ideas of how everything should be proper, doing with this odd past relationship?

Finally she confronted him without mentioning the letter. She waited until after dinner, when he'd folded his newspaper and was sitting on the couch, half-watching the news, and holding a sleeping Brittany on his lap. She cleaned the kitchen, wiping all the surfaces, and stacking the glasses upside down, as per Nick's unofficial kitchen policy, in the cupboard. Then, for a few moments, she relished the simple sight of Nick holding his infant daughter on his lap.

But the urgency in her would wait no longer.

"Nick," she said, forcing herself to sound casual.

He looked up at her half-expectantly and half-chastizing that she had interrupted his concentration. He cocked his

head at her, as if challenging the importance of this interruption.

Allison forced herself to shrug. "The other day, I was
just thinking about Sophia, wondering what's happened to
her and where she is now."

His eyes bored into her, and a sudden smile erupted on
his lips. "You are worried about where she is?"

Allison tried to shrug aside her intensity. "No . . . not
worried. I was just thinking that we hadn't seen her for a
while."

His smile broadened. "You are concerned that I might
see her?"

"No . . . not concerned. Just wondering."

"Wondering." He leaned back his head and laughed.

"So, do you know where she is?"

Now he delicately lay a still-sleeping Brittany on her side
on the couch with her head on a sofa pillow. With exaggerated steps, he came up behind Allison. He began to
tickle her spine, agonizing, probing tickles that caused her
to laugh without dispelling her anger. "Do you want to
know where Sophia is? Sophia Sophia Sophia," he said,
tickling her, until she finally began to laugh.

"Yes," she said finally.

"Sophia is my friend," he said simply, his arms envel-
oping her waist. "She came to this country at the same
time I did. We have much in common. We both learned to
speak English at the same time. She is my—how do you
say it?" His smiled crinkled and he gazed off to the side.

The word *lover* floated agonizingly in Allison's thoughts.

"Buddy," he said abruptly, laughing mysteriously at the
word itself.

Do you talk to her? Do you see her? Do you love her?
Questions rose in Allison's mind, but she sensed he would
laugh at whatever she said. And he would tell her nothing.

Memories of Josh and his clandestine phone calls began
to plague her thoughts, and she watched and listened. The
days passed like summer hours—flexible, elastic, and free
as long as she met Nick's requirements for a spotless house
and sumptuous food. There were long walks with the

stroller, early evenings lying on a blanket on the lawn, relaxed barbecues with a host of fresh fruit, burgers, and sal-
ads in big bowls. Nick sometimes invited friends of his,
men with white-toothed smiles, who spoke only Hungarian
and nodded at Allison with European dignity. But Nick
never mentioned Sophia. There was only one time when
Allison answered the phone and a woman with a foreign
accent said she had the wrong number.

As closely as she observed, she couldn't detect any
change in their marital climate. And when she became pregnant again, months later, she let herself believe all was well
and she was finally living her dream. There was still no
sign of change when Nick again rushed her to the hospital,
and she again gave birth to a beautiful dark-haired girl who
captivated her as much as her first three children. And once
more she seemed to sense that her opportunities to name
children might be limited. Her second child with Nick
would bear the listlike name of Jennifer Jacqueline Gigiana,
called Jenni only minutes after her birth.

Jenni was four when Allison began to admit to herself
that living in Nick's home and having their daughters did
not completely fulfill the image of the dream she'd always
wanted. No matter how often she bought matching sheets
and towels, stitched drapes, or added accessories, this was
still Nick's house. She kept the house according to Nick's
specifications, cooked the meals he wanted, and took care
of his children. She gradually began to understand that she
was fitting the description of his dream.

But she continued on, until the day she found play tickets
in the top drawer of his bureau. She didn't ordinarily look
in Nick's drawers—they were boringly perfect if nothing
else. He still wore cuff links, starched shirts, and rolled his
underwear like white cotton sausages in his drawer. She'd
simply found a folder of Sen-Sen he'd dropped, and knew
that he always kept them in a small bowl next to the cuff-
links.

The tickets were in the bowl. Two tickets, torn in half,
to *The King and I*—a play she'd never seen in her life.

But Nick had.

That night she fixed pork chops the way she'd finally learned pleased him, dressed the girls in the dresses he liked, and waited.

She held the tickets up in a tight fist, so he couldn't wrest them away.

"What are these, Nick?" she asked.

He looked close with mock seriousness. "Tickets," he said simply, then pushed himself back from the table, running to tickle and wrestle with Brittany and Jenni. Watching him laugh and make the girls squeal, Allison hesitated. Could she risk disrupting this?

She waited again, until the girls were in bed, and the only sound in the house was the hum of the air conditioner.

"Nick, I want to know about those tickets."

"They're old—from a long time ago. I'm not even sure what they would be for. I should throw them away."

"They're for *The King and I*. A play. I didn't see it, but there are two tickets here. Who went with you?"

He pretended to think hard. "Don't remember. Long time ago. Doesn't matter." He turned down the bed, climbed in, and turned away from her.

"It was Sophia, wasn't it? You took Sophia to a play."

He didn't face her, but he didn't answer, either.

"Nick."

He still didn't answer.

"Nick, I'm calling a counselor in the morning."

He turned over in a mad rush and pointed his finger at her. "Sophia is my friend and that's all. What I do with my friends is none of your business and has nothing to do with our life."

"So you did take Sophia." A sickened sense that Sophia had never left her husband's life filled her with dread. "Nick, I have to call a counselor. I can't go on like this. You're not faithful to me."

"As your husband, I order you not to," his finger thrust at her again.

Feeling tingles of fear, she looked straight in his eyes. "I don't take orders from you," she said simply, knowing fully at that moment that orders were what he'd given her for years.

Chapter Thirteen

Sitting in the counselor's office, she tried to recall which incidents hurt the most and held the most significance in the slow decline of their relationship. She told of the night he said the pork chops she made "tasted like wood," and threw them out into the garbage, and how, in his anger, he banged a carton of a dozen eggs so hard against the Formica countertop that they bounced upward, landed on the ceiling and dripped onto Allison and Nick's heads as they screamed at each other without stopping.

Beneath the counselor's expressionless gaze, Allison swallowed. All the years of tension over his ironclad rules came together in one phrase. She said simply, "I don't even have a thought that isn't his."

"That's not true," Nick shot back. "What about when you get in my drawers and interfere in my personal business?"

"And—" Allison held up her hand to fend off the attack. "He has never told me he loves me."

Nick's face reddened with rage, and he pounded his fist against the counselor's desk to punctuate each sentence. He shouted, "I love her! I take care of her! I pay the bills! What is the problem here? Why does she want to cause so much trouble in our life together?"

The counselor cleared her throat. "Perhaps your expectations for the relationship are different. In our sessions, we will explore these expectations.''

"Explore . . .'' Nick dismissed the counselor with a wave of his hand, then pounded the table again. "I pay the bills. I am a good father. I am a good husband.''

The counselor said, "For the next six weeks, you will attend separate sessions.''

At first Allison was startled when the counselor didn't dismiss her ideas the way Nick always did. Speaking about her longing for a family, Allison savored the counselor's calm, nonjudgemental replies. She was able to talk, for the first time, about the two children she lost.

"I lost my son when he was two years old. My father took him. I gave up my daughter because I didn't have a father, or a home, or anything to give her,'' she began bravely, feeling her throat tighten in the preliminary stages of weeping.

"That must have been very painful for you,'' said the counselor.

"I never knew that the hurt wouldn't get better. I don't know what I thought would happen. I must have sensed I wouldn't stop loving them. My son was torn from me, but I gave up my daughter in hopes that she would have a better life.''

"Have you undergone counseling for these losses?''

Allison shook her head. "No. I thought that my experiences were the result of taking a left turn in life.''

"Have you tried to find your children?''

"I've been told that my son is happy in his adoptive home and that no information could be released. I didn't feel it was right for me to find my daughter. I felt I shouldn't disrupt the home she has now.''

"Please be assured that your feelings are very normal. I know that until just recently, women weren't given counseling to deal with those feelings. Somehow it was assumed, even by the professional community, that they would go on with their lives smoothly, without recrimination. Yet thousands of others have felt what you are feeling now.''

Allison shook her head. ''Once, I bought a Christmas ornament. An angel. I asked the store owner to write 'Sam' on the toe, for my daughter's initials, Sara Anne Morgan. I wrapped the ornament in Kleenex and kept it in a special place. And once, when I moved out of an apartment, I left a marble egg there. We had a marble egg when my son was little, and I hoped somehow that he would find it.''

''You worked to cope with your feelings.''

Allison again shook her head sadly. ''But they still hurt.''

''That is actually very healthy. So many mothers who place children for adoption block out all their emotions. They hold the pain inside forever. By talking now, we can help you cope with the pain.''

Allison smiled wanly. It had already helped to address the feelings she'd held within for so long. Yet she sensed that the counseling wasn't bringing her back toward Nick.

Before they met in another joint session, the counselor stressed that if she didn't express her real feelings, the painful issues in their marriage wouldn't be addressed.

''Now that our children are in school, I'd like to get a job. I'd like to be a teacher's aide, utilizing the skills I gained while being a nanny,'' Allison said bravely, in their third joint session.

''A job! You!'' Nick laughed. ''I pay the bills. You are my wife. What do you need a job for?''

Allison realized that all the counseling in the world wouldn't help their marriage. Their relationship was over. When she actually moved out of the house, there were many echoes of that long-ago day when she crawled out her window at Victoria's. Again, she was leaving a beautiful home that was perfectly neat and filled with beautiful furniture. This house was also filled with emptiness. The shallowness of their relationship was brought home to her during a final meeting with Nick and both of their attorneys.

Nick's lawyer spoke first, presenting her with an offer her soon-to-be ex-husband had designed.

"My client proposes to pay you the amount of child support while retaining custody of the girls himself," said the attorney. "May I say, Mrs. Kovacs, that this is a very generous offer."

"What?" Allison could not believe what she'd heard. "He wants me to give up custody in exchange for a few dollars every month?" Suddenly the room swam before her eyes.

She forced herself to look at him as she spoke. "Nick, nothing in my life has hurt me more than the loss of my two older children. You don't know me at all if you think I could give up our girls."

"How would you take care of them? I would look out for them. I am their father."

"And I am their mother. They need me and I need them more than any of us need your money."

"This woman is being unrealistic," Nick insisted. "She has only worked in a hamburger joint and as a baby-sitter. There's no way she could give my daughters the proper upbringing like I could."

"Even though my jobs were not prestigious, I worked many hours and supported myself," said Allison. "And there are issues here I haven't addressed, such as—" Allison was going to mention "the possibility of infidelity," but it seemed Nick knew what was in her mind, and when he raised his hand in protest, something caught at Allison's heart. There was, underneath the brusqueness, something sympathetic and touching about this man who naively thought he could rule the world as long as everything went according to his orders.

She was suprised how loudly her voice emerged. "We aren't bad people—either one of us. It's just that he's a typical European husband who oversees his home. I was a feminist before they came up with the word. I've been on my own since I was sixteen. We just couldn't know that we wouldn't work out together until we tried it. And we've been trying it for ten years. The trouble is—both of us still want to call the shots. And I think we always will.''

There was a stunned silence in the room that seemed to last forever.

Finally Allison spoke softly. ''There's one thing we've never argued about—until now. That's our girls. We both love them very dearly. And he is a good father. I give him that.''

''You might want to consider joint custody,'' said the counselor.

No one protested that thought, not even Nick, who looked at Allison with an expression of interested curiosity. She walked out of the counselor's office alone and waited for her bus. When Nick drove up beside her, and gestured for her to get in the car, she first pretended to look beyond him. Instead of loudly insisting she get in, he simply drove away.

After that day in the counselor's office, Allison's life was at first oddly quiet. There were no phone calls from Nick, telling her what she should be doing. She found an apartment, in a good location for schools for the girls, and applied for work as a teacher's aide. Yet when Nick called to ask if he could take the girls out for the weekend, and meet her for lunch the day before, she felt an odd sense of trepidation.

They went to her favorite seafood restaurant, and he ordered the shrimp she usually liked.

''How are you?'' he asked simply. It was hard to read his expression.

Allison looked off to the side. ''I'm starting a new job as a teacher's aide in a about a week, and we've found an apartment.'' Finally she looked in his eyes.

''About the apartment . . .''

Allison steeled herself, sensing he was about to criticize the place where his daughters were now growing up. To her surprise, Nick glanced in all directions, then leaned close to her. ''I have some money to give you. You could use it for a down payment on a house.''

''Money?'' She shook her head. ''We agreed that the

child support payments would be made every month. I have no problem with the terms.''

"I'm selling my house. I will give you some of the equity.''

Instantly this idea fell into the realm of Nick's taking the helm, directing her life as if she were somehow too inept. Allison laid down her fork in protest. "No—you owned the house before I lived there. You made all the payments. I'm not entitled to any equity.''

"My daughters are.''

"Then you can provide that for them when they are older.''

"I would like them to live in a house now.''

Allison sighed. The quiet before this afternoon was really only a lull before the storm.

"I don't want your money,'' she said simply. "We'll be all right.''

Now Nick shifted uncomfortably. He said, "There is something else I need to tell you . . . before the girls have their weekend with me.''

What was he about to prescribe for her now?

At last he sighed. "Sophia is now living with me.''

Anger, fury, and finally futility built inside her. She couldn't resist. "I was right. All the time, when I thought I knew, I did know. You were having an affair all of our marriage.''

"No! No! We have only been together since you left.''

Allison leaned close. "Don't ever lie to me again,'' she said simply, tossing her napkin next to her plate and standing quickly. She left the restaurant without looking back.

When the girls came home from their visits with Nick, and talked about Aunt Sophia, Allison tried not to let them see that the phrase brought her pain. They couldn't guess that what hurt the most was her realization that "Aunt Sophia'' was a long-time acquaintance of theirs. While she and Nick were married, he'd simply forbidden the girls to mention Sophia—but now that he was single, they were allowed to speak of her openly. Allison kept telling herself that at least she would never look back with longing.

There was an air of exhausted accomplishment after she finished her first year as a teacher's aide. She'd made it a year alone, once again. The rent for the apartment was paid, and the girls finished the year with good grades.

She started her second year feeling confident. She loved working with children, and teaching made her feel as if she was making a difference in their lives. After work she came home to her apartment to take care of Brittany and Jenni. True to his word, Nick showed up every weekend, exactly on time. There were days when she could spot Sophia sitting in the far side of the car, a scarf demurely tied over her hair and her hands folded in her lap. There were times when she felt a streak of loneliness, but it was milder, subtler than the feeling of being trapped under Nick's rule.

She told herself that once again, she would make it alone, and this time her children would be with her. She dropped them off to their school each morning, then drove to her own job, confident in their safety until she returned to pick them up at the end of the day.

At first she thought she noticed the man because of his clothes. There was a classiness about him that reminded her of her growing-up years—he always wore suits and ties, and sometimes a vest. His shoes were shined. Was it his full beard or the gold-rimmed glasses that made her think he looked like a professor? She saw him more than once in the school office. He didn't seem to work there everyday, but each time when she saw him, he was speaking to the school counselor. At first, she told herself, she was simply curious about what this man was doing at her school.

She asked Maggie, the secretary. "That's William," Maggie said.

"Why is he here every once in a while?"

"His kids go here. And he works for the city. The CETA program. For low-income students."

Allison sighed. "He doesn't look low-income himself."

Now Maggie smiled at her. "Think he looks all right, do you?"

"Those suits—" said Allison. "And his voice is classy, too."

Maggie nodded. "He's divorced."

Allison felt herself blush. "I am, too. And he probably spends all his time taking care of his kids, just like me."

For seven months, whenever she saw the man in the school office, Allison found her eyes drifting toward him. He was just interesting, she thought. How many men who worked for the city dressed like that? And he looked so confident and at peace with himself. Like it didn't matter what the rest of the world did. He would stay okay and unruffled.

She wasn't even aware he was in the building the day Maggie said, "Come here, Allison, I want to show you something."

She followed obediently, thinking of the plants in Maggie's office, and thinking that Maggie probably wanted to display an African violet or Boston fern. Instead, Maggie took her to the main office, where William sat reading a copy of *Saturday Review*.

Allison flushed. William looked at Maggie, who said, "William has tickets to the ballet on Friday. Would you like to go, Allison?"

"Does he want to ask me?" Allison questioned, looking at Maggie rather than William.

"He does," said William .

"Then I'll say yes," Allison answered. She was surprised to be filled with a flood of delicious tingles, along with the blush that seemed to last all the rest of the day, until she went home to Brittany and Jenni.

William actually wore a tuxedo with tails to the ballet. His handsomeness left Allison shy and tongue-tied. But as they were sitting in the loges, waiting for the curtain to lift, she found that he talked easily, telling her he had season tickets and had attended this particular dance company's performances for eight years, since he'd retired from the military, where he lived in Turkey and Germany. They went to an opera together three weeks later. Then there were picnics on the beach, and lunches out, during which he always held her chair for her and asked what she wanted to order so he could inform the waiter. She realized that his classy dignity was a part of her dream that she'd never even dared to envision.

He kissed her in the car, in front of her apartment, after one of their Saturday picnics.

"There's something I need to tell you," Allison said, her heart already racing.

"Yes," he said, glancing gently at her. His brown eyes gleamed behind his glasses.

"It's about my family. I don't just have Brittany and Jenni. I lost two children before."

"Oh. I'm very sorry. How old were they when they died?"

She breathed. "They didn't die. It's a long story. But I feel like I need to say that I don't think I could get involved in a relationship until I resolve my feelings about them. I'd like to find them—at least my son."

"So there was a son—and a daughter."

"Yes . . . it's hard to explain. I lost Rafe when he was older. My second husband left me and I was only seventeen. My father took him away and put him in foster care. There was supposed to be a hearing—but no one ever told me."

His hand grazed hers. "You could protest the legality of that . . . even now."

"I-I didn't pursue it for a long time. He's in another family, and I thought I should let him grow up there, without interrupting that."

"But he's an adult now—isn't he?"

She nodded, feeling her lip quiver. "It's harder now—that I know he's grown up. It's as if I can't stop thinking about it. As if there's no reason to stop me."

There was a long silence. William sat back against the car seat. She watched him breathe and look straight ahead. He's thinking of how to let me down easily, she thought.

"It's okay," she burst out suddenly. "I know I'm in a weird situation. You don't have to ask me out again." Her words blared loudly in the silent car. Seconds inched by, and finally she reached for the car door handle.

"Wait—" William reached out and took her hand. "It's just very odd that you would tell me this."

Allison looked at him quizzically. "I've had a strange life," she said.

Now William shook his head. "No—that's not it. It's just that—I've lost a daughter, too. I hardly ever tell anyone about her. It's hard for me to talk about her. And even though I have three other daughters, and two sons, she's never left my mind."

"She died?" Allison asked.

"No." William shook his head and closed his eyes. Then he looked straight ahead as he spoke. "It was a long time ago—in the service. She'd be twenty by now. I fell in love with her mother." He paused. "When Mary became pregnant, the military said I couldn't marry her—because I am a man of color."

Allison gasped, then smiled gently at him.

"It ate at me. I never forgot. I hardly ever tell anyone, because it's so painful to talk about."

Allison shook her head. "I didn't mean to force you—to talk about something that makes you so sad."

"No—no," he said, taking her hand. "When you told me about your children, it lifted my hurt for just a minute, to know that I'm not alone. Someone else understands what I'm feeling—"

"The hurt never goes away," Allison finished, and a moment later he hugged her.

They kept dating. There were more ballets, opera nights, picnics, and long lunches. She discovered that beneath his classy dignity was a man of both sensitivity and confidence who was still recovering, both financially and emotionally, from a bitter divorce. For the first time in her life, she took the lead in a relationship, trying to buoy him up with encouragement from her own long years of conflict, and occasionally, with a little money from her meager savings. Yet as four years passed, she never doubted that he was worth it, and she eventually knew that her dream could finally come true if it were his, too.

"I think we should get this thing together," she said, one night in her apartment, where they were leisurely watching a ballet, this time on television. Brittany and Jenni were now in their teens, off with friends.

He frowned the gentle frown she knew so well by now, and looked around the room. He made a curious face and shrugged. Then, suddenly, understanding dawned and he asked, ''Is this when I'm supposed to do this?'' He got down on one knee, and held his hand out to Allison. She giggled helplessly, couldn't speak.

''Miss Allison,'' he said, with exaggerated formality. ''Will you do me the great honor of becoming my bride.''

''It would be my great honor to comply with your request,'' she said, dipping to her own knees beside him.

They were married in a Unitarian church, just the two of them, alone, without any worry over bridesmaid or witnesses, or who would give her away. Eight more school years passed, with their understanding of each other's lives growing as time mellowed their togetherness. There was an ease about being with William that she'd never felt before—it was a revelation to understand that often the best moments in her marriage were the calmest, where there was a sense of understanding and empathy. And if she wanted excitement, well, at least they never stopped going to the ballet and the beach.

Chapter Fourteen

It was nearly the end of their ninth year together, and almost the end of school year, when she returned home late after a faculty meeting. William greeted her at the door with a tenuous smile.

"There's a young man who has been trying to reach you—he called three times."

Allison set her books on the bed as she was suddenly filled with an electric charge. "William, I know who it is—" she said, although William couldn't hear her from the living room. Allison closed her eyes as all the longing, pain, and anxiousness of the past years flowed over her in waves. It couldn't be, could it?

It was two days later when another call came.

"Allison McGarry?" asked a friendly, open voice.

"This is Allison," she said, and her knees immediately shook like tree branches in the wind. She hadn't been Allison McGarry for almost twenty years. Who knew her now that would call her by that old name? Unless—

"This is Rafe Romero," said the voice, and Allison's eyes closed in ecstasy, relief, and euphoria. Tears edged from her eyes. Now her whole body shook. She heard the young man breathe.

"I don't exactly know how to say this—" Now Rafe paused.

Yes! Allison wanted to shout. Yes!

"I really don't know what to say, except that I believe you might be my birth mother."

"Yes! I'm sure I am," Allison finally said aloud. "I didn't want to lose you, and I've thought of you every day." She inhaled as a fresh flood of tears cascaded her cheeks. "Where are you?" she said, her voice breaking. "Can I see you now?"

A nervous laugh. "I'm probably about ten minutes from your house. I drove by last night."

"You drove by! Why didn't you come in?"

"I—didn't know how you would feel about me. I knew you gave me up, and I didn't know what happened to your life after that."

"I didn't give you up—" Allison wanted to tell her son that she wasn't the one who gave him away, but revealing that his own grandfather took him and relinquished him seemed too hard to explain in this heady moment.

"Just come see me now," she said finally.

As soon as she hung up, Allison dashed to the bedroom to fix her hair, put on makeup, and don her classiest pantsuit. What would Rafe think when he saw her?

The doorbell rang. Allison opened the door and gasped. When Rafe was little and she held him, she always thought that he looked like either Antonio or her own father. Brown eyes, black, serious eyebrows, and bronzed-peach skin.

But the tall young man at the door had her face.

Her round eyes and peach-plump cheeks. Her smile.

"Rafe," she held out her arms, and he said, "Wait."

Confusion invaded her emotions. Wait? She'd spent half her life waiting to find him again. But then she realized he held one hand behind his back. Slowly, carefully, he extended his wrist, and she saw what he held.

He said, "I think you left something behind besides me."

Allison stared at Rafe's grown-up palm. In it was a china marble egg, the same egg she'd left behind in one of her long-ago apartments. A silent wish of desperation that he might find her again someday. Looking at it, Allison felt chills.

"How did you ever . . . ?"

He smiled her smile again. "Total coincidence. No explanation, except that I've been looking a long time, and it was the first path of yours that I crossed."

"But how—"

Suddenly how didn't matter. She walked up and hugged him, feeling his warmth in her arms as she hadn't for almost twenty years. Above her, he said calmly, "I'm getting married. I wanted to find you before my wedding."

"Married?" She smiled at him, in dizzying disbelief. "You're old enough to get married?"

His smile turned thoughtful. "My father is coming—and I'd like you to be there, too."

"Your father—" Surely he had to mean the father who raised him, who adopted him. She gave him a slightly confused look.

"Well, both of them actually. But I think the one you know is Antonio."

"Antonio? You talked to Antonio?" Again, she thought she should probably say that Antonio left her behind in Mexico and never came back. But she was in too much awe for such a complicated explanation.

"Yes. I found him first. Through the child-support records."

"Child-support records?" This sounded crazy, as if there must be a mistake.

"He paid child support to the foster care system for years, even though he never saw me. . . ." Now she saw tears on Rafe's face. "Even after he couldn't find you—"

Now Allison's mouth dropped in astonishment. "He told you he couldn't find me? After I came here alone and never saw him again."

Now Rafe touched her shoulder. "He tried to find you. Like I did. For years your mother told him you moved without a forwarding address. That's another reason why I waited to call you. I didn't know how you'd react if you really tried not to be found all these years."

If what he said was true, then it was Victoria who had kept them apart, Victoria who never wanted her to be Antonio's wife. How could her mother have done that?

Rafe blurted, "Antonio says you're still married. That there's never been anyone else for him, and there never will be. He's still trying to find you. I'm supposed to let him know where you are."

Allison was stunned. All the nights she spent alone, exhausted after peeling potatoes. All this time . . .

She asked slowly, "When is your wedding?" Then she looked up into his warm brown eyes, and gave him a tearful smile. "I'll be there whenever it is. I'd stop my life to be there."

Rafe smiled back at her. "It's the day after tomorrow," he said simply.

That night Allison mulled aloud as William listened calmly. She knew her father took Rafe. Now it looked like Victoria had steered Antonio away from her. Antonio thought they were still married, and Rafe was getting married in two days. As she spoke, Allison was grateful for the genuine empathy on William's face, and she sensed she wouldn't have missed meeting him for anything, even if Antonio had stayed by her side forever.

In the sea of candles and people talking in the church foyer, Allison at first didn't recognize the older woman in the navy dress suit, who walked quietly up to her and took both of Allison's hands in hers. Allison was startled to see that the woman was crying.

"Mi niña," she said.

Now Allison started shaking. "Maria," she said slowly. "You look beautiful." During the time she'd lived in Mexico with her mother-in-law, the woman was draped in widow's black. Now, with her classy suit, makeup, and a new hairstyle, Allison realized what a beautiful woman she was. As were all of Antonio's family, with their fair complexions and red highlights in deep brunette hair.

"I knew I'd see you again," said Maria, and the two hugged. Then tentatively Maria took Allison's hand and led her through the crowd to where a tiny woman with a cane sat on a straightback chair.

"This is Antonio's grandmother," said Maria. "She has waited to see Rafe ever since she knew he was born."

The tiny woman spoke in soft, rushed Spanish.

Maria took Allison's hand. "She is eighty-seven now. She says she always knew she would live to see her grandson, Rafaél."

Allison bent over, took the tiny woman's hand. She saw that faith and hope shone from her eyes. "I've waited forever to see him, too," she said.

She felt a hand at her back. Thinking William must now be behind her, Allison stood. And turned to face Antonio. A rush of emotion filled her, and it was as if her insides melted. There was tender recognition in his eyes and a gentle smile, this handsome man whose ebony hair was now flecked with gray. Staring at him until he took her in his arms, Allison knew she'd never stopped loving him.

I love William, she thought. And I still love Antonio. It's possible to be in love with two men.

And as Antonio held her and spoke softly, both in Spanish and English, she knew that if William and Brittany and Jennifer somehow weren't there, she could go back to Mexico with Antonio, and Maria, and work in the dry-goods store as if she'd never left.

But twenty years had gone by.

She gently broke away from their hug, took Antonio by the hand, and led him into an alcove at the side of the church.

"Antonio—it is so wonderful to see you," she said. "I never thought I would see you again."

"*Mi esposa*—my wife," he said, moving to take her in his arms.

Instead of allowing herself to be enveloped within the hug, she forcefully reached out and grasped his hand. "Antonio, I need to tell you. I'm married to someone else."

His look held pain. "But we are married. You are my wife."

Allison took a deep breath, then forced herself to look

into his brown eyes. "I had to divorce you. I never wanted
to. But I thought you left me—I waited a long time and
you never came back to the States."

"I never would leave you. I will marry one time in my
life."

"But I thought—you never came back to me, after our
son was born. You never sent for me to come back to San
Luis."

"I returned to the States to get you as soon as I could
get my passport. Your mother told me you moved away.
Left no forwarding address."

Allison gazed at the years of pain in Antonio's eyes. "I
looked for you, too. My mother said you never sent a letter."

"I didn't need to send a letter. I was here looking. Calling on the phone. Trying to find where you lived. I went
to your mother's house at least five times, until she
screamed at me never to come back."

"If I had known . . ." Allison said.

"And I kept paying child support for our son. I thought
you would know about that."

"No," Allison said, still reeling at Antonio's words.
"When I tried to find Rafe, they said I was too young to
keep him. . . ."

Suddenly William was at her side, and she was more
aware than ever that she and Antonio were standing here
alone in the deepening dusk. She stepped back and took
hold of William's arm.

"Antonio . . . this is William . . . my husband."

She glimpsed a look of instant pain cross Antonio's face.
In the irony of the situation, she could think of no other
way to introduce the first man she ever fell in love with.
"William," she said. "This is Antonio . . . who was also
my husband."

The two men stared at each other uneasily, and it was a
long moment before they shook hands. In that moment she
knew she was in love with both of them, and always would
be.

William said, "You're Rafe's father."

Antonio nodded.

"It's been a great relief for Allison to find her son. I myself have a daughter that I'd like to search for."

"A relief to me, too," said Antonio.

Allison said, "I think we'd better be getting back to the wedding guests."

But when the two men continued talking, she left and went back by herself. In the rush of laughter, hugs, food, and swishing skirts, it suddenly struck Allison that there were only two other people still missing. Her daughter and William's.

In the days after the wedding Allison's emotions rode a roller coaster. She was filled with both euphoria that Rafe was back in her life, and renewed pain for the years that they had lost. When he confided that he planned to go Mexico to work with Antonio, she again felt mixed feelings— happiness that he and his father would be together and sadness that he would once more be far away. Allison said, "It's so hard for me to let you go. Please don't ever get lost again."

Rafe hugged her. "You know that I'll be back. . . . With Antonio's business, I'll need to travel to the States quite often."

"Antonio's business?" Allison was curious.

"You know he's a land baron?"

"I didn't. I knew about the dry-goods business."

It turned out that the dry-goods business was only the beginning—Antonio's family owned half of San Luis, which he planned to share with Rafe. Allison was tempted to call Victoria and tell her she didn't know that she was throwing away a wealthy son-in-law twenty years before. Now her feelings toward Victoria were as much curiosity as anger. What made such a beautiful woman so cold and so cruel that she never wanted to see her grandchildren? Where in her life did she turn a corner and leave all the love and caring behind?

During the next six months she and Rafe began to build their relationship. It was a unique experience, she thought, to have such a close biological tie and no history of life together. She felt like she wanted to call him every day—yet at the same time didn't want to intrude in his life. Once, he put his mom on the phone, the one who raised him. Allison was suddenly overcome with tears. "Thank you for taking care of my son . . . our son." She managed to say before a lump filled her throat.

"Thank you for sharing your wonderful boy with us," said his mother. "I'd like to met you someday."

She was frequently euphoric at seeing and talking to Rafe again, yet also plagued by her painful emotions returning—the bereftness of being without him all those years. She realized there was so little she knew about him—what was his favorite food now? Where did he go when he had a day off? What made him lose his temper? It was like meeting a childhood friend again and discovering how they had changed. More than anything else, she felt an all-encompassing sense of relief at completing this unfinished business in her life. There's no way I could have died and left this earth without seeing him one more time, she thought to herself.

But her happiness made her feel the pain of missing Sam all the more. Was there any way she could see her once, too? Just one time? To know she was all right? Allison called a friend who was an attorney. She wore her best dress to his office.

Her friend folded his hands and asked, "How could I help you the most?"

She told him, "My son, who was taken from me, has just found me. It was like being born again . . . as if I was a new person. I felt as if a weight was lifted from me." She paused as her voice broke. "I didn't know my feelings would be so strong. It was as powerful as when he was born the first time." She waited, gathered her thoughts. "I know I don't deserve this. But now I'd just like to see my daughter once before I die. Even if I could just see her standing across the street somewhere, and know she was alive. I don't feel I have the right to interfere in her family."

"She was also taken from you?"

"No. After my son was taken, and my life was ripped to shreds, I didn't feel I could offer her anything. I didn't have a job or a family, and even my son was gone. I didn't want to bring her into the trauma I was going through. So I gave her up for adoption."

The lawyer asked, "Was this a private adoption?"

"Through an agency. I signed her away at birth."

The lawyer shook his head. "That's tough. You could try to get a court order for the file to be opened . . . but you've said yourself what the court would say. That you might disrupt her life. If there were a medical reason, or if you were the child looking for the parent . . ." He paused, then said, "Possibly, with thousands of dollars."

Allison thought of William's long battle in his divorce, the war that cost all his savings. She thought of Brittany and Jennifer, and their young families, who could use her financial help. She thought of her long-lost daughter, who might not appreciate being found. Then she shook her head. "I wish I could feel comfortable spending thousands. I know how much I want it, but wanting doesn't free up the funds."

Her friend patted her arm. He said gently, "Let me know if circumstances change. But in the meantime be comforted that you did what you could to give her a good life."

"If I saw her, I'd know that for sure." Allison stood and shook the lawyer's hand.

One night, a year later, her neighbor rang the doorbell.

"Mrs. Johnson? I got a phone call today, from someone looking for a Allison McGarry. Your name isn't McGarry, but you are the only Allison I know who lives around here."

She handed Allison a scrap of paper that was crumpled, as if it had been stuffed in a purse. "There's no name?" Allison asked, gazing down at the phone number.

"Sorry. That's all I got."

"Was it a man or a woman? What did the person sound like?"

"A woman. Professional. Businessy. And somehow I got the idea the call was urgent."

"Thanks," said Allison, who could feel her heart pumping unexplainably. She was filled with a rush of adrenaline and could hardly wait for the woman to leave so she could call. Yet it was already after eight P.M. She looked down at the unfamiliar number. It was an area code she'd never seen before.

She dialed "0" and asked, "Where is 941?"

"Florida," said the operator automatically.

Florida. Allison felt the hair on the back of her neck stand on end. Coral Gables, Florida, was the last place she knew where Josh lived. Was it possible that . . . ? Was there any way . . . ?

Taking a breath, she dialed the whole number. It rang three times, before a youthful, friendly male voice said in a taped message, "Thank you for calling International Locator. Our office hours are from nine A.M. to five P.M., Eastern standard time . . ."

International Locator. It sounded like some sort of missing-persons agency. Allison was stunned. She closed her eyes as the adrenaline rushed again. Butterflies filled her stomach. Wasn't there only one person in the world who would want to locate her?

She called the number again the next day, where the vice president, Arliene Dunn, said there was a young lady who wanted to reach her . . . who had tried for years on her own without luck, until she found this company. . . .

Allison only half-listened to the friendly words. A young lady. Looking for her. Tried for years. Wanted to find her . . .

When the woman asked what she was thinking, Allison fought to catch her breath. Then she said, "I've wanted to meet her again since the day she was born."

Sitting in the audience at the *Rolonda Show*, Allison was scarcely aware of the crowds of people sitting around her who clapped wildly when the music started. She herself could hardly sit still as Rolonda introduced Troy and Arliene Dunn of International Locators. She closed her eyes quickly and started shaking as Arliene told Sam's story. Only the girl's name wasn't Sam now. Her name was Tara.

Allison looked up and tears streamed her face as a beautiful young woman with her sister's coloring and Josh's height and bone structure walked onto the stage. When her own sister, Susan, patted her back gently, she realized she was hyperventilating. She fought to sit in the chair while her legs shook with anxiousness.

The young woman spoke clearly and distinctly, in a voice that sounded like Susan's. "I always wanted to meet my birth mother and tell her I've had a good life. I want to let her know that if she wants to meet me and get to know me and my daughter, we want her to know we'd love to meet her."

If, thought Allison . . . If. If you only knew how much. She gripped the armrests of her chair and waited.

"I'd like to ask anyone out there who might know where Allison McGarry is, or any way that I might find her, to please call Rolonda." The voice was so sincere, so hopeful.

Arliene Dunn turned and looked out into the audience. She smiled in Allison's general direction. "Tara, I think there's a woman out in the audience who might be able to help you. . . ." she said.

Allison was shaking so much it was hard to stand. But once she did, she ran up toward the stage. Arliene called out, "Tara, meet your birth mom, Allison Johnson."

Allison was still running when her feet hit the stage. A sob choked from her throat as she saw tears cascading from Tara's eyes. The two met in a tight hug that was filled with electricity. My arms have been empty for twenty years, Allison realized. I've longed for her each moment until then. She felt Arliene's gentle hand on her shoulder and heard her say something about "take some time to get to know each other."

As they still clung to each other, Arliene led Allison and Tara off the stage and into the green room, where they talked for hours. In the days that followed, Allison discovered that Tara, like her former self, was a struggling single mom with a child that she put first in her life. She felt a sad wistfulness along with the understanding that she would never be Mom, but it was far overshadowed by gratefulness that at least the daughter she gave up was now back in her life. "Our relationship will never be the same as the one you have with your mom, because I didn't raise you. But at least we know each other now," she said, before one of their hugs.

It was a few months later when Allison realized she'd finally found the dream she'd waited for so long. She was standing with William at Tara's wedding, dressed in a black dress that accented her brown hair. She watched as a tall, dignified young man in a well-cut suit entered the room. He'd taken about ten steps when he caught up with Tara. The two spoke briefly, then trembled as they embraced in a long, tender hug. When they turned slightly, Allison gasped with joy, seeing that the young man was Rafe, who had told her there was a small chance he might fly in from Mexico. The headiness of the moment filled Allison, and she felt her heart beat in her chest. "This was what I really wanted all those years—all those nights of working late, all that time of struggling alone. I didn't even dare hope for this—having all of my family together in the same room, sharing the love I always felt for each of them." With tears on her face, she turned to William, and saw that he was crying, too. Her gaze drifted to where Brittany and Jenni sat talking companionably at a table. A wistfulness filled her heart, and she knew that there was one task left. Taking William's hand, she leaned over and spoke softly, her lips near his ear and her cheek against his. She said, "I want you to feel what I'm feeling right now. And you will. We're going to find your daughter next." Squeezing his hand, then leaning to give him a quick hug, she stepped calmly away from him and with fresh tears, took Rafe in her arms for a welcoming embrace.

The Son They Never Forgot

Chapter One

Laura was excited that the wedding plans were finally set. She and Tommy were leaving tomorrow to go to Tennessee to get married. If you were under twenty-one and lived in Arkansas, as they did, that's where you crossed the state line to get a marriage license. Laura packed as many of her clothes as would fit in the white Lady Tourister suitcase. She breathed a sigh of relief that her parents were gone on a week-long trip.

When the suitcase was full, she looked around her at the high-ceilinged, white-walled room where she had lived since she was four years old. That was when the Milligans had rescued her from the orphanage and later adopted her. She still remembered coming to this big, mansionlike house on weekends before they decided to add her to their family. She felt as if she were moving into the king's castle. The older she got, the luckier Laura felt. The Milligan family sheltered her, she knew. She shivered at the thought of telling them that although she was madly in love with Tommy, the real reason they were getting married right away was that she was pregnant.

She sensed that the fact that she was in love, and that Tommy was the only man she ever had sex with, wouldn't soothe the wounds the pregnancy would cause. The Milligans raised her to be a good Catholic—and good Catholic girls didn't have a baby if they weren't married. She had just finished business college, receiving her two-year medical secretary certificate. Her life was set to move ahead to a career. And she always thought she'd marry Tommy someday, later, when they were both older than nineteen. But now this. . . .

When Tommy told his mother that he and Laura were leaving the next day to get married, the softness of his mother's voice couldn't temper the devastation of her words. Sitting in her rocking chair, she abruptly turned to face Tommy. She said, "Don't marry Laura . . . it's not your baby."

Tommy felt like someone slugged him in the stomach. "What?" he asked in disbelief.

The older woman shook her head, rocking in the chair where she sat every day to look out the living room window. A few agonizing seconds later, she stared at him with icy blue eyes. "I always meant to tell you . . . when you were older. I'm sorry, Tommy. But it's the truth. You can't have kids. You had an illness when you were little."

"Mom . . . no. I can't believe Laura would be with somebody else. She never dated any other guys."

"Face it . . . she did . . . tell her to go find the real father."

Speechless, Tommy stared at his mother, who rocked silently in the humid, quiet spring afternoon. Having made her pronouncement, she stared straight ahead. He thought of asking which illness, what happened, but the horror of the moment rendered him mute. Minutes later he stumbled down the steps of his mother's house, carrying the suitcase he packed the night before. He opened the trunk and lifted the suitcase inside. What could he do now? His emotions fought inside him like a pack of dogs chewing at each other. He felt devastated at his mother's words, angry at both her and Laura, guilty over causing pain to two women he loved so much. And oddly, he felt relieved and angry at himself for seeing this as a possible out. As he drove to where he and Laura were supposed to meet, he admitted to himself that he really didn't feel ready to be a dad, to work a steady job, to be stuck in all the things that adults did.

But he loved Laura. He'd probably marry her later anyway. Why not now?

He saw her parents' car, with her suitcase sitting high in the back. She smiled and waved with an expectant look, her reddish-blond hair shining in the sun. He parked the car and got out. His feet felt leaden with each step as he moved closer. The sun glinted off her teeth as she smiled at him. Even her blue eyes looked happy and sparkling. Yet his mother's words haunted his every breath, added painful weight to every step he took. When he reached the car, he spoke without thinking, not knowing how his mind formulated the words.

"You can call me an asshole . . . but I can't marry you."

"What?" For a second, the world stood still before her face crumpled in shock. "What do you mean?" When he didn't answer instantly, she demanded, "Are you kidding me? What are you saying, Tommy?"

"Mom told me I can't have kids. I had an illness when I was little. I'm sterile."

Laura shook her head in protest. "You know you're the only guy I've been with. It's gotta be yours."

"She says it's not. And I trust my mom. She wouldn't lie to me."

"Well, she just did."

"I believe her. She likes you okay. She wouldn't say something like this unless it were true."

He shook his head and looked away from her, out into the bustling Little Rock street, where cars passed and people entered the downtown shops. Moments later Tommy forced himself to turn back to Laura's stricken face. "She just told me now. I'm sterile. The fact is, I couldn't get a dog in heat pregnant."

Laura spat back, "It's yours, Tommy, you know it is. It happened that night—" Her voice broke and he could see tears course down her cheeks at the same time her anger boiled over. Before he could say another word, she turned, started the car, and pushed her foot to the gas pedal. She took off so fast he was afraid she'd hit half the cars on the street before she got to the corner.

He felt sick. And lost. Deep inside, he wondered if his mama was wrong. Memories nagged him—he was sure Laura was a virgin the first time they slept together. She said he was her first love, and he believed her. As he trudged back to his car, loss, loneliness, and guilt poured over him in waves. He thought of all the times they talked about getting married, all the parties they went to together. It was hard to imagine himself being without her. And now, he admitted to himself, he felt like the baby was probably his, too. His mother never said anything about any disease before.

Down the street he saw a father walking with his little boy. Now his own boy might never know him. Tommy squinted back tears. Then he took his suitcase home, where he began to repack it to get ready to go to South Carolina to serve in the army instead of just going to Tennessee for a three-day weekend to get married. He'd been granted a three-day leave pass for the wedding, but now there was no wedding, and he had to report for duty. He sensed that in the nights ahead, memories of this bleak day in downtown Little Rock would haunt his mind.

Laura just drove. She couldn't say where or for how long she sat numbly behind the wheel, turning corners and racing down streets. She didn't hear the radio blaring. She didn't see the street signs passing. Finally, with no idea how many hours had passed, she somehow drove back to the huge Colonial house where she'd lived since she was four.

When she thought back to being little, before she was adopted, Laura remembered the fire. The heat that surged down her arms and legs and the smothering smoke that made her cough and choke. She and her mother and eight brothers and sisters were crowded into an apartment in a poor part of town. Even before she could read, she understood that her family was too poor to take care of that many kids. Her mother stayed home with the children, and always seemed to have a baby on her lap that needed care. Her father's only work was as a pin setter at a bowling alley.

Everything was scarce—food, time, and room to breathe in the small apartment.

The fire was the last straw, according to the state of Arkansas, who took away all of Mama's nine children and placed them in orphanages. Laura remembered that the orphanage where she ended up was a huge building, filled with babies born after the war. If you were lucky, families came to take you out for a visit, and if you were even luckier, a family took you home permanently to adopt you. At night she tried to imagine being chosen to go to a family's home, and wondered what that house might be like. Would there be lots of brothers and sisters like she had now?

One day she was playing with a group of other children when a family chose her to stay with them for the weekend. "That one there—she looks like an Irish girl with that strawberry hair," said a friendly-sounding man. Bryan Milligan looked Irish himself, with blue eyes and black hair. Laura packed her three outfits in a cardboard shirt box and Bryan Milligan took her hand to help her into his big Cadillac so they could take her for a two-day visit.

She gasped when she saw the imposing Colonial house with the huge concrete pool in the backyard. Looking up, she saw a woman walking over to her. She sat and stared at the first black person she ever saw. The maid, whose name was Lula, smiled at her, and Laura felt horrified fascination at the black woman's white teeth and pink tongue. She screamed in terror, which partly dissolved when Lula took her in her arms for an all-encompassing hug. At that moment, she knew she had a home.

Laura's warm memories were abruptly chased away as Tommy's devastating announcement replayed in her head. How could he say that he couldn't marry her? Even the first night, when they flirted over the intercom at a friend's apartment building, they found that chemistry flowed between them. That night a bond began that seemed as if it would last forever. But it was shattered now.

Laura opened the front door, then walked into the silence of the house. Again she was grateful that her parents were away. If they were here, she'd surely break down and seek refuge in their loving embrace. She couldn't do that. She was still pregnant, and she knew that would destroy them. She had to figure out what to do.

As the next day passed she cared for her grandfather, who lived with their family. She fed him and washed his clothes. She decided she would wait to make her escape until she knew her parents were on their way back from Florida and he would be safe a few hours or so without her. Numbing her emotions, she began to pack her clothes and belongings into her blue Chevy Nova. Her mind was made up—no way would she bring this disgrace on the parents who'd rescued her from the orphanage, cared for her all her life, and sent her to college. She made a frantic call to her friend Kay in California.

Her voice sounded breathless and revealed the anxiety she felt. "I've got to get away. I'm desperate. If I come out there, will you help me find a place?

"You need to get away before the wedding? Aren't you busy getting ready?"

"No." Laura's eyes closed and she fought to speak past the tears that threatened. "There isn't going to be a wedding."

"What?"

"He dumped me. And I'm pregnant. I have to get out of here."

"How could he dump you? He seemed like a nice guy."

"His mother told him he's sterile. Blood's thicker than water."

There was a pause. Then Kay said, "Ricky is there now. In Little Rock. He wants to come back out here. But he doesn't have a car."

"I have a car," Laura said quickly.

"But there's all his stuff. And your things, if you're coming out here to stay."

She thought of the packed Nova. It was filled to the brim. "I just won't bring as much . . . and do you think there's any way he could sort of . . . travel light, too?"

"Hmm . . . maybe. And maybe you could stay with us, until you get a job or whatever."

Laura's mind flashed a warning signal that this arrangement wouldn't be as simple as Kay made it sound. Yet what other choice did she have? She sighed. "My parents will be back on Saturday. I'd like to leave before then."

"I'll have Ricky call you," said Kay.

After she hung up the phone, Laura's emotions warred. She felt relief at the thought of leaving before her parents came home. Yet that relief was a candle in the darkest night she could ever imagine. She wasn't getting married. She wasn't going to be Tommy's wife, or have a father for her baby. She felt as if she were drowning in a sea of despair, with no life raft in sight. Part of the time she wanted to call Tommy and scream at him, saying, "You know it's yours, come on, you miserable coward!" Other times she imagined that she had somehow left him alone with his own set of sad feelings. She wasn't used to not talking to him. When she tried to think of a friend she could share this crisis with, his familiar face always came to mind. There were moments where she almost picked up the phone. They'd been a couple for so long. More than three years now. She never thought they'd be apart. Now, they couldn't even speak to each other.

She grew anxious when three days passed without Ricky calling. She debated leaving alone, maybe even getting a small motel room in town and calling him from there. She had to leave before her parents got home. She could drive to California alone, she reasoned, but she'd never driven anywhere by herself. Her idea of traveling was carefully orchestrated trips her father engineered each summer. Upscale restaurant food. Suites in hotels. First-class air flights. The idea of managing all that on her own seemed impossible. If only she could ride with someone who'd traveled alone before. . . . Finally, fighting off panic, she called Kay and asked for Ricky's number. Then her thoughts still warred. What was the right thing to do? She only knew she couldn't stay here.

It was after two P.M. when she called the number Kay

gave her, yet when Ricky answered the phone, it sounded as if he'd just woken up.

"Yes—"

"This is Laura Milligan, a friend of Kay's. She said you need a ride to California?"

A grunt. Shifting in the sheets. Clearing his throat. "Thought I'd just take the bus."

"But aren't you moving there? Don't you have all your stuff to take?"

"Hmm . . . not sure yet."

"I need to leave now . . . tomorrow or the next day. Any chance that would work out for you?"

A lot more sheet-shuffling. "Tomorrow. No way. It's my last day of work. I'm getting my paycheck."

"The next day?"

"Uhh . . . maybe . . . I don't know."

"I need to know right now. I have to leave."

"Call ya back . . ." he said. He hung up and Laura said, "But you don't have my number," into a dead receiver.

She spent the rest of the day packing, and went to a gas station to see if they had maps of California, but they only carried the surrounding states. She wondered if the one hundred dollars she'd saved would last until she got there. This wasn't the way it was supposed to be. She and Tommy should be on their honeymoon now, celebrating and relaxing at a hotel with a swimming pool in Tennessee. Then they would come back and find an apartment. She'd use her recent business college degree to work in business until the baby was born. It was all planned so neatly. And suddenly yanked away.

Later that night she called Kay, trying not to sound as if she were begging and desperate. "Ricky said he'd call me back . . . and he didn't. I need to know if I'm going. I have to get out of here before my parents come home."

Kay said she'd call him. Then Laura had nothing to do but wait, think, and worry. Should she call a bus company? Ask about airline tickets? See if she could find someone else who needed a ride? She checked everything she packed until midnight. Then she lay on her bed, and was nearly asleep when the phone rang.

It was Kay. "He says to pick him up at 6:00 tomorrow morning,"

Laura fought to fully wake. She rolled over and looked at the clock. She knew she'd be awake at six, because she probably wouldn't sleep all night. But what about the car? Did he have his stuff packed? Shouldn't she talk to him herself and arrange things, like who would drive, how they would pay for gas, how long they would travel each day? Her mind floundered, until she thought of her mom and dad. She just had to leave. Period. She would have to work out the other details as they came along. She thought of writing a letter to her parents, just a goodbye letter without mentioning the baby. But her heart hurt at even the thought.

Chapter Two

She knew within the first hour of sharing her car with Ricky that she should have tried to make this trip alone. Ricky was a silent, ominous presence behind the wheel. He drove so fast that she clung to the armrest after he swore at her for bracing herself against the dashboard. He wanted to drive all day without stopping—finally she was forced to protest that she would get morning sickness if she didn't take a break to eat. She wanted to stay in a cheap hotel while he argued that they should sleep only a few hours in the car. He gave in on letting her eat occasionally—she conceded the futility of trying to find cheaper lodging than the car. But still they argued all the way across the country, and there were times when she wondered if it would be easier to simply drive across the median and become a head-on collision victim rather than battle him the rest of the way. She had to admit that he knew his way around a map, and as the mileage signs flew by, she found momentary relief on seeing that they were actually making progress.

He wanted to sleep at a campsite in the Nevada desert instead of stopping at a motel. She gave in when she realized she'd already spent twenty dollars that day, and he said he had a bedroll she could use. They'd already split the three-dollar fee when she realized he meant they should share the bedroll, too.

"I thought you said you had one I could borrow."

He pointed angrily. "This one."

"I thought you meant an extra one."

He gestured with fury at the packed car. "Where would there be room for an 'extra one' in that piece of junk!"

"I'm not sleeping with you," she flung back.

He stuck his long, sharp-nosed face into hers. "Don't worry. I wouldn't touch you if you were the last piece on earth."

With that, he ceremoniously undid the bedroll. They lay back to back, crammed in the small nest of quilting. She stared at the stars for what seemed like hours, until the sky began to lighten. It seemed like she'd scarcely fallen asleep when he nudged her awake and said, "Time to hit the road." She opened her eyes to a sky filled with sun.

They slept back to back for three nights before they reached Los Angeles. Laura silently gazed at palm trees and tall buildings as cars raced beside them. She could tell that Ricky was looking for an address when she blurted suddenly, "There's a place I need to go."

"Kay said you were living with us."

"No . . . well, I might have to go somewhere else."

He swore. "Well, where is it?"

"I-I need to find a phone book."

He exhaled noisily, exasperated. Then he pulled up sharply, and she thought he might order her out of the car. But she saw he pointed to a phone booth. She climbed out of the car, and, with shaking fingers looked up the number for Catholic Charities. The number in the phone book looked as ordinary as any other, but she knew if she dialed it, it would change her life forever. She recalled Becky Stanton, an older girl who she knew vaguely back home. She remembered hearing the rumor that Becky was pregnant, and one day she'd walked behind her in the school hall. Though it was meant to be a whisper, she'd heard Becky's friend ask, "Will you be showing by the end of the year?" Then she heard Becky answer, "Hope not." Every day after that, she'd stared at Becky, wondering how it must feel to walk with the hundreds of carefree students in the school and know that you carried a hidden secret that someone might find out at any moment.

Now she knew how it felt. Where was Becky Stanton now?

She stared at the phone number without dialing.

Ricky honked once, then leaned on the horn until it screamed.

Laura closed the phone book and ran back to the car.

"Well?" Ricky demanded, a sneer in his voice.

Laura swallowed, looked straight ahead.

Now he leaned forward and stared into her eyes. "Where to, bitch?"

She swallowed again. "Your place," she murmured, her voice almost inaudible.

For the next weeks she stayed in Ricky and Kay's apartment as her money dwindled. On the days when she awoke with morning sickness, she ran for the bathroom, turned on the water, and hoped they wouldn't hear. One night, when Kay and Ricky were arguing in the next room, she heard Ricky mention her, and ask how long she planned to stay with them. Kay lowered her voice to a whisper, and Laura felt helpless and out of place in this apartment. She thought of her parents, who'd been home for more than three weeks now. What did they think when they arrived home from their trip and found she was gone? The next afternoon, when Kay and Ricky left the apartment after another argument, she dialed the familiar number.

"Hello?" Were those tears in her mother's voice?

"Mom, this is Laura—" Her voice broke at the first word, although she fought to sound calm. Her knees shook and she felt her throat tighten with impending tears.

"Oh . . . oh . . . thank God! We're worried sick!"

"Mom . . . I didn't want to upset you—"

"The police are searching for you right now! Why didn't you at least call—"

"I couldn't, Mom. . . ."

"Lula told us maybe you and Tommy ran off to get married, but then we called Tommy's mother to see if she'd heard anything. When she said he was in South Carolina without you, we didn't know what happened. . . ."

"I'm sorry, Mom . . . I couldn't call you . . . it hurt too much."

A pause. "You and Tommy . . ."

"He broke up with me, Mom. He dumped me."

"Oh . . . I hoped it wasn't something like that. Well, you've had your fights before, and maybe you'll get back together. . . . Don't worry about it. I'll call the police right now and tell them you're coming home."

"I'm not coming back."

"Don't be silly. Come home and rest. You'll get over it."

"I need to stay away for a while. And I'm never speaking to Tommy again."

"You say that now . . . but maybe you'll feel differently later. And if you don't, it isn't the end of the world."

"Yes, it is, Mom."

"Don't say that . . . you're still young. When are you coming home?"

"I'm staying with Kay for a while. . . ." Laura swallowed. "I'm in California."

She heard her mother's gasp as if she were in the next room. "My Lord, Laura. What were you thinking? How did you get there? At least you're all right. But why don't you come back here? I'll have Dad send you a plane ticket."

"I need . . . a break . . . I have to go now. . . ."

"Wait, Laura. You're not safe out there alone. Give me your phone number and address."

Laura heard her mother rummage in a drawer for a pencil. She swallowed. "I'll call you, Mom. Gotta go now."

"Wait!" she heard her mother say, before she dropped the phone in its cradle and the silence in the apartment roared around her. She'd never felt so alone in her life.

She decided to apply for a job at Palm Embers, a fancy restaurant where the waitresses wore uniforms that looked something like French maids, with white lacy aprons. The dishes served in the restaurant bore exotic names, like beef en brochette.

She wore her only dress to the job interview. She gargled with Ricky's Scope, hoping the interviewer couldn't tell she'd been sick again that morning. Walking to the interview, she tried to pretend she was just a girl back home, applying for a job that would give her money to go out to lunch and buy sunscreen and a Jantzen swimsuit.

The interviewer was a woman in her fifties who appeared to be trying to look either younger or classier. She was unsuccessful on both counts. She wore big earrings, a lot of makeup, her dyed red hair piled high on her head. One of her false eyelashes was leaning off her eyelid like a car tilted on two wheels as it turned a corner too fast. Her first look at Laura was obviously dismissive, and she held up a hand as Laura moved to sit down.

"You can stop right there," the woman said. "There are no summer jobs."

Laura finished sitting down. She licked her lips and said, "I don't want a summer job."

The woman emitted a throaty sigh. "I've heard that before. We spend hundreds training them and they work for three months. It's a waste of money, just like it's a waste for me to spend my time talking to you now."

"I want to work more than three months. I need a job . . . for good," said Laura.

The woman glared at her in disbelief. "You look like a high school kid to me . . . maybe college at the most."

"I graduated from business college. I'm nineteen. I've just moved into an apartment and I need to work to pay my rent." Laura told herself it wasn't a lie. She did move into Kay and Ricky's apartment.

"Whaddya graduate in?"

"Medical Secretarial," Laura said hopefully. "I know I could operate a cash register."

The woman's glare continued. "Medical Secretary? Why are you applying here? You should have a secretary job."

"I looked. There aren't any right now." Now Laura's face flushed with a statement that really was a lie.

"But as soon as you find one, you'll go. No, thanks."

"No . . . no . . ." Laura fought for her words. There was no way she could say she didn't want to get started in a job in her field and have her coworkers discover she was pregnant and had to leave. Drawing herself up, she calculated. It was now June. She was two months pregnant. Anywhere she worked, they'd know within a month. She sat back, and looked straight into the woman's eyes. "I could promise at least six months." A nagging doubt reminded her that this was if she worked up until her due date.

"What happens then?" the woman asked quickly.

"What?" Laura asked.

"What happens after six months? That's not very long."

Laura glanced around the room uneasily. What could she say now?

She settled back in her chair, folded her arms in her lap. "I won't miss a day," she said, with a surprising and slow intensity. "And I'll work every night if you want. And the truth is, I have nothing planned for six months from now." That was true. She had no idea what she would do after the baby was born.

The woman seemed to weigh her determination. She exhaled in frustration. Laura saw the long eyelashes move as the penetrating gaze traversed her small frame, then settled on her face. Sighing and popping her gum, the woman opened a folder. Laura glimpsed a schedule of some sort.

"Can you start today?" the woman asked firmly.

"Right now," Laura said. "This minute."

"Come in Wednesday. Two o'clock. That's when training starts. Paycheck after two weeks, can keep your tips immediately. Name?"

"Laura Milligan."

The woman wrote down her Social Security number, glanced absently at her driver's license, and asked her to fill out an application with a few details . . . her address, date of birth, last school year completed. The woman took the application from her, then closed the folder with a snap.

"Wednesday . . ." she said.

"I'll be here." Laura smiled, meeting the woman's gaze, although she felt like shriveling up inside. Well, at least she now had a job.

Chapter Three

After she started working, Laura realized she had no idea how tired it would make her. She worked until midnight, fell into bed, then experienced the rocky nausea of morning sickness as soon as she woke up about ten the next morning. She ate crackers until she felt better, but then it was time to go to work again. She was too tired for almost everything else.

As weeks, and then a month, passed, she gradually realized there was no way she could bring a baby into this life. Who would take care of the baby while she worked? And if she didn't work at this job, there'd be another. And how much would a baby-sitter cost?

She thought, with longing, of the big white Colonial house where she grew up. There was plenty of room for a baby there . . . but good Catholics didn't have babies when they weren't married. She shuddered at the thought of hurting her parents like that—they deserved so much better after all they'd given her. They'd think she was no better than her mother, who had nine children and was dirt poor. She remembered enough of her life before the fire to know that she didn't want her baby to grow up hungry. Thoughts of her own rescue through adoption continued to nag at her.

On her day off she looked up adoption agencies in the

Yellow Pages. The name Catholic Charities stood out right away. A slogan in italics read *Serving good Catholic families throughout the United States*. She found the number she'd written down before, then phoned for an appointment.

Laura woke late the next morning. She refused to ask Ricky for a ride to Catholic Charities, yet cringed at spending three dollars for a cab. She watched the cab meter in despair as her money ticked away. Yet at the same time she sensed that the cab ride was the first peaceful silence she'd felt in weeks. For just a few moments she basked in the firm warmth of the leather seat, the cooperative quiet of the cab driver, and the freedom to look around her without interruption as buildings and streets slid by.

The cab stopped all too soon in front of a tall, imposing redbrick building with few windows. A square white sign said simply CATHOLIC CHARITIES OF CALIFORNIA. Laura stared. She sat motionless inside the cab until the driver said, "This is it, miss."

Laura eased herself out of the cab, which sped off instantly. She stepped closer to the building. Sighing, she stood at the heavy wooden door for a long time before she found the courage to open it.

When she gave her name to a nun dressed in a black habit who sat at a reception desk, she was quickly ushered into a small office room. She studied the crucifix on the wall until she felt she knew each crevice in the metal. Finally an older nun opened the door and came to sit at a desk that faced her.

"How may we help you today?"

Laura's thoughts swam. What should she say now? "I'm pregnant," she said simply.

The nun looked away as she spoke. "As you may know, this is a boarding home for unmarried mothers. You are welcome to stay here while you complete the pregnancy. You may also know that the church believes that if a marriage is impossible, adoption is the proper choice."

Laura swallowed. What was the right response? "I'm thinking about adoption. . . ." she managed.

The nun continued, "It's very hard to decide . . . you will

be offered counseling here, if you choose to stay.''

Suddenly Laura's tears welled. This was so different from where she thought she would be now. ''I have nowhere else to go,'' she admitted. ''I'm staying with a friend, but I can't bring a baby there.''

The nun took her arm. ''Let me help you,'' she said.

The room Laura shared with thirty other unwed mothers was small for the number of beds it held. There was only room for a nightstand between each two beds. She was surprised there were so many girls in the same sad situation. One girl was only eleven years old—a victim of rape. Another was the daughter of a famous country western singer. All day they crocheted baby blankets, listened to an occasional health lecture, and were advised by the nuns that they were doing the best thing they could for their babies.

''The families are already happy that you have made the decision to be here,'' said Sister Clarissa, talking before the group who sat on their beds in the dormitory. ''They will provide your child with so much more than you could ever give him.''

Tentatively Laura raised her hand. When the nun smiled placidly and nodded, she asked, ''Will they honor my request that he be raised Catholic?''

''Yes.'' The nun smiled and nodded again.

''And what about another request?'' Laura persisted.

Now the nun looked at her questioningly.

''I'd like to request that my baby be given his birth father's name. I'd like him to be called Robert Thomas.''

Now the nun didn't answer right away. ''We can inform them of your request. They know that you are giving them a precious gift, and they may choose to honor your wish.'' She reached down and took Laura's hand with her cool fingers.

Laura clung to both the words and the sister's hand, yet at the same time wondered how a stranger could love her baby as much as she did.

During the day, she tried to crochet a yellow baby blanket. At night she often lay awake and listened to the other girls around her, breathing, snoring, talking in their sleep.

Every once in a while, she woke to find a girl missing who went into labor in the night.

It was in the middle of the night when she herself felt a jarring, knifelike pain that tore abruptly through her insides. At first she thought she simply turned her body the wrong way and pulled a muscle. When she moved onto her side, there was a catch in the middle of her stomach, as if the baby didn't quite move along with her. Then, even though she lay still, it tore through her again.

Fear locked Laura in an icy grip, and she looked around to see if anyone else was awake. There was no sign of movement, and the only sound was the even breathing of the twenty-nine girls in the other dormitory beds. Laura tried to lie as still as possible. The pain again. This time she couldn't hold still.

She dragged herself out of bed and leaned against the wall as she eased out of the dormitory room and inched down the hall, step by step. The hall was dark and vacant, lit only by night-lights every few steps. She was almost to the end when the pain racked her again, gripping her like a vise that wouldn't let go. She closed her eyes and clenched her teeth. As soon as she thought she couldn't stand it another second and was about to scream, the pain subsided slightly. But minutes later the inner scraping started again. What was she supposed to do? No one ever said anything about going into labor in the middle of the night.

At the end of the hall she passed the empty classroom where the health lectures were held. The pain seemed to hang on, stabbing her. When she was on the brink of a scream, it ebbed only slightly, then more, until it was gone, leaving her sweaty-faced and gasping.

The pain caught her halfway down the stairs, and again she leaned against the wall, cupping her stomach with both arms, trying to think thoughts that could somehow take her far away.

She said a quick prayer. Then she inched down the rest of the stairs, half gasping and half holding her breath. She reached the foyer where visitors waited. Parents and friends with sad and sympathetic looks sat on those chairs. She never had a visitor. She wrote home, saying she was out here working and trying to take her mind off the fact that she and Tommy broke up. She had written that she was okay, the weather was beautiful, the change of scene was doing her good. She never said anything about a baby.

Another pain. Like the knife again, cutting deep through her body until it turned into a vise that twisted her insides. She doubled over, held her stomach. When she reached the door to the nun's quarters, she pounded on it until she heard the lock turn.

Even through the haze of pain, she saw Sister Mary Josephine's frown. She was breaking rules, she realized. Out of her room after midnight. Out of her room wearing only her bathrobe. She breathed in as a sea of sweat swam on her face.

"I'm in labor," she gasped.

"Laura? You're not due for another two weeks."

"I'm in labor . . . now."

"You're sure?" the nun asked.

"I'm in terrible pain," Laura almost screamed as another spasm seemed to punctuate her words. Finally the nun took her arm and led her to the bed. She called the hospital, then woke the nurse who stayed at Catholic Charities. Sister Mary Josephine took Laura's hand and led her to the nurse's office

"On your back," the nurse said in a firm, clinical tone. This much was familiar from the three checkups she'd been given since arriving here.

"She's dilated," the nurse confirmed. "About four centimeters."

Only four centimeters, and it felt like her insides were ripping out? Laura knew that babies were born at ten centimeters. She had so far to go.

The nun took her arm and led her out of the building to the station wagon in back of the dormitory. "Your suitcase," she asked urgently.

"It's in my room."

"I'll get it. You wait here."

Before she stepped into the car, Laura gazed around her. Somehow this night seemed blacker than any other in her memory. It was like the whole world went away and left her here alone in this nightmare of hurt. In the lull before another pain, she thought of the baby and whispered, "Please don't leave me." She thought of Tommy, of her parents. She was supposed to be a new bride now.

Just as another pain began to streak through her body, she heard footsteps. Someone opened the car door for her, and she let her body drop slowly on the backseat. Two nuns climbed in front, and Sister Anne turned the key. The engine spun to life, and the nun shifted gears fast enough to throw Laura against the cool leather.

Even though this was Los Angeles, the city seemed deserted, streetlights the only interruption to the solid wall of blackness. No one in the car said a word as they sped through the ebony night. When another pain pierced her, Laura gasped and held her hands over her belly. How could this go on much longer? Why did she feel like her entire body was being torn to shreds? Suddenly she felt wetness below.

"Something's wrong—I'm bleeding," she called out to the two women in the front seat.

The station wagon ground to a halt in a section of town filled with banks and office buildings.

Sister Anne leaped out of the car, and opened the door beside Laura. Cool air rushed in, freezing the sweat on her face. The nun touched her arm, forehead, stomach.

"The whole seat and all your clothes are wet. I think your water broke." Sister Anne patted Laura's arm.

Amid her torment, Laura was filled with a brief moment of wonder. It really was happening, the way they said in all the health lectures. Then sadness draped her mind like a sudden cloud. Her baby was almost gone.

The station wagon roared into Saint Ann's Hospital, and the two nuns eased her out of the car. A cool breeze made her shudder. She was soaked from the waist down from her own water.

Sister Anne dashed into the hospital, and almost instantly, Laura saw three men and two women running toward the car pushing a stretcher. Moments later she was lying on her back in a labor room.

It felt as if the pain would never stop. She screamed, railed at Tommy, at the nuns, at life, at herself. For seven hours the pain racked her, and she cried to her parents, Tommy, and God.

Then Heaven gave her a gift. It felt like the earth moved as all the churning inside her focused on one last, skin-splitting pain. She felt the weight she'd carried all these months leave her body in a single wave. Then she heard a tiny, thin cry. Her eyes flew up to catch sight of her baby. Tiny, purple, wet, and perfect. His eyes and bulb-fists squeezed shut. A shock of dark red hair on his tiny head.

Laura struggled to sit up, to drink in the sight with her eyes. The nurses quickly wrapped him in a white blanket, and as they left the room, she heard a last, tiny, heart-shredding cry.

"No—" Laura said aloud. "I can't do this."

A nurse looked back at her in alarm.

"I can't," Laura sobbed. "I can't just let him go."

She heard rushed voices in the hall. Then Sister Anne came and sat by her chair. The nun took her hand. Moments later she said, "You know that the family who raises him will give him everything you can't provide."

"I would try really hard. I still have a job."

"The baby doesn't have a father. He'll be reminded of that his whole life. And what will your parents say?"

"I just can't say goodbye."

"Don't think of it as saying goodbye. You're not giving him away. You're giving him the gift of a secure and happy life."

"But I'll never see him again."

"Just think of him as being safe, with a family who loves him."

"A good Catholic family?"

"Yes, that is a wish we will honor."

"Not a broken home."

"No—all candidates for adoption have long, enduring

marriages. And we will make a special effort to choose a good, Catholic family. Rest, Laura, and try to gather your strength. You will soon start a new life."

"I can't leave. I have to see him baptized." She scrambled to sit up in the hospital bed. "And I want a baby picture of him. Please give me that."

The nun sighed. "It's not our policy to allow you to see the baby after the birth. It only brings more pain."

"Please—it's the only way I'll feel peace." Laura folded her arms in determination. "I won't leave this hospital until I see his baptism. I know they do it in the chapel downstairs. The other girls told me."

The nun shook her head. "That's never been done that I know of. . . ."

"I won't go until I do."

Sister Anne shook her head in frustration, then left the room. Laura waited for her to come back. One hour passed. Two. Twelve hours after the birth, someone brought her a dinner tray with chicken soup, a roll, salad, vanilla pudding, and a can of 7UP. She ate the food listlessly, finding little comfort in the familiar flavors. As the night wore on, her discouragement increased. A nurse came in after dinner, took her pulse, checked her episiotomy stitches, said, "Looks good," and left the room. Occasionally she heard footsteps in the hall, but they never turned in her direction. Her spirit plummeted as hours passed. Her baby was gone. There was no hope.

She lay awake until after midnight, the television in her room droning on unwatched. The hospital nightgown felt limp around her still-puffy frame. She didn't want to look in the mirror, and only eased her weary body out of bed to use the bathroom. Finally, late into the night, she drifted into a fitful sleep, noises outside in the hall occasionally interrupting her blank dreams.

No one woke her in the morning. When she opened her eyes, the room was already filled with sun. A breakfast tray sat on a cart by her bed. She ate the cold toast and and drank the warm orange juice. After she pushed the food away, she decided to erase her pain by going back to sleep.

Though her stitches throbbed with a mild, burning itch, the greatest pain was in her heart. It all happened so fast and now tiny Robert Thomas was gone. She lay on her bed and jerked once in her sleep. She was dreaming of that day in the car, and Tommy's words in her dreams were as sharp-edged as ever. "I can't marry you. It's not my baby."

Suddenly someone jostled her shoulder. Her eyelids fluttered, then she saw a nurse looking down into her face. The nurse put her lips close to Laura's ear and whispered. "Come right now. Your baby's about to be baptized."

Laura yanked herself out of bed so fast that her stitches pulled, but she hardly felt the pain. Her awkward walk didn't stop her from moving quickly beside the nurse. The hall seemed to go on forever. There was no nursery on this floor of this hospital for unwed mothers. The babies were kept somewhere far off, where no one could hear their cries. Was this nurse sneaking her off somewhere secretly? Should she duck down and try to be quiet? Laura wasn't sure, but she followed as eagerly as her wounded body could move. She was about to see her baby.

They turned abruptly and faced heavy double doors with gold crosses. The nurse led Laura inside to a room filled with silent black-draped nuns. Laura was conscious of wearing her hospital gown. She hadn't combed her hair, and its strawberry-blond length fell like a ragged rope to her shoulders.

She was looking around nervously when, abruptly, someone placed a warm bundle wrapped in a blue blanket into her arms. She gasped in surprise and wonder. It was her baby. Gingerly she lifted a corner of the blanket to gaze into the tiny, golden-peach face. Her finger traced a strand of the wispy, carrot-colored hair. She reached under the blanket to envelop the tiny, warm fist inside her own hand. Without thinking, she leaned forward, pressed her face against the soft bulge of the baby's sweet-smelling cheek.

Suddenly a hand was on her back, and Sister Anne, reached over to scoop up the baby and take him from her. No. Not yet. Laura felt a silent scream rise inside her, along with tinglings of helpless panic. Then a wrenching that left her arms empty and aching.

The nurse beside Laura nudged her, and she looked up to see the priest pouring water over her baby's head. The child's sweet, soulful cry rose and echoed to the high and distant cathedral ceiling. Laura's tears streamed as she watched a tiny nun she didn't know take the baby from the priest and leave the chapel.

No! No! Not now and not ever!

Laura was shaking and she fell back onto a chapel bench.

Sister Anne walked to her, stood at the edge of the pew, and held out her hand. Laura grasped the cool flesh, not even bothering to wipe away the freshest flood of tears.

Sister Anne looked in Laura's eyes. "It takes a brave person to do what you just did. You've demonstrated what real maturity is: to give something away that you want very badly, but you know would be better off if it were in the hands of someone else."

Despite her anguish, the words sank in. She was silent as the nuns led her out the door of the chapel and back into the hospital. In the horrifying silence of her hospital room, she felt achingly alone. No one came in to see her. Staring out her window, she watched daylight fade to afternoon, and then dusk. In the midst of her sadness, she wanted to tell someone that a momentous event had taken place in her life. She thought of calling home, or her friends, or the people at work. None of them seemed right. Finally she opened her nightstand and drew out Tommy's address.

She wrote,

Dear Tommy:

Your son was born today. He weighed 7 lbs. 6 ounces. He has your eyes and your chin. He is an absolutely beautiful baby. His birth was hard, but as soon as I saw him, I forgot all about the pains. I gave him up for adoption. I'm having a really hard time thinking that I won't ever see him again. I waited to leave the hospital until after I saw

him be baptized. I've requested that his parents name him
Robert Thomas, after you. He is our son.
  Laura

After writing the letter, she packed her suitcase and
walked out of the hospital without a word to anyone.

Chapter Four

Tommy was sitting on his bunk at boot camp when the letter came. His son was born a week ago. A rush of thoughts filled his mind. His mother would say that Laura was lying. She would tell him to tear the letter up, that Laura was probably trying to trap him. But he knew differently. He was a father. He had a son. Though nothing in the sterile military atmosphere around him had changed, his life would never be the same.

He tried to picture what his baby looked like. He imagined himself playing golf with his son, teaching him to drive a car, and showing him how to take a picture with a camera.

But something about his mental pictures was unrealistic. The image was fuzzy. The son in his mind would never know him. A ripe sadness filled him. He thought about writing back to Laura, but what could he say? Nothing that would ease her pain . . . or his own.

That night he went out and got drunk. The drinks burned, but didn't brighten his outlook. He couldn't leave behind the ache that lay inside.

Sally McFarland never thought she'd feel this happy again. Not while there was still pain from losing Christy, the little girl she and her husband, John, had adopted. The heartbreak from when Christy's birth mother changed her mind and took the baby back was still a fresh wound. They'd never really said goodbye. Christy still hovered in their hearts.

Yet now tears cascaded down Sally's face as the social worker handed her the blanket holding the baby son she never imagined would someday be hers. She drew back the covers to discover a tiny, red-haired doll whose sweet beauty instantly took her breath away.

"Oh—" She gasped. "He's gorgeous." She continued to gaze into the smooth, round-cheeked face until she sensed the social worker's restless need to leave. "How old is he?" Sally asked quickly.

"Four months," said the social worker. "He's been in the foster home since he was born. I have a box with his things."

Later that day, looking through the box, Sally discovered a picture of her baby boy shortly after birth. When she turned the photo over to see who the photographer might be, she discovered that someone had written *Rusty, 1 month* on the back of the photograph. Rusty. She said the name again and again, liking the way it sounded. She and John decided long before that if they ever had a boy, his name would be Robert John McFarland, Junior. They'd christen him with that name, Sally knew. But gently touching the baby's wispy red hair with a finger, Sally sensed that Rusty was the perfect nickname for her new little boy.

"I love you, Rusty," she said, touching his cheek to hers. A tear dropped on the baby blanket, and Sally inexplicably thought of the birth mother who gave her this precious gift.

Laura was alone in the apartment. Ricky and Kay went out for breakfast. They invited her along, but she relished these few minutes to herself. She finished last night's dishes, put in a load of laundry, and was studying the want ads, trying to decide if she could apply for a job using her medical secretary training.

Still, it was hard to think of anything but the baby. Was

he napping now, or was he restless in his new mother's arms? Laura prayed for peace for him.

She knew there was no way she could bring him back to this apartment, or to her family's home in Little Rock. There was no other way. But this hurt so much. And it wasn't getting better.

The doorbell rang.

She walked to the peephole and, looking through it, glimpsed two unfamiliar men in suits.

"Who is it?" she asked.

"Catholic Charities," said an official-sounding male voice

A shiver of fear darted through her. What could be wrong now? Was something wrong with the baby?

Laura flung open the door to greet the two formidable-looking men.

"Catholic Charities," one of them repeated.

Puzzled and fearful, Laura stepped aside and let them come in.

They instantly took command of the room, one sitting in the middle of the small Naugahyde couch, and the other filling the velveteen easy chair.

She herself got a chair from the kitchen.

"We're looking for Laura Milligan," the man on the couch said determinedly, opening a briefcase and setting it on the couch beside him.

"I'm Laura," she said meekly. "Is something wrong?:

"Let me confirm your identification," said the man. "You are the Laura Milligan who recently surrendered a baby boy at St. Ann's Hospital?"

Laura nodded. "But if there's any problem with the adoption, I'd be happy to take him back," she said. "I was in an orphanage myself, and I know that sometimes there are children that no one wants—"

The man interrupted her abruptly, his voice louder and more determined than hers. "Your baby is very much wanted. Many babies given up for adoption in California are mixed race—part black or Hispanic. There are hundreds—thousands—of families who are longing to adopt an all-white infant. Your son is settled in his new home, a good Catholic home with a mother and a father.''

The man's penetrating stare bored into her, and she felt both anger and relief. So her baby was all right. But why were these men here?

"So what do you want me to do now?"

"The problem is that you left the hospital without signing the adoption papers. You could be charged with abandonment, ma'am. Leaving the hospital without caring about the welfare of your own newborn baby."

"No," Laura pleaded desperately. "I care about him so much. I was having such a hard time giving him up that I didn't even think. They let me see him be baptized, and then they took him away."

"They tell all of you unwed mothers about signing papers in the Catholic Charities home. You knew what you were doing," the man accused, leaning closer as his face reddened.

"No . . ." It was the only word that still rose in her weary mind.

The man stared angrily in her eyes, then fumbled in the briefcase.

"I have the papers with me. You are in violation by not signing them the other day. They're here for you to sign now. If you don't, I have no choice but to report you to the police."

The papers looked official and absolute. Termination of Parental Rights. Permission for Child to Be Adopted.

Laura took the pen from the man's hand, wrote her first name, and then stopped. "I can't just sign away everything like this."

The man sighed, shook his head. "I have a paper here that states you lived in the Catholic Charities unwed mothers' home for four months, during which time you received counseling and chose adoption. Now what is the problem here?"

"There's something I need."

"Here are the papers. Everything is in here."

"I want a picture of my baby."

Now the man's sigh turned to anger. "That's not our policy. You're aware of that. You know that things like that can keep you from getting on with your life. It's best not to dwell on what happened to you, so you can move on."

"I want it and I'm writing it on the paper with my signature."

Before she wrote her name, she wrote a phrase above the signature line that read *Catholic Charities agrees to provide a picture of the child to his mother, Laura Milligan.* Then she wrote her signature.

"I can't guarantee anything," the man said.

"It's on the paper. It's part of the agreement," she insisted. "And I'll get a lawyer if I have to."

Now the man sneered at her. "Good luck. You're lucky we didn't just throw you in jail." He stood and gestured at his partner. Then he shoved the the papers into the briefcase, clicked it shut, and walked toward the door. He slammed it with an equal force that hit like thunder and left Laura reeling in her tears.

Laura went back to work at the restaurant and stayed in Kay and Ricky's apartment. She found that what the nuns said was true—that by not having a baby to take care of and stay up with in the night, her physical recovery proceeded quickly. Yet still, her body felt like a traitor to her as it healed—how could it so simply forget the pain that was etched on her heart? She thought of baby Robbie every day. Where was he? Was he crying for her? Was he healthy and growing? She still wrote letters to Tommy, which were really letters to her own consciousness.

Dear Tommy,

Our son is five months old. I wonder how much he's grown, and if he's smiled yet. The one time I saw him, he had your mouth. And your eyes. Tommy, he was so perfect. I'm so sorry you never saw him. If you did, there would be no way you could deny he was your son. I still wonder what would happen if things had worked out between us. I can't hate you, no matter how hard I try; you are still a part of me.

She always stopped for a moment before she signed her name. She remembered the casual notes she wrote him before, when she always signed "love." It didn't seem right any more, so now she chose from "yours truly" and "sincerely."

She always stared at the letter a long time before she slid it in the envelope and mailed it to where Tommy was stationed with the army.

Tommy never knew what to think of the letters. There didn't seem to be a way to answer. How could he tell her that the pain rode inside him, too? That maybe a week, or even a month might pass, without thinking of his son, but other times he thought of him several times in a single day. At first he threw the letters away after he read them, but it was like they burned in his mind, so eventually he kept them, buried in the bottom of his footlocker. Reading this last letter, he tucked it with the others, and called Mary Jo's phone number. What would Laura think if she knew he was dating? Would Laura ever guess that when he called Mary Jo to ask her out for dinner, something inside him was tempted to say, "Hey, girl, did you know you're dating a man with a kid out there somewhere?"

Chapter Five

Laura called Catholic Charities a few months after the men visited her apartment.

"How may we help you?" asked a friendly voice.

"It's about an adoption," Laura said.

"Are you seeking to place or adopt a baby?" asked the voice.

"I already did," Laura replied.

"I'll transfer."

"Post-adoption services," said a voice that sounded like Sister Anne.

"I surrendered my baby several months ago, and I have a question about it."

"What is your question?"

"I'd like to know where my baby is."

Silence.

"Did you stay here in our dormitory before the birth?"

"I did."

"Then you know that all such information is legally sealed. There is no way other than a court order for you to receive such information."

"I just need to know that he's all right."

"What is your name?" the nun demanded.

"Laura Milligan."

She heard shuffling, and a file drawer being opened.

"The adoption placement was successful. There were three home visits before the placement. The couple already have an older child and are happy that she will have a sibling."

"He has a sister. . . ." Laura burst out, then slapped her hand over her own mouth.

She heard the metallic file drawer at the adoption office slam shut. "I've already violated policy by telling you anything. Now go along, as they told you, and start your new life."

She thought of her baby every day, and the pain was constant. Even though she didn't usually drink, one night after the restaurant closed, she found herself walking into a bar called the Main Event and ordering a beer, and then another. The pain over losing baby Robbie didn't exactly go away, but at least it felt fuzzy for a little while. As days passed, she still kept thinking of Robbie, but now found herself going to the Main Event at least three times a week in search of a way to somehow forget.

One morning, when the bleak emptiness of the apartment and memories of last night's argument between Kay and Ricky seemed overwhelming, she thought about moving back home to the big white house where she at least felt welcome to stay. At the same time she hated leaving the state where she knew her baby was living. She didn't dare move away without taking one more try at finding out where baby Robbie was. She scanned the Yellow Pages and made an appointment with an attorney who advertised that his rates were lower than others. She donned the one dress she'd brought from Arkansas and combed her long hair back into a ponytail.

When Laura said that she wanted to find out anything she could about the child she gave up, the attorney sat back in his chair and pursed his lips.

He shook his head, then spoke in a direct voice. "Adoption records are sealed by the court. Have to a get a court order, have a compelling reason," he said simply. "Didn't they tell you that at the agency?" The man's piercing blue eyes stared into Laura's.

Her fingers pressed together as she fumbled to translate

her emotions into words. "I think I probably didn't realize how this would feel . . . to give him away and never see him again. It's like he's died, but I know he's out there somewhere and he might be crying for me. I knew I couldn't take him home—I couldn't even tell my parents. . . ."

"Then why do you want to find him?" The man's blue eyes held frustrated puzzlement. "Most everyone would say you did the right thing. And how could you change that now? You're not married, are you?"

"No . . ." Laura sighed. "I just can't stop thinking about him, and I wonder if there is any way I could get him back."

Now the attorney frowned and shook his head. "This is a hard one. Best interest of the child and all of that."

"I want his best interests, too."

The attorney shook his head again. "Those papers you signed are binding. I'd have to ask for ten thousand up front, and couldn't guarantee a thing. But I might find something . . . where he is or something like that. No way I could say I'd get him back."

Ten thousand dollars. He might as well have said ten million.

Laura fought the impulse to say that if she had that much money to spare, she might not have given her baby to Catholic Charities.

"I'll think about it," she said.

The attorney nodded at her. "It's a hard task," he said, then stood to show her out. "I'm sorry."

She kept thinking about the tiny red-haired baby. Each day she pictured him laughing, sleeping, and lying beside her at night. She kept visiting the Main Event, where the beer would numb her pain, but it wouldn't make her forget.

One night, as she sat staring into her beer mug, loud strains of the song "Boogie, Boogie Down Broadway" somehow bored into her mind past her sad thoughts.

She looked up and caught sight of the band—two young

men playing guitars, a drummer, and a lead singer she couldn't stop looking at. He had brown eyes, curly brown hair, and managed to smile even while he was singing and dancing. Laura blushed and felt a stab of electricity when he caught her eye and winked.

She turned away and brought her attention back to her empty glass. The music ended, and moments later the lead singer sat beside her. "Two beers," he said confidently, starting to laugh as he softly touched her arm.

She was too shy to even look up. "Already had mine for the night," she said.

"You're gonna make me drink both of these?" he asked, pushing one glass toward her. He leaned close until she could smell his sweat along with his citrus aftershave. When she sneaked a look at him, his smile eased into a wide grin. "Aw, come on, tell me your name," he said.

She raised her eyes slowly, looked at him through the glass. "Laura," she said softly.

"Mine's Bryan," he replied. When the jukebox started playing, he said, "Ya gotta dance with me. This is the only dance all night I'm not up there with the guys." He gestured at the empty stage.

"Why you lookin' so sad tonight, pretty lady?" The words were almost a song in themselves, and they brought a lump to her throat. Because she knew that her voice would break if she spoke, Laura simply stood. She held still as he draped a warm arm around her waist and took her hand in his. As he touched her waist, she thought of the flesh there, still loose, almost flapping. Could he tell she'd just had a baby? She blushed at the thought of him guessing her secret.

"Why're your cheeks so red all of a sudden?" he asked as he leaned back to look into her face, grinning at her. "Am I a bad enough dancer to embarrass you?"

Now a nervous giggle escaped her lips. "N-no," she managed.

"There's her smile—knew she had to have one. Know she's got to have a phone number, too. If you give it to me right now, before the music ends, maybe I can memorize it while I'm walking up to the stage.''

Now the blush seemed to fill her whole body, and she felt sweat prickle her sides.

''Come on . . .'' he said again.

As she smiled and shook her head, her lips quivered. ''Don't know you well enough,'' she said finally.

The stage suddenly lit up, and a man stepped to the microphone, shading his face with his hand. ''Bryan—'' he called out in exasperation. At that moment Laura sensed that flirting with a woman in his audience was something Bryan did more than once when he was supposed to be on stage.

She watched each confident step he took up the aisle, noting that his Levi's were tight against his waist and legs. He looked out in the audience and grinned, and, like the man who called out to him, he held his hand against his forehead to keep the light out of his eyes. He seemed to scour the audience with his glance, and she wondered if he were searching for her. As soon as he started to sing, a slow romantic song that made her tingle to her toes, she stood, picked up her purse, and ran outside. She was sweating as profusely as the night she went into labor. And then she realized, for a brief few minutes, she hadn't thought about the baby. Unsettled, and feeling a bit guilty, she walked home, mindless of the dangers of the dark.

For a few weeks Laura stayed away from the Main Event, forcing herself to go home to Ricky and Kay's apartment after work. But she soon realized the two of them had grown to appreciate their evenings alone—and she hated the feeling of tiptoeing around the apartment, trying to stay out of their way as they ate, fought, and watched television. She spent long, uninterrupted evenings alone in her room, without a word from her two roommates. A sad loneliness filled her and hovered over her thoughts each night as the end of her work shift neared. Where could she go now? She had never felt more alone in her life.

• • •

One day when she came home from work, she was surprised to open an envelope from Catholic Charities among the rest of her mail. What could they possibly be writing to her about now? Didn't they have everything they wanted from her? She eased her fingers under the envelope flap. She reached inside and slid out what appeared to be a blank piece of paper. As she unfolded the paper, she gasped as she saw that it held the baby picture she had requested but never thought she would receive.

"Oh!" A cry escaped her throat, and the picture fluttered in her hands. Gulping a deep breath, she flattened the photo on Kay's glass coffee table with both hands so she could drink in the details. Her baby. He was beautiful, and alive, and much bigger than the day she held him for the baptism. He was wearing a yellow romper and miniature tennis shoes and was sitting propped against a background depicting a blue sky with clouds. A shock of apricot-colored hair fell across his forehead. His arms, legs and cheeks were plump and pillowy. She closed her eyes and held the picture to her heart. She opened her eyes again quickly, as if the photo would somehow go away. She ran her finger over his strawberry hair in the picture, lifted it and kissed his cheek. "You are real. . . ." she said.

She kept the picture in her drawer, where she could get at it easily. Sometimes she looked at it five or six times a day. Then sometimes, she would purposely take a break from looking at it, so that when she opened the drawer again, it would seem new, as if it were the day she first received it in the envelope.

She usually looked at the picture before going to work and when she got home. Walking out of Palm Embers and thinking of baby Robbie, she looked up and saw the marquee for a new band at the Main Event. When she realized the new sign meant Bryan had moved on, a fleeting mixture of sadness and relief flooded her mind. She opened the big wooden door of the bar and walked in. Almost instantly someone grabbed her arm.

"There she is—I got her!" a male voice exclaimed, and

she looked up to see Bryan's happy grin as he held her wrist.

"I thought you were gone," she said, hoping her disbelief didn't sound rude.

"Last night here," he explained. "They put up the new signs for the weekend. So you get to see my last performance." He swung her arm. "Last show's the best of all the game, right?"

"I really should go."

"No, you shouldn't. I'm asking you for a date, for right now—and for after I get off. You're not busy, or you wouldn't be here."

"I'm not exactly busy, but I'm not really free, either."

"You're meeting another guy here?"

"Well, no . . . I'm just sort of getting over somebody."

Now he swung her arm again. "I can help you with that. . . ."

"I don't think so."

"Why not?"

"Well . . ." she swallowed, and her throat closed. Seeing the panic in her face, he gestured for her to sit beside him at one of the vacant bar tables. Onstage, other members of Bryan's band were beginning to set up their equipment. "I better let you go get ready," she said finally.

"No—tell me what's wrong," he insisted.

Suddenly her sadness forced itself out, after being held back for months. Her throat seemed raw and aching as she said simply, "I had a baby."

"You mean you're married? You're trying to tell me you've already got a husband?"

She shook her head as two tears squeezed from her eyes. "No. He left me at the last minute. I even had my suitcase packed."

Two band members dressed in black walked up to Bryan. One cuffed him on the shoulder. "Need your help up there, guy."

He waved them off, saying, "Just a sec, man. I'll be right there."

Laura shook her head as if she could shake the tears

away. "You'd better go. And I better go home, now."

As she slid her chair back, he planted one hand over hers, his grip firm so that her fingers could not move. "You're not leaving," he said firmly.

So she sat there, that night, and other nights during other months when Bryan's band came back for return engagements. After he was through playing a gig, he took her out to restaurants that were open late, to midnight movies, for walks along the beach. He was sort of fun and frantic and she had to admire his electric energy that contrasted sharply with her own limp despair. Gradually she began to admit to herself that she looked forward to seeing him and that his effervescent personality gave her a lift. That he was the only person who knew that she'd given up a baby seemed to bond them together, too. But still—

"I need to tell you something," she said one night as he was half-listening to her, and half-joking with Freddy, his manager.

"Yeah . . . what?" he said, patting her leg. "We can head out here in a few minutes."

"That's sort of what I needed to tell *you*. I'm heading out. Moving. I've been evicted."

"So you need to find an apartment?"

"No . . . I'm going home . . . to Arkansas."

Now he gestured to Freddy to excuse the two of them, took her hand, and walked out into the lobby with her. He backed her against a wall, pinned her hands gently back against the gold wallpaper and said, "Now tell me that again."

"Ricky and Kay—who fight every minute—told me they're getting married and they want the place to themselves. I have one week to get out."

"We'll find you a place."

"No, I can't stay here. This is where I had my baby. I need to go somewhere else for a fresh start."

"But you can't go to Arkansas. I don't have any gigs set up there."

"I'm sorry—" She reached out, took his hand. "Let's have our last night out tonight."

"No," he said. "You're not going away."

"I have to."

"We'll get married, and you can go on the road with me."

"No." She shook her head, memories of her last proposal rising within her. "I've heard this story before. Only last time I was supposed to get married and live on an army base. I believed that and look what happened. Better we say goodbye now."

"No," he said again, shaking his head fiercely. "We'll get married after the gig at ten. I'll set it up for tonight and you go on the road with me to Chicago next week." He smiled at her.

"Oh . . . I don't think so . . . maybe I'm not supposed to get married. It didn't work out for me before."

"It's working out this time—" He pointed a finger at her as he headed back into the room where Freddy was waiting. "Tonight at ten-thirty."

"But I—" she said lamely.

"Stay right there," he ordered.

They got married on the Main Event stage, under the hot lights that made her blink. This wedding didn't seem to be even remotely connected to the lavish ceremony she'd always envisioned in the big Colonial house in Arkansas. She wore the cotton navy pantsuit she had worn to work, because he wouldn't let her go home to change. The only witnesses were Freddy and the other band members, and the justice of the peace insisted on a higher fee because he had to work on location and after hours. They toasted with beer, and she didn't have so much as a corsage or a ring. But seeing Bryan's intent look when he said, "I do," and feeling the warmth of his kiss, she suddenly felt like this unexpected turn in her life might work out to be a move toward happiness.

In the coming weeks, as they headed out on the road to Chicago, St. Louis, Memphis, and Nashville, she realized that her grief was ebbing slowly as the miles passed and Bryan finished gig after gig. She kept the photo of Rusty in the pouch in the lid of her suitcase. Some days, she took it out to look at it more than once, and other days, she only glimpsed the red-haired baby's face before she went to bed for the night.

Chapter Six

As *"Boogie, Boogie* Down Broadway" ended, Laura was startled, when Freddy, Bryan's manager, came over and sat next to her at the table next to the stage. After their eyes met, he cupped his hand, pressed it against her ear, and whispered loudly into it. "I need to talk to you." Seeing his gesture, she stood, and followed him out into the lobby of the concert hall.

He paced without looking at her, massaging a gum wrapper into the carpet with the toe of his glistening black boot. His shiny black hair fell onto his sweaty face, and he swished it away with a jerk of his head. He clasped his arms behind his back, against the black Levi's jacket. He walked a few steps away, then trudged toward Laura, head down, as if he couldn't look at her. He stepped close, nearly bumping her, and then he looked up. Shrugging, he said, "The thing is—girls like Bryan."

"No kidding. Tell me another one." Even as she made a mocking face at Freddy, she somehow sensed she should be nervous about what he was about to say.

"The girls come here to see Bryan."

"I never thought they came to see you," she said, hiding her rising worry behind her laugh.

"They buy records and tapes, and go to concerts because they like him. They like to think about him."

"I didn't think they went for the exercise." Somehow the lightness left her voice.

With a wave of his hand, he said, "I don't know any other way to say it. The girls want to think Bryan is available."

"He's not." Laura held up her hand with the wedding ring he'd bought her last month. The gold ring looked like a metal cigar band with a big diamond in the middle.

"They come 'cause they think he is. They don't wanna come see some old married guy. That's boring. They know you got him and they can't have him. They want to see some young, good-looking guy that they can have fantasies about—and think maybe their wish could come true. You know, that he might ask them out and fall in love."

"They can wish all they want, but Bryan's mine."

"We gotta hide that, though, to keep Bryan's career going. Every girl that comes here has gotta think he's about to ask her out any minute. If she thinks that, she keeps buying his records and going to his concerts and thinking a romance is about to start between 'em any minute. If she think's Bryan's married, she's gonna look for some other guy that's not. And he'll *lose money. And so will you.*"

She frowned at him. "I don't understand why you're telling me this. I know girls like Bryan. I don't do anything to stop them. Except the ones that try to take him to bed."

He sighed in elaborate exasperation, and his voice rose. "The thing is, you gotta stop coming down to the club at night. You scare the girls off. And that scares money off. And that hurts Bryan." He punctuated each phrase with a stabbing pointing finger to her shoulder.

Suddenly she shook with anger, and she shoved him away with both arms. "I'll do what I want. You aren't my boss. You can't tell me how to live my life. I'll be there if I want to—"

"You'd better not," he thundered back, shouting into her face. With a sigh, he forced himself to speak with exaggerated politeness. "This is a very competitive business, see. And anything that cuts the competition down, we have to do. And if that means you stay home, you stay home.

What's the big deal? You get to see him after work every night anyway.''

She thought of the hundreds of girls. And what Bryan might do if she wasn't there to remind him of her presence. She said, "I can't stay away."

Again, the stabbing finger. "If you won't listen to me, I'll tell Bryan he's got to keep his wife in her place. You're stupid. It's your own income you're cutting off."

"It's my own marriage I'm watching out for." She was still shaking as she turned and walked out of the club. She could feel his eyes on her as she pushed open the heavy door, and stepped out into the warm summer night without looking back. Shaking with anger and worry, she went home to the apartment to wait for Bryan. It was after midnight when she heard him ease open the front door as quietly as possible.

Taking a breath, she called out, "You don't have to do that. I'm awake."

She heard him toss his keys on the kitchen table, hang his jacket in the closet, and seemingly take forever to walk back to the bedroom to her.

"Freddy told me to stay out of the clubs," she said flatly after he entered the bedroom and stood in the dark.

"Oh . . . he's just thinking of work. Wants to make all the money he can."

"Wants all the women to get to you. . . ."

"You're the only one gets to me." He flicked his tie at her in the darkness, then began to unbutton his shirt.

"No, Bryan . . ." she said, for the first time ever. "I know all those girls throw things at you—pass you their phone numbers—"

"It's just part of the gig. No big deal . . . don't let Freddy bug you. . . ."

"But what about that time I found an earring in the backseat?"

"I can't stop them from trying . . . they're the ones that pay the bills." He hung up his shirt, turned, and spoke with an iron firmness she'd never heard before. "It's all work. Part of the job. Nothing like you and me. Forget it and take

Freddy's advice." He slid his pants off, climbed into bed, and turned to face away from her. "You just have to trust me," he muttered.

"I can't, Bryan. I know Freddy's right. The girls really go for you."

"If you can't trust me, it's your problem . . . not mine. . . ."

She lay there in the dark a long time, long after she heard him start to snore.

After that she couldn't say why she took Freddy's suggestion and stopped going to the clubs where Bryan played. But whether they were in town or on the road, if he played at a club, she waited until he left their house or the hotel room, then she went out to a different club. She hardly noticed her surroundings—whether the club was spacious or cramped, whether the band played rock or country, or whether anyone else noticed she was there. And each time she drank more, going past the two beers to three or more, not noticing how much any more than she noticed the shape or color of the stool where she sat.

Then there was the night she got staggering drunk, and felt the pavement give way beneath her as she began the seemingly endless walk to her car. She fell, skinned her knee. When she tried to stand, shimmers danced in front of her eyes, and she tried to focus on buildings and road signs, but could not. She nearly fell again a few times before she finally leaned against the side of a building and inched her way along.

In the car she sat a long time, leaning back, her eyes closed. The screaming horn of a passing car roused her, and she put the key in the ignition. Scores of oncoming cars zipped by as she tried to ease out from the curb. She waited through an entire song on the radio until the street was empty and dark. Then she turned the steering wheel and swung wildly out on the road, crossing the median and narrowly missing a Jeep that whizzed past. She didn't brake fast enough as she approached a light, then slammed her foot on the pedal as the car edged frighteningly close to a

Cadillac stopped in front of her. A few blocks later she swung wide in a turn and found herself face-to-face with a sea of car lights and blaring horns heading in her direction. She was now on the wrong side of the road. She yanked the steering wheel back, swerving the car across the road where it slammed the curb with a jarring, scraping thud that knocked her chin against the steering wheel and mashed her thigh against the gearshift. Then she sat, dazed, in the mangled car as lines of other cars surged past, honking at her to move her car out of the way.

She only half-heard the honking and swear words thrown in her direction. More sober now, she began to cry. Her eyes stung, and all her joints ached. She felt blood dripping from her chin, and her thigh throbbed in pain. She stared out the window and realized she had no idea which street this was, how late it must be, or where she was before she turned onto this street filled with office buildings and parking meters. She stared out the window a long time before she slunk down in the seat, determined to wait until morning.

At first she hardly felt the hand on her shoulder. The touch blended in with the pain that seemed to scream throughout her body. But then, someone began to tap insistently near the shoulder seam of her blouse, and she stirred, shaking her head and groggily battling to open her eyes. The shimmers were still there, along with dizziness and aches. She'd almost fallen back to sleep when a voice cut through her pain and the early morning stillness.

"Miss." A man's voice, firm and forceful. When she didn't respond, he kept tapping at her shoulder. Her eyelids felt like they were made of cement, but she concentrated on forcing them open to see who this person was who demanded her attention.

Her eyelids flickered, then finally made it fully open to stare at the navy blue uniform of a policeman. "Miss!" he demanded again, this time pressing harder against her shoulder blade.

"Yes?" she said, staring out, trying to see his eyes through the tinted glasses he wore.

"Are you hurt, miss? Should I call an ambulance?"

"I don't know," she said. "Just a minute." Touching her chin, she felt that the blood there was now dry, a grainy powder. Her fingers gingerly played against her thigh, where needles of pain ignited. "I don't think I need an ambulance," she said.

"We need to report the accident. Please step back to my car with me," he commanded.

Sitting in the car beside him, she saw he was holding a chart on a clipboard.

He said, "Wait a minute—your eye looks blackened. There's a big bruise."

"I'll look at it when I get home."

"Does your head hurt?"

She stopped to consider. "Everything hurts, " she said finally. "I'm still in pain from losing my baby." As they sat in the car her words poured out in waves and he didn't interrupt anything she said, about Tommy, about Bryan, about coming here to California, and saying goodbye to her baby and feeling all alone now.

She talked until she felt as if she'd told him everything that happened in her life. Finally she looked into his face, realized she was talking to a real person, and said, "I'm sorry."

He cleared his throat. "I think you need to talk. Probably to someone besides me. I can tell you've been through a lot. But right now, we need to fill out this accident report. Can you show me where you were traveling?"

She shook her head. "I couldn't really say. But probably straight—I mean I don't think the car was facing a different way before I hit the gutter."

Now his voice acquired a hard edge. "Were you drinking last night?"

She was suddenly aware of her rumpled clothes, a staleness hovering in her throat and mouth. Her hand flew to her hair, which she sensed was unruly and wild. Could he smell her breath? Or her clothes?

"Yes." she said finally, staring at her hands lying limp on her rumpled skirt.

He sighed. "I could arrest you for reckless driving. And for driving while intoxicated."

"Please—I didn't—"

He held a hand up as if to ward off her response. "But I think what I'll do is to give you a warning and advise you go to counseling. And try to get past this crisis without alcohol. Next time, you might not just hit the side of the road."

She was silent as he climbed out of the car. He winced at the dent above her tire. Then he kneeled and pulled the fender straighter. "You should be able to drive this now," he said.

"Thank you," she said simply. "It felt good to tell someone what I'm going through."

He nodded crisply. "Just don't let me find you out here another night."

She drove home listlessly, her head aching as she heard the scrape of the bent fender against the tire. She imagined falling into bed and wanting to sleep for a week.

She was surprised to hear music and see lights on in the apartment. Her headache and exhaustion seemed to intensify as she thought of having to talk to people rather than just going to bed.

She opened the door and a long whistle erupted at her. "Hoo-ee! Where's she been all night?"

"Looks like she's been in a fight or something."

It was Bryan and Freddy and a couple of the band members.

"For your information, I was in a car accident."

Freddy jumped to his feet. "Yeah, look at her. She's beat up, all right. Look right here—" He ran his fingers along a bruise at the side of her face. Her anger rose and she slapped his hand away.

"You won't let me come see you, so I have to go someplace!"

She was surprised to hear anger in Bryan's voice, too. "You could stay home and watch TV. You could go to a friend's house. You can stay out of the clubs."

"No, I can't. I can't stay here and think of all those girls after you. I have to get out."

"It's too dangerous. You're turning into a drunk! You'll total the car and kill yourself next time."

"If I do, it'll all be your fault." She flounced away, but not before a sob racked her, and she began to cry, for herself, for her baby, and for her marriage to Bryan, which now seemed sad, desperate, and hopelessly bleak.

After that, although her anger held, she never went back to a club at night. In cities across the United States she'd spend the night in the hotel coffee shop, or wander aimlessly near the hotel, looking in shop windows or buying cheap fast food. How could anyone ever think it was glamorous to be married to a rock star? What was appealing about it when all she could do was stay away from him?

Chapter Seven

Whenever they left Los Angeles, she thought of Robbie, her baby. Somehow leaving the state and distancing herself from him geographically felt like leaving him behind all over again. As long as she stayed in Los Angeles, it seemed as if there was somehow a chance that she might see him again. Maybe she'd be filling a bag with oranges at the grocery store, and glance over to the next cart, and catch a glimpse of a red-haired three-year-old licking a sucker. Or maybe she'd stroll through the boys' department at Penney's, and see his mother buying him a new pair of jeans. It was even possible that he lived somewhere close by, and one day she'd see him out mowing the lawn and riding his bike. It was her only hope.

She kept her baby's picture in the top drawer of her dresser. By now one edge was ragged from the constant touch of her fingers, and once she'd accidentally bent the lower right edge when she closed the drawer fast. She didn't take it with her on the road—when she came back and looked at it, it was like meeting Robbie all over again. Seeing the picture was as close as she could get to calling him on the phone and telling him his mother still loved him.

She often lost track of time when they were on the road. There was no calender to look at, and she and Bryan never discussed the itinerary. She was often half-asleep when he came in late at night, either high with excitement or exhausted, smelling of cigarettes and beer. Still, she couldn't fall deeply asleep until she felt him climb into bed beside her. Consequently, she often slept in the next morning, ate a late breakfast, and went out for a walk. It was something like when she went on trips with the Milligans growing up. One long, unstructured day followed by another. The days blended into one another, stretching out until she lost track. Her hours were filled with riding in the van to the next city where the band was booked, registering at the hotel, swimming in the hotel pool, and eating in restaurants, sometimes with Bryan and other times alone.

She almost forgot the tour was going to Little Rock until she began to see the exit signs on the freeway. Without thinking, she said, "Bryan, take me home. I want to see my house." She talked with her parents briefly by phone from each new city, but hadn't been back to visit her house since she left.

"The guys are tired, Laura. We've got to get to the hotel to check in."

"It would only be five or ten minutes out of the way. Please. I'll just sleep there tonight." As soon as she saw familiar sights, she was filled with a strange, longing ache that culminated in a sweet sadness. How long was it since she talked with her parents and told them how she felt?

She held her breath as the van drove closer and closer to the freeway exit. Would he let her go visit? She was prepared to beg. To her surprise, Bryan gestured to the left, and the car headed up in the direction of her house. Soon she saw the wide streets, big lawns, and carefully tended gardens that she remembered from growing up. When the van finally turned in at the driveway she hadn't seen in three years, there was no way she could stop her tears. Somehow their warmth was comforting against her cheeks. The massive white-columned house looked bigger than in her memory—and definitely more beautiful and majestic. Her shoulders were shaking, but she didn't struggle to hold them still, nor did she lift a hand to brush aside the tears that flowed until they dripped off her chin. She only drank in the heavenly sight of her old home and wondered if there was any way she could somehow disappear inside the house, inside the life she knew before, and never come back.

Someone said, "Forget the motel. Let's just check in here. . . ." but Laura didn't bother to look to see who it was, even after someone else laughed.

"I just need my small suitcase," she said, and when Bryan grumbled, her head didn't even turn in his direction.

She rang the bell and waited for someone to answer the door. She swallowed, wondered what she would do now if no one was home. Suddenly Lula opened the door, caught sight of her, and screamed. A fresh flood of tears drenched her cheeks as she and Lula clung to each other, sobbing until it seemed they would never stop.

"What you doin' here?" Lula asked, stepping back and surveying Laura from head to toe.

"I'm here to visit for the night."

"You ought to come back to stay." Lula enveloped her with her arms again, and Laura once more felt the reassurance that nothing bad could happen with this woman in the world. With their arms about each other's waists, they turned and headed into the house. Laura called over her shoulder to Bryan, who stood in the driveway, "Go on to the hotel. I'll be here. Come back and get me tomorrow." She heard someone slam the door of the van and then glanced briefly back again as the engine caught and the van surged out of the driveway.

She and Lula walked down the hall into the living room, where her mother and father sat on the couch. Why didn't she see how beautiful her mother was when she herself was a child? Why did she never sense the pain her mother must have felt at never being able to have her own baby? Understanding flooded over her as she comprehended what heroes these two people were, and how rare and fortunate she was even to know them.

They rushed to hug her. "Laura!" her mother exclaimed.

"It's been so long! I've missed you so much. I wondered if you'd ever come back."

"I wanted to—but with Bryan's schedule . . . this is the first time I could get here."

"How long can you stay? We'd love to get all of the family together," her father said.

Suddenly fear enveloped her, and she wondered if her family would somehow guess what she'd been through if they saw her. Yet at the same time, a visit with her secure, serene past seemed like a warm bath in the midst of a sea of upheaval.

"Let me call Bryan—at the hotel," she said. When he told her the gig was three nights, the thought of three days at home seemed like a welcome retreat.

Yet during the second day, as she stood limply at the end of the couch, she glimpsed her father's blue-eyed penetrating gaze. He kept looking at her until she fumbled with the collar of her shirt and finally sat down. He was still staring. When their eyes finally met, he said, "You look different."

A lump in her throat. "You just haven't seen me in a long time."

He shook his head. "It's not that. You've changed."

"My hair is longer?" Her heart thudded as she flipped the strawberry tail of hair upward.

"No—" Now he stood and stepped toward her. "You've gained weight or something. Around your waist."

She folded her arms over her stomach, tried to shrug him off.

But his stare continued. "You look very different. Like you gained three sizes. My little girl who was always so tiny. What happened?"

Her shrug was now halfhearted and a sour taste found its way into her mouth.

"You were our skinny little girl. Now you're as big as your cousin Janet. How can that be?"

"Daddy—" Her voice broke, and all the pain she held since the day Tommy said he couldn't marry her filled her mind with a rush. Her chin wobbled with emotion. "Oh, Daddy—Daddy. I didn't want to tell you."

Now concern accompanied the curiosity on his face. He looked old, tired, and worried about her.

"Daddy, I look like this because I had a baby. It was the worst thing that's ever happened to me, and I feel so bad. I couldn't tell you and that's why I had to leave. . . ."

She'd never seen her father cry before, but now large, round tears escaped his eyes and his lips trembled as he fought to press them firmly together.

"Laura—" He held out his arms to her, and she went into them, feeling small like she had as a girl, yet sensing she never again would be as safe and free as in those early years. Her mother came up behind them, and a fresh flood of tears soaked Laura's face as her mother's gentle hands caressed her hair, her shoulders, the small of her back.

She couldn't say how long they stood that way before they walked to the couch and sat, their sobs and sniffs mingling in the silence.

Her mother put her arm around Laura's shoulders. "When did you have the baby, dear?"

Laura's lips quivered. "Two and half years ago. In January."

"In California?"

"Yes . . . at the Catholic Charities Hospital . . . St. Anne's. Mama, they promised they would give him to a good Catholic family."

"You gave him up for adoption?"

Laura nodded, shivering underneath her mother's arm.

"Oh, honey, I'm so sorry you had to go through this. But—you know that we adopted you. We must have faith that a family who loves him as much we love you will now raise him. Him . . . the baby is a boy?"

Laura nodded.

"My grandson," said her father.

Laura said, "A boy, and Tommy's mother said it couldn't be his, because he is sterile . . . but I swear I hadn't been with anyone else . . . until I got married."

Now she pressed her face into her mother's shoulder, felt

her mother's shoulder blade absorb her sobs. She knew tears were falling, dampening her mother's blouse. Once she felt her mother sigh, but none of the three of them made a move to get up off the couch until it was nearly dusk.

For the next two days no one mentioned the baby. Her mother nurtured her as if she was ill, asking Lula to serve Laura's favorite casseroles and let her sleep late in the morning.

She woke up on the third morning to find her mother sitting at the end of her bed, the way she did when Laura was a child. The look of pure, gentle concern on her mother's face brought tears.

"He was a beautiful baby, Mama," she said.

Her mother touched her hair. "So were you. A beautiful little girl. I still remember."

"He had red hair like Daddy always likes, and big blue eyes. . . ."

Now she saw a tear on her mother's face.

"I probably shouldn't talk about him."

"No, you should. . . . It will help you sort things out."

"The thing is, I know he is their baby now. But I still feel like he's mine. I keep wondering if he's crying for me."

Her mother's face crumpled, and Laura thought back to her own past. "Oh, Mama. I need to say something. I want you to know that I'm so glad you took me in. I think my birth mother did the right thing. She couldn't take care of me—and I couldn't take care of Robbie when he was born."

Her mother's hand reached out. "Laura, there's something I never told you. They told us, at the orphanage, that your mother would walk down there and stand behind a tree across the street. She would wait for hours, just hoping to catch sight of you—" Her mother's throat caught. "But she never crossed the street. She knew you were our baby, but she never forgot. That's what you're feeling now. It's normal. It's okay."

Laura couldn't speak.

"I'm sure your mother has never forgotten you, either,

Laura.'' Her mother patted Laura's knee and rose. "I know I never could. I've been waiting years for you to come back and see us. I just wish I could have been with you when the baby was born.''

"I saw him be baptized, Mama. I heard him cry.''

"We can still pray for him. We can keep him in our hearts . . . and maybe you will see him someday.''

"I tried to get him back, Mama. I even went to a lawyer.''

"If you are meant to see him, someday you will. . . .''

"He'll be a gorgeous man. He'll have Tommy's smile. . . .''

"And your red hair. A good combination.'' Her mother squeezed Laura's fingers and stood. "We were lucky to get you, Laura.''

"No . . . I was the one who was lucky,'' Laura managed before her throat swelled and she knew she was about to cry.

When Bryan came to pick her up the next day and her mother hugged her at the door, she truly didn't want to let go. She longed for a day from her childhood—shopping downtown and buying new shoes, eating in the mall tea room, coming home to watch cartoons until her mother fixed dinner. Thinking of the days gone by brought a sweet sadness, making her wish she'd appreciated the days of her youth more while they took place. "Come back soon,'' said her mother. Though her lips smiled, there was no way she could hide the sadness that hovered in her eyes.

As she and Bryan set out on the road again, Laura was filled with a deep sadness knowing that her mother shared her feelings. Her mother, who had saved her from the orphanage, the last person she hoped to hurt, but probably the only person other than her birth mother who could understand how she felt. Before, it always seemed that she could go back home sometime and be a little girl again if life became too rough. But now that her mother knew her secret, it was as if a torch were passed. Now she'd felt the truly adult pain of giving up a child the way her mother had felt the hopeless sorrow of never being able to give birth. She could no longer turn back. She could visit her home again, but there was no way she could once more become the little girl she used to be.

Dwelling on her sadness, she continued to lose track of the time and days she spent in the van. Late nights, restaurant meals, and a calm resignation in her relationship with Bryan. Nearly three months passed before she suspected that she might be pregnant.

Chapter Eight

Tommy, who everyone now called Tom, headed out of his job at the computer company and walked briskly to his car. The end of this day was like the end of many others. After lunch he started looking forward to the bottle of vodka in the glove compartment. He started drinking it on his way up the interstate, and by the time he was ten miles from work, he was already high and looking forward to a night in his BarcaLounger. He continued to drink during the six o'clock news, becoming increasingly drunk on his way to a blackout. But no matter how much he drank, no amount of liquor could erase the memory of the son he never saw. Laura still wrote to him sporadically—months or a year could pass, or he'd get a letter after receiving one three weeks before. He never wrote back. He couldn't let her know that he thought his mother was wrong all those years ago. He didn't have to see the baby to know in his heart that he was the father.

Just like the letters from Laura, thoughts of his son rose sporadically. When he was golfing, he'd see another father and son playing golf together and he would wonder if, had things happened differently, that could be him and his son. He mostly pictured his son as a baby in his mind, yet there were times when he calculated how old he'd be now, and tried to imagine what he looked like.

He was thinking of the baby today as he sped along the freeway. He didn't see the flashing red light behind him, or hear the siren when it first blared into a whine. He zoomed along even as the sheriff's car surged up behind him, then drove alongside him in the next lane. The officer honked his horn, frowned, and angrily gestured at him to pull over.

Tom gradually slowed the car to a stop. Looking in his rearview mirror, he caught the disturbing sight of the sheriff's car behind him, the red light still revolving on top even after the scream of the siren died. He watched as the sheriff wrote on a clipboard, stepped outside his patrol car, and strode up to the side of Tom's car. Tom waited until he got there to roll down his window.

"Driver's license," the sheriff demanded.

Tom cursed his fingers for shaking as he reached in his pocket to draw out his wallet. He opened it and handed it to the sheriff. An eternity passed as the officer studied his license.

"Step outside, sir," the sheriff's voice barked.

Tom eased himself out of the car, then fell in a heap against the closed driver's side door.

"Been drinking?" the sheriff snarled the question.

Tom didn't answer.

"And I clocked you at ninety."

Tom couldn't remember the last time he looked at the speedometer. What could he answer?

"I'm citing you for speeding and DWI."

"I'm almost home. I'll—I'll slow down," Tom said.

"How far is it to your home, Mr. Dutton? I see here you live on Crandall Avenue."

"It's off the next exit," Tom said. Actually, it was two more exits before he usually left the freeway, but if he slid off the freeway now, he could drive home on the side streets.

The sheriff seemed to weigh his decision. "So you work out this way? Take this road home every day?"

Tom nodded.

"I'm out here every day, too. Mr. Dutton. I'll be watching. And next time it won't be just a ticket. It'll be your license. And the next time it'll be jail.''

Shaken, Tom climbed in his car. He trembled, his fingers drumming against the steering wheel. After the sheriff drove off, he breathed a sigh of relief. And as soon as the patrol car was out of his sight, he opened the glove compartment and took another slug of vodka. It was true. He was almost home.

That night his wife, Carol, was searching through his pants to send them to the cleaners when she found the ticket. It shook in her hands when she brought it out to the living room and waved it at him.

"Tom!" she said in both a firm and scared voice. "This is serious."

By now he was just coming off his afternoon drunk and dismissed her with a wave of his hand After all, she was standing in front of the TV.

When she didn't move, he groaned, "I talked to 'im. It's okay."

"It's not—" He could hear that a swell of emotion was rising in her voice. "Tom, you drink way too much and you can't handle it. You'll get killed."

He shook his head.

"Tom, you have to stop. I can't stay here with you if you're like this."

For the first time since she spoke, his eyes focused on hers. "I'm all right!" he shouted back at her. "You don't have to tell me what to do. And as far as that goes, when are we going to have that baby we talked about two years ago?"

Now it was Carol who backed away, through her spotless and elegant living room into the perfectly organized kitchen.

Tom stumbled out into the kitchen after her. "We were going to have a baby, remember. What's happened to that?"

He finally caught up with her in the bedroom, where she stood silently folding towels in neat thirds. "I said, what's happened to that?"

She looked up at him, her small chin quivering. "I don't want to have a child, Tom. Not now, not ever, and not with you."

The words stunned him, hit him like a slap. Carol never wants to have a baby. He always thought they'd have a child, now that they were getting older and were financially ready. He suddenly realized that after the one discussion where they decided to wait until later, they hadn't talked about it in years. Now he knew she never intended to get pregnant. She didn't want his child. She didn't want him. His emotions from that long ago day with Laura surged back over him, and he had chills. Now he knew how she felt when he rejected her.

Chapter Nine

A contentment settled over Laura as the days in the van passed. As she grew gradually more pregnant, sitting and watching the country go by outside her window seemed an appropriate way to wait for the baby. Yet she kept thinking of Robbie. Where was he now? Was there any way he could possibly sense that he was about to have a brother or sister? If she concentrated in her mind, was there some way Laura could communicate that message to him?

In ways she felt more alone than she ever had in her life. Being pregnant seemed to separate her from the band members—no one joked and jostled with her the way they did before. And when the band canceled its next trip to Little Rock, Laura was surprised to feel relief rather than regret, somehow knowing that this pregnancy would also refresh her parents' memories of the earlier, sadder birth.

As the baby grew inside her and she got bigger, she worried more about Bryan and the female fans that threw themselves at him. She found a bracelet in the van one night, and another time, a pair of girl's moccasins. There were phone numbers with no names written on envelopes and pads of paper. A few times too often, the caller hung up when she answered the phone.

But Bryan was asleep beside her the night she felt like her insides were suddenly burning up with pain. She lay awake in the dark a long time listening to him breathe. When the scraping pain streaked through her once again, she caught sight of an array of stars through a crack in the curtain. She focused on the stars, imagining them as the painful needles that seemed to prick the inside of her stomach. She wished that Bryan would sense her pain, wake up, and ask what he could do to help. But he slept soundly. She had no idea how late he came in the night before. Laura just lay there and waited for the pain to subside, finally she turned over and fell asleep.

The pain again. Like an ice pick scraping, and then a vise, tightening, twisting her stomach.

"Bryan," she said.

He lay like a brick in the bed, soft whistle-snores evenly punctuating his breathing. Her voice had no impact on the even rising and falling of his chest. She waited, lay on her back, stared again at the stars.

The pain, even sharper, jarring her insides.

"Bryan." This time she poked at his shoulder, leaned up, and half-whispered in his ear.

Bryan mumbled in his sleep, turned over, and settled back as if he would never wake.

She shook his shoulder, patted his cheek, and didn't stop touching him. "Bryan . . ."

"Whaaa?" His eyes blinked like a candle's flicker, then closed again.

Now she raised her voice as the pain again sliced through her. "Bryan, I'm having the baby!"

He shuddered, shook, and abruptly sat up, palming the sides of his face with both hands. "What?"

"The baby, Bryan. I have pains one after the other. The baby's going to be born any minute."

He jumped up off the bed, fumbled on the bureau for his keys, then searched under the bed for his shoes. Sliding his feet into the loafers, he again fought to wipe sleep from his eyes. "Let's go."

"I'm not dressed."

"The baby's almost here—let's go!"

By now her stomach felt like she had a never-ending

cramp. She struggled to slide into the huge maternity Levi's without tripping whatever lever caused the pain. Bryan took her arm almost roughly, steered her through the night to the van. The inside of the van smelled of beer, smoke, and stale food. She struggled to hold her stomach still lest any movement start the pain again. She guessed they were half-way to the hospital when a huge pain like a sword cut through her, twisting her uterus as if it would never let go. How did other women cope with this? Laura thought of the only thing she'd ever seen another woman do. Her scream, painful and pleading, pierced the night.

"Stop that! You scared me to death!" shouted Bryan. He pulled the van over to the curb. "Are you going to make it?" he asked her.

She shook her head, waved him off.

"Do I need to find someone right here?"

"No . . . just drive."

When they arrived at the hospital, Bryan ran in to get some help. Almost immediately, men with a stretcher raced to the van.

"Here," they said, easing her on to the white, blankety softness. Someone touched her forehead with a cool hand, and she felt another hand on her wrist. As the stretcher surged toward the emergency room door, the pain increased. She felt someone rip off her jeans and cover her with a blanket.

"It will feel like a bit of ice at your back, and possibly a prickle around your knee," someone said. There was a poke near her spine, then, moments later, her legs numbed, feeling heavy as sandbags. The pain now seemed to be buried, submerged, no longer on the attack.

A doctor's face hovered over her. He smiled and reached beneath the blanket. "We'd like to have you push," he said. Push? The anesthetic made it feel like her insides were made of rubber. Pushing was like trying to gain footing on a slippery sidewalk. She pushed until her head shook. Sweat sprang on her forehead

"Again," said the doctor.

Gripping the handrails, she pushed until she felt her body would split in half.

Then, suddenly movement, a surge between her legs. Wetness, then weight, then a squall.

"There she is!" the doctor called out cheerfully, as if this were the Miss America Pageant. He held up the tiny, purple-pink bundle. Tiny pillowy cheeks. Strands of wet, rust-colored hair. The new baby looked exactly like Robbie.

Tiffany Ann Stewart. Robbie, you have a sister. I pray that you will see her someday.

Suddenly, she remembered Bryan. She looked around for him. His familiar grin was topped by eyes filled with awe. "She's gorgeous!" he said. "Can I hold her?"

Was this the man who never held a baby before? Laura sighed with the realization that her husband appeared to be, once again, in love. If only this new affection for his daughter could somehow quell the constant need for other women. Despite the look of pure ecstasy on his face, worry and anxiousness still inhabited Laura's mind as if they might never leave.

Laura struggled to stretch the tape across the diaper's two corners as the speeding van bumped and jostled. As months passed, Laura kept wondering why no one ever told her how hard it would be to take a baby on tour. How a messy diaper could stink up the van for hours until they stopped for a lunch break. How other hotel guests would complain if Tiffany cried too long at night. Or how the other band members would get angry if she cried during the day when they were trying to sleep. Or what it was like to pack a baby's things to travel, and to have her baby sleep in a different crib every two or three days.

Laura grew weary from worry, nervousness, and exhaustion over being up with a new baby. She didn't have any strength left to worry if Bryan had girlfriends. Finally she insisted that Bryan get an apartment in Los Angeles, where she and the baby would stay while he the band toured. What difference did it make if she was on the road or not? She was still forbidden from going to the clubs where he played.

Because she and Bryan were together so seldom and she thought she always took precautions, Laura was shocked to discover that she was pregnant again. Her worry over Bryan's traveling life was tempered with a kind of serene pleasure that at least Tiffany wouldn't grow up alone. For a few months Laura basked in being pregnant. She mixed herself fruit shakes, read long novels with her feet propped up on a stool, and spent hours lying on the bed studying the simple beauty of Tiffany's face.

Her second birth was completely different from the first two. Knowing Bryan was on tour and her labors were fast, the doctor checked her into the hospital to induce the birth. Through the calm haze of a local epidural anesthetic, she felt both excited anticipation and sad memories of Robbie's emergency birth in the hospital. Now he would be three . . . no . . . three and a half years old. She pictured him dressed in a baseball hat and striped T-shirt, a redheaded boy with a friendly smile. The image was so real in her mind that she was startled when the doctor smiled at her. "We're heading for the birthing room," he said, in a hopeful, light-hearted tone.

Her second baby was also a girl, this time with wisps of blond hair. Laura named her Amelia. As thrilled as she was with a second daughter, she couldn't help but think of her only son, out there somewhere, who now had another new sister. She called Catholic Charities again and again, trying to think of new ways to pose the question about how her son was doing. The response was always the same—that there was no way anyone could open the file for her.

As five years passed, and she saw Bryan only every few weeks, Laura clung to her love for the two little girls. Though their father was gone, they were always there for her, hugging her at night while the three of them watched TV, eating dinner together at the kitchen table, keeping her company while she cleaned the apartment. When Bryan came home, his excitement in seeing the girls always gave her hope that possibly their marriage would never be threatened by the women she suspected he still saw on the road. His love for his daughters made her think that maybe someday they would be a family, with a house in a suburban neighborhood, and a father who came home every night to have dinner.

In a way it made sense the night Freddy told her the band would be staying at his apartment after arriving back in town at two A.M. Whoever was driving the van would probably appreciate just being able to stop at Freddy's rather than having to stop at everyone else's apartment.

But Laura was uneasy. She tried to quiet a rising tide of worry as she tucked the girls in bed. Then she called the sitter over and asked if she would be willing to stay all night. She closed the apartment door silently and headed out.

It felt strange to drive at night again, and reminded her of her earlier days when she'd drive from one club to another, stop to spy on Bryan, and stay until Freddy frowned at her. She felt a bittersweet nostalgia for those days when being the wife of a rock musician still held the hint of hope, romance, and excitement.

She found a parking space right in front of Freddy's place. When a man in front of her entered the apartment building door and held it for her so she didn't have to buzz, she moved quickly, thinking that now she could surely surprise Bryan.

She knocked on the door quietly. When there was no answer, she waited, shifting from one foot to the other. She knocked again. Still no answer, and no sound. She began to feel foolish, thinking maybe they hadn't even arrived yet, and now she had paid a baby-sitter and driven all this way.

She was turning to leave when the door suddenly thrust open. It was Bryan dressed in his bathrobe. He obviously tied it in a hurry, and through the slit, she could see he probably was naked moments earlier.

"Surprise!" She rushed forward to give him a hug, but felt as if she slammed into a brick wall when he held her off, gently urging her back toward the door as if he wanted to push her outside.

"What's the matter, Bryan?" She asked, worry and concern rising in her voice. "I haven't seen you in three weeks. I came down here to—"

"You can't stay here. This is Freddy's place."

"Then come home with me—you can see the girls when they first wake up—

"Shh!" Bryan placed a finger to his lips and hissed harshly.

There were sounds from behind him in the apartment. "Bryan, what is it?" The voice sounded curious, concerned, and definitely female. Laura stared in horror as a slim, young, dark-haired woman stepped past Bryan, tying her bathrobe as she finally caught sight of Laura.

"I'm his wife," Laura muttered through clenched teeth at the young woman.

"Bryan?" the young girl's initial look was startled, but her shock dissolved into a half-giggle that made Laura's blood boil.

"You never asked to come down here. You're supposed to stay away from me while I'm working," Bryan said, now stepping backward to try to urge the young girl back into the apartment.

"*This* is work, Bryan?" Laura's voice rose to a shout, and she heard a door open down the hall. "Bryan, I'm leaving you. This minute—"

"Oh, Laura, wait—"

"I'm taking the girls. We'll be gone first thing in the morning—"

"Not the girls—" Bryan protested, but Laura didn't answer. As tears dripped along her cheeks, she ran back to the car. She knew she would drive to the house and start packing the moment she got there. There was no way she could sleep tonight.

Chapter Ten

Tom sighed in despair. Was it his drinking or her not wanting to have kids that finally broke up his first marriage? He couldn't say, and the truth was, neither he nor Carol took time to ask. Now he was married to Sally, and she was an alcoholic, too. They fought, but not about alcohol. And at least drinking wasn't affecting his work. As materials manager for a major corporation, the promotions were sure and steady. He now was responsible for millions of dollars in computer inventory. All that, and he often came to work drunk or coming out of a drunk. It should have been satisfying to pull off the ruse, but really, he felt like he'd sort of earned it. Somehow, he managed to do all his work and keep drinking.

Like this morning. He had a meeting with his boss and the human services manager. He was probably getting another promotion, though his evaluation wasn't for seven months.

However, there was an air of dread from the moment he stepped into the boardroom, although it was just Clint Ames and Ray Tanner. The three of them played golf together every other Friday. Why didn't they just talk to him then? What was this meeting all about?

"Hello, Tom. We need to talk to you about something serious."

"What's that?" Probably an inventory overload or maybe somebody up on four missed a deadline again. But why were they calling a meeting?

"Tom, we have reports that your performance is unacceptable for this level of management at the corporate level. . . ."

Sweat streamed down Tom's side, yet at the same time he felt numb. He sputtered, "Reports? I'm an outstanding employee. Ten years of promotions and outstanding evaluations—"

"Tom, the information in these reports cancels out any positive recommendations you may have in your file. We don't care about those. We have information that you were drunk at work on many occasions."

"I couldn't do my job if that were true! You know that!"

Now Ray, the human services specialist said, "Isn't it true you've been coasting on your job? We have a witness who says one day you could hardly read a report. And look at this signature." They passed him a document where his signature slanted down, off the line. The lines in his name were sharp, jagged, rather than curved.

Tom protested, "I don't know who's trying to get me in trouble, but . . ."

Now they handed him a pile of documentation. There were dates, times, signatures. They stared at him, challenging him to offer an explanation. What could he say? He was drunk almost every day. What excuse could he possibly give?

He started to say, "I'm sorry if there's been some confusion . . ."

But Ray shook his head before he even finished the sentence. "This isn't a 'sorry.' These activities require disciplinary action. . . ."

A chill of fear darted down Tom's spine. What could they do to him now?

"You guys just don't appreciate how important I am . . . all the accomplishments I've made for this company."

"We don't care about that right now. We're talking about you coming to work drunk. There are changes you have to make if you want to avoid being terminated.''

"Terminated? I'm an outstanding employee. Look at my evaluations.''

Clint waved him off, then shouted at him. ''A drunk is not an outstanding employee!''

Tom sat and stared, unsure what would come next.

''We're placing you on ninety days probation. You have to meet with your boss every week, and you will be alcohol and drug tested without warning. If there's any evidence that these activities are continuing, you will be fired immediately. Do you understand?''

What could he say? Tom felt a sick, sinking feeling in the pit of his stomach.

''Your job is on the line. Can I state it any plainer?''

Tom shook his head. He stared at the floor until the two men stood. He waited for one of them to pat his shoulder, to say something about his long and successful work record. Or their friendship.

But no one said a thing until Ray gruffly spat, ''Get back to work now.''

Months later, when the new boss took over, Tom knew instinctively that he'd better hide his drinking. He stopped going to the bars after work and just grabbed a bottle of gin or vodka to take home, where he passed out in his BarcaLounger.

Tom knew his drinking was a problem, and he couldn't handle his alcohol as he could in years past. It used to be that he could drink and enjoy the high for four or five hours before blacking out, but now the high was as quick as a match flame, only nanoseconds of feeling good before he passed out and lost track of time. What was happening to him? Where did the fun go? Sometimes he wondered if either he or Sally would rely so much on booze if they'd ever had kids. He found it sadly ironic that his first wife didn't want children, and now Sally seemed to be infertile. The only child he had was the son he'd lost so long ago. Even now, a day or two could pass without him thinking of Robbie, but then he'd feel a rush of longing hit him several times in a single day. And that's when he needed to drink the most. At least when he passed out, he temporarily didn't feel the pain.

The call came at work, one afternoon, when he was sitting at his desk, thinking again of the bottle of vodka or gin in the glove compartment. It was Sally, whose voice was surprisingly clear—obviously she was spending a rare sober afternoon.

She said, "Tom, I have bad news. They rushed your mother to the hospital."

His pulse quickened. "Was there an accident?"

"No, Tom." There was a long pause. "The way the doctors explained it to me, she's what is called a 'wet brain.' " His wife's voice caught. "Her organs just won't work anymore from the alcoholism. Tom, she's dying."

Quitting drinking never crossed Tom's mind until the hospital told him his mother was dying. Even then, it was hard to imagine never taking another drink; the idea felt almost like never taking another breath. So he pushed the possibility to the back of his mind, until Sally found the treatment center. Then, after they both entered treatment, it appeared that drinking was the glue that held the marriage together. After they both got sober, the divorce allowed them to abandon the unhealthy enabling they'd carried on for years. Free from alcoholism, they were both free to start new lives.

At the treatment center they told Tom that the odds that he'd stay sober after the first time in rehab were only two percent. Lots of people went through treatment centers again and again—they kept backsliding. They told him that one way to help cling to sobriety was to help other people. But why didn't anyone say how scary this was going to feel?

Tom's hands felt clammy as he approached the podium. The treatment center audience looked like a cross section of the United States. There were patients and their families. Men and women in Sunday dress, casual Levi's, and a cou-

ple of patients in hospital gowns. This should be less intimidating than when he spoke at a conference at work, yet
somehow he sensed that there was much more at stake this
time.

Standing at the podium, Tom cleared his throat and
straightened his tie. He said, "People tell me that if I stay
sober, I'll be blessed with a serenity and peace of mind."
He cleared his throat again. "That's what I hope for. That
will be a new feeling for me. In the past, I didn't want to
be anything but an alcoholic. I didn't want to grow up.
Didn't want to accept responsibility." He thought his knees
had settled into stillness, but at the thought of his next
words, they started fluttering like wind-filled tree limbs. "A
prime example of all this is . . . well I'm going to talk to
you today about one of my deepest, darkest, innermost secrets. I'm telling you now"—he closed his eyes quickly,
grasped the sides of the podium with both hands—"that
twenty-six years ago, I fathered a child I've never seen. I
didn't take the responsibility to raise him. He was placed
for adoption, and I'm sure he has a great family . . . but I'm
without my son, my only child."

How did the son he lost end up taking over so much time
in his talks to the groups of recovering alcoholics? Tom
didn't know. The first time he mentioned the son he gave
up, he practically shivered. But now, after a few introduc-
tory comments, his talks were all about his son.

It was the beginning of another talk. He shifted weight
at the microphone, then said. "People ask how I'm still
sober, seven years later, after one time through treatment.
I want to thank you for that. You, and all the other people
in the groups where I speak. I owe my sobriety to you . . .
and to one other person." He caught his breath. "I have a
boy I've never seen. I couldn't take responsibility for him
back when he was born. I was still a boy myself. Twenty
years old. But I'll never forget him. I still love him. He
never left my mind. But now I know what it means to lose
a son. And to be responsible. . . ."

After he finished speaking, floods of people came up to

congratulate him. He couldn't help but wonder if someday his son would shake his hand.

Usually he gave at least one talk a week. They told him that, so far, he was one of the rare 2 percent who stayed sober after one rehab treatment. Tom continued to notice that more and more of his talks centered around Robbie. After telling his story for what seemed like the hundredth time, he said, "I don't know if there's any way I can ever see my son, but if I do, I'll try to explain everything to him."

He abruptly caught sight of a woman near the aisle, on the second row. She was crying. Not just dabbing her eyes, but weeping. Even when he described how his treatment helped, and he overcame his addiction, the woman's shoulders still shook with sobs. When his talk was over, and the crowd rushed up to congratulate him, Tom was surprised to find that his curiosity about the woman lingered. As politely as he could, he extricated himself from the well-wishers who commended him, shaking his hand and patting his shoulder.

The woman was still seated, now discreetly dabbing her eyes and sniffling. When he approached, she stood and walked up to him. He saw her glance quickly from side to side. "Thank you for your talk," she said. "I never told anyone . . . just my sister that I stayed with during those months . . . but I gave a baby girl up for adoption . . . sixteen years ago." A fresh sob racked her body, and Tom felt his own lip quiver with emotion.

"I don't think I did the wrong thing," the woman protested quickly. "But I do think that trying to cope with the pain is one of the things in my life that started my drinking. . . ."

Tom turned away as his own emotions flooded, but the woman caught his arm . . .

"You're the first person I've ever told about this. I have to thank for you letting me know that maybe I can get help. . . ."

Tom felt his own tears rush. But the warm feeling in

knowing that he'd helped someone lasted far longer than his sadness.

After his second divorce Tom seldom dated. Instead, he began giving his two talks a week at AA meetings, discussing the son he never knew, again and again. Once, over dinner, he said to a woman he was dating, "I'd like to meet my son."

She frowned at him. "That's crazy."

"Why?" he asked, surprised at her reaction.

"How old is he?" she demanded.

Tom pretended to calculate, though he knew the answer by heart. "Twenty-six," he said.

"You can't just walk back into someone's life after almost thirty years . . . it's not healthy. Just let him go on with his life. He might even be married with kids by now."

"Are you saying I look old enough to be a grandpa?" Tom demanded.

Her laughter broke the tension, but Tom sensed this was probably their last date.

Chapter Eleven

Laura ached with loneliness after the divorce from Bryan. Her love for her girls and the hope of seeing Robbie someday were the only reason she moved through the seemingly endless days. She moved back to Little Rock, rented a house, looked for a job, and spent any free time she had with the girls. The last thing she thought she wanted now was a romantic relationship that might threaten the fragile balance of her life. She didn't think of John Wyatt as a romantic possibility when she first met him at a dinner party. But then, she'd pretty much crossed romantic possibilities off her future completely.

John was older and more serious than she was—and seemed to sense the emptiness in her life. He called the woman who threw the dinner party and she told him Laura was a single mom struggling to make her home here. He never asked her out on a date, but soon began appearing at her house, like a mature genie out to grant everyday wishes that would take the despair out of her life. She told him she was recovering from her divorce and couldn't even think about a relationship now, but that didn't seem to scare him off. Neither did her warnings that she couldn't repay him, and he should probably look for a woman more in his financial bracket. He shrugged off her rebuffs, and kept hanging around, paying her billss, taking her car for repairs, making sure she had a turkey at Thanksgiving. Sometimes she thought John thought of her as a daughter—other days she wondered if he considered her his girlfriend. He kissed her more than once, but it hardly felt romantic.

But when he dismissed her protests that he was doing too much for her, Laura didn't have much strength to fight his kindness off. Having someone always look after her needs felt so opposite from trying to grab bits of time from Bryan when he happened to be in town. And it wasn't like John was totally supporting her. She was working full-time. She lived at her own house, even though he took her to see his huge home that she thought of as "The Mansion." It had an indoor pool and he had a maid—sort of like what she was used to growing up. He had three Malamute dogs that he loved. She never could decide how she really felt about John. It was just that he was always there—like a safety net—to catch her if she, Tiffany, and Amelia fell through the cracks. It felt as if all she could do was thank him profusely and hope that her appreciation filled some kind of need in him. Guilt over the relationship haunted her, yet she felt that rejecting his kindness would hurt him more than she could imagine.

So after two years of this bland, yet secure relationship, she felt safe and comfortable. And when he said he didn't feel well and didn't want to go to her friend Carma's New Year's Eve party, neither of them thought it strange when she chose to go herself.

She arrived late, and there was only one seat left on the couch, next to a black man. She felt a twinge of—was it unease?—sitting beside him. Her first thought was that he was pretty good-looking for a black guy, even if he was a little chunky. But she was always taught that races shouldn't mix, so she didn't give her feelings a second thought as he laughed at someone's joke and passed her a tray of hors d'oeuvres. When his knee accidentally bumped hers, she again felt some sort of twinge. She reasoned that maybe she felt uneasy being out alone—and this was her first party in a long time.

Mike, the man sitting beside her, started talking to her

as if they knew each other for years. He told her that he worked at US West and was divorced, with three daughters. She was telling him she had two daughters when someone shouted that it was nearly midnight. Someone else shut off the lights, saying there were fireworks going off outside. Laura was thinking of John, home alone, probably asleep, when Mike started kissing her. His kiss was insistent and probing, and she felt embarrassed, excited, and totally confused. What was this? A black guy kissing her? What were these feelings? Could he feel the sparks that surged inside her?

Home again, she stared at herself in the mirror. There was a flush to her cheeks that wasn't there when she left the house that night. And a rush of sexual excitement that she couldn't deny.

But Mike was black. She thought of the day she first saw Lula, the maid, when she was five. That black skin and that pink tongue. She blushed with the understanding that she didn't see the color of Mike's tongue tonight. But she could still feel it in her mouth.

She waited two agonizing weeks before she called her friend Carma.

"I told him you were married," her friend said.

"What?" Laura asked, her cheeks flushing with unwanted emotion.

"You know you won't date a black guy."

"You're my best friend—how could you do that to me!" Laura sputtered.

"You mean you do want to date him? How many times have we talked about dating black guys? You said you never would, so when he called, I told him you were married."

"He called?"

"Well . . . yeah. Day after New Year's."

"And you didn't tell me?"

"I thought I was doing you a favor."

It was two more days before she summoned the nerve to call the number Carma gave her.

"Hello," Mike said.

A fresh rush of electricity spiraled through her, and she could feel his kiss all over again. She giggled and tried to force herself to talk.

"Hello?" Mike questioned, sounding a little friendlier.

"Hi," Laura said.

A long pause. Then, "Is this the married woman?"

Now she almost split with laughter. She caught herself quickly. She said, "I'm not—"

"I know. You don't date black guys. Well, I don't date women who are *married*."

A rush of embarrassment soared to her brain. So Carma had told him she didn't date black guys. What could she say now? "I'm not married," she said.

"Well, I'm still black."

"Well . . . I'd like to come and see you."

"But you don't want to date me. I'm okay to talk to, be friends with, and that's that."

"Well . . . no."

"I'm not okay to talk to?"

"You're okay, Mike."

"Are you sure you're not married?"

At first she told herself they weren't really dating, because she'd always been warned against interracial dating. So she told herself that the nights of movies, dinner, concerts, and long walks were really just two friends getting together—two friends who kissed at the end of the evening. But then one night when John wanted her to go a movie with him, she knew she wanted to hold the night open for Mike.

"So can you go with me?" John asked.

" I don't think so . . . don't think I can."

"Need a sitter for the girls? I could ask—"

"That's not it, John. I feel really bad about this, but you are forcing me to admit something."

"Admit something? What do you mean?"

"I don't know how else to say this. We've always been good friends, but now there is someone else."

"Someone else? Who? I wondered where you were all those nights when no one answers your phone."

A long pause. "I didn't think you were in love with me. But I kept hoping. . . ."

"I didn't mean to meet Mike. It started when he kissed me. . . ."

"He forced himself on you?"

"No . . . no . . . not like that. He kissed me on New Year's Eve, and I knew I was attracted to him.

"That night . . . I knew I should have gone with you. . . ."

"There was nowhere else to sit but next to him."

"What are you going to say to your mom and dad?"

She waited as long as she possibly could to tell her parents. There was no way she could call them on the phone and tell them, so she sat down to write a letter.

Dear Mom and Dad,

I'm writing to tell you some news. I met a nice guy and I'm getting married. Oh, well, no more beating around the bush. I better just tell you. His name is Mike Harris, and he's an Afro-American. I know you won't approve. I can just hear you. But the truth is, I already gave up a baby and I can't give up anyone else that I love this much. That's all I can say.

    Love,

    Laura

Chapter Twelve

Laura prepared for over a week for this, trying to get as much work done in the office as possible to offset the black hole that emptied her soul this one day every year. She woke with a feeling of dread, and knew almost before she opened her eyes that it was the twenty-sixth of January again. Robbie's birthday. The paralyzing sadness hovered over her as she struggled to dress for work. Though she knew logically that he was now twenty-six years old, in her mind she still saw him as the baby she held one time.

Combing her hair in the mirror, she knew she would cry if she met her own eyes in the glass reflection. She wondered what Robbie would be doing today to celebrate. Did he have a wife and children who planned to take him out to dinner? Or would the family who raised him have a special dinner at home with his favorite dishes? Would there be a cake with candles? Presents wrapped in colorful paper and topped with bows? Was there any chance that he would he somehow think of her, and know that he was on her mind?

At work she was useless, just staring into space. She sat still a long time at her desk. Somehow, the the piles of data entry and letters to be written couldn't command her attention. She went to the watercooler more than once. The rest room. She picked up an assignment, then set the papers back down, fingers shaking. She made two phone calls her boss asked about, then cleared the clutter from her desk. At least she'd worked extra hard the three previous days.

It was about an hour before lunch when she sensed some sort of commotion at the front door. Usually, she'd be so involved in her work that she never noticed the noise any-one else made and didn't see any other people until they were standing beside her desk. But this was January 26.

Some of the women were giggling, and she found herself oddly curious. Unable to turn away from their laughter, she walked to the front office to discover the source of their mirth. There were about ten women, standing in a circle, laughing, talking, smiling. As she stepped closer, and saw the focus of their attention, Laura closed her eyes in terror. No. Not today. Any day but today.

She wanted to turn and run. But by now, there were others standing behind her. She turned her head to the side, looked at the floor, and concentrated on the squares in the tile pattern.

"Are you all right?" She heard genuine concern in the voice, and her glance lifted to meet the gentle brown eyes of Amy, who worked two aisles away.

She nodded quickly, even as her jaw quivered. "I'm fine," she said.

"Isn't he cute?" Amy pointed.

Laura forced herself to look up.

It was Roz, the newest member of the team, visiting dur-ing her maternity leave. Now she held her tiny baby up to her shoulder. From where she stood, Laura could smell baby powder, see the soft quilted blankets and almost feel the smooth flannel of the baby's miniature yellow night-gown. When Roz held the baby's pillowy cheek to her face, Laura recalled with bleak and desperate clarity the one brief moment when she was allowed to hold Robbie and feel his warm, smooth skin against hers. Now she began to tremble as her arms seared with an aching emptiness. She turned and pushed past Amy's curious glance. She strode down the hall quickly, stopping at her boss's office.

Adam stood as she stepped inside his office. His frown showed both concern and curiosity. "Laura? What's the matter?"

"I need to go home." Her hand shook jaggedly as she fought with the clasp on her purse and finally emerged with a Kleenex. She patted the tissue against her eyes, and when she glanced down at the crumpled mass, she saw that mascara granules clung to its surface. She sniffed and shuddered deeply. She said, "I can't stay."

"Are you sick? Why are you crying?"

Another long shudder filled her body and left her feeling chilled. "There's something I never told you. When I was twenty, before I ever worked here . . ." She stopped. She looked up into Adam's face. Did anything in his seemingly normal wife-and-two-kids life approach the horror of her long-ago loss?

He prompted, "What happened?"

She sniffed. "I had a baby son. My only little boy. The boyfriend I was going to marry said it couldn't be his at the last minute . . . but it was . . . he was the only guy I was ever with. . . ."

"Laura." She looked up to see concern in Adam's well-sculpted face. "That must have been terrible."

She shook her head. "Worst moment in my life."

He waited.

She squared herself in her chair. "I gave him up for adoption."

Adam's face stayed motionless. No comment.

Laura picked at a piece of lint on her skirt, then forced herself to confront those cool blue eyes again. "I need to tell you . . . the thing is . . . today's his birthday. It's always my worst day."

He didn't say anything.

"And—" She raised a hand to her forehead, dropped it back down when it started to shake. "Adam . . . I could have made it through today. I got dressed and rushed down here. But when I saw that new baby . . . all my emotions came back." She sniffed as a fresh flood of tears drenched her face. She swallowed and gritted her teeth.

The next words fought their way from her throat, leaving a dull ache. "I can't stay. I won't get anything done . . . I don't know how to explain it anymore."

He looked at her for a long time. She felt her eyes blink, a tear stick to her lashes until she wiped it away. Her lip quivered.

Adam sighed, reached into his desk drawer, and drew out a pad of paper. She watched as he wrote quickly on the paper, then stopped. He wrote again, then tore the paper off the form and handed it to her.

She'd never seen a form like this before. At the top it said, "Emergency Leave Authorization." He'd filled in the blanks, giving her the rest of the week off with pay.

"Oh." Her flood of relief escaped in that single syllable. She swallowed again. It was a few moments before she could say, "Thank you."

He brushed aside her words with a wave of his hand, then picked up a clipboard on his desk and began to study it. Taking two steps toward the door, she stopped. "Thank you," she said. He didn't look up. She walked out of his office, down the back hall where no one could see her, and left the building.

It was on her second day off that she was watching *Oprah*, letting the time drift by as she sat on the couch. There were no sounds from outside. The neighborhood was quiet with adults at work and children at school. Today, Oprah was featuring adoption reunions. Laura sat still on the couch and watched. How would it be to meet her son on television? Watching the show, she cried as birth mothers embraced children they'd never seen in their lives. It was comforting to be able to cry in the privacy of her own house. At the end of the show, Oprah interviewed Troy and Arliene Dunn, who owned International Locator, a worldwide search company. Could someone like that find Robbie? Laura recalled the long-ago lawyer who requested $10,000. When she couldn't pay, nothing else happened. But she only wasted a little of her time. What would she lose if she called the search company now?

All the fear and anxiousness of twenty-six years coalesced in her mind and her hands trembled as she dialed the number she saw on *Oprah*.

"International Locator," said a businesslike, yet friendly-sounding operator.

"I'd like to find my son," said Laura, closing her eyes to blink back tears, and gripping the phone with both hands.

"How long has it been since you last saw him?" asked the woman, friendly and impersonal.

"I only saw him once . . . when he was baptized . . ." Laura's words rushed, and as she told the story, she scarcely thought of the person who was listening. She only saw Robbie's sweet little face and felt the cold emptiness in her heart.

"I think of him every day," she finished as a sob choked its way from her throat.

The voice paused. "Would you consider appearing on a television show and possibly making a plea to find him?"

For just a moment Laura envisioned throngs of people, all gazing at her as she stood under the lights. She was a shy person, but there was no contest.

"I'll do whatever it takes," she said. "But there is one thing—I don't want to interfere with whatever family he has now."

The woman from International Locator said, "That's great. I'll get back to you."

For hours afterward Laura was warmed by the possibility that it might somehow happen.

Three days later a television producer called.

"Would you be willing to fly to New York to make a plea on our show?" asked the woman from the *Maureen O'Boyle Show*.

"In a heartbeat," said Laura. "But I can't afford it right now."

"All your expenses will be paid," said the woman. "We have an opening right before Christmas. . . ."

Flying on the plane reminded her of the traveling days with Bryan. Arrivals and departures, changing scenery, restaurant food that tasted the same all across the country. But at the same time, she knew this trip would be like no other in her life. Neither the spacious hotel suite with its panoramic view of New York City nor the limousine ride could distract her from her raging emotions. She sat in the green room at the television network, crying and snacking on peanuts and soda pop as minutes seemed to drag. When a production staff member wearing a microphone came and brought her out onto the stage, fresh tears spilled across her face. She fought to remember the words she'd rehearsed all night in the hotel.

Maureen O'Boyle said, "Meet Laura. Laura has wanted to meet the son she gave up for adoption twenty-six years ago. Do you think of your son often, Laura?"

"Every day," Laura managed.

"And I understand you've tried to search for him yourself?"

Laura said, "I made a few phone calls to Catholic Charities. No luck."

"And you'd like some help from us today?"

Laura nodded. "That would be wonderful."

Maureen cocked her head sideways. "Laura, what would you say to the people who are going to try to find your son?"

Now Laura struggled to remember the thoughts she'd rehearsed for hours. "I'd tell them I love him very much. I think of him every day. But I know he has his own life. I don't want to intrude on the family he has now. But if he is willing to meet me, nothing could make me happier." Her voice broke as she repeated, "There's nothing I want more."

Maureen's voice revved up. "Well, Laura, I have great news. I have a Christmas present for you. . . ."

At that moment the house lights dimmed, and someone projected two slides on a screen. Laura gasped. It was the face she longed for all these years. Her strawberry-blond hair. Tommy's fine-featured face and even smile. Though the features never formed quite this surely in her mind, there was no question. This young man was her son. Hers and Tommy's. Her tears flowed nonstop, blurring her vision so that she felt, rather than saw, the young man hugging her.

Laura blinked, stared in awe at the smiling face. She said, "You're my baby."

The young man nodded, grinned broadly. "I'm Rusty," he said.

In the green room she discovered that Rusty liked cameras and archery, and that he had a wonderful life with two parents who raised him in the Catholic church according to her request. She learned that he was an airplane mechanic, and his girlfriend's name was Holly. As much as she wanted to keep talking to him, there was a phone call that she couldn't wait another minute to make.

Her fingers trembled, and she was surprised she still had the number memorized.

A rush of relief and excitement filled her as she said, "Tommy, I have someone here who wants to talk to you."

She paused a moment, waiting for him to ask who was on the line. When he didn't say a word, she handed the phone to Rusty.

"Hello?" Rusty asked tentatively. A few moments later, he said, "This is he."

Laura waited for some sort of response, a quick denial and a hang-up. But Rusty stood there, listening for a long time to whatever Tommy was saying to him. She saw him nod his head, then use his hands when he talked the same way Tommy always had. Abruptly he laughed. "Oh, absolutely," he said. "Right . . ."

Gradually Laura began to feel that she was intruding on a private conversation. She left the green room and shut the door behind her. She stared out at New York City below, the sea of yellow cabs, throngs of people on the sidewalk, buildings almost frighteningly tall. Waves of validation flooded her mind. Before she handed the phone to Rusty, she wished she'd said, "I was right, all those years ago, the day you left me. You have a son, and there's no way you can turn back now."

Chapter Thirteen

Standing at the airport, Tom felt that this pounding in his brain was probably the worst headache of his life. Thinking back to all the meetings in his long business career, he knew he'd never before felt this same urgency. It was as if he couldn't wait one more minute. He always thought he'd know Rusty anywhere. But now, he wondered, would he really recognize the son he'd never seen? He and Laura stood together as the crowd deplaned at the Little Rock airport. There were tons of people he knew weren't the right one—older women in hats, bald men, families. They stood and waited. A long line of people passed them. It looked as if everyone was gone. The flight attendant was counting tickets. Everyone seemed to be walking toward baggage claim. But then the last young man from the plane walked into the terminal.

Tom was stunned at the resemblance—it was his own face he saw on this young man. My gosh . . . it's my twin, he thought.

Beside him, Laura said with confidence borne of years of pain. "Yes, Tommy, I was right all this time. You do have a son."

Her words barely graced his mind, scarcely penetrated the intensity of this heady moment. Tom cleared his throat. "Rusty," he called out, and the young man turned. With the same smooth, easy gait he'd glimpsed in glass doors all his life, Tom's son walked toward him.

All the years of anxiety, curiosity, guilt, and sadness descended over Tom in a wave. His throat filled and tightened. When was the last time he cried like this? Without a word he and Rusty embraced.

The next morning, when Tom was preparing coffee, he wondered how Rusty liked his coffee.

With cream, like mine, came his unbidden thought.

When Rusty sat at the table, Tom asked, "How do you like your coffee?"

"With cream," said Rusty innocently.

Moments later, as the two men ate, Rusty suddenly said, "That was weird, about the bathroom."

"The bathroom?" Tom frowned quizzically. He recalled carefully laying out towels and a travel-size toothpaste.

"Yeah . . ." Rusty smiled, and for the thousandth time, Tom caught himself staring at the planes of Rusty's face. And the hands—just like his own—with big palms, but small fingers.

"Well—what was weird about it?" Tom asked, and this time he caught Rusty watching him gesture with his hands, the same way Rusty did.

Rusty giggled. "The Coast soap. Same kind I always use, I just like the way it smells. And Edge shaving cream. I never buy any other kind because I have—"

"A tough beard, but sensitive skin," Tom finished for him.

Now the two men laughed together. As they finished eating, Tom said, "I have to tell you, Rusty. Seeing you at the airport was the greatest moment of my life. But it had to happen the way it did. It was like a script—"

"I know, man," said Rusty, still grinning, not guessing that Tom was about to say something serious.

"What I mean is, all this happened the way it was supposed to."

Rusty nodded, smiling again.

"I have to say, you were lucky you weren't there at the first. With Laura and me. For us to get married would have been the most wrong thing in the world.'' Tom cleared his throat. ''A small tornado, ready to turn into a big one and wreck a lot of lives. What I'm trying to say is—you benefitted from not being there.''

Rusty nodded sagely, and, not for the first time, Tom was struck by the vast ocean of peace that filled this young man.

''I mean, look at you—calm, smart, all grown up . . .'' Now Tom smiled. ''And I gotta say, you were a gift to the McFarlands, but you're a blessed and lucky guy that they selected you.''

Rusty's grin drooped, and he blinked. His eyes filled. ''Don't I know it.'' He wiped away a tear, then looked up. Peaceful again already. ''Hey, do you think there's any way someone could find the baby girl that they lost?''

''When the adoption fell through?''

Rusty smiled. ''Yeah, right before me. Little Christy. I know my mom kept thinking about her. She'd probably just like to know that she's all right.''

''If they could find you, I'd think they could find her. . . .'' Tom's smile wavered with emotion. ''I mean— if it's supposed to happen.''

Across the table Rusty nodded.

It was the night of the family reunion with all the aunts, uncles, and cousins. A day full of smiles, tears and hugs.

But neither Laura nor Rusty smiled now.

They concentrated, sitting across from each other at her kitchen table. First she beat him at backgammon, after not playing the game for fourteen years. Now they were in the middle of Sorry. The simple rhythm of the game was soothing. Roll the dice. Move your token around the square board. If someone else's token landed on you, start over.

This time Rusty was winning. When he sent her blue token back to the start, he looked up at her. Their eyes met.

''I was worried,'' said Laura, hoping he'd sense she wasn't speaking of the game now. ''When I left you in Los Angeles as a baby. Thought it might be a place where lots of crime happens. I hoped and prayed you'd be safe.''

"L.A.'s great," Rusty said.

"I thought you might drink, or get on drugs. But you never did."

Rusty shook his head. "Never did. Was an altar boy too long, I guess."

"You're clean. Sober and clean," said Laura.

Rusty laughed again. "I'm a mechanic. I get grease on everything. My mom—uh, Sally—used to die over my laundry."

Laura caught the awkwardness of his words. She said, "Don't call her Sally. She's your mom. I'm Laura."

Rusty threw the dice. They played three times before it was time for bed. He would spend the next day with Tommy. This week was the way it would be if they'd married, then divorced, Laura thought. One day at the reunion and playing games with her. The next day golfing with Tommy. Then shopping with her. Then the movies with Tommy.

We have joint reunion custody, she thought.

The three of them stood at the airport.

"Meet halfway next time," Rusty said.

"I'll bring your sisters," said Laura.

"I'll pay for the Holiday Inn or whatever," said Tom. The son he'd never seen before this week slugged him good-naturedly on the arm. Then he hugged him. Tom watched Rusty hug Laura.

Realizing the plane was about to take off, Rusty started running. The same loping gait as mine, Tom thought. Abruptly, fifty feet from them, Rusty turned, still moving. "See ya, guys!" he shouted.

"In six months—" Laura called out.

Tom drove Laura to her house. He drove back to his own huge old-fashioned home, which seemed empty to him as he sat alone in it the next day.

It was three days before Tom went back to work. He stopped in Personnel. When the clerk looked up at him, he said, "I need to change the beneficiary for my life insurance."

The clerk raised her eyebrows questioningly.

"I need to add my son to the policy," he said.

She smiled. "Your son? I never knew you had a son."

"I knew," he said. "I always knew."

She started to laugh, and Tom smiled with her. Then he held out the picture so she could see it. It was the two of them, he and Rusty on the golf course. Rusty practicing his swing. The two of them, with the same lanky stance. Then he handed her the other picture. A portrait of just Rusty.

"He looks just like you!" the clerk exclaimed, studying the picture, then looking up into Tom's face.

"I know," he said again.

Moments later he took the elevator up to his office. He walked through the door, glanced around at the papers, the blinking light on his answering machine, the pen set, the awards. He moved everything aside on his desk, so the top was free and clear. He set the two framed pictures there, at the head of his desk, where everyone in the world could see them.

WHO WOULD YOU LIKE TO FIND?

My name is Troy Dunn, and I am the CEO of International Locator, Inc., the organization who helped reunite all of the wonderful people you just read about. Over the past decade, we have reunited thousands of families worldwide and continue to do so at this very moment. We would like to help you find a lost friend or family member as well. Who knows, you might be our next great story!

I feel everybody has somebody they have lost touch with. Someone that they would love to see one more time in this short life we live. Who is that person for you? Is it an old classmate, a teacher, someone in the military or perhaps a former coworker or neighbor? Perhaps you are one of the twenty-seven-million Americans affected by adoption (our specialty), and you want to find your biological family?

Whatever the case may be, we can help you find that special someone and bring closure, answers and, hopefully, joy to your life and the life of your family. Contact us and see if we can help you. We will evaluate your situation and recommend the best, fastest and least expensive route to help you find that missing person.

There are several ways to contact us. Pick your preference:

By telephone: Call our world headquarters at (941)574-1799
Our toll-free information line is (800)BigHugs

By Internet: Visit our Web site at http://www.BigHugs.com
(While there, check out our FREE reunion registry!)

By mail: Write to us at International Locator, Inc.
2503 Del Prado Blvd.
Cape Coral, FL 33904
(This is the slowest way to correspond with us, so be patient.)

Thank you for reading this wonderful book by our good friend Carolyn Campbell. Look for the other books in this series coming soon to your favorite bookstore. I wish you the best of luck in your search for friends and family, and encourage you to never give up. We have a saying in our office, "You can't find peace until you find all the pieces."

God Bless,
Troy Dunn
CEO
International Locator, Inc.

PENGUIN PUTNAM
online

Your Internet gateway to a virtual
environment with hundreds of entertaining
and enlightening books from
Penguin Putnam Inc.

While you're there, get the latest buzz on
the best authors and books around—
Tom Clancy, Patricia Cornwell, W.E.B. Griffin,
Nora Roberts, William Gibson, Robin Cook,
Brian Jacques, Catherine Coulter,
Stephen King, Jacquelyn Mitchard,
and many more!

Penguin Putnam Online is located at
http://www.penguinputnam.com

PENGUIN PUTNAM NEWS

Every month you'll get an inside look at our
upcoming books and new features on our site.
This is an ongoing effort to provide you
with the most interesting and up-to-date
information about our books and authors.

Subscribe to Penguin Putnam News at
http://www.penguinputnam.com/ClubPPI